In the early years ~~~~~~~~~~
Grosvenor is only seventeen when both her
heart and her home life are broken.
Blamed for a family scandal, she is
banished to Portugal by her adoptive
parents to make her home in a small
mining community, run by members of her
family she has never met. Initially
unhappy, she is soon bewitched by the hot
climate and equally torrid passions of those
around her: the uncle who loves her, the
aunt who hates her and the Englishmen
who pursue her. But most of all she is
captivated by the ramblings of her aged
grandmother.

For Joanna has stumbled upon another
family scandal – one that will lead her into
the mysteries of the past, into danger – and
towards a new and lasting love . . .

Also by Pamela Oldfield

The Heron Saga
THE RICH EARTH
THIS RAVISHED LAND
AFTER THE STORM
WHITE WATER

GREEN HARVEST
SUMMER SONG
GOLDEN TALLY

THE GOODING GIRL
THE STATIONMASTER'S DAUGHTER
LILY GOLIGHTLY
TURN OF THE TIDE
A DUTIFUL WIFE
SWEET SALLY LUNN
THE HALLIDAY GIRLS
LONG DARK SUMMER

The Passionate Exile

PAMELA OLDFIELD

WARNER BOOKS

A *Warner* Book

First published in Great Britain in 1993
by Michael Joseph Ltd
This edition published in 1994 by Warner Books

A CIP catalogue record for this book is
available from the British Library.

ISBN 0 7515 0472 6

Printed in England by Clays Ltd, St Ives plc

Warner Books
A Division of
Little, Brown and Company (UK) Limited
Brettenham House
Lancaster Place
London WC2E 7EN

For Victor Allan
who was there as a boy

With grateful thanks to Jack and Josephine, Tony and
Cidalia, John and Madge, and Jorge

Chapter One

WITH HER EYES TIGHT SHUT Joanna counted to ten and was astonished. She counted to ten again but it continued, so she went on counting. Twenty ... thirty ... she reached fifty, and still it had not ended. Although the year was young the sun was warm, and she felt a fine perspiration break out on her skin. Opening her eyes, she stared into Mark's face as he laboured above her. His blue eyes were shut, sweat glistened on the peachy skin and his full lips were parted as, with each thrust, he gasped with exertion. Averting her eyes from his face she stared grimly up into the green of the tree which cast its shade over them ... A hundred! And still the ridiculous situation continued with no apparent sign of conclusion. How long did it last? Was it always like this? No wonder women spoke of 'a wife's duty'.

She bit her lip, stifling the cry of dismay and the reproaches that craved utterance. The fierce disappointment which swept over her was like a wave of icy water which carried her away and left her joyless, stranded on the shores of her expectations. If this was physical love it seemed there was to be no rapture, no wondrous revelations. It was all a trick, and she had been taken in by it. Her own gullibility sickened her and she almost ground her teeth in helpless rage.

'Mark!' she protested, wondering why he did not bring the unhappy event to a discreet end, but he shook his head, apparently annoyed by her interruption. Yet he did not appear to be enjoying himself either. A fresh thought struck her, increasing her anxiety. She must be doing something wrong – although, in fact, she was doing very little. But what on earth *should* she be doing? She had finally given in to months of pleading because she loved him, but her sacrifice was proving worthless. Tears filled her eyes as the extent of her stupidity dawned on her. Excitement was replaced by apprehension, and she was so engrossed in her own thoughts and anxieties that when he suddenly gave a high-pitched groan and rolled off her she was taken by surprise.

For a few moments Mark lay back exhausted, then he turned his head and began to kiss her shoulder. 'Oh, my sweet Joanna!' His face looked relaxed and strangely flushed in a way that was unfamiliar. He looked *satisfied*, so perhaps he had enjoyed their lovemaking. So why was it different for her?

'Joanna!' he murmured, smiling up into the tree, and she suddenly felt a fierce urge to shake him. Saying nothing, she sat up and began to rearrange her clothes, tugging down her skirt and petticoats, fumbling to fasten the buttons with fingers that trembled.

'You were so beautiful!' he told her, but she regarded him dispassionately as he lay beside her with his head propped on one hand. She tried to answer with something noncommittal, but no words came so she remained silent and turned her head slightly so that he should not see her face. If he cared to look, she was sure her disillusionment would be plain to see, and she did not want to hurt him. She sighed deeply. So *that* was what all the fuss was about! She wondered why anyone bothered. Yet gossip had it that Mark had taken one of the maids – and not once but a score of times. Presumably Lizzie had somehow managed to *enjoy* the experience – or had Mark persuaded her with the promise of a shilling each time.

Clasping her hands round her knees, Joanna stared straight ahead and considered the possibility that there was a knack to making love which the maid had mastered. Perhaps there was some way to find all that discomfort pleasurable. If so, it was incredible.

'Incredible!' she repeated.

'What did you say?' Mark gazed up at her and he suddenly seemed altered in some indefinable way. Did she still love him, she wondered.

'Nothing!' she said.

'I thought you said—'

'I didn't speak.'

For a moment he eyed her intently and she felt herself colouring slightly. Her sins were multiplying, she thought. First adultery and then a lie.

'Did you like it?' he asked.

Did she like it? A variety of images floated through her mind: a tree root had pressed itself painfully into her spine, Mark's weight had all but crushed the breath from her body, and she had felt helpless and vulnerable throughout.

'It hurts!' she said, her tone accusing. 'And it's boring!'

To her annoyance he appeared quite unmoved by this criticism, treating her verdict as a joke and laughing delightedly. He tidied his rumpled clothing, took a large white handkerchief from his pocket and, with infuriating unconcern, began to dab the sweat from his face. It began to dawn on her that many of her illusions about him had suffered a fatal blow. To her, his twenty years no longer added up to an aloof maturity which she had been more than ready to admire; the shared sin had reduced him to a little boy who has done something naughty without Nanny's knowledge.

'I mean it!' she insisted. 'It was horrible!'

But was it actually adultery, she wondered? Mark wasn't married . . . yet, although he was betrothed and due to be married in the autumn – October the third, to be exact. It

3

was to prevent this marriage to the pale and haughty Isobel that she had finally given in to his demands. Briefly, now, she tried to imagine Isobel trapped beneath Mark's body. Presumably for her it would be worth it to be married to a wealthy young man from a 'good' family – and, of course, as a wife it would be Isobel's duty to produce a family to carry on the Grosvenor name.

Mark reached out, gently lifted one of Joanna's dark curls and put it to his lips. Then, releasing it, he put a finger under her chin and said, 'Joanna, you are a sweet, funny little thing but I adore you.'

'Then will you marry me and not her?'

'No. I can't.'

'Or won't!'

'Joanna, you're my *sister*!'

'But you don't love her?'

'No.'

'Would you marry me if you could?' He had professed his love many times, but had never told her what she most wanted to hear – that he *would* marry her in preference to Isobel if circumstances would allow.

'Don't ask me to be disloyal,' he said.

'But you have asked me to ... to be immoral! And I have! Why can't you be just a *little* disloyal?'

'It wouldn't be chivalrous.'

'*Chivalrous*! What about all this?' She waved her hands to indicate their predicament. 'Is what we've just done chivalrous?' Her voice sounded thin and she felt like a nagging wife, but there was so much at stake and she did still love him. At least she hoped so. The suspicion that her feelings towards him might be irrevocably changed filled her with alarm. Her secret love for Mark was the brightest thing in her life. 'I wish it were true,' she said soberly. 'I wish you were my real brother! Being your real sister would be better than nothing.'

'Instead you are my black-eyed beauty!' he laughed. 'Isn't

4

that enough?' Brushing the last of the leaves and grass from his trousers, he leaned towards her and kissed the side of her face. 'And one day you'll be somebody's wife,' he added.

He jumped to his feet and held out two hands to help her up, but she remained where she was, looking up into his amused blue eyes, wishing desperately that she could turn back the clock.

'Come on, Jo!' he urged. 'It struck three ages ago and you know how Mama will fuss if you don't turn up for tea.'

'She's not my Mama!' Ignoring his hands, she scrambled unaided to her feet and shook her skirts irritably.

'Joanna! Don't be such a misery,' he urged. 'So you didn't like it! It hardly matters. I expect you were dying to know what happens. Women are never told anything until it's too late. And now you know. Anyway, women aren't supposed to like it the way men do.'

He pulled her towards him and for old times' sake she did not protest. She told herself that he still loved her; that he was still the one member of the family who cared for her. Mama hated her; Papa tolerated her and poor, plain Dorcas was jealous of her. Suzanne was only five and hardly counted. Only Mark was really kind to her; in Joanna's eyes, he was her champion.

He went on, 'Don't spoil what's left of the holiday, Jo. We're going on a picnic tomorrow and—'

'Fort Salses *again*!'

'You *like* the fort!' he protested. 'At least you've always claimed to like it.'

'But we go there every year!'

She was suddenly determined to find fault, as though her dissatisfaction with their lovemaking was somehow casting its shadow over the rest of her existence. The annual holiday in France, always such an adventure, now seemed dull and parochial. The old French fort, tucked away between sea and plain, no longer intrigued her. Mademoiselle Thiraud, their French tutor employed for the holiday, had lost a little of her glamour. The delights of French cuisine had paled. 'I'm tired of France!' she exclaimed and was aware of a growing sense of loss.

'Joanna! There are times when I could cheerfully shake you!' Mark shook his own head wearily. 'Why do you have to be so difficult? Nothing has changed.' When she did not answer he said firmly, 'You will enjoy the picnic, you know you will – and then on Thursday we are going to Lamalou-les-Bains to visit Jeffery. We've never been there before!'

He looked at her hopefully, and with a huge effort of will she held back a scathing comment about his old school-friend whom she had never met and had no reason to dislike. Why *did* she feel so terribly hostile, she asked herself. The truth was that circumstances had cast her in the role of a victim and she sometimes took a vicarious pleasure in the pain of knowing that she was a foundling. At other times, the mystery surrounding her real parents plunged her into a period of genuine depression which made her difficult to live with. They had died together in a boating accident soon after her birth, and she could scarcely recall a time when she had not felt vaguely resentful and suspicious. The news that Mama and Papa were her adoptive parents had been broken to her by eight-year-old Mark when she was five. From then on the passage of her childhood years had been disrupted by her own furious rages and periods of near-hysterical tantrums and the doctor had diagnosed a brain fever brought on by the original shock of Mark's disclosure. Now seventeen years old, she had almost grown out of what Mama referred to as 'her awkward ways', although her anger had been replaced to some extent by occasional moods of deep depression.

'Jo!' Mark shook her hands gently. 'You're miles away.'

'I'm sorry,' she said, momentarily subdued. She had

never blamed Mark for the trauma she had suffered at his hands, choosing instead to see him as a champion of truth. Mark, to atone for his revelation, had assumed the role of protector and comforter, and their closeness as children had developed into something deeper. Joanna had never expected to feel this tremendous loss of respect for him and it frightened her. She suddenly forced a bright smile, snatched up his hand and kissed it fiercely, hoping that by so doing some of the passion she had felt for him would return. With her lips pressed to his hand she waited, but was finally forced to admit that, for the moment at least, the magic had gone.

Mark, with a wry shake of the head, took her hand in his and without another word she allowed herself to be led back towards the path. She was aware that he was watching her from the corner of his eye, and suddenly he put an arm round her shoulder.

'You do still love me, don't you?' he asked.

'Of course I do!' She did not meet his eyes. Surely she still loved him? Life would be so empty without her love for Mark.

'I promise you it doesn't matter,' he told her earnestly. 'I mean what happened just now, between us. It would have happened sometime with someone ... your husband, I suppose. So why not now, with me? There's no harm done, nothing to grieve over. And Joanna – not a word to anyone?'

'Oh, no!' She was shocked. This was to be their secret.

'No one else must know,' he insisted. 'We agreed. You promised.'

They climbed the sloping path and reached the lawn. Ahead was the house which the family rented each year for the Easter holiday. Its warm walls under a red-tiled roof blended effortlessly into its background; the windows behind the wrought-iron balconies were shuttered as usual against the sun. She had always loved it, had considered it her second home and had often fantasized about owning it. More than once it had featured i her dreams, and always it had been a reassuring haven. Now, to her dismay, she saw that the house, along with Mark, had lost some of its charm and she longed suddenly to be back in England.

'Joanna . . .' He had stopped walking and she looked at him sharply, aware of a subtle change in his manner.

'You do remember your promise, don't you, Joanna? I mean the exact words?'

'Yes?'

'Even if someone finds out about us—'

A cold fear clutched at her heart. 'Finds out? But how could they?'

'They can't, Joanna, but just in case they did. Someone might have been watching.'

'Spying on us? Oh, Mark!'

'I'm certain they weren't, but just in case. You promise not to tell who you were with – you do promise that? You do remember that you swore on your dead mother's grave?'

'I remember, Mark, but you swore too.' She was becoming anxious, alarmed by his expression. He had sworn on the grave of one of his favourite housemasters, a certain Julius Tobin, who had been killed falling from a train in the Austrian Alps.

'It would be worse for me, Jo, because of Isobel and being betrothed.'

She nodded, telling herself resolutely that no one could have seen them – although how could either of them be certain of that fact? She had closed her eyes throughout the ordeal and Mark had been facing downwards. They *could* have been seen!

Before she could voice this terrifying thought there was a shrill cry from the terrace as Suzanne called them in to tea.

Mark said, 'Perhaps we shouldn't be seen coming in

together. You go on in and I'll go round to the side of the house and in through the other door.'

Awed by his caution, Joanna agreed reluctantly.

Watching him hurry away she whispered, 'Oh, Mark!' and then made her own way across the lawn to the terrace where five-year-old Suzanne, falling into step beside her, began at once to scold in her mother's voice.

Joanna said crossly, 'Oh, do be quiet, you baby!'

Suzanne, who would one day be a beauty, protested, 'But everything's ready and waiting!'

'So? Are the cucumber sandwiches going to get cold or something?'

The sarcasm was lost on Suzanne, who considered the question seriously. 'The tea will,' she said at last.

'Then Mama will send for a fresh pot. You really are a ninny!'

The child's lips trembled but Joanna hardened her heart, in no mood to be generous. She had finally tasted the forbidden fruit and found it unappetizing. Worse, in the process her beloved Mark had toppled ignominiously from his pedestal and her world was in ruins. Surely, she thought miserably, today was proving to be the worst day of her whole life.

*

Throughout tea Mark eyed Joanna cautiously, expecting his mother to remark at any moment on the girl's high colour, but to his relief nothing was said. He came to the conclusion that his mother had noticed nothing unusual about Joanna's behaviour and thanked God for it. Already regretting the incident in the woods, he felt guilty and confused. He also worried that Joanna would unintention-ally betray him or, worse, that she would find herself with child and be forced to reveal the name of her seducer. He bit into a cucumber sandwich and sighed. It had all started as something of a joke when, aware of Joanna's infatuation

9

for him, he had teased her about her innocence. When she first offered to prove her love he had been tempted, and the idea had grown in both their minds until the inevitable had happened. At the time it had seemed an amusing conquest, but now he was full of regrets. He had a very real affection for the girl and recognized that he had behaved badly towards her. If Joanna found herself 'in the family way' it would be a disaster – a terrible scandal which would affect the entire family. His marriage to Isobel would be impossible. And to be fair, he was quite fond of Isobel, even if she was rather self-centred. Compared with Joanna, she definitely lacked spirit, but she would make a very suitable mother for his children.

Why had he been such a fool? He had treated his poor Joanna like a common servant! He sighed again. The truth was that had she not grown up as part of his family he might well have preferred her to Isobel, but since he could not marry the girl he should have shown some restraint. But there! It was done, and he must find a way of ensuring that his foolish indiscretion did not ruin them all. Certainly, Isobel must never know what had happened. In his mind's eye he saw the effect such news would have. The haughty face would turn pale with shock; the thin mouth would tighten with anger; the cool grey eyes would darken with the hurt of rejection. Her mother would never forgive him, and her father would probably threaten him with a horsewhip!

Joanna turned to him a little breathlessly and he forced a smile to his lips. As he did so a further complication occurred to him. Like all well-bred girls, Joanna would be unaware of the signs of pregnancy until some of the facts were revealed to her on the night before her wedding. If she *was* with child she would be ignorant of the fact until it was too late. He knew that it was possible for a woman to 'lose' a child if she wanted to, but only if it was accomplished in the early stages. Somehow he would have to alert his mother to the possibility, so that she could keep an eye on Joanna and ask any questions that needed to be asked ... Damnation! It was becoming more complicated by the minute. Suddenly an idea came to him. Suppose he told his mother that he had seen Joanna with a young man in the wood and urged her to be sympathetic.

'Mark!'

They were all staring at him, expecting him to answer a question he had not heard.

'Sorry!' he said easily. 'What did you say?'

Joanna tried to catch his eye, but he pretended not to notice. Dorcas said, 'Mama says we might set off to the fort a little earlier tomorrow. Do you agree? Could you drag yourself from your bed by nine-thirty?'

'Can you?' he countered.

Suzanne said, '*I* can. What is nine-thirty?'

While Dorcas was explaining that it meant half-past nine, Mark helped himself to another sandwich and considered his idea. Were there any snags? As long as Joanna did not know who had betrayed them, he would be safe. Joanna would only break her promise if she discovered that she had been deceived, and he must see that that never happened. His mother would suspect various young men in the vicinity, but they would never suspect *him*! It was perfect.

He felt a little calmer. As long as he handled the revelations carefully it would work. Smiling, he held the plate of cakes towards Joanna.

'A lemon cake? Your favourites!'

She met his gaze and held it fractionally before answering, 'Lemon or chocolate. I like them both.'

Suzanne said eagerly, 'I like raspberry buns best. Why can't we have raspberry buns, Mama? Why do we have to have lemon cakes? I hate lemon cakes.' To disprove this she took one and bit into it heartily.

Her mother frowned. 'Eat daintily, Suzanne! How many times do I have to tell you?'

Mark said, 'The answer to your question, Dorcas, is yes, I can get up early. And will. So is everyone satisfied?'

'I expect you are!' Joanna said, and gave him a smile that was at once artless and full of meaning. The innocent words held a wealth of meaning for him. He glanced anxiously at his mother, but fortunately she appeared not to have noticed the slight emphasis Joanna had put on the word 'you'. Secretly amused by her impudence, he nevertheless felt a prickle of unease at her boldness. His mother was no fool, and a few more such remarks might well register with her and set alarm bells ringing. He took a deep breath to calm his nerves. The sooner the whole matter was done with, the better it would be for all of them. Joanna had always been unpredictable and she could easily overplay her hand. There was no time to be lost; he would speak to his mother at the first opportunity.

*

While in France, Joanna kept her diary behind the oak chest in the bedroom she shared with Dorcas; the chest was so heavy that the servants rarely moved it. The narrow space between chest and wall accumulated dust and the occasional cobweb, and there was also a damp patch on the wall which was the original reason for the positioning of the chest. The diary, therefore, was also prone to damp but as Joanna eased it from its hiding-place the next morning, she blew away the dust, wiped the slim volume on the hem of her dress and riffled through the pages to find the last entry.

'What to say?' she murmured as truth struggled with a desire to salvage what she could from her ruined dreams. She crossed to the table, so inconveniently placed away from the light and very inferior to the exquisite roll-topped bureau which Aunt Agatha had given her for her twelfth birthday. The present was so lavish that it had caused quite a stir among the family, who seemed to disapprove, but it had made Joanna review her opinion of the ageing spinster who lived on the other side of Folkestone.

Now that the time had come to write in the diary Joanna dared not reread the previous day's entry, for it would point up the wide gulf which existed between her expectations and the reality. Seating herself on the stool she reached for her pen, dipped it into the ink and, turning to the next page, wrote: '*15th April, 1912*'.

Now that the moment had come to commit the facts to paper, doubts crowded in. Suppose someone found and read the diary? She would be in serious trouble and, worst of all, Mark would think she had betrayed him.

'Darling Mark!' she whispered, filled with a great sadness that the romance had been so rudely shattered. She decided she would have to describe the events obscurely so that no one but herself would understand the true meaning.

> I am no longer a child but a disenchanted woman whose heart is broken . . .

She supposed it was shattered beyond repair, but if that were so then the rest of her life would be nothing but a sorrowful postscript.

> . . . I must remake my life from this moment on, carrying my heartache close to my very soul . . .

If only she had a close friend in whom to confide. But her closest friend was Mark and she could hardly reveal her despair to him. He would laugh and call her, 'My funny little foundling', and her tragic moment would be spoilt.

'Why did it have to be so awful?' she demanded aloud. If it was always that way, then she did not relish the idea of a husband. Perhaps with another man it might be more enjoyable, although she could not imagine how the act could be improved. A faint smile suddenly lit her face as she thought of the hated Isobel and imagined the shock she was in for on her wedding night.

'And serves you right!' she said. Had Mama and Papa not been so blind, they might have considered the possibilities of a union between Joanna and their precious son! For a moment Joanna imagined a scene in which she declared herself with child. That would put the cat among the pigeons! A new thought struck her. Perhaps when a child was intended the process of lovemaking was somehow different and much more enjoyable. Was that it? She felt warmed by this sudden hope, and continued:

> Today we are going to the fort for our French picnic. Baguettes, squashy Camembert from the farm, apples and nuts and 'le vin rouge' from Monsieur Dupard's vineyard. Always the same picnic, yet for me it will never be the same again. For I have lost . . .

What exactly had she lost, she wondered, apart from her virginity? She still had her faith in God, and her health, and her adoptive family and friends, but she had surrendered part of herself and must therefore be a different person. Since she certainly did not feel enriched she must be the poorer – but in what way?

> . . . my innocence.

Yes, that was it, exactly. She sighed.

> M. winked at me at breakfast, but otherwise said very little. I wonder what he is thinking today. Is he pleased that it happened or does he regret it? . . .

Abruptly she sprang to her feet as Dorcas's footsteps sounded on the wooden stairs. By the time she entered the room the diary was back behind the chest and Joanna was busily tidying her hair.

Dorcas had inherited her father's looks; she had mousey hair and hazel eyes that were marred by a heavy forehead and brows. Without a word to Joanna, she snatched up a brush and began to tug at her hair impatiently.

Joanna said, 'I shall sit next to Mark.'

Dismayed, Dorcas whirled to face her. 'But it's my turn!' she protested. 'You sat next to him last year. You promised! Oh, I shall tell Mama!'

'Baby!'

'I'm not, but it's not fair! You're a hateful beast, Jo, and anyway I shall remind Mark. He'll know whose turn it is. So there!'

Joanna adopted what she hoped was an expression of disdain. 'You really are the most infantile creature—' she began loftily, but Dorcas had thrown down the hairbrush and now rushed off in search of her mother.

Joanna regarded her reflection soberly and said, 'I should sit next to Mark, Mama, because he has had carnal knowledge of me.' She whispered the words, savouring the 'carnal knowledge'. What a dreadful thing she had done, but she had done it all for love. 'He has had carnal knowledge of me,' she repeated. Yes, that is certainly what she ought to say; that would put an end to their nagging. They would know then that she was a force to be reckoned with and not a nameless nobody. But of course it was impossible. Mama would clutch her heart and swoon, Mark would throw a fit and Dorcas would go red in the face and burst into tears. Only Suzanne would be unaffected, for she was too young to understand. For a moment Joanna was tempted by this melodramatic vision, but in her heart she knew she could not go through with it. The whole day would be spoiled; the whole holiday would be ruined and Mark would never forgive her. She might even be banished from the household for ever. No, for Mark's sake she would keep her own counsel. Their secret would be safe with her.

She gathered up gloves and parasol and followed Dorcas down the stairs and out on to the road where the servant, Louise, was stowing the picnic hamper in the boot of the carriage. Dorcas, almost in tears, was complaining to Mama about her. Mark glanced at Joanna and, to her surprise, did not immediately smile as he usually did.

Mama also caught sight of her and said sharply, 'It was most unkind of you, Jo, to upset your sister. You know it is her turn to sit with Mark. Whatever has got into you?'

Opening the parasol as roughly as she could, Joanna rested it on her shoulder and twirled it angrily. 'Dorcas is not my sister!' she declared.

Mama gave her a warning look and said, 'Now don't start that again, Joanna! You are old enough to know better. Really, you are the most ungrateful child.'

'I'm not a child! I'm seventeen.'

Dorcas said shrilly, 'I don't want you for my sister, so there!'

Joanna ignored her.

Suzanne, not to be outdone, said, 'Nor do I! Why not, Dorky? Why don't we want—'

Joanna told her loftily, 'Little girls should be seen and not heard, Dorcas.'

Mama said, 'Get into the carriage, Joanna, before I lose patience with you. You will sit between me and Suzanne, and that's an end to it. And put on your gloves. If Papa were here he would—'

'I wish he were!' Joanna made no move towards the carriage but tugged at the offending gloves. 'Then we need not be jammed together in the carriage like sardines in a tin. We would have to take the dog-cart as well, and Louise could travel in it with Dorcas and Suzanne—'

Dorcas glared down from her place in the carriage. 'Why should I have to go with Louise?'

'Because—' Joanna broke off suddenly as she felt the pressure of Mark's hand on her right arm.

He whispered, 'Let it go, Jo! For me!' and then handed her up into the carriage. Dorcas was already installed, as was Suzanne. After a moment's hesitation Joanna seated herself next to Suzanne with as much aplomb as she could manage. Mama joined them, then Mark sprang up to sit beside a beaming Dorcas. At the front of the carriage, Stevens, the coachman, was collecting up the reins and Louise scrambled up beside him. The touch of Mark's hand had restored Joanna to a good humour and she suddenly smiled at Dorcas.

Dorcas stared back suspiciously. 'What are you laughing at?' she asked.

'I'm not laughing, I'm smiling!' Joanna turned her head fractionally so that her smile encompassed Mark. He had once told her that her smile was like the sun after rain. He grinned back at her and her spirits lifted. He still loved her! There was still a chance that he would change his mind about Isobel. Suddenly the day seemed brighter. She had prayed hard the night before and surely God had listened to her impassioned plea; she would leave the matter in His capable hands and everything would somehow turn out for the best. For the present, they were going to the fort and she was going to enjoy herself.

Stevens glanced back and said, 'All set now, are we, ma'am?' and Mama nodded.

'Giddy-up, there!' Stevens' whip touched the mare's rump lightly and she broke into a leisurely trot. As the carriage gathered speed Joanna tickled Suzanne's leg and then denied all knowledge of it and pretended it must have been a mouse. When Suzanne giggled delightedly Joanna felt the tension within her fade and gave herself up to the motion of the carriage. As she did so Mark caught her eye and smiled again, and Joanna felt the day grow rosy with promise.

Chapter Two

THE VISIT TO THE medieval fort was timed to be the high spot of the holiday each year. It was also a sign that the stay in France was almost over, and for Mary Grosvenor it heralded four fretful days of washing, ironing and packing in preparation for the family's return to England. Although she welcomed the conclusion of the holiday there was the long journey home to be borne, and she hated the sea when it was at all rough. The Easter holiday was the only time of the year when she did not have the support of her husband, Maurice, since his work on the estate could not be interrupted for so long a period. At least, that was his excuse. Mary suspected that he simply preferred the too rare pleasure of solitude, and she sympathized with him.

Today, as usual, the ride had been long and uncomfortable, but she silenced the complaints of the children by her oft-repeated assurance that a little suffering was good for the soul. In fact, she herself was heartily relieved when the lagoon appeared to the left of the road, signalling the end of their journey. Fort de Salses was situated a few miles further on, just outside the small town of Salses and surrounded by vineyards. The fort itself was ringed with grass, but as this might be damp the family had learned to bring rugs on which to sit. A large white cloth, spread upon the ground, would serve as a table.

'Down you get!' Mary told them as the carriage rolled to a halt and Stevens wiped the sweat from his face.

'And we're all in one piece!' laughed Dorcas, reminding them of a previous excursion which had ended disastrously with the loss of a rear wheel.

Mark helped Joanna down while Stevens did the same for Dorcas. Louise managed the descent unaided and began at once to open the boot and take out the rugs and the cloth. There would be no plates; instead, they would manage as best they could with a large napkin. Mary insisted that this was a peasant picnic. The more genteel picnics which they enjoyed in England were altogether different, but the charm of this occasion lay in its informality. While Louise unpacked the hamper, the family stretched their legs after the long drive. In spite of the heat Suzanne raced across the grass, screaming with delight, and Dorcas, forgetting her superior years, ran after her.

'Girls! Your parasols!' cried Mary, but they pretended not to hear and she shook her head. 'Dorcas will be as freckled as a bird's egg,' she muttered despairingly, 'but will she listen? She will not!'

Mark did not answer and she glanced at him briefly, registering his distracted air and the narrowed eyes beneath the straw boater. He was watching Joanna who had wandered off alone towards the vines but Mary, turning to follow his gaze, saw nothing unusual about the girl's appearance. At least, she thought, she had had the sense to take her parasol and she was walking demurely, bothering no one. Perhaps, after all, she would do them credit. Thankfully, she was very different now from the small fiery creature she had once been. With a smile Mary remembered her as a child – dark eyes flashing, voice shrill, quick to anger, but with a generous heart. And with an abundant energy which frequently made Mary long for the children's bedtime and the prospect of a little peace and quiet.

Joanna had been the very opposite of their own fair girls

with their docile temperaments and obedient ways. Poor Joanna! Even now Mary could find it in her heart to pity the child, although she had frequently doubted the wisdom of taking her into the family. On rare occasions Joanna could be warm and loving, but even as a young girl she had kept her own counsel; had never allowed anyone to get really close to her. With the exception of Mark, of course. In Joanna's eyes Mark could do no wrong.

Suddenly she said, 'Joanna will be quite beautiful in her own way.'

'You think so?' Mark's tone lacked enthusiasm.

'Don't you?' She looked at him, surprised. He had always championed the girl, for some reason; making excuses for her wild behaviour and laughing at her worst excesses. Mary had always found this very irritating, but had schooled herself not to show it. Now, when she expected him to agree with her complimentary remark he seemed unwilling. She told herself that she would never understand her son and would be relieved when he was safely married. Isobel would be a much needed restraining influence. Mark had been the apple of his father's eye, the longed-for son and heir, and Maurice had indulged him, forgiving his occasional deceits and ignoring his faults. She suspected that Mark was no saint where women were concerned, but her husband had scoffed at her fears, explaining that a young man must sow his wild oats. Now, however, he was to marry the sober and sensible Isobel, and Mary's relief was almost tangible. With her son safely out of the way, they could concentrate on finding husbands for the girls. First Joanna, then Dorcas and, eventually, Suzanne.

She busied herself with the picnic but a small doubt now niggled at the back of her mind. Mark had seemed a little quiet this morning, she thought, and hoped he was not going down with a fever. As usual she had insisted that while in France they drink nothing but boiled water or wine, but it was just possible that he had contracted something.

Unless he was bored ... That was more likely, she concluded. Mark had outgrown the family holiday some years ago, but had been too kind to say so. Mary had been tempted to leave him at home with his father, but then she would have been in France with only Stevens in case of emergency and that would have been most unsatisfactory.

'We should have persuaded Isobel to join us,' she said.

'I'm glad you didn't.'

'Mark!' Her tone was reproachful. 'I thought you were fond of Isobel – I mean, really fond.'

He shrugged his shoulders and in Mary's mind a new doubt surfaced. Not a rift between Mark and Isobel, she thought, suddenly afraid to ask. 'She's such a sweet girl,' she said.

'Mmm!'

'You don't sound very sure?'

'Of course I'm sure.'

'She's beautiful, Mark. I sometimes wonder if you deserve her.' It was true, she reflected. Isobel had that look of fragile bone china which epitomized the English beauty and Mark would be envied. Not that she *was* fragile. She had a good brain and knew how to use it. Yes, she would be good for Mark.

As Louise placed bread and cheeses on the cloth, Mark suddenly moved closer to Mary and took her arm.

'A word in your ear, Mama,' he said, his voice low. 'Away from the servants.'

Startled, she repeated, 'Away from the servants? But why?'

'Please, Mama!'

She looked at him in alarm. 'A word about what?'

'Just walk with me a moment,' he said, and after a brief hesitation she allowed herself to be led to one side so that the servants could not overhear them.

'What on earth is this about?' she asked, her anxiety increasing.

'It's about Joanna.' His expression frightened her. 'I'm afraid, Mama, that I have something disturbing to tell you.'

'Disturbing? About Joanna? Oh!' In spite of her efforts to remain calm, Mary's right hand crept to her heart. Her son was looking at her with a sombre expression.

'I've heard something, Mama. Something rather serious.' He avoided her eyes. 'Information which . . .' He sighed heavily. 'It seems that yesterday she was seen by someone in the woods.'

'In the woods? But Mark, what's wrong with that?' Already her throat had tightened. Intuitively she longed to cover her ears, unwilling to hear whatever Mark wished to tell her.

'It seems she was not alone in the woods but . . .' He raised his eyes to hers, his reluctance obvious. 'I'm afraid, Mama – well, to put it bluntly, she was with a young man!'

For a moment shock robbed Mary of speech. As the realization of his words sank in she was horribly aware that this was one of the disasters she had dreaded during these past years – that the wild, headstrong child would somehow bring disgrace upon the family. Although she had never consciously considered it before, Mary now knew that the possibility had always been there, pushed to the back of her mind. Joanna, the cuckoo in the nest!

'Joanna and a young man? I don't believe it!' Mary clutched at his arm. 'She wouldn't! And anyway, she doesn't know any young men. You must be mistaken, Mark; it can't have been Joanna!' Yet even as she protested she knew it was possible. Joanna alone in the woods with a young man! Oh, yes! It was certainly possible.

'It can't be true!' she said again, but with less conviction than before. Mother and son regarded each other unhappily. 'How do you know?' she asked at last. 'Who told you, Mark? Can we trust whoever it was? They might have been mistaken!' She was already wondering how to break

22

the news to her husband. A letter would not reach him in time and, in any case, it might be better to tell him in person on her arrival home. A small, mean thought came to her. Now Maurice would have to accept that all those years ago she had been right. He had over-ridden all her doubts, had insisted that the child came to them and, against all Mary's better judgement, she had allowed herself to be persuaded. It seemed her reservations had been founded on common sense after all; she had been right to hesitate.

As Mark remained silent she repeated, 'I must know who told you this. Surely you can see that? I shall have to know everything before I tell your father.'

Mark bit his lip. 'I will only tell you if you promise not to blame Joanna. You know what a child she is. I mean a serious promise, Mama. On oath. On your mother's grave!'

'Oh, Mark! Don't be so ridiculous!'

'Then I can't tell you.'

She recognized the stubborn look settling on his face and said, 'Oh, very well, then. I swear it. Now who saw them? Who told you this?'

'I did, Mama. *I* saw them.'

She caught her breath. 'You? Oh, Mark!' She stared at him wide-eyed. 'You saw them and yet you did nothing?'

'I saw them from a distance, Mama, and at first I had no idea it was Joanna. I was amused – I assumed it was one of the village girls with an admirer, and no concern of mine, but then I saw her coming back to tea – somewhat dishevelled, I have to say. I recognized the clothes she was wearing too. It was Joanna, Mama. I'm sorry but there's absolutely no doubt in my mind.'

She stared at him fearfully. 'And the young man?'

'I didn't recognize him. They were too far away.'

She thought she sensed a hesitation before he answered, and now pressed him again. 'You are sure you didn't recognize the man?'

'Quite certain.'

'He won't look me in the face,' she thought suddenly. He *did* recognize him! 'You mustn't protect anyone,' she insisted. 'If you know who it was, you must tell me. It's your duty, Mark.' Her mind raced. There was the son from the nearby farm . . . or maybe the young doctor who had attended Suzanne when she was stung by a bee . . . or the young English artist staying at the Auberge le Marin . . .

'The artist from the Auberge!' she cried. 'Was it him?'

'No, no! It wasn't him.'

'The young doctor?'

'I tell you I didn't see his face!'

'Then how can you know for certain that it wasn't the doctor if you weren't near enough to—'

'You will have to trust my judgement!'

Startled by the sharpness of his tone, Mary bit back an equally sharp reply, reminding herself that for Mark it must have been a terrible shock. He had always been Joanna's favourite and now, it seemed, he had been ousted. No doubt his pride was somewhat dented. But Joanna in such a compromising situation! She was beginning to feel a little faint and put a hand on her son's arm to steady herself. She must find the strength to deal with this revelation until she could confer with her husband. Maurice would know what to do for the best.

'And they were – I mean, she . . .' She stopped, unwilling to put her worst fears into words. It was unthinkable that they had been – *physically* involved. She could hear Dorcas and Suzanne laughing, and Stevens was talking to Louise, but their voices seemed to reach her from a great distance. The horses whinnied gently. It was all so unbelievable. The fort picnic was so special to them – and now Mark had ruined it! No! Not Mark. She must not blame her son for having to impart such awful news. It was Joanna who had ruined everything. She felt a wave of resentment towards the girl.

Mark said quietly, 'They were definitely – how shall I put it?'

She swallowed. 'They weren't – indecorous?' The word sounded ridiculous even to her own ears. 'Oh, Mark! You know what I mean.'

'Yes, Mama. I know what you mean and yes, they were. Very indecorous!'

'But if you were so far away . . .'

'I'm sorry, Mama, but they were definitely – oh, poor Joanna! She is so vulnerable. You must see that she has been led astray.'

'Oh, my God!' She raised her head with an effort and looked across at Joanna who had now been joined by the other two girls. In her cream lace dress she looked quite charming and so demure; so innocent!

'I thought it best to tell you, Mama.' He looked at her anxiously.

Mary nodded distractedly. 'Of course. And thank you, Mark. It must have been hard for you.'

Dorcas began to run towards them, flailing her arms like the sails of a windmill, shouting that she was starving. Poor Dorcas and poor Suzanne. It seemed that Joanna would bring shame on them all. As Dorcas reached her she threw her arms around her mother's waist and Mary bent to hug her. Joanna must not be allowed to spoil the girls' chances, she thought, but what was to be done? Thankfully she knew that if there were unpleasant decisions to be made her husband would be the one to make them. It would all have to wait until they reached home.

Forcing a smile, she held out her arms to Suzanne who had followed her sister. Joanna was walking towards them at a more leisurely pace but Mary turned her head away. In her present state of mind she felt quite unable to give the wretched girl even the ghost of a smile, and was glad that Mark greeted her with a laughing remark about the temperature of the wine. A favourite phrase of her long-dead grandmother came back to her with horrible clarity.

'It will all end in tears!'

*

By 2 o'clock the picnic food had disappeared down hungry throats and the soporific effect of the wine was beginning to wear off. A slight breeze had sprung up as one by one the members of the little party discovered fresh energy and mustered enthusiasm for the longish tour which awaited them. The exploration of the fort would be led by the official guide, who paused frequently to pass on relevant information. On a warm day, the hour-long walk could be very tiring but at least the interior was shady. Joanna hoped there would not be too many questions, for they delayed the guide and extended the tour. She was feeling a little happier now. The familiar surroundings and Mark's kindness were overlaying the trauma of the previous day with a veneer of serenity, and for the time being she could pretend to herself that all was well.

Once inside the fort she stood patiently with the rest of the family as the guide, resplendent in his grey uniform, waited for late arrivals to swell the group. The awareness of her sin had faded a little in Joanna's mind and the sharp sense of disappointment had given way to one of resignation. At least she was here with Mark, while the hated Isobel was miles away on the other side of the Channel. She would make the most of the last few days of the holiday and would reconsider her life when she returned to England. Mama bent to reprimand Suzanne, who was fidgeting from one foot to the other, and the little girl's face crumpled ominously. Joanna moved closer to Mark and whispered, 'What's the matter with Mama? She seems rather short-tempered all of a sudden.'

He shrugged. 'One of her headaches, I think.'

'Did she say it was a headache? I saw you two plotting.'

'We weren't plotting, just talking.'

26

'But what *about*?'

From the corner of her eye Joanna saw the guide beckoning impatiently to a noisy family of four who sauntered through the gates, blinking in the sudden gloom.

The guide called to them, '*Dépêchez-vous, s'il vous plaît, messieurs, mesdames!*'

But they shouted back, refusing to be hurried, determined to buy their guide-book and postcards, arguing amongst themselves as they searched for money with which to buy their tickets.

In a low voice Mark said, 'If you must know, someone saw us yesterday.'

Joanna's heart almost stopped beating and her rolled parasol slipped from her fingers. When Mark bent to retrieve it she caught sight of Mary's face and saw the tension there. As he returned the parasol to her she whispered, 'Saw us! Who could have seen us?' and was annoyed to hear that her voice shook.

'Mama won't say, but it hardly matters, does it? What matters—' He stopped abruptly as Suzanne ran towards them and snatched at Mark's hand.

'I want to walk with you!' she told him. 'I don't want to walk with Mama.'

Mark said, 'Not now, Suzanne.'

'But I *do*!' She stared up at him with the appealing expression which experience had taught her would melt the hardest heart.

Joanna waited desperately, hiding her anxiety as best she could. If Mama knew, then shortly Papa would know also . . . She felt frightened by the speed of what promised to be her downfall. Or was she exaggerating the threat to her secure little world? She wanted to think so. 'Melodramatic Anna' had been Mama's nickname for her as a child when she had made mountains out of molehills. Perhaps she was doing that now, but if so then why did her heart thump so fiercely? She drew a deep breath and let it out slowly.

Mark said, 'Go back to Mama, Suzanne.'

'I won't!'

Joanna gave her a little push. 'We're talking,' she said. 'Mark will walk with you later.'

The small mouth puckered disconsolately. 'I want him to walk with me *now*!'

Joanna gritted her teeth. 'Well, he doesn't want to walk with you so go away, Suzanne!' The words sounded harsher than she had intended and she was at once contrite, but the little girl suddenly gave in. She put out her tongue at Mark and then ran back to her mother.

Mark said, 'Whoever it was who recognized *you* did not identify *me*, thank God – but you promised, Joanna, that you would never tell.'

'I won't tell! Never! But – oh, what are we to do? What will happen to us?' A new idea came to her and she seized upon it easily. 'Will Isobel be told?'

'Of course not. Why should they involve Isobel? I told you – they didn't see me. Only you.'

For a moment the gloom of the castle interior seemed to press in upon her, crushing her spirit. She felt that she was drowning in a sea of trouble from which she could never be rescued. And Mark was to get off scot-free! She had always felt that life was unfair, but now she was certain of it.

'*Dépêchez-vous, messieurs, mesdames! Ah! Nous sommes toutes prêtes? Bon!*'

He led the way, with the chattering group behind him. Sick at heart, Joanna fell in behind the rest with Mark beside her.

'I'll never betray you,' she whispered as they moved out into the sunlit courtyard, 'but what am I to do? You'll have to help me, Mark.'

'Ssh! Not now, Joanna.'

He turned a look of feigned interest towards the guide and Joanna also tried hard to look attentive. To force down her panic she concentrated on the rapid French and attempted to translate it into English.

In earlier times the wide square had served both Spanish and English armies as a parade ground. Now it was empty except for a well in the centre. Joanna listened to the guide's familiar patter, aware of the awed glances of those who had never seen the fort before.

'. . . *élevé au cinquième siècle, sur la route Romaine* . . .'

Loudly Dorcas translated for the benefit of her younger sister: 'Built in the fifteenth century on the Roman route . . .'

'Don't tell me! I know!' cried Suzanne furiously. 'Tell her, Mama! I know what he's saying!'

'She does not!' Dorcas crowed. 'She's hopeless at French. Mam'selle said so.'

'Leave her alone, Dorky,' Mama said irritably. 'You do this every year, and you know she hates it. If she doesn't understand, that's her problem.'

'But if she doesn't understand the guide, there's no point in bringing her to the fort!' Dorcas insisted, unwisely pursuing her point. 'We should leave her at home to work on her lessons. Mam'selle says she's lazy. Mam'selle says—' She broke off as her mother reached forward suddenly and slapped her hand with considerable force.

'Mama!' She began to cry at once – loud, noisy sobs deliberately designed to cause the utmost embarrassment. She succeeded dramatically. The guide paused in mid-sentence, annoyed by the interruption, and everyone in the group turned with interest to watch the antics of the eccentric English family. Mark groaned and Joanna turned away to hide tears of mortification. This was all her fault, she thought guiltily. She understood the reason for her mother's changed mood, and now Dorcas would go into a sulk and the day would be spoiled. There seemed to be no end to the repercussions of yesterday's fiasco. For a moment there was no sound except for the girl's shrill sobbing, but then Mary apologized to the guide in her fluent French. Mark moved to stand beside Dorcas and whisper something soothing in her ear; Suzanne, a little unnerved by the atmosphere, hurried to take Mama's hand and Joanna found herself alone. Looking at Mama's white face, she felt a moment's compunction.

Mollified, the guide began again, rattling through the dimensions of the fort, the thickness of the walls, the quantities of food and wine consumed by the military garrison which had been quartered within the walls. When he had finished the little crowd nodded its appreciation of the information and he managed a tight smile. With a final stern glance at the English party he said, '*Suivez-moi!*' and they obediently followed him out of the courtyard, up a flight of stone steps and along a passage.

Joanna lagged behind, trying to avoid another glimpse of Mama's unhappy face. One thousand men had been garrisoned in the fort and Joanna tried, as she did every year, to imagine them hurrying about their everyday duties. She leaned back against the stone wall and closed her eyes, but this year the images eluded her. Letting the group move on without her, she struggled with the sense of isolation which now threatened. Her lips moved silently: 'Help me to be brave!' Seventeen had once seemed a very sophisticated age, but Mark's few whispered words had reduced her to a child again. There was so much trouble ahead and, since she could not possibly betray Mark, she would have to face it alone. Her one hope was that the confrontation might be delayed until the family reached England. Somewhat ingenuously, she wondered if they might overlook this one error. If they would, she told herself, she would never disappoint them again. She would promise anything they asked of her. *Anything.* She would be a model daughter, a daughter they could be proud of.

'Joanna!'

She opened her eyes hastily to see Mama glaring at her

from the curve in the passageway. 'What are you playing at now, Joanna?' she asked. 'We are all waiting for you.'

'I'm coming!' Joanna told her quickly.

Mama stood back to let her pass but as she did so, she said, 'I have heard some very disturbing news, Joanna. I shall have to talk to you later.'

Joanna took a quick look at her face and was not reassured. Mary's lips were compressed and her eyes were hard and unforgiving. The last of Joanna's fragile hopes immediately evaporated.

*

The summons came just before 9 o'clock and Joanna went downstairs with a heavy heart. Mama sat alone in the large room, her hands clasped in her lap, a glass of red wine on the small table beside her. There was no sign of Mark and Joanna did not know how to interpret his absence. She was relieved that her humiliation would not be a public affair, but the suspicion remained that he had simply chosen to avoid the unpleasant confrontation.

Mary pointed to the chair on the opposite side of the fireplace where a small fire burned smokily. 'Sit down, Joanna, and say nothing until I have finished.'

Joanna obeyed, trying to hide her nervousness behind a defiant expression. Whatever happened, she must not incriminate Mark.

Mary took a deep breath and for a moment Joanna felt sorry for her. She could imagine how hard it was for her mother to deal with such a calamity, and admired her for her prompt reaction to the unwelcome news. Her sympathy, however, was quickly withdrawn; her own troubles most certainly outweighed Mary's, she reminded herself.

'I have heard from someone who shall not be identified that you were seen with a young man in a compromising situation in the woods. This was the day before—'

'Who was it?'

'I don't intend to tell you – and I asked you to remain silent while I—'

'But you trust this person?'

'Of course I do. Why, do you deny it?' Mary looked at her with the beginnings of hope.

'No.' Joanna wondered who it was that Mary could trust so completely. Louise or Stevens, perhaps? But no. They would keep their own counsel. Servants knew their place.

'If you don't deny it, then please be quiet and allow me to finish.' Mary's face was very pale and again Joanna felt a sneaking regret that she should be the cause of so much anxiety. She had let them down; she had let herself down, too, and that was her greatest sorrow.

'Apart from the fact that such behaviour is extremely unsuitable for a young woman in your position, I wonder if you know how dangerous it is to ... to have ... to allow such—'

She faltered, but Joanna refused to help her. She had been told to remain silent and so she would.

'What I am trying to say is that certain ... close relations with a young man might result in ... might bring about – depending on how far these ... what familiarities you may have—' She put a hand to her throat, her agitation plain to see.

Joanna said abruptly, 'Yes, I did allow him to—' and then found to her annoyance that she, too, was unable to find the words to confess the deed. 'We did it, but there will be no consequences. I mean, no child.'

'But how can you possibly know that?' Mary demanded. 'I do hope this wretched man has not misled you, Joanna. There is really no way you can be sure.'

'But *he* was sure!'

'Oh, Joanna!'

There was a long silence and Joanna felt a flutter of doubt. Had Mark misled her? Surely not. She would never believe him capable of such a mean action. 'He would not have lied to me, Mama. I know it. You need not fear that I shall produce a child. I know we did wrong, but at least —'

'Joanna! Have you not listened to what I have been saying? There is *no way* to be sure. Life is not that simple, believe me, and if you are with child – though God forbid it! – you will break your father's heart! And mine. After all we have done for you, I cannot understand how you could allow this to happen. I have to know who this man is. You must tell me his name so that your father can write to him.'

As Joanna opened her mouth to protest, Mary silenced her with an angry wave of her hand and went on, 'He must be told that this must never happen again, and he must be made aware that if you are with child he must make an honest woman of you. If he is a suitable person, that is. I trust he is a gentleman?'

'He is.'

'And his name?'

Joanna pressed her lips together and stared stubbornly at her mother.

'Joanna! I insist.'

'You cannot force me to tell you. I have sworn not to reveal his name.'

'What nonsense! I insist that you tell me. Is it the artist, Frank Whatever-his-name-is?'

'No, Mama!'

'Then it is the doctor who attended Suzanne? He at least is a reasonable, personable young man. Is it him, Joanna? You will have to tell us some time, so why not now? Your father will insist on knowing his name. You could hardly have expected to keep the affair secret.'

'It's not an affair, Mama. It is over.'

'Over? Oh, you silly girl! You may think it over, but there may be years ahead of you during which you will learn that such folly is not so easily dismissed. Do you mean you no longer love this man?'

33

'I shall always love him. I mean that I shall never be able to be his wife.'

Mary's eyes widened in horror. 'You don't mean that this wretched man is married already? Oh, no! Not even you could be that foolish!'

Joanna cursed her careless words. She must not allow her mother to guess that her own son was the 'wretch' to whom she referred so frequently. 'I shall not say any more,' she said quickly.

'Indeed you will, Joanna. You will tell me his name and then I shall know the worst.'

'It is over. There is no point.'

'Joanna! I tell you again that you have been tricked by this wretch. It may not be over. Your father will go mad when I break it to him. Poor Maurice, he will take it very badly. How could you treat us all so shabbily?' She stood up suddenly, clasping and unclasping her hands. 'Please, Joanna. Tell me. It will be best if you do. How can we help you if you refuse to co-operate? You must see how impossible it all is.'

'I don't need help, Mama. It is over, and it will never happen again. No one need ever have known except for that Peeping Tom! Why don't people mind their own business? Why stir up all this trouble?'

'You refuse to tell me his name?'

'I have sworn a solemn oath not to do so.'

Angry colour surged into Mary's face and she lifted her hand as though to strike Joanna, who instinctively stepped back. Mary's arm fell and tears filled her eyes. 'You see how your stupidity has affected me?' she cried. 'First you break my heart, and then you make me so angry I could— Oh, Joanna!'

She sank down on to the chair and began to sob while Joanna watched helplessly. After a moment she knelt beside the chair and tried to put an arm around her mother's shoulders.

'Don't!' sobbed Mary with a twist of her shoulders. 'Don't touch me! Just go away before I say something I shall regret.'

With tears pressing at her own eyelids Joanna stood up and hurried from the room. She saw Mark standing half-way along the hallway and wondered if he had been listening. As she ran up the stairs she heard him call her name, but for the first time in her life she suddenly hated him.

Chapter Three

FOR JOANNA, THE REST OF the holiday was a nightmare of alternate hope and despair. Hope, when Mark assured her that he would do all he could to persuade his parents to be lenient. Despair when, in her heart, she knew that nothing he might say could save her from retribution of some kind. More than anything she mourned her fall from grace. She had never been a favourite, except with Mark, but the family had treated her well and she had considered herself one of them. Now she felt like an outsider and the more she considered her position, the more she realized exactly how much she had to lose. Her few stolen moments with Mark had somehow assumed a significance she had never anticipated; the indiscretion had become a crime. The excitement had been nothing more than a foolish error of judgement – and a dangerous one at that. But what could they do to her? They would punish her, she was sure of that, but what exactly could they do to her? Surely they would never turn her out into the street! However grave her crime, they would never abandon her – would they?

For several days after their return to England she turned the problem over in her mind, dreading the fateful summons from Papa and yet anxious to know the worst. They even despatched Mark to seek her out and, the final irony, to try to persuade her to name her seducer! On reflection, it seemed to Joanna that there were two ways open to her. She could admit to having made a foolish mistake, be totally abject and throw herself on their mercy. Or she could insist that, although the 'affair' was at an end, she loved the man and had no regrets. The former might save her from total disaster; the latter would probably serve no useful purpose. It was not even true, for her feelings towards Mark had changed and that saddened her. Suffering in silence for someone you loved was a noble thing to do, but his insistence that his share in the episode should never be revealed had wounded her. He maintained that his marriage to Isobel must go ahead – which was obviously sufficient reason why the truth should remain hidden – but still his reluctance to share the blame smacked of betrayal.

Of course she could break her part of the bargain but, though tempted from time to time, her pride would not allow it. *She* would do the honourable thing even if Mark faltered. It occurred to her that she might be sent to live with Aunt Agatha in Folkestone, which would be tolerable if dull. There seemed no good reason why her aunt should assume the burden of a disgraced niece, but it was a remote possibility. After all, her aunt *had* given her the beautiful bureau and several other expensive gifts, so she must entertain some kindly feelings towards her. Briefly Joanna considered the possibility of having a child, but reassured herself that that was not very likely. She had heard the servants gossiping among themselves about the sister of the cook who had similarly fallen from grace on more than one occasion; she had remained childless. It seemed that there were people, Agatha included, who never did produce offspring. For a while she brooded on the idea that she would bear Mark a handsome son, and that the haughty Isobel would prove unable to have any children. Mark would then be forced to beg Joanna to allow him to adopt her child. Or, better still, Isobel would fall from her horse and be killed and then Mark would be free to marry again. He would reveal that he was the father of Joanna's son and would wed her against the wishes of his family. They might even elope! Unfortunately these scenarios had only a limited appeal, since Mark had fallen in her estimation and no longer appeared entirely eligible as a husband. She was beginning to believe that there must be others more chivalrous who might replace Mark in her affections.

Joanna's patience finally evaporated and she wrote in her diary:

> I cannot bear the suspense much longer. Why doesn't Papa send for me? If he is punishing me by this delay it is too cruel. Perhaps they do not know what to do with me. If they do not send for me by tomorrow evening I shall demand to speak to Papa myself . . .

*

That same evening Mary and Maurice sat in the library, sipping brandy but comforted not at all by its warming properties. Mary clasped her brandy glass with both hands and swirled the golden liquid with quick, nervous movements. She stared into the fire, her eyes dark with worry, glancing only rarely towards her husband.

'You must see, Maurice,' she insisted unhappily, 'that nothing must be allowed to spoil our own children's future. He may be your brother, but that is no reason why he should not shoulder his responsibilities. At the very least, he must be told what has happened.'

Her husband sighed heavily and shook his head, apparently unconvinced by the argument. She regarded him with exasperation. Maurice Grosvenor was the oldest of the three sons and, since the death of his father many years earlier, had assumed the role of head of the family. His mother, Clementine, was still alive but lived in Portugal

38

with another son, Elliot, who at sixty was one year younger than Maurice. Agatha, the only daughter, was a year older.

'I don't care to burden him—' Maurice began, but Mary interrupted.

'But what about us? Why should we be burdened? Why should we bear it alone? What have we done to be punished in this way?'

He tutted irritably. 'It is not a matter of guilt and punishment; it is a matter of responsibility. We adopted the girl and we look upon her as our own. We can't suddenly try to shift that responsibility at the first hurdle.' He threw back his head, finished the brandy that remained in his glass and poured himself another.

Mary said, 'Do keep a clear head, Maurice. That's your fourth.'

'I can count, thank you, Mary!'

She flushed at his tone. 'It won't help us if you cannot think clearly.'

As though to prove how little he cared for her rebuke he emptied his glass again, but as he reached for the decanter Mary sprang from the chair and snatched it away. She carried it to the side table and set it down, then turned to face him.

'Just tell me what we are to do,' she demanded, 'and then you can drink yourself into oblivion! I say we send the girl to Elliot, whether he likes it or not.'

'He *won't* like it!' He glared at her, his face flushing with anger. 'What is he going to tell Catherine? What will it do to their marriage? Don't you care?'

'Not particularly!'

'No, you might not, but that's because you're jealous, Mary, and always have been. Jealous of the bond between us. Jealous of the strong family ties that exist between one brother and—'

'Piffle!' Her look was scathing. 'I have put up with this tale of brotherly love for too long, Maurice. You did what

39

you did from cowardice, not love. You were too afraid of the scandal, too afraid of what your precious Mama would say. Oh, yes, I'm not as stupid as you like to believe, Maurice. Your mother would have turned her back on Elliot if she had known what was going on – and well you know it! When she did find out, you simply stepped in to prevent an unpleasant incident because neither of you had the courage to stand up to your domineering mother.'

His prolonged silence satisfied her and allowed her anger to cool a little. Seeing his obvious confusion, she even began to regret her outburst, and when she spoke again her voice was less strident. 'I am not saying that I was unwilling to take her in, Maurice. I did so long for a girl, and we didn't know then that we would have two of our own. And she was such a funny little scrap.' Her face softened. 'So tiny, with that mop of dark hair and those big brown eyes. No, I don't really regret it, not even now. You know that. Nobody could ever accuse me of harbouring any ill-will towards the girl. I have done my best to treat her just like the rest of the children, though God knows it has been difficult at times. Joanna has been more trouble than the other three put together. Oh, don't give me that look, Maurice. You know it's true.'

At last he nodded and she thought suddenly how very tired he looked.

'I know,' he said. 'You were wonderful about it all. I've always been grateful – but I *know* Elliot, and I knew how hard it was for him. Mother has always been a forceful character, and he never could stand up to her, even as a boy.' He sighed. 'Poor Joanna.'

'Poor *Joanna*? What about poor us?'

'I know, and I accept that she hasn't been an easy child. But we do love her, Mary, in spite of her wild ways.' He looked at her for reassurance. 'Don't we? Don't you?'

For a moment Mary was silent, then she nodded unwillingly. 'I love her, but I won't let her ruin our own children's lives. If she is with child—'

'If she is, then we certainly shouldn't abandon her!'

'I'm not suggesting we *abandon* her! I'm not saying we should send her to a home for fallen women, Maurice. I *am* suggesting we send her to her father! Let Elliot take a turn with her. He can tell Catherine any tale he chooses; he can say he is doing it to help us – just as you helped him all those years ago. He doesn't have to confess it all.'

'But if she is with child? What then?'

'Then we shall all have to think again. But she may not be, and I see no reason to anticipate a disaster which may never happen. Oh, please do see reason, Maurice. They only have Leo to consider, while we have two daughters to marry. I think we have done our share, and your brother should be eternally grateful that we have done it so well – until now,' she added lamely. 'And we can hardly be blamed for what happened.'

'Then who is to blame?' He stood up and moved to pour himself another drink.

Mary bridled defensively. 'Well, certainly not me, Maurice. You cannot lay the blame at my door. I can't be expected to keep the girl on a leash, for heaven's sake! We could not possibly expect that someone would take advantage of her in such a place. I would have staked my life on it that no one there wished her harm.'

'It must have been the artist,' he said. 'Artists are so bohemian – like writers. It couldn't have been the doctor; he would have too much to lose. The farmer's son is already married, and surely would not risk his wife's wrath if he set his cap at an English tourist. I'm sure it was the artist, but we shall never prove it.'

Forgetting her earlier reserves about the brandy, Mary now poured herself another and swallowed a large mouthful. 'Mark is sure it was no one he recognized,' she repeated, 'but when he tackled Joanna she refused to say who it was. She would only say who it *wasn't*! She is as stubborn as a mule and always has been.'

'We should not have left Mark to do the talking.'

'But Maurice, he offered to talk to her; it was his idea. He suggested that since he is closer to her than either of us, there was more chance of him discovering the truth. And he was right, Maurice. If Mark could not wheedle the truth out of her, we will stand no chance.'

He looked at her and she watched him uneasily.

'What I don't understand,' he said slowly, 'is this. If the man was not known to us then he was a stranger, and if she was seduced by a stranger against her will, why did she not come running to us to complain of what must have been . . . rape?'

'Don't, Maurice! That horrible word!'

They looked at each other unhappily as it hung in the air between them. Mary knew that one last possibility remained. One unpalatable possibility had not been discussed and never would be, if she had her way. If Joanna had given herself *willingly* to someone she knew and trusted, that could only be one person. But that was unthinkable. Neither of them, she knew, dared even contemplate such an explanation. If such a shameful thing had happened, they had best remain in blissful ignorance. The silence lengthened uncomfortably, then Maurice poured himself another brandy and said roughly, 'My sixth, if we're still counting!'

She stared at him without replying until he shifted his gaze, unable to bear the expression in her eyes.

At last Mary said carefully, 'We shall never know the truth of the matter.'

'Probably not,' he agreed.

'Never!' she repeated. 'You know what I'm saying, Maurice?'

He whispered, 'It's not possible, Mary. No, I won't believe it. Never!'

'Not Mark!' she said, but she framed the words soundlessly. True, Mark and Joanna were not brother and sister but . . . No! It was not possible.

She stared at her husband until he nodded. 'Maybe better that way,' he mumbled.

'And we shall not talk about it to her again.'

'No. We have done all we can.'

'Ah. I see.'

'We shall send her to Elliot – and pray!' She pressed home her advantage. 'It's agreed, Maurice?'

'I suppose so.'

His weakness angered her. 'For God's sake, Maurice, pull yourself together! I am asking you, yes or no? Does she go to Elliot? Don't leave me to manage alone. You must write to Elliot and tell him that we are sending her. Don't ask him, *tell* him. Say that we are not prepared to—'

There was a knock on the door and she stopped abruptly.

Maurice called, 'Come in!' and Joanna entered the room.

Her face was white, her hands were clenched and her face was set in the rebellious expression they both recognized. Before either of them could speak she had pulled herself up to her full height. For a moment she appeared speechless, but when she did speak the words tumbled out in a trembling rush.

'I want to say that I'm sorry about what happened, but I can't undo it although I would if I could – and I know you'll never forgive me so it's no good asking, but I want to know what's going to happen to me?'

Maurice began, 'My dear Joanna . . .' but Mary, suspecting that he would weaken, gave him a sharp look and took control of the situation herself.

'We do not wish to discuss the matter, Joanna,' she said briskly. 'Not one word. It has been decided that you are going to stay with your Uncle Elliot and Aunt Catherine – for a long holiday.'

It took a moment or two for Joanna to digest this information, but when she did her mouth quivered.

'But they live in Portugal!'

'They have often asked that you should visit them, and it now seems a good time to accept their kind invitation.' Mary ignored the surprise on her husband's face and willed him to keep quiet. She saw with pleasure that Joanna was shocked.

'I'm going to *Portugal*?'

They both nodded.

Joanna looked stricken. 'But for how long?' she asked. 'What about Mark's wedding? That's in six months' time!'

Mary fought down an image of Joanna six months into her time and said, 'For at least a year!' Even if by some miracle the girl was not with child, it would do her good to realize the extent of her folly. Joanna's face had crumpled and her look of rebellion had been replaced by something very like fear. She looked from one to the other and apparently saw no chance of a reprieve.

'When?' she asked dully.

'As soon as we can book a passage on a suitable ship. And we shall tell everyone that you are going for a holiday.'

'A *year's* holiday!'

Maurice said, 'Elliot will make you very welcome, my dear,' but spoiled it by adding doubtfully, 'I'm sure he will.'

Mary saw the gleam of tears in the girl's eyes but hardened her heart. 'It is not the end of the world, child,' she said. 'The mine is quite civilized. It is called San Domingos and there are—'

Joanna swallowed hard. 'And if I refuse to go?' she challenged.

Mary's lips became a thin, hard line. 'You are going!' she told her. 'And there's an end to it!'

*

Joanna sat on the swing which hung below the sycamore and pushed herself slowly to and fro, watched curiously by a dove in the boughs above her. A week had passed since her parents had broken the news of her banishment to the wilds of Portugal, and she was still totally unreconciled to the idea and desperate for a way out. Whenever she tried to imagine herself in a strange country she felt sick and cold, although she would not admit to being frightened. The family were all behaving as though she was about to set off on an exciting expedition, but Joanna refused to show any enthusiasm. For her own part she did not once refer to her visit, and her replies to the comments of others were terse to the point of rudeness. She had considered running away, but there was nowhere to run to except Aunt Agatha in Folkestone and they would soon find her there. Mark was being very sweet to her, but even he was trying to persuade her that she would enjoy herself in Portugal.

'Traitor!' she whispered to the absent Mark, and her opinion of him sank even lower with the knowledge that he was not fighting for her to remain in England. She sensed that he was relieved at the prospect of her departure, and that hurt her more than she would admit. They all wanted to get rid of her.

She glanced up as Suzanne danced towards her, her small face bright with excitement, a pair of new white shoes dangling from her right hand.

'Look, Joanna! Look! My shoes for the wedding. Real kid leather with buttons. Don't you adore them?'

Joanna stabbed a toe into the grass and set the swing going again, refusing to glance at the shoes which were an unfortunate reminder that the wedding would take place without her.

Suzanne's voice grew shrill with indignation. 'Stop, Joanna! I want you to see my new shoes. Stop swinging!' She made an ineffectual grab at the rope as it passed her but missed.

'Leave the swing alone, Suzanne. You'll hurt yourself.'

Although her tone was harsh, Joanna felt a lump in her throat as she looked into the child's face. What would they tell her about her big sister? What lies would they concoct to spare her the shame of Joanna's predicament? And suppose Suzanne somehow learnt the truth – would she ever respect her again? She had never realized how much she cared about the family who had adopted her, and now she felt vulnerable. It was so unfair. She had made this one terrible mistake, one error of judgement, and it was going to ruin her whole life. For a moment she almost hated Mark, not for his part in it but for escaping without a stain on his character. If anything, it was being enhanced by what had happened. Everyone seemed to admire him for the way he was dealing with the situation, and the fact that he continued to treat Joanna as a normal person and not as a monster. Mama was no doubt grateful to him for offering to 'talk to' Joanna, and for taking upon himself such a distasteful task. Yes, she thought miserably. Perhaps she should hate Mark. Perhaps she should try to hate all of them, for then their disapproval would hurt less. Maybe she would be better off with Uncle Elliot and Aunt Catherine unless they, too, treated her like a leper. If she hated them and San Domingos, where could she run to?

'Do you like them?' Suzanne demanded hopefully.

Joanna glared at her. 'They're just shoes!' she said.

The small face crumpled. 'They're not! They're my wedding shoes!'

'How can they be *your* wedding shoes, you ninny? You're not getting married. It's not *your* wedding.'

Suzanne's blue eyes filled with tears and she opened her mouth to protest, but at that moment they heard Mary calling them.

Glancing behind her, Joanna saw that Mama was waiting on the terrace with a visitor – an elderly lady dressed entirely in black. It looked like Aunt Agatha, and Joanna

46

slipped from the swing reluctantly. Was she going to be paraded in front of the whole family, she thought resentfully. Had her aunt been informed of her disgrace, or was Mama keeping the bad news from her? Slowly Joanna followed Suzanne across the grass, hoping that her face did not reveal the turmoil she felt inside. To her relief the old lady greeted her as warmly as usual. She had once been a handsome woman, but now her face was lined and her grey eyes faded. Her back, however, was ramrod straight and she was never ill. She had told Joanna once that she 'couldn't be bothered with ill-health'! Joanna managed a smile and said, 'Hullo, Aunt Agatha. This is a nice surprise.'

For some reason Agatha positively beamed at her and said, 'I had to come as soon as I heard about your trip to San Domingos. It's so exciting. Oh, how I envy you!'

Mama said, 'Aunt Agatha spent some years at the mine and wants to tell you all about it.'

Suzanne waved her new shoes in front of the old lady. 'These are my wedding shoes, Aunt Agatha. They're white kid with buttons. Don't you think they're pretty?'

Agatha took the proffered shoes and examined them carefully. 'Fit for a princess!' she declared as she handed them back and Suzanne, turning to Joanna, allowed herself a broad smile of triumph.

'You see, Joanna!'

Discomfited, Joanna nodded.

Agatha turned her attention to Joanna with a smile. 'I have asked your mother to indulge us with lemon tea on the lawn, Joanna. You and I are going to have a little talk. I want you to know all about the mine. Oh, I do so wish I could come with you!'

'Can't you?' Joanna asked, thinking how nice it would be to have an ally in the camp.

Agatha laughed. 'I'm afraid Catherine and I are like water and oil; we don't mix well, even with a shake-up! So

I'm afraid you will be the only one to enjoy that marvellous place – but you can write to me, if you will, and tell me all about it.'

Joanna suddenly recognized the ploy. It was so obvious, she thought bitterly; they were using the old lady to break down her resistance to the scheme. She said sharply, 'I don't want to go. It is Mama's idea.'

'She thinks it will be good for you, Joanna, to be—'

'No, they don't! They think it will be good for *them*! They want to get rid of me!'

But Agatha did not rise to this bait. Instead she took hold of Joanna's arm and began to lead her across the grass towards the table and chairs which were grouped in the middle of the lawn.

Mama called after them, 'I shall send out some tea and biscuits but don't eat too many, Joanna, or you will spoil your appetite.'

Joanna's mouth tightened at this remark, since she had been eating very little for the past week in the hope that she would go into a decline and be too ill to travel.

Five minutes later she was eating biscuits as fast as she could and Agatha was pretending not to notice as she poured the tea. For a few moments they busied themselves with the lemon slices and the sugar, but throughout the little ritual Joanna was aware that her aunt was regarding her critically. So they *had* told her!

'You look rather pale, Joanna!'

'I dare say I shall survive – but no one will miss me if I don't.'

Agatha appeared not to have heard these remarks and went on as though Joanna had not spoken. 'There are shadows under your eyes. Aren't you sleeping?'

'No.' She took another biscuit and her aunt also took one and dipped it into her tea to soften it.

'You must excuse me,' she said. 'I'm having trouble with my teeth. I can expect nothing better at my age, but I do so hate going to the dentist. All that rinsing and spitting; it's quite disgusting.'

Joanna decided to say nothing. If her aunt had been dragooned into 'talking Joanna round', she would not make it easy for her.

Agatha settled back in her chair and smoothed the silk of her skirt. 'I was twenty-five when I first went to San Domingos. I had just been married, and my husband was a mining engineer from Camborne. You know where that is?'

Joanna nodded, determined to contribute as little as possible to the conversation.

'It's in Cornwall,' her aunt told her, undeterred. 'He studied at the School of Mines in Redruth. San Domingos was his first appointment, and he was so proud.'

In spite of herself Joanna was intrigued – not by the mention of the mine, but by the details of her aunt's brief marriage. She knew only that the husband had died within a year of their wedding.

The old lady turned to Joanna. 'I doubt if you can imagine me as a young bride?'

Joanna did not try.

'I was so afraid!' she laughed. 'I thought Portugal was the end of the world. Well, I suppose it was in a way. Charles was the son of my father's friend. Have you heard them speak of William Warren? William Warren and Edmund Grosvenor were close friends; they were at Harrow together.' She looked into Joanna's face and waited for her response.

'I've heard the name,' Joanna conceded at last.

'He died of malaria. Poor Charles. He was very bright and had a brilliant career ahead of him. Everything to live for.' She shrugged.

So malaria was rife in Portugal, thought Joanna. Probably they were hoping she would die of it! Absentmindedly she took another biscuit.

49

'I've been many times since, of course. It is so beautiful. You will love Portugal, Joanna. You may not want to, but you will.' She looked at Joanna earnestly. 'I can assure you, you will fall in love with it.'

Joanna munched solidly on her biscuit, refusing to comment, but the silence lengthened to such an extent that at last she felt obliged to break it. 'A mine doesn't sound very pleasant,' she said.

'Oh, but it is!' Agatha's voice was full of genuine enthusiasm. 'The miners do the work underground, naturally, and I daresay their lives are difficult but—'

Joanna seized on the idea. 'Poor wretches!' she said. 'I daresay they are little better than slaves!'

She was gratified to see that this barb had struck home.

'Then you would be wrong, Joanna!' Agatha tried to hide her irritation. 'The miners earn much more at the mine than they could earn anywhere else. They are actually envied by their countrymen for their standard of living. The company looks after them very well, and some of them manage to save a little money. Many of them own their own rifles – the Portuguese men are great hunters, and it is very prestigious to own a rifle.'

'But mining must be horrible, dangerous work,' Joanna insisted, determined to believe nothing good about the place. 'Dangerous for the workers, but not for the English.'

Her aunt frowned. She appeared to be counting to ten and Joanna felt a pang of remorse. It was not her aunt's fault that she was being sent away. She had only herself to blame. And Mark, of course.

'There are occasional accidents,' Agatha admitted, keeping her tone level, 'though few fatalities, thank the Lord. But enough about the miners. You will not be joining the Portuguese workers but the English community, and for them it can be very civilized. Very elegant.'

'It sounds boring.' Joanna ignored the hurt look on

Agatha's face and went on, 'What on earth do you find to *do* at a copper mine?'

'To do? Oh, so many things! You can ride, you can boat on the lake – they've dammed the river. You can paint, of course. The countryside is wild, but so beautiful! Let me see, where are we now? The last week in May. Oh, yes, by the time you get out there it will probably be late June and there will still be a little green left. The sun will not have parched everything . . . And you can play the piano—'

'They won't want me there!' The words burst out and instantly Joanna regretted them.

Gently Agatha laid a hand on her knee. 'Visitors are always welcome,' she assured her. 'The English community is so small – no more than nine or ten families. A new face is a tremendous excitement. You will be invited out every night of the week! There is a tennis court and—'

'I meant Uncle Elliot and Aunt Catherine. They don't even know me!'

'Oh, but—' Agatha stopped abruptly, then said, 'They will make you welcome, Joanna, believe me. Your uncle has spoken to me more than once, expressing an interest in you and wishing you could visit.'

Neither spoke for a while as Joanna considered this information and poured a second cup of tea for them both. Suzanne appeared but Aunt Agatha shooed her away, saying that she and Joanna had important things to talk about.

At last Agatha said, 'I was last there eleven years ago, but there won't be too many changes. Elliot still writes regularly to me. Charles is buried there of course, in the English cemetery, and on the anniversary of our marriage Elliot sees to it that there are flowers on the grave.'

'I'll put some there for you.' Joanna made the offer without thinking, regretting it immediately. If she showed the slightest interest in the place, they would feel that they had won.

'Thank you, dear.' Agatha accepted her offer with a smile. 'You have a good heart. Your uncle will be—' She stopped abruptly and shook her head. 'Your Aunt Catherine, however, might be a little cool at first. She is a difficult woman. But don't let her upset you. We all have our faults, and the truth is that Catherine can be very selfish and she has a sharp tongue, but we all know the old saying about sticks and stones!'

Joanna's heart sank, but she said nothing. So Catherine would hate her? Well, she, Joanna, would hate her in return.

'The Barratts are still there,' Agatha continued. 'John Barratt is the English doctor and he has a wife, Sarah. Charming couple, and he's a good shot, too. He might teach you to shoot. And they have a son, Paul. He must be in his twenties now; he's gone into the assaying department.'

'Assaying?'

'The ore has to be assessed for quality before it is shipped out. All metals are assayed. The copper content of the ore at San Domingos can vary from $1\frac{1}{2}$ per cent to 10 per cent!' She laughed. 'You can see that I was married to a mining engineer. He used to rattle off all these impressive facts and as a dutiful wife, I pretended not to fully understand. Actually I understood a great deal, but you know what men are. They like their women to be decorative and not too intelligent. I didn't want to be labelled a "blue-stocking"!' She smiled. 'There is a laboratory there and a very fine one it is, too. Mason and Barry have spared no cost where the mine is concerned. You will be surprised . . .' She threw a few crumbs to one of the doves who had wandered over enquiringly. 'Of course, poor John wanted his son to be a doctor too, but his interests were elsewhere. He's very clever, however; a nice lad when I last saw him.' She eyed Joanna speculatively. 'You will be much in demand with the young men!' she told her.

Joanna tried hard not to be cheered by this remark. 'I'm not interested in men,' she said. 'I doubt if I shall ever marry.'

'Oh, really? What a shame! Still, it takes all sorts and it's not compulsory. I could have remarried, but I never did.'

'I don't much like men – or children.' Joanna waited in vain for her aunt to argue with her, but she merely laughed.

'Just as well, then, my dear. More men to go round for the women who *do* want husbands!'

Joanna said firmly, 'Well, I'm dreading it and I think it's too unkind of them to send me away when I don't want to go.'

Agatha looked at her for a moment with her head on one side, and Joanna found it hard to read her expression.

'You should go, Joanna. It's right that you should see Portugal; that you should know the country and its people.'

'I shall hate it!'

Her aunt shook her head as though this remark amused her. 'Seventeen, Joanna,' she said, 'is a difficult age to be. Neither girl nor woman. The world can look very odd through seventeen-year-old eyes! I was very unhappy when I was seventeen. My parents were determined that I should become engaged to Charles, and I gave in, but I hated the idea. I was sure I could never love him, but later on, of course, I understood and I was grateful. He was a wonderful husband and we had a perfect marriage . . . Poor, dear man.'

Joanna glanced briefly at the old lady beside her, trying to imagine her as a young woman, defying her parents' wishes, refusing a handsome suitor. She thought it rather ridiculous to insist that she had had a perfect marriage. There had hardly been time for anything to go wrong.

Agatha pursed her lips thoughtfully. 'And then there's my poor Mama, your Grandmother Clementine. A very sad case.'

'I've never met her.'

'No. She never did like the sea, and they had a bad trip out; she was very ill – mal de mer, of course. She vowed she would never cross the water again and she never has. She still lives with Elliot and Catherine, but she is very difficult. Not intentionally, poor soul, but because her wits are going. A creeping dementia, Dr Barratt called it, and there is nothing to be done about it. They could send her back to England and put her into a nursing-home, but Elliot won't hear of it. Whatever his faults, one must admire him for that.'

His faults? Joanna wanted to ask what these were, but thought better of it.

'They can afford a nurse who lives in, naturally, but I suspect that our Mama's death, when it comes, will be a merciful release to them all. Not least to her. We all hope we can end our lives with a little dignity, but it isn't always possible.' She sighed deeply, then tutted to herself. 'But I am supposed to be encouraging you, Joanna,' she confessed. 'And here I am telling you about your poor grandmother and depressing you.'

'It doesn't make any difference,' Joanna told her. 'I'm going whether I want to or not! I just have this terrible feeling here—' She laid a hand dramatically on her heart. 'A feeling that I may never come back!'

This was intended to alarm her aunt, but instead it produced a broad smile. Agatha took Joanna's smooth hands in her own gnarled ones.

'Oh, Joanna! My dear girl! Once you discover Portugal you may never *want* to come back!'

Chapter Four

ELLIOT GROSVENOR'S HANDS SHOOK slightly as he re-folded the letter, aware of his wife's presence across the breakfast table. He was a thick-set man who, because of the extra weight he carried, looked older than his brother Maurice, who was one year his senior. Not that this bothered him in the least. He was a self-satisfied man, pleased with his position in society and well aware of his business talents. As General Administrator at the mine he was responsible for the overall view of every aspect of the community, although he delegated authority to a number of specialists. The mining operation went ahead under the supervision of Steven Benbridge. Assaying was Oliver Jackson's department. Transport of the ore by train to the river at Pomerao and its subsequent loading on to the barges was overseen by Senor Louro. The company's agent in Lisbon was Senor Andrade. Elliot knew and trusted these men. He kept a sharp eye on everything that happened in his small kingdom, and believed totally in himself and his abilities to manage.

Only in one area was his confidence lacking, and that was in his marriage. Catherine was beautiful, but ruthless, and he sometimes regretted his choice of a wife. She was considerably younger than he, and still slim and attractive; he knew that some of the younger, single men found her desirable and had finally come to terms with the fact that she occasionally returned their affections. Over the years he had longed to confide in her about a youthful love affair but had never dared. The secret of his illegitimate child was one he had longed to share, but his mother had insisted that if he confessed to Catherine before their marriage he would most certainly lose her. After his marriage he realized that she would never accept the fact that he had a daughter. As far as anyone knew, Joanna was a foundling. Maurice and Mary had adopted her, and no one need ever be any the wiser. He owed them a tremendous debt of gratitude, and now that they were asking him to take the girl 'for a year or so' he knew he must accept. But how to convince his wife that he should accept this responsibility when she had no knowledge of their relationship?

Catherine glanced up from her own letter and said curiously, 'A penny for them!'

Unprepared, he mumbled something vague and said, 'And your letter?'

'From cousin Alice. Reams and reams of it. She's laid up again with her old trouble and is no doubt whiling away the time writing letters to all and sundry.'

He looked at her as she spoke. Her smooth brown hair was swept up on top of her head, balanced impeccably upon the slender neck of which she was so proud. He had often wanted to tighten his hands around it, but had somehow refrained. She frequently reminded him of the fragile china figurine which had adorned the mantelpiece in his mother's room; a flamenco dancer in swirling skirts with a tambourine held above her head. Now, in Catherine's large grey eyes he recognized the hint of insolence which had become habitual over the years.

He resisted an overwhelming urge to say, 'I have had a letter from Maurice. My daughter is coming to live with us!' That would send the colour into those porcelain cheeks! Instead he slipped the letter into his pocket, fearful that for once she might ask to read it. She never did; she showed very little interest in his affairs and for that, at least, he was grateful. The mine was his life and she no longer attempted to interfere in any way. She liked to say that they simply shared the same house; that she led her own life.

He wanted to delay telling her what was in the letter, but what was the point? Catherine had to know. A seventeen-year-old girl was going to be a considerable disruption to their lives. She might also prove a challenge to Catherine if she was as attractive as Agatha had once suggested. He dreaded breaking the news to his wife, yet he longed to see the girl. Joanna. The name was as near Juanita as he had dared go, and then they had had to pretend that it was Agatha's choice, not his.

He became aware that Catherine was speaking to him and said, 'What did you say?'

'You never listen to me, Elliot! Am I so terribly boring?'

'Of course not! My mind was elsewhere.'

'It always is! I sometimes wonder why you married me. Or anyone else, for that matter.'

'Oh, not that again, please!' He saw her mouth tighten in the familiar way and wondered how long it would be before her beauty faded. Would she be easier to live with then, he wondered, or harder?

'I said that I shall not be in to lunch, Elliot. I am going to the library and then on to Mrs Jackson. We shall go into Mertola in the wagonette with Teresa, as her girl needs another pair of shoes. The girl has proved very good around the house and her English is passable. I wish I could say the same about Liliane, but I fear she is ill-equipped up here!' She tapped her forehead and sighed. 'Mrs Jackson has much better luck with her maids than I do.'

Elliot said nothing, although he might have pointed out that the lady concerned probably spent more time training the girl and less time on her own vain pursuits. Liliane, the daughter of one of the miners, was proving remarkably slow to pick up the ways of the household. Fortunately Christina was still with them, and hopefully would be for some years to come. She had been trained by Elliot's mother and her English was very good. As though in answer to his thoughts, the door opened and Christina herself came in to clear the table. Catherine told her that there would only be one for lunch, but that the doctor and his wife would join them for dinner at eight.

As Catherine folded her napkin and slid it into the silver ring, Elliot suddenly made up his mind. He would tell her now before his courage failed.

'Before you go . . .' he began, but she had already risen to her feet and was regarding him impatiently.

'Well?' She looked at him in surprise. 'What is it?'

'This letter . . .' He produced it from his pocket and held it aloft. 'It is from Maurice. He wants to send Joanna out to us, for a holiday.'

It was out. Now the sparks would fly! Slowly Catherine sat down again. Christina, sensing the tension, glanced anxiously from master to mistress, then quickly piled the crockery on to the tray and left the room: aware and discreet, as a servant should be.

There was a moment's silence.

'Then he will be disappointed,' said Catherine.

'I want her to come.'

'Maybe you do, but who will have to entertain her? It certainly won't be you, Elliot, for you will be busy at the mine as usual. She will be no trouble to *you*, but I shall find her a tiresome nuisance.'

'How do you know that?' he asked. 'You don't know the girl.'

'Exactly! And I don't want to. And I think it a great imposition that your brother even asks. What happened to good manners? What happened to waiting for an invitation?'

'I want her to come, Catherine.' His voice shook slightly and he swallowed nervously. He could not refuse Maurice's request without a very good reason, but he did not want to refuse. He wanted with all his heart to see his daughter. He had pushed her to the back of mind for too long, but he could no longer deny his need to see Juanita's child.

He stared into Catherine's furious face and thought, not for the first time, how unattractive she became when angry. 'He says she has had an unfortunate affair of the heart,' he told her.

'An affair of the heart?' She gave an exclamation of contempt. 'She has been jilted, you mean? Oh, really, Elliot!'

He went on as though she had not spoken. 'The doctor recommends a complete change of scenery—'

'Then why don't they send her to Bognor Regis or somewhere? Why send her to us?'

'Perhaps Maurice felt that she needed to be with family. She is only a child.'

'A child does not have unfortunate affairs of the heart, Elliot! The truth is that she is mooning about the place, refusing to eat and casting a gloom over the entire household.'

'Perhaps it is worse than that. Perhaps the shock has made her ill.'

'An invalid, you mean!' She rolled her eyes heavenwards. 'An invalid who will want my undivided attention from morning to night! Certainly not! I shall not play nursemaid to your wretched niece. Your mother is bad enough! Do you want to turn the place into a hospital?' She stood up. 'She is *not* coming, Elliot, and you must tell your brother so.'

He stood up also, clumsily, sending his chair toppling backward, tossing his napkin on to the table as though throwing down a gauntlet. 'She *is* coming, Catherine. I want her to come. Maurice would not refuse us if Leo needed help. You know that very well.'

'Leo never needs help.'

It was true, he reflected with a flash of pride. Leo, their only child, was a precocious boy for his eleven years. He regularly travelled alone to San Domingos from England, and had done so since he was eight years old. Put in the care of the purser when he boarded the ship in Liverpool, he was met in Lisbon by the company's agent. The boy was confident, if not fearless, and Elliot worshipped him. His school reports were glowing in the areas of sport and work, with the exception of mathematics. His teachers' only complaint was of his independent spirit which led him into a variety of scrapes. Elliot hoped they would never knock that spirit out of him.

Elliot repeated, 'She is coming, Catherine, and you will, I trust, make her as welcome as any other guest.'

A variety of emotions flitted across Catherine's face and he was suddenly alert to a subtle change in her demeanour. It was very slight, but where Catherine was concerned his intuition was rarely at fault. She looked down at her hands, always a sign that she was hiding something.

'Perhaps . . .' she began tentatively. 'That is, I might be persuaded, Elliot, if . . .' She walked to the French window and stared out on to the patio. He moved to stand beside her and together they looked out on the sun-drenched orange trees. These now bore their first crop, but they also carried the sweet-smelling flowers that would bear fruit again later in the year. Juan-Carlos was picking oranges into a basket, but when he caught sight of them he smiled broadly and raised the broad-brimmed hat which he always wore. Catherine raised her hand and gave him a gracious smile. Elliot nodded briefly, his mind on the problem of Joanna's visit.

Catherine said, 'If only you would promise to spare some time to spend with her, Elliot. If the burden did not fall quite so squarely on to my shoulders I might be more willing. I know you hate to refuse Maurice . . .'

He tried to see the expression in her eyes but with an adroit movement she turned and passed him, leaving him at the window alone. He turned and watched her at the table as she smoothed a few crumbs into a small heap.

Elliot hesitated. She was manipulating him again, but he was not sure why. He wondered what she would gain by his acceptance of her terms. What would she do with the time she gained, he wondered bitterly. Was there another admirer on the scene who would enjoy more of her company if he undertook to spend time with his niece? For a moment he felt a surge of anger, but then reminded himself that he was hardly in a position to cast stones. Whatever wrongdoing his wife might be planning, he had committed the ultimate sin of abandoning Joanna and her mother; he had kept his unhappy past a secret from Catherine. He sighed heavily as the familiar guilt pressed down on him for a moment, then straightened his shoulders. Did it matter to him any more if his wife's attentions were directed towards another man? Did he care that she no longer loved him? If he was honest he would admit that their marriage had ended years ago; that they remained together for the sake of convention and convenience. If Catherine did not agree to Joanna's visit and he forced the issue, she could make life very uncomfortable for the poor girl, and he knew he could not bear that. Should she take a positive dislike to the girl, she would make life totally unbearable. Dared he risk it? If Joanna came to San Domingos, he wanted her to be happy – happier than ever she had been with Maurice. Suddenly, with a rush of anguish, he knew that he wanted her to love him more than she loved her adopted father. He needed her to soothe the ache in his heart and give meaning to his life. He wanted her to stay at San Domingos for a long, long time – perhaps for ever. Time passed as he wrestled with the problem.

Catherine said, 'Are you ever going to speak again, Elliot, or have you been struck dumb?'

With an effort he looked at her. 'I'm sorry. I was thinking.'

'You were miles away.' She smiled suddenly, a sure sign that she was winning, he thought.

'She could travel out with Leo. They would be company for one another.'

The idea of his son and daughter travelling together was altogether delightful and his reservations melted away. He realized with relief that she was agreeing to the visit, and it had all been much less fraught than he had expected.

'That is a splendid idea!' he said.

'And you promise to take her off my hands?' Her smile was artificially bright.

'I do have a mine to run!'

'But you will try?'

'I will try, but I won't promise.' But he knew he would spend every moment he could spare with her.

Catherine said, 'She will have a great deal of time on her hands, Elliot, so she can spend some of it with your mother instead of me. The nurse needs a break from her occasionally, and I am finding it increasingly wearisome. She can also help Liliane with her English and Leo with his arithmetic.'

He said gruffly, 'Don't let's make a drudge out of her, Catherine! She has been through a difficult time and is in need of rest, remember.'

'A drudge? Oh, Elliot! What a hateful thing to say!' The familiar pout followed – a beautiful pout which had younger men trembling at her feet. 'You just don't understand these things. She must not be allowed to brood on her broken heart. A love affair is rarely fatal, but the afflicted do show a morbid tendency to droop around the place. I don't want a wilting lily on my hands. We will be doing her a favour if we keep her mind occupied.'

He hesitated. Was this another reason for Catherine's unexpected change of heart? Where his wife was concerned he was never sharp enough. His mother used to say that she 'runs rings round you', and it was true. For himself, he had given up caring, but for Joanna he must be on his guard. It might be that Catherine intended to exploit the girl to punish him for his insistence? If so, he would have to find a way to thwart her. He made up his mind that he would personally attend to whatever was necessary for the girl's happiness – and he must stop thinking of her as 'the girl'. She was Joanna, his daughter, and she was coming to San Domingos.

As Catherine swept from the room, he began to smile, and he was still smiling when Christina returned to finish clearing the table.

*

My dear Joanna [he wrote],

I received your father's letter this morning, suggesting that you might spend a few months with us here in San Domingos. It will be our great pleasure to have you here, so please be assured of your welcome.

Although we have a large number of men working at San Domingos they are mostly Portuguese. There are only fifteen English people on the staff, but some of these have families out here. I expect your father has told you something about the mine. Although he has not visited us for many years we keep in touch by letter. Your aunt Agatha will also be able to tell you about our life here.

Catherine tells me that she will be delighted to have your moral support. At present we are training a new maid, Liliane, a young Portuguese girl who is the daughter of one of the miners. She is rather slow to respond, and we hope that you might be able to help her with her English.

Your grandmother is also looking forward to your visit. Unfortunately she is not always entirely lucid, but you must not let that alarm you. When she has a good day we get a glimpse of the fine woman she used to be. She, too, will appreciate your company; it always stimulates her mind to see a new face.

We have arranged for you to travel out on the SS *Lanfranc* on the 26th June. You need have no fears for the sea journey, for the steamship is one of the Booth fleet, modern and very sturdy. Your journey coincides with that of your cousin Leo, who returns from his English prep school for his annual holiday. Because of your age I have reserved two adjacent cabins, and I hope that you and Leo will get along. My son is very bright for his age and very independent. He is used to travelling alone so will not need supervision – in fact, I suspect he would resent it! His teachers find him a little precocious for an eleven-year-old, but my own feeling is that it is no bad thing.

If the crossing is without incident you should make the train connection at Lisbon without any difficulty, but if the ship is delayed Senor Andrade, the company's Portuguese agent there, will book you into the Durant Hotel, so have no anxieties on that score. We have a new assistant mining engineer joining us shortly, and he may or may not travel out on the *Lanfranc*. His name is Andrew Striker, and he is newly qualified from the School of Mines at Redruth.

Please pass on my good wishes to your parents and assure them that we shall look after you to the very best of our abilities.

Your affectionate uncle, Elliot

Joanna read and re-read the letter, a little comforted by its enthusiastic tone. At least someone wanted her. She was not particularly thrilled by the prospect of her cousin's company, but there was always the possibility that Andrew Striker would also be on the ship.

She mentioned this last item casually to Mark in the hope of arousing his jealousy, but he appeared unmoved by the news. He was, in fact, apparently unaffected by the coming parting and Joanna found this demoralizing. Surely, she reasoned, he could pretend that the prospect saddened him, but she rarely found the opportunity to be alone with him so was unable to reproach him for his indifference.

The day of departure approached with startling rapidity, and she could not help but recognize the relief in her mother's voice when she went down to breakfast on the morning of the 26th. The entire family was present in honour of the occasion, but to her surprise Joanna found herself unable to eat. The food seemed to stick in her throat and she was aware that all eyes were upon her. She thought irreverently that 'The Last Supper' must have been something like this. Or perhaps, more appropriately, 'The condemned man's last breakfast'!

It was a great relief to find herself, several hours later, on the deck of the *Lanfranc*, whose slim lines belied her 6,000 tons. Her mother had accompanied her to the ship and a helpful steward showed them to the little cabin and warned her to expect 'a bit of a swell' when they left harbour. The sight of her own name on the cabin door had an air of great finality and gave Joanna a moment's panic. She felt like a mutineer being set afloat in uncharted waters, never to be seen again, and quickly reached for her uncle's letter which she kept in her jacket pocket. It gave her a certain reassurance and she was able to smile and nod in reply to Mama's cheerful comments. So far there had been no sign of young Leo, although the steward assured them that 'young Master Grosvenor' had already come aboard.

'Probably hiding!' Mama suggested. 'You know what boys are like. He will declare himself when he's ready.'

Silently, under her mother's critical gaze, Joanna unpacked the clothes she would need for the voyage – most of her belongings were in the cabin trunk which would be taken separately to San Domingos. Carefully she laid out the silver brush and comb that Aunt Agatha had given her as a 'going-away' present. She felt tearful and unable to speak, and desperately wished to be left alone to weep in private. Her mother, however, evidently felt obliged to stay with her until the last moment, talking cheerfully about trivialities and repeating various instructions until Joanna wanted to scream. She was heartily thankful when several blasts from the ship's single funnel warned passengers and friends alike that it was time to leave harbour. Loudspeakers urged all those who were going ashore to do so without further delay. Mama gave Joanna a quick embrace and said, 'Now be sure to write, Joanna. We shall need to know that you are safe and well.'

It seemed to Joanna that her mother could barely hide her relief and she suddenly found her voice. 'And if I'm not safe and well?' she asked, her voice shaking.

'You will be, my dear!'

Joanna looked at her mother with passionate longing but there was to be no reprieve. After a brief hug Mama moved to the cabin door, but Joanna remained where she was. Mama paused and looked back in surprise.

'Aren't you coming on deck, Joanna, to wave goodbye?' she asked. 'It's always exciting.'

Joanna shook her head. 'I don't need excitement,' she said, 'and I don't like goodbyes.'

She stared accusingly at her mother, who started to protest but then changed her mind.

'Well, God bless you, my dear,' she said uncertainly.

Joanna gave a slight nod but said nothing.

'Joanna . . .' She hesitated. 'We do love you, you know.'

The words 'Do you?' sprang to Joanna's lips but, in her present state of mind and so near to tears, she dared not risk a confrontation. Instead she muttered, 'I know.'

She closed her eyes as her mother retreated unhappily

along the passageway, then closed the door and leaned against it. Her tears, when they came, scalded her eyes and loneliness enveloped her like a dark shroud.

*

The ship's ropes were cast off within two minutes of the advertised departure time and the moment the vessel was under way Joanna felt marginally stronger. All ties with home and family were now severed and she must rely on her own resources. She washed her face in cold water to remove most of the telltale blotchiness, but could not hide the redness of her eyes. But what did it matter, she asked herself fiercely. There was no one to care or even to notice except an eleven-year-old boy, and she cared little enough for his opinion. He still had not put in an appearance, for which she was grateful. She was hardly in the mood for precocious small boys, although the kindly attentions of a junior mining engineer might help to soothe her ruffled feathers. She decided to ask the steward if a Mr Andrew Striker was on the passenger list.

When she judged the excitement of the departure to have died down Joanna finally ventured on deck. It was a novel experience to be entirely alone and it dawned on her gradually that for the first time in her life she was 'the mistress of her own destiny'. The phrase, culled from a magazine, thrilled her and, without realizing it, she straightened her back and met the eyes of her fellow passengers without flinching. The fact that nobody else knew the reason for her journey was a bonus she had not appreciated until now, and it gave her a wonderful feeling of freedom. She might be anyone – the daughter of an earl, a famous singer or even an heiress! If she kept her own counsel she could become something of a mystery. If she cultivated an enigmatic smile the other passengers might whisper among themselves about her . . . But then, of course, she was not travelling alone; there was the precocious cousin to think about. Young Leo would be sure to reveal all. She kept an eye open for a boy who might fit the description, but saw no one. Coming across the passenger list pinned prominently on one of the deck noticeboards, she was vaguely disappointed to find no one by the name of Striker.

The afternoon passed pleasantly as she explored the ship, discovering a small library, a cocktail lounge and a games room where a young couple, possibly newly-married, were playing chess. Dinner was served at 7 o'clock, and by that time Joanna was very hungry; she was one of the first in the dining room and was shown to her table. Seeing three unoccupied chairs, she mentioned this and the steward smiled.

'Master Grosvenor will be along soon, ma'am. He never misses a meal. The other couple are suffering a little "mal de mer" due to the choppy sea and are remaining in their cabin.'

The steward, resplendent in a newly-laundered white jacket, beamed down at her in a way that suggested he was impressed and Joanna's spirits rose. She ordered veal in a cream sauce with creamed potatoes and carrots, and was still waiting for them to arrive when a small boy slid on to the chair opposite her and examined her with unabashed curiosity. Joanna, for her part, studied him in silence. She saw a boy, smaller than she had expected, with ruffled brown hair and startlingly large grey eyes. He was wearing a suit of light-weight tweed with a Norfolk-style jacket; she had glimpsed knickerbockers and socks as he slid on to his chosen chair.

Referring to the empty chairs between them, she said at last, 'I don't have the plague, you know.'

'I should hope not!' he replied promptly. 'Almost a hundred thousand people died of it, you know, in London alone. It was a horrible way to die. They had these awful swellings called buboes—'

'Thank you!' she said sharply. 'I'd rather not hear about it at dinner, if you don't mind.'

He shrugged his shoulders. 'You raised the subject. I thought you'd be interested.'

'Well, I'm not.'

At that moment the steward appeared with Joanna's meal and set it down on the table.

Leo said, 'Hullo, Mr Parsons. Here I am again!'

The steward smiled at Leo and said, 'Welcome aboard, sir. I have received your diet sheet, as usual. I take it I am to ignore it, as usual?'

Leo nodded and said, 'I'll have whatever my cousin's having; it looks edible.'

Joanna said, 'It's veal with—'

'The veal,' Leo ordered and the steward hurried away.

Reaching for the cruet, Joanna asked, 'What's this about a diet sheet?'

He waved a hand airily. 'Oh, that! It's a diet sheet prepared by Old Mother Hubbard; she's the matron at my prep school. Steamed fish and stuff like that. I give Mr Parsons a few bob and he tears it up. I'm quite old enough to decide what I want to eat, but I daresay matron thinks she's doing her best for me.' He stared round at the half-empty dining room. 'All queasy, poor things. I'm a pretty good sailor myself. How about you?'

'I've never been to sea before,' she confessed, 'but I feel fine at the moment.'

'I'd like to know how they'd all get on if we ran into a bad storm.' He looked at her slyly. 'We do, sometimes, you know. Force eight or nine! The ship rolls alarmingly. People fall over and break their legs.'

'Thank you for the warning.' She attacked her food eagerly, pleased to find that her appetite had returned. When Leo's meal arrived they ate in silence for some time, Joanna wondering what he had been told about her.

As though reading her mind, he said abruptly, 'I thought you'd be older – you know, more grown-up. Papa said you'd had an unhappy love affair, but you don't look old enough to me. What does that mean exactly? I mean, what was unhappy about it? Did he die, or shoot himself or something? There's a boy in my house at school whose father blew his brains out. Or was it an unsuitable match? People are always making those, it seems. Were you jilted at the altar?'

Disconcerted by his directness, Joanna stammered something about her affections not being returned and understood what the boy's father had meant by the word 'precocious'.

Leo leaned forward and waved a forkful of food at her. 'You shouldn't get involved with love and all that stuff – it's a waste of energy! I read a book once about this man who was a great warrior and tremendously strong and wise. But he never got mixed up with women.' A piece of carrot fell on to the tablecloth and he stabbed it absent-mindedly and put it in his mouth. Chewing and speaking at the same time, he went on earnestly, 'You see, he knew that he needed every ounce of strength to do battle with the evil in the world. If he once dissipated his strength, he'd be lost; his power would wane. That may be why you look so peaky.'

'I don't look peaky!' she exclaimed. 'And don't wave your food about.'

'I shall if I want to. And I *do* want to. Your eyes are all red. I bet you've been crying!'

'Well, you're wrong! I haven't. And mind your own business.'

He grinned suddenly. 'Now you're telling lies! You see what love does for you! I shall never fall in love. Never!'

Joanna said severely, 'Well, that will save some young woman from a fate worse than death!' And was surprised by his delighted laughter which rang out across the dining room and caused many heads to turn in their direction.

'You're quite funny,' he told her. 'Most girls I know are very boring.' He glanced down and saw with surprise that his plate was empty. He raised his right hand and snapped his fingers and Mr Parsons was with them instantly.

'Was the veal to your liking, sir?' he asked.

'Yes, thank you, Mr Parsons.'

'Treacle tart, sir?'

Leo nodded. To Joanna he said, 'You should have some. It lines your stomach. Old Mother Hubbard says we should chew each mouthful twenty times. It aids digestion, but I find the food is cold before you have a chance to finish it. So I don't.'

'I noticed. Do you always have treacle tart?'

'When it's on the menu. Mr Parsons is very good; they always seat me on one of his tables.' He grinned. 'So that he can supervise the diet!'

When the treacle tart arrived it was covered with custard and piping hot, but Leo set about it immediately, blowing energetically upon each spoonful before entrusting it to his mouth. The plate was empty in a matter of minutes and he then slid from his chair.

Joanna looked at him uncertainly. 'Shall I see you later?' she asked.

He considered the suggestion briefly, then shook his head. 'I've got things to do,' he told her and hurried away in the direction of the door leading out on to the deck.

The steward, who had reappeared, smiled after him. 'Young Master Grosvenor is a bit of a spark,' he said, 'but you can't help liking him.'

Cautiously Joanna murmured something non-committal. 'A young spark' might well be an apt description, but she was not at all sure she liked him. He certainly might prove a force to be reckoned with.

Chapter Five

THAT NIGHT JOANNA LAY ON her bunk, in what she hoped was a languid pose, pen in hand, and considered her diary entry for the day. So far she had written:

My first night ever at sea. The ship rolls a lot but the motion has not affected me so far. I wonder what Mark is thinking, now that I have left him. He cannot be as sick at heart as I am, but I dare say he is grieving in his own way and dare not let anyone see it. Poor Mark. I think now that I am glad I shall miss the wedding. I do not want to see him wed to that cold, calculating fish they call Isobel. She may be very rich, but money alone will not make him happy – and she has such round shoulders!

Leo is an odd boy but I need not see much of him. He keeps himself occupied and only appears at mealtimes. The young engineer, Mr Striker, has not appeared and is probably going to travel on a later ship. Not that I care a jot, but he might have been interesting company.

Aunt Agatha has given me a set for my dressing-table: a brush, comb and mirror, and very elegant. I heard Mama say to her that it was 'too extravagant' a gift and not necessary, but Aunt A. said, 'The child must have some good pieces of her own.' It was very kind of her. I wish she had come to see me off instead of Mama. Then I would have gone on deck to wave 'Goodbye'.

I have a new green skirt and jacket (very pale) in a lightweight cloth, and a new riding-habit. Also some new, rather pretty underclothes including two night-dresses and matching negligée, one in a peach satin (the nicest, and which I'm wearing tonight) and one in a floral design. I showed them all to Dorcas in front of Mark and said jokingly that it was almost a trousseau, but he didn't laugh and Mama glared so at me that I wished I had kept quiet. Dorcas was envious, but pretended not to care for the colour of my suit and said it would not go with my colouring. Not that I value her opinion, but I wanted Mark to visualize me in my finery. Perhaps he did ... I shall never know. And a new parasol in white silk with fringing because the summers are terribly hot in Portugal and Mama does not want me to ruin my complexion. If she really cared she would not send me to such a godforsaken place, but when I suggested this she snapped my head off. In some ways I am glad to see the back of her.

I am so desperately tired; not so much physically, but in my mind. I cannot seem to keep my thoughts still for a moment. In some ways I wish this voyage could last for ever so that I need never arrive at the wretched mine. The very name San Domingos depresses me. All those men slaving away underground, and all for a bit of ore so that rich people can have copper saucepans. I am simply dreading it in spite of all Aunt A.'s efforts to persuade me otherwise. Hidden away in the Portuguese hills, I might as well be dead! I know I shall hate it. And yet what is left to me back in England with Mark gone ...?

There was a knock at the door and she hastily slid the

diary under her pillow. 'The boy wonder returns!' she thought caustically as she got up to open the door. To her surprise and consternation a young man stood there, smiling shyly, a panama hat clutched in his hands. For a moment she stared at him, assuming he had come to the wrong cabin. Hastily she wrapped the peach negligée around her.

'Miss Grosvenor?'

'Yes, but—'

He held out his hand. 'I am Andrew Shreiker. I believe we are both heading for the mine at San Domingos. I'm the new mining engineer – a very junior one actually. I have just graduated.'

He was a little taller than Mark and his hair was almost black and flopped over his eyes, which were light brown. His face was a little angular, but otherwise he was not unattractive and despite her broken heart, Joanna felt her spirits rise at the sight of him.

She hesitated, then said, 'I thought your name was Striker?'

'It rhymes with Striker.'

'Oh, I see.' The comment sounded very unworldly, but she could not think of anything sophisticated or witty to say although she was longing to impress him. 'I . . . I'd better not invite you in.' She glanced down at the peach negligée.

'Oh no, no!' he agreed hastily. 'I simply wanted to introduce myself. I looked for you at dinner—'

'I was eating rather early; I was so hungry.'

'Ah! I ate about eight. Habit, I suppose.'

'So how did you find me?' she asked. 'How did you know I would be on the ship? Did my uncle tell you?' She was pleased to see from his expression that he found something to admire in her. If only Mark could be here to see it also, she thought regretfully.

'I didn't know,' he told her. 'Young Leo Grosvenor

74

tracked me down. Said his father had got my name wrong. He's been tracking me for most of the day and I was getting a bit annoyed, to tell you the truth. Every time I turned round, there he was with that earnest expression on his face. I didn't realize until he spoke up who he was. The son of my boss! Good job I didn't give him a ticking-off! He told me you were also on board. Quite a reunion, in fact. The San Domingos contingent!' He laughed.

Joanna said cautiously, 'What did Leo say about me?'

He looked surprised by the question. 'Nothing, really. He said you were in the cabin next to his and why didn't I introduce myself? He also suggested that I might ask the dining-room steward if I could change my place and sit with you both – that is, if you wouldn't object and the other people would agree to move.'

'I wouldn't mind!' Joanna said quickly and then, regretting the speed of her answer, added, 'At least, I see no reason why you shouldn't join us if Leo wants you to.'

He smiled again. 'Then I'll see what I can do about it tomorrow morning ... Now I'd better let you get your rest.'

She nodded. 'Until tomorrow then.'

'Good night, Miss Grosvenor.'

'Good night, Mr Shreiker.'

She watched him to the end of the passageway and then closed the door. Her over-riding thought was, 'Thank goodness I'm wearing the peach!'

*

During the early hours of the morning the sea grew calmer, and there were more passengers at breakfast than there had been at dinner the previous night. When Joanna entered the dining room she was disappointed to find that the other two people at their table, an elderly couple, had recovered from their sea-sickness and were eating lightly-buttered eggs. Leo was also there, munching his way through a large plate of kedgeree while recounting a gory tale about a monster from the depths of a volcano which emerged at intervals to scour the surrounding countryside for human flesh. His listeners viewed Joanna's arrival with obvious relief and immediately took the opportunity to change the topic of conversation to something safer. Of Mr Shreiker there was no sign.

'Probably fallen overboard,' Leo suggested with relish in answer to Joanna's question. 'He won't stand much chance of being rescued if he has.' He rolled his eyes dramatically. 'The captain told me last year that even if they know where a person goes overboard they then have to take account of the current, the prevailing wind, the speed at which the ship is sailing and all that stuff. Plus – you might be eaten by a shark!'

Joanna ordered egg, bacon and kidneys and searched the room for the young mining engineer. 'Perhaps he's ill,' she said, 'or doesn't eat breakfast. Some people don't.'

The elderly lady volunteered the information that a niece of hers had eaten nothing for breakfast but a single slice of brown bread. 'For her entire life! Can you imagine?'

Leo asked with interest, 'Was she of sound mind?' and, assured that she was, suggested that perhaps she had an abnormally small stomach and did she die young?

'She did, as a matter of fact!' the elderly lady exclaimed. 'She went into a decline and died just before her twentieth birthday. They said it was consumption.'

'Starvation, most likely,' said Leo.

Joanna said, 'Well, you won't suffer that fate! You eat enough for two people!'

'I have to,' he explained. 'They starve us at school and I have to build up my strength while I'm on holiday.'

He finished his kedgeree and asked Mr Parsons for three crumpets and some Oxford marmalade. The elderly man asked Joanna what she was going to do in Lisbon, but before she could answer Leo told them that she had been crossed in love and was going to a mountain hideaway to recover. While Joanna was trying to correct this somewhat melodramatic interpretation, Leo finished his breakfast and disappeared. Almost at once his place was taken by Andrew Shreiker who, it appeared, had simply overslept. After brief introductions the elderly couple got up to go and Joanna saw the head steward talking to them, presumably asking them if they would mind moving to another table. Following their encounter with Leo, Joanna felt that they would probably welcome the suggested change.

By 10.30 Joanna found herself strolling on the deck with the new mining engineer, listening to his life story. He had grown up in Camborne in Cornwall, in the heart of the tin and copper mines, and had followed in the footsteps of his miner father.

'A real miner,' he told her, 'not like me. He hefted a pick for eight hours at a time by candlelight. Eight hours at the rock-face. Gruelling work in that heat!'

'Heat? Is it hot underground? I should have imagined it cool and damp.'

'You'd be wrong. At least in the Cornish copper mines. They're dry and they get uncomfortably hot; in fact, the temperature rises by one degree for every hundred feet you go down. If you're working on a level that's five hundred feet below ground level and it's seventy up top – well, it doesn't take much working out! Some of the large mines are thousands of feet deep! One of my jobs is to deal with that problem – the heat and the stale air. We have to use pumps and they're being updated all the time. Oh, dear! Am I boring you?'

'Not at all; it's very interesting. You sound terribly knowledgeable! It must be fun to have a career. Men have all the luck.'

He laughed. 'Don't tell me you'd like to be a mining engineer!'

'Maybe not that, but something more interesting than waiting around for a husband!'

'Lucky man!' he said slyly and she felt herself blush.

He went on quickly, 'My great-grandfather also worked down the mines for a while, but then in '49 he went to California, looking for gold. He found plenty, but like so many others he spent it as fast as he found it and came home without a penny! I never met him, but I'm supposed to take after him in looks.' They stopped to lean on the ship's rail, gazing out over the sea. 'My mother said she wasn't having that for me. If I was to go underground, I was to be an engineer and study. Her father died in a rock-fall, and my father's health gave out when he was thirty-eight. Sulphur fumes and backbreaking work from the age of fourteen. He just wore himself to a shadow; he died when I was ten, but I can remember how frail and grey he was.'

'Did you have any brothers?'

'No. Three sisters, all older than me.' He glanced at her. 'What does your father do? Is he also connected with San Domingos?'

Joanna shook her head. 'My adoptive father has some shares in the mine; all the family do. But I don't know who my parents were. You probably won't believe this but—'

'Of course I'll believe you, Miss Grosvenor.'

'I was found one morning in a basket on the doorstep of my aunt's house. Aunt Agatha was a widow by then, and living on limited means, so I was taken in by her brother's family.'

He was looking at her with amazement. 'A foundling? Good Lord! How exciting!'

'I should hardly call it that!'

'Oh, but it is!' he insisted. 'It means you could be anybody!'

'It means I am nobody!' she corrected him.

For a moment he allowed his hand to rest comfortingly on her shoulder. 'No, I mean it. I think that's tremendous! Fascinating! I mean, presumably you have a nice home and

78

an adopted family, but you also have this wonderfully mysterious past! Don't you see how romantic it is? I envy you, Miss Grosvenor. Honestly, I do.'

Joanna wondered uncomfortably how impressed he would be if he knew just how she had repaid her adoptive family's kindness, and was thankful that talkative Leo did not know all the facts. Taking a sideways glance at her companion's face, she saw that he was genuinely enchanted by her story. His eyes shone and she thought suddenly how handsome a couple they made. If only there was a photographer handy she could send a photograph back to the family, so that Mark could see her with this attractive escort. Surely that would make him jealous! For a moment she allowed herself the delightful fantasy of Mark arriving at San Domingos in a week or two to declare himself a fool for ever agreeing to her banishment, and vowing to renounce the obnoxious Isobel for ever. And she, Joanna, would greet him with civility but a certain detachment and declare that she was needed in San Domingos and might decide to remain. Mark, hollow-eyed with grief at her rejection, would return to England. He would confess everything about that fateful afternoon in the woods and reproach his parents for sending her away, for failing her in her hour of need.

'Miss Grosvenor?' Andrew Shreiker was waving his hand in front of her face.

'I'm sorry. What were you saying?'

'I was asking if we might meet again, after we have both reached San Domingos? I shall not be there as quickly as you will.' Seeing her surprise, he said, 'After Lisbon our paths diverge, I'm afraid. You and your young cousin, being family, go by train to Vila Real and then by steamer up the Guardiana. I, being a humble engineer, will make my way by train to Beja and from there by mule to Mertola and—'

'By *mule*! Surely not?'

He laughed. 'Oh, yes!' Her reaction obviously pleased

79

him. 'I see you are disappointed, Miss Grosvenor. May I take a little comfort from that? And hope that we might find an occasion once we reach San Domingos—'

'Yes, yes!' she said impatiently, 'But why shouldn't we all travel by steamer together?'

He gave a little shrug. 'No doubt the expense involved. I assure you I am quite content with the arrangement, Miss Grosvenor . . .'

'I could ask the company agent at Lisbon!'

His expression changed to one of alarm. 'Oh, no, Miss Grosvenor! I would not presume – that is, you must not dream of such a thing. It would do me no good at all if the authorities – that is, your uncle – thought I was trying to obtain favours. He would be incensed, and rightly so! I beg you not to think of it!'

Reluctantly she agreed, but brightened almost at once. 'But we could come with you!' she exclaimed. 'That would *save* the company money. They could not object to that. It would be an adventure! I'm sure Leo would agree.'

But it seemed that this scheme also met with his disapproval. He explained carefully that the journey would not be suitable for a young lady. Or a small boy. 'There are wolves in the hills and Lord knows what else! Wild boar. Bandits, maybe! And a longish trek by mule! I'm quite sure your uncle would be furious if I encouraged you in such a wild notion. Please, Miss Grosvenor, do try to see it from my point of view. Imagine if any harm came to you!'

Joanna sighed. 'I seem to be something of a liability,' she said crossly.

'You could never be that!' he told her. 'In fact, I cannot imagine you ever being anything but charming. Utterly and terrifically charming!'

The look which accompanied these words left Joanna in no doubt that she had made a very good impression on the young engineer. His next words, spoken very softly, confirmed her conclusion.

'I think I'm falling in love with you, Miss Grosvenor. Would you mind very much?'

Did she mind! She was delighted, but her conscience was cautioning prudence. 'Certainly I am very flattered,' she told him, 'but we have only just met. It is rather hasty, don't you think? I mean that you might change your mind when you—'

'I doubt it, but you are right. I must not tell you how much I admire you. So I won't.'

She laughed. 'Mr Shreiker!'

'I must not tell you how meeting you has restored my broken heart.'

Now she was intrigued. 'Your broken heart? But you have not mentioned this before.'

'I have not been entirely frank, Miss Grosvenor. I was in love with a young woman for six or seven months, but although she claimed to return my affections she would not consider marriage because she would not leave her parents.' He sighed. 'I suspect they persuaded her against her better judgement. They warned her of the climate and the food and the malaria. She was their only child and they didn't want to lose her; they frightened her away from me.'

'How sad.' She looked at him thoughtfully. 'But isn't seven months a very short time to be sure of your feelings?'

'Not for me!'

'And it broke your heart?'

'Naturally.'

She could not suppress a smile. 'Yet here you are declaring yourself in love with someone else!'

He shrugged. 'What can I say? Except that perhaps Fate knew best. Perhaps Fate decreed that I should meet you on the SS *Lanfranc*. I like to think so.'

Joanna's excitement was tinged with regret that she was not the innocent young woman he obviously thought her. But perhaps he need never know. Perhaps – and her hopes rose a little – perhaps there had been some improprieties between him and his young lady? Even a few indiscretions would do, she thought wistfully. If he were leaning ever so slightly from his pedestal, the gap between them would be lessened and she would feel a little happier. But then, what did it matter? It would only be relevant if she fell in love with him, and that had not happened yet. He was cheerful company and his admiration soothed her wounded pride, but she must not take him seriously. It sounded as though Andrew Shreiker fell in and out of love with alarming rapidity, and she dare not risk a second rejection. She smiled.

'We must wait and see,' she told him, deciding reluctantly that the exchange of confidences had gone far enough. 'Meanwhile, I suggest a game of cribbage in the Games Room. What do you say?'

'How could I refuse such a simple request?'

She beat him easily and he insisted that he had not 'allowed' her to win, although she was not entirely convinced. But she had not abandoned her earlier idea, and that evening she went in search of Leo to suggest that they might somehow miss the train to Vila Real and so be forced to accompany Mr Shreiker on the alternative route. Although Leo was not averse to the idea, it seemed impossible to arrange. The company's agent in Lisbon would meet the *Lanfranc* and escort them personally across the River Tagus on the ferry to the train terminal at Barreiro. There he would see them installed in a first-class compartment and would wait to wave them off.

'It's more than his life's worth to let us escape!' Leo told her. 'He would probably get into trouble with my father if he lost us. But we shall reach San Domingos before Mr Shreiker and could ride out to meet him when he gets to Mertola. That could be fun.'

And with that she had to be content.

*

As Leo had predicted Senor Andrade, the company's agent, was waiting on the jetty to greet them, in passable English, as they disembarked. It was after eleven at night and the jetty appeared eerie, lit only by a few flaring gas-jets. Most of their luggage would go by the route Mr Shreiker was taking, so Joanna and Leo had nothing but a travelling-rug and their hand luggage. Senor Andrade had brought a brown-paper parcel, a small hamper of food and a cushion for Joanna, assuring her that even the best train seats became uncomfortable during a long night.

After a hurried parting from Andrew Shreiker, who was to spend the night with the agent and his wife, Joanna and Leo were escorted to a small rowboat which was to take them across the estuary to Barreiro and the waiting train. This crossing, too, was a somewhat alarming event, conducted by a silent oarsman who stood in the stern and wielded a single pole. The river was wide and full of noises – the harsh cry of night birds, the slap and gurgle of water, the mournful sound of a ship's horn far out in the darkness. The atmosphere so affected them that even Leo appeared subdued and they conducted what little conversation there was in hushed whispers.

The station at Barreiro was similarly eerie, and Joanna's earlier optimism started to fade. Stumbling along behind Leo and Senor Andrade, she began to feel threatened by the unknown which seemed to press in on her from all sides. Her stomach was rumbling with hunger, and the role of victim which she had originally sketched for herself seemed more apt with each passing minute. After the bustle and glamour of life at sea, the present situation was by contrast unexpected and somewhat depressing. For the first time since she had parted with Mama, Joanna truly felt that this trip was going to be the punishment her parents had intended.

Leo, however, regained his spirits as soon as they stepped ashore and he now plied Senor Andrade with various questions about the mine which he answered as well as he could. By the time the whistle blew for their departure he was his old self again, and Joanna was full of admiration for his resilience. They waved until the station had been lost to view and then settled down to make themselves as comfortable as possible. Fortunately the carriage was only half full and nobody sat opposite to them, so they could stretch out their legs. The first-class carriage was less than luxurious and did nothing to alleviate Joanna's mood. The only light came from three lanterns which swung overhead, and the windows were covered with a layer of dust. Joanna found herself wondering what the other carriages were like. Their travelling companions consisted of a middle-aged Dutch couple, a large Portuguese family with seven well-behaved children, an elderly lady and her paid companion and three wizened men of indeterminate age who argued continuously. Three crates of chickens had been pushed into the far end of the carriage and a cat in a wicker basket mewed plaintively.

The seats were of wood covered with thin matting and Joanna was grateful for her cushion. Leo stowed the parcel beneath Joanna's seat and opened the hamper.

'We'll eat first,' Leo told her, in a voice that brooked no argument. 'We can eat everything, because every time the train stops there'll be local people selling fruit and nuts.' Evidently the contents met with his approval, for he gave a little whistle of appreciation and went on, 'Cold chicken, hard-boiled eggs, tomatoes, chocolate and lemonade. Good old Andrade! He knows what I like.'

He divided the food with expert fingers and handed Joanna a large napkin which she draped across her lap. He also offered her various paper packages containing her share of the meal, and without preamble they both fell on the food like two starving mongrels. By the time she had wiped the last crumb from her mouth, Joanna felt considerably happier.

The train rattled and swayed along the track and outside the moon shone on the unfamiliar landscape. When Joanna lowered the small window and glanced out she saw very little that reassured her. Leo took it upon himself to enlighten her.

'Cork trees, almonds and olives. Stuff like that. Boulders and little stunted bushes. You might get a bit of soot in your eye if you keep looking out.' He stared at her for a moment and then said, 'What does it mean to be no better than you should be? Do you know?'

Joanna felt the colour rush to her cheeks and was grateful for the dim light. So Leo knew more about her than she had imagined! She wondered who had told him.

'Not really,' she hedged. 'I suppose it means that someone is – well, not exactly . . . er . . . virtuous.'

'That's what I thought.' He sighed. 'Does it mean that the person is bad through and through?'

'Oh, no! Not that bad!' she protested. 'I mean, a person could do something that was worse than they realized at the time, and when they did realize how bad it was it was too late . . .' Her voice faltered. '. . . And then the bad thing can't ever be undone . . . So the person . . .' She stopped abruptly. Why on earth did she have to explain herself to a boy of eleven? 'Why do you ask?'

He stared intently at his shoes. 'I overheard Grandmother talking to Papa. They were both very angry and didn't know I was listening; they were walking in the garden and I was tracking them. It was about a year ago when Grandmother was more herself.'

Joanna's thoughts whirled. He could not possibly have heard about her own fall from grace a year ago because it had not happened then.

Joanna hesitated. 'Were they talking about anyone you know?'

'They were talking about Mama,' he said simply.

*

Tired though she undoubtedly was, Joanna found it impossible to sleep, and envied her young cousin. Leo had wrapped himself in his blanket, curled himself on the narrow seat and was now fast asleep. Joanna tucked the blanket around her legs and leaned back, but the jolting of the train seemed specifically designed to keep her awake. One by one the other passengers followed Leo's example until finally she could tell by the assorted snores and grunts that she was the only person left awake. For a time she tried to write in her diary, but the erratic movement of the train made it impossible to produce anything legible and she gave up in despair. Outside the moon continued to reveal the wild countryside through which they were passing, and occasionally a distant glimmer of lights in the vast darkness hinted at a remote settlement of some kind. After what seemed like hours, the train slowed down and stopped with a clanking of wheels and screeching of brakes guaranteed to waken all the passengers. Startled, she glanced across at Leo who was unwrapping himself and rubbing his eyes.

'Where are we?' she asked.

'In the middle of nowhere!' He grinned at her sleepily. 'The driver's hungry!' he told her. 'We'll have about twenty minutes while he eats his picnic. I'm going to stretch my legs!'

She stared at him. 'In the dark?'

He put his head on one side. 'Well, I shan't exactly be stretching my legs! If you see what I mean.' He indicated their fellow passengers and Joanna noticed that all the men were jumping down from the carriage and disappearing into the undergrowth alongside the train.

'Oh! I see!' She felt herself blush slightly, and immediately became aware of her own need to relieve herself. Leo pointed to the parcel which Senor Andrade had given them.

'Use that,' he told her. 'I'll be at least ten minutes. I

usually have a few words with the driver. Then empty it out of the window there.' He pointed to the window on the other side of the carriage and said, 'Honestly, it's the only way.'

With another grin he jumped down to join the men and Joanna reached unhappily for the parcel. Inside was a cheap tin chamber-pot. For a moment she hesitated, until it became apparent from the sounds going on in the rest of the carriage that this was, as Leo had said, 'the only way'.

Five minutes later the deed was done and the pot wrapped up and restored to its place under the seat. One by one the men returned and there was a great shuffling and murmuring before they all settled themselves once more. Leo declared himself wide-awake and suggested a game of 'I Spy' to which Joanna reluctantly agreed. The train continued its journey and more time passed. When 'I Spy' ended both Leo and Joanna managed to doze, but to Joanna the night seemed interminable and there were moments in her half-dreaming state when she doubted if morning would ever come. It was just beginning to grow light when the train stopped again and immediately all was bustle and excitement. They had halted at a little village, and at first glance Joanna thought that the entire population must have turned out to meet the train. The large family from their carriage left the train to a tumultuous welcome from what appeared to be rest of the family, and were led away amid tears and laughter to a waiting wagon into which they all scrambled.

Leo rummaged in the hamper for the two mugs and jumped on to the rickety boardwalk which doubled as a platform, at once in his element among the sellers of fruit and nuts. The men wore bright shirts, dark trousers and leather boots; they also wore wide-brimmed hats and even wider smiles. After a moment Joanna followed Leo on to the platform and was at once surrounded by smiling faces and out-thrust hands offering oranges, lemons and figs. A young woman, barefoot but brightly dressed with a red shawl over her head and shoulders, drew Joanna's attention to a nanny-goat which she led by a long rope. She mimed drinking but Joanna shook her head doubtfully. At that moment, however, Leo appeared with the mugs and nodded vigorously.

'*Si, si!*' he told the woman. '*Leite, se faz favor!*' and held out the mugs.

The goat's milk was warm, with a strange but subtle flavour which was not unpleasant, and Joanna realized with the first mouthful just how thirsty she was. They bought a few oranges and figs, then it was time to set off once more. When the train finally reached Vila Real their journey had lasted just over twelve hours.

The town was the frontier post between Portugal and Spain and was situated on the mouth of the River Guardiana, in itself the dividing line for the two countries for a few miles at least. Joanna felt tired and unkempt and was longing for the luxury of a hot bath. The fact that their travels would soon be at an end cheered her, but she was full of apprehension about her reception at the mine and her thoughts returned again and again to the family she was about to join. Leo's remark about his mother had made her uneasy. Still, on the other side of the coin there was the new mining engineer and his obvious desire to see her again. Leo had said they would go to meet him at Mertola, and she wished she had paid more attention to the map in which Aunt Agatha had tried to interest her on one occasion. She recalled that it was the nearest village to San Domingos, but how near was that?

Leo, for his part, was growing more excited by the hour at the prospect of rejoining his parents and talked non-stop to Senor Pavao, the company's man at Vila Real, who met them from the train and saw them safely installed on the *Rona*, the spruce little steamship which would take them up-river. Even this, Joanna learned, would not be the end of the journey. The steamship was going to the little port of Pomerao where the company's narrow-gauge freight train would await them. A special carriage would have been added for them and this would take them the last twelve kilometres to San Domingos.

While Leo chatted with the captain, Joanna watched with mixed feelings as the ship chugged its way up-river. The sun was already quite hot and the sunlight gleamed on the water and shone hazily through the greenery along the banks. Leo pointed out several observation posts which allowed both Spain and Portugal to keep watch on their neighbour and, hopefully, to prevent smuggling.

'See the goatherd? There, Joanna! With all those goats. Dozens and dozens. They eat a lot of goat here. Don't pull such a face, Joanna. They do! They eat it young and call it *cabrita*. That means kid!'

'Poor little things!'

He rolled his eyes at her reaction. 'It's delicious,' he insisted. 'Christina makes it sometimes. It's called *sarapatel* – made with the meat, tripes, lungs, liver and heart.'

'I don't believe you!'

'It's true! They even add the blood!' He laughed at her expression. 'Don't worry, you'll love it.'

Joanna allowed him the last word. Watching the alien scene slide past, she felt a wave of homesickness. When would she ever see England again? How could she ever return without their permission? She would be a virtual prisoner! The familiar panic began to rise but, swallowing hard, she closed her eyes and prayed frantically for courage with which to meet whatever the future held in store for her. Nothing Aunt Agatha had told her had prepared her for the feeling of desolation which clutched her.

'It can't be that bad!' she told herself silently. 'And Leo will be there – and Mr Shreiker. And if it *is* that bad I'll survive somehow. I must!'

She breathed deeply to try to calm her ragged nerves and then, as the *Rona* nosed its way round yet another bend in the river, she straightened her back and stared grimly ahead.

*

From the Portuguese side of the river, Pedro Picarra watched the *Rona* pass. Swarthy, dark-eyed and silent, he watched the frothing wake behind the little steamship and the white steam that came from the funnel. The boat was to him a thing of great beauty and power with its rumbling roar and puffing smoke. He saw it often as he wandered along the river-bank with his herd of goats and, when this happened, he mentioned it casually to his wife who had never seen such a thing. She had never seen Spain, but he had only to stare across to the opposite bank of the river. He knew all about the boat, too; it was going to Pomerao and then it would go back south to wherever it came from. Vila Real, some said, and that was possible. Sometimes he wondered how it would feel to be in the boat, but he had no wish to try it. He knew about Pomerao and the trains that ran from the river to the mine at San Domingos. He pitied the men who slaved in the darkness below the ground; they worked for the foreigners and were sometimes punished by them. If they were late for work they were punished. If they complained about their conditions they were punished. When they were broken and ill the foreigners paid them money, but it was never enough. Pedro knew all this because his wife had a brother who had a friend who worked in the mine. It was a well-known fact that in 1888 at Rio Tinto, the Spanish mine, soldiers had fired on striking miners and killed many of them. The mine was a cruel master. Yet one day his wife had urged Pedro to give up his herd and become a miner. 'You will earn more money,' she told him. 'You could buy a gun and shoot a wild hog.' Pedro had laughed at her. What did women know about such things? He did not want their money, he wanted to be his own master.

A slight movement at the water's edge caught his eye and his response was swift. 'Uh-hah!'

It was not a word but a sound, meaning 'Take care!' The old nanny-goat was blind in one eye and less sure-footed of late. She had stepped too near to the edge of the water, but at the sound of his voice she drew back with a startled toss of her neat head. He smiled. The goats understood him; they trusted him and in his own way he loved them. They were his life, his responsibility. The men at the mine knew nothing of this; they thought only of the money the foreigners paid them. In Pedro's eyes they had nothing, but he had twenty-nine goats and by the autumn there would be more. Maybe three more; maybe four. The steamer rounded the bend and gradually the sound faded. He shook his head in wonder at it. The river was smooth again, as though the boat had never been. Men are like boats, he thought; they make waves and they puff, and then they die, and it is as though the world has never seen them. Waving his stick, he called to the leader of the herd and the goats turned their backs on the water and began to climb.

Chapter Six

ELLIOT GROSVENOR RAN A HAND through his hair and tried to concentrate on the papers on the desk in front of him. Dockets awaited his signature, letters demanded answers, projects needed his approval, bills had to be paid and lists drawn up. He needed two pairs of hands, he thought irritably, and eyes in the back of his head. The paperwork never diminished, no matter how many hours he spent on it – and he spent more than was good for his health. He had been up at six this morning and in the office by seven o'clock, desperate to clear some of the accumulated papers, eager to solve some of the outstanding problems. It didn't help that he had recently lost his senior mining engineer, who had reached the age of sixty-five and promptly headed for England. He had promoted Steven Benbridge and had engaged young Striker, but he had yet to arrive. Benbridge could not fairly be expected to do the work of two, but he was trying damned hard.

'Damned hard!' he repeated aloud and picked up a list of names at random. He stared at it without seeing it and put it down again. His gaze fell on a letter he had dictated earlier to the Bucyrus-Erie agent in Lisbon, demanding delivery of the new steam-shovel which was already ten weeks overdue. Work in the open-cast area of the mine had been slowed down and the new machine was vital if the year's target was to be reached. The report for the shareholders would include the cost of the new plant, and there must be a corresponding increase in production to justify the expenditure. No good explaining to them that the promised machine had not reached San Domingos. It was his job to see that it did! He re-read his letter, wondering if it should be more strongly worded. Perhaps he should threaten cancellation of the order, but if he did that a replacement order from the Spanish firm would take even longer. After a moment he threw down the letter. His mind was not on his work and that, too, irritated him, for he prided himself on his dedication to the job and was proud of the way he controlled his little kingdom. With a little snort of annoyance he pushed back his chair and crossed to the window, his footsteps muffled by the carpet which the company had provided. Mason and Barry had spared no expense, he was the first to agree. The kingdom they had created in the wilderness of the Alentejo was one that was the envy of the entire country, if not the whole of Europe. That was the way Elliot saw it, and that was how he would describe it to Joanna. She would be impressed.

'By God, she will!' he muttered. He would bring her here to his office in the Palacio and he would show her the little community over which he held sway. The Palace! So called because the administrative offices were housed in the largest building. Not palatial by other standards, but certainly so when compared with the tiny white terraced dwellings which housed the miners. Rows and rows of them, providing homes for the thousands of men who dug copper pyrites from the honeycomb of underground galleries that ran deep beneath the surface – a separate existence, hidden from the rest of the world. Thousands of men for whose welfare he organized the rest of the facilities which Mason and Barry had provided: hospitals for the sick, a school for their children, a church for their devotions.

'A model mine!' he told the absent Joanna. 'Visitors come from far and wide to see how it's done. To see and inwardly digest.' Once a young journalist had come out from Cornwall to write an article about that 'little England in a foreign land'. And a good article it was, too, which had inspired many young Cornishmen to learn the trade and try their luck on foreign shores. Doctor Barratt had framed the article and hung it on his waiting-room wall to remind his patients how lucky they were.

Elliot stared out across the tree-lined 'praca' but saw in his mind's eye the sprawl of buildings and sheds, the train and its loading bay, the mounds of discarded rock, wood and coal. An unlovely sight to some, perhaps, he reflected, but he would make Joanna see it through his own eyes. She would see the beauty he saw in the coloured rocks revealed by earlier excavations and now stained by wind and rain; the blue-green of the copper against the rust-coloured earth. Through the open window the familiar sounds drifted in on the light breeze: the clatter of wheels, the clang of metal on rock, the continual whine of the winding gear which hauled the loaded trucks from the tunnel, the shouts of men and the occasional whinny of the inevitable mules.

He picked up the draft of his speech to the shareholders which would shortly be read to a packed hall in London: 'the highest yield ever . . . possibilities of further exploration in the immediate neighbourhood . . .' He would mention the fire briefly in passing. It was slow-burning and they had it under control. It was no hazard to life or limb; not a fire at all in the true sense of the word, but a smouldering mass of hot ore which had leaked sulphur fumes and self-ignited. They would never understand. Enough for the shareholders to know that it was not affecting their profits! That was all they cared about, and rightly so.

There was a knock on the door and he called, 'Come in!'

The secretary, a young man, entered with the day's post. He handed over the letters and then said, 'Doctor Barratt says that the young chappie from the lab has definitely got malaria.'

'Malaria! At this time of year!' Elliot glared at him as though holding him personally responsible.

Unabashed, the young man smiled. 'That's what the doctor said, but the symptoms were—'

Abruptly Elliot lost interest. Coming to a sudden decision, he held up his hand. 'I'll hear the details later. I shall be out of the office for an hour or so. I'm going down to Pomerao to meet my—' Just in time he remembered: she was *not* his daughter. Or at least, she was, but no one must ever know. He was shocked by his carelessness and felt cold with fright. It only needed one careless word and the gossip would start; the deceit was going to be much harder than he had expected. He swallowed hard. 'To meet my son,' he amended, 'and my young niece.'

He fancied the secretary's eyes gleamed with sudden interest. 'Your niece, sir?'

'Joanna.' Rightly interpreting the other man's expression, he said, 'She's my brother's girl. Nearly eighteen, and I'm told she's going to be a beauty! So ...' He tried to anticipate anything that might happen during his absence. 'If there's a problem with the assaying, tell them to hold on to the ore until I can sort it out ... And if Senor Elias puts in an appearance, send him off with a flea in his ear! The man's becoming a pest! Now be off with you!'

Impatiently he hustled the man from the room, then called him back. 'Send a message to my wife, will you?' he told him. 'Say that I won't be home to lunch. I'm going to Pomerao to meet them!'

*

The ore that was mined at San Domingos was not treated in any way before being shipped off to its two destinations.

One of these was Swansea in Wales, the other was Pensacola in Florida, and it was in these towns that the ore was smelted and the copper finally extracted. The ore that came up out of the San Domingos mine was loaded on to trucks and sent by rail to the port of Pomerao, about twelve kilometres away. Today Elliot intended to travel on the small passenger carriage that was being tacked on to the line of trucks which waited in the siding. Samples of this ore had already been assessed and lighters would be waiting on the river at Pomerao to receive the ore and carry it down to Vila Real.

The driver, squatting on his haunches in the shade of the rear engine, rose to his feet when he saw Elliot. He touched the brim of his hat and said, '*Bon dia, senor!*'

This meant 'Good morning' and Elliot acknowledged the greeting with a nod as the driver indicated the carriage that had already been coupled.

'*Bem!*' Good. Elliot pretended to glance along the line of trucks, but in fact he was in a fever of excitement to be gone. He would reach Pomerao much too early, but he would be that much nearer to his daughter . . . and son, he thought guiltily. His son was home for the holidays and the boy's cheerful presence always brightened Elliot's days. On the frequent occasions when he wished he had never married Catherine, he had to remind himself that she had given him Leo and for that he could excuse much.

Seeing that Mr Grosvenor had arrived, albeit earlier than expected, the staff bestirred themselves and, with much shouting and waving of flags, the train set off with Elliot in solitary splendour in the carriage. It was some time since he had been to Pomerao and he watched eagerly as the track ran through the countryside towards the river. It passed through a narrow cutting and over an embankment, then crossed a little stream by way of a stone bridge. Further afield the rolling hills were purple with heathers and a small herd of long-horned cattle grazed among the stunted bushes. The train passed through the shade of a clump of pine trees and past a windmill. Elliot saw it all through Joanna's eyes. She would appreciate it, she would be enchanted. Please God, let her love Portugal.

When at last the track levelled out for the final approach into Pomerao, he put his head out of the window to try to see the village through fresh eyes. The rows of whitewashed houses shimmered in the heat as they clung to the steep side of the gorge. Their red roofs would only be visible from above. Washing fluttered from poles thrust out of the windows. With a final whistle the train slowed, clanking to a halt in front of the lowest row of houses. The engine of the train was now perched perilously above the dark green waters of the Guardiana, for the jetty at Pomerao had been built right out over the river. The track on its wooden decking was supported on iron pillars which plunged down through the water and mud to find the rock. This 'aerial' construction meant that the ore could be delivered straight from the wagons into the holds of the lighters, three of which now waited below.

As Elliot stepped down, mopping his face with a large handkerchief, Senor Louro advanced to meet him with hand outstretched. Tall and thin, with a large moustache, his small dark eyes missed nothing. He was a man in whom Elliot put a great deal of trust and so far the agent had never disappointed him. After an exchange of greetings, Elliot told him in fluent Portuguese that his son and a niece were expected on the *Rona*. Senor Louro offered hospitality to while away the time, but Elliot was too restless to accept and chose instead to pace up and down along the waterfront, supposedly keeping an eye on the loading which now went ahead. From time to time he took out his half-hunter watch and stared at it in disbelief, for the time had never passed so slowly as it did now. At last, however, his patience was rewarded. The familiar chug-chug of the steamer's engine preceded the vessel round the bend in the river and Elliot, shading his eyes with his hand, saw two figures at the ship's rail. A moment or two later, as the *Rona* neared the landing-stage, he could distinguish Leo from his companion and got a long-awaited glimpse of the child he had never seen.

*

As one of the crew leaped nimbly ashore Joanna wished that she looked more presentable, but the unfamiliar heat so early in the year had caught her unawares. Her hair felt lank and she was conscious of a fine film of perspiration that clung to her skin beneath her unsuitable clothes.

As the crewman tied up Leo said, 'My father and Senor Louro,' and reached for his luggage which gallantly included the parcel. Joanna followed him down the gangway and while Leo was being hugged by Uncle Elliot, Senor Louro shook her hand gravely and said, *'Benvindo a Sao Domingos!'*

'That's "Welcome to San Domingos,"' Leo translated. 'Only we're not there yet. This is only Pomerao.'

He struggled free from his father's embrace and excitedly darted up the slope towards the village, leaving Joanna face to face with her uncle. He took her outstretched hand, but then pulled her towards him and kissed her.

'Welcome to San Domingos!' he echoed. 'I hope you will be very happy with us. Your visit means a lot to me . . . You will never know . . .'

A little overwhelmed by this enthusiastic welcome, Joanna smiled nervously and said, 'It's very kind of you to – to take me in at such short notice. I was afraid—' To her annoyance she found herself stammering awkwardly. 'That is, I feared it might be inconvenient . . .'

She faltered to a stop, for he was looking at her in a very intense way which she found unsettling. What was he looking for, she wondered? Signs of repentance? Lingering traces of her disgrace? Was he afraid she might prove a bad influence on his precious Leo? And where was the aunt who was 'no better than she should be'? Surely she would normally be on hand to greet her son, yet Leo had not remarked on her absence. As though reading her mind her uncle said, 'Your aunt has a sick headache this morning. She finds the climate rather tiring.'

Joanna nodded. He looked older than she had expected, but she could see a faint resemblance to her father. Remembering her manners with an effort, she said, 'My parents send their love and best wishes. Dorcas asks when she can come to San Domingos; she was most insistent that I ask you that.'

'Ah! Little Dorky! No doubt she has grown into a fine young lady?'

'She is fifteen now.' Joanna forbore to mention that Dorky was as plain as a pikestaff.

He appeared to have forgotten that he was still holding her hand, and she disengaged it as politely as possible. Seeing that she did so, he gave an embarrassed laugh. 'You must forgive an old man!' he said. 'I have been so looking forward to your arrival. Ah! I see they have finished unloading the ore and the train awaits. And Leo is ahead of us – impatient as ever! No doubt eager to get home and starving as usual. He eats like a horse, that boy of mine, yet he doesn't grow much. It must all go to feed his brain! Come along, my dear.'

As he led the way towards the carriage Joanna said, 'Leo has been a most amusing companion.'

'Leo! Oh, yes! You found him precocious, no doubt?'

'Only in the nicest way. You must miss him when he's in England.'

'We do indeed. But now we have *two* young people to brighten our lives. Your grandmother is aware that you are coming.' Seeing her surprise, he said, 'She has her moments, thank the Lord. It is a great tragedy for her. She was such a tower of strength to all of us when we were growing up — a fine example of English womanhood, if you will excuse such an old-fashioned phrase. Now she lives mostly in a shadowy world of her own, full of confusions, poor soul. But then, quite suddenly and just for a few hours, she is herself again!'

Just then Leo leaned out of the carriage window and shouted, 'Does Senor Pedro still have the stallion, Papa?' and without waiting for an answer asked, 'And has anyone seen a wolf lately?'

His father laughed good-humouredly as he helped Joanna into the carriage. 'Yes and no!' he answered. 'And to the rest of your questions I say, "Wait and see!"'

As the train with its empty wagons drew away from the jetty, Joanna settled into her seat and crossed her fingers. She had met her uncle and he seemed reasonably agreeable; he had not referred to her fall from grace, although that did not mean he would not do so later. He must be a fond father, though, if he had taken time off to meet his son at Pomerao. If only her aunt could also prove a pleasant surprise! She claimed to have a headache, but Joanna wondered if this was an excuse to delay their meeting as long as possible. Perhaps she, too, could invent a sick headache and go straight to bed when they arrived. But no, there was no point in putting off the evil hour. Aunt Agatha had said she could be very difficult, and Joanna wanted to know the worst.

'Is my aunt in bed?' she asked. 'Will I see her today?'

'Oh, you'll see her.' Her uncle smiled. 'She's looking forward to meeting you. It's just the heat; it can be very oppressive. I hope you'll find it bearable.'

Leo said, 'Of course she will, Papa. She's a girl, not a woman.' To Joanna he said, 'You'll like it here. Everyone does.'

And Joanna smiled and hoped desperately that he was right.

*

Her first glimpse of her new home was reassuring. A neat one-storey house, whitewashed under a roof of red tiles. It was one of a number of such houses, each with its own wrought-iron gate revealing a garden where palm trees waved over a riot of mimosa and geraniums which scented the air delightfully. The houses appeared to encircle three sides of a small park, in the centre of which she saw an elegant wrought-iron bandstand. This was empty at present, but a few chairs hinted at the presence somewhere of bandsmen.

Leo waved an airy hand. 'The praca.' He pronounced it 'prassa'. 'We can walk here on Sundays and listen to the music. The ladies love to parade themselves here! Ouch!' He ducked, grinning, as his father aimed a playful cuff at his head.

Her uncle said, 'We provide the bandsmen with uniforms and the instruments. They are mostly Portuguese and very proud to be members of the band. What they lack in talent, they make up for in enthusiasm. There's great competition for a place in the band.'

They went in through the gates and Leo disappeared round the back of the house, leaving Joanna to follow her uncle into the delightfully cool hallway. At once a small, elderly maidservant appeared, wiping her hands on her apron and holding them out in welcome to Joanna, who took an immediate liking to her.

'You like Portugal!' she told Joanna firmly. 'You like very much. Portugal very good place!'

'Of course she will like it,' said Elliot.

The interior of the house was cool and white and simply but tastefully furnished in the Portuguese fashion – dark polished wood and intricate carving. There were striped woven mats on the tiled floor and decorative plates on the walls. Before Joanna could take it all in there were steps behind her and she turned to see a slim, elegant woman with grey eyes and brown hair. She wore a dress of pale lemon and looked remarkably unruffled. By comparison, Joanna felt like a scarecrow in her dusty, crumpled travelling clothes. A smile on Catherine's beautiful face did nothing to soften her expression, which Joanna read as thinly disguised hostility. She felt her throat tighten as she, too, forced a smile.

'Hullo, Aunt Catherine.'

'My dear Joanna! So here you are at last.' She gave Joanna's cheek a brief and unenthusiastic peck and added, 'Now I see why my husband saw fit to miss his lunch! Your father played down your charms in his letter.' She made the compliment sound like a slur and Joanna knew that her worst fears had been realized. This woman did not want her here. Perhaps they had argued as to whether or not she should be allowed to come. She searched for something else to say but remained stupidly silent. To hide the uncomfortable moment Elliot said heartily, 'We are all hungry, Catherine. I'm sure Christina can find us something to eat.'

Christina agreed quickly and hurried away as Leo reappeared and said, 'Grub? Oh, good. I'm fading away!' and they all laughed gratefully.

Seeing that her aunt still regarded her with apparent disfavour Joanna struggled to retrieve her waning courage. She must on no account let this woman see how frightened she was.

She said, 'I'll try not to be a burden to you, Aunt Catherine.'

'Oh, my dear, you *won't* be a burden.' Catherine glanced at her husband. 'Elliot is convinced that we shall find you a useful addition to the family. We all know what they say about idle hands and there will be no time for the devil's work here. Do you sew?'

'Yes.'

'Some of the pillowslips need—'

'Joanna has had a long journey, my dear!' put in her uncle.

Catherine's laugh rang out. 'Elliot! There is no need to mollycoddle the poor girl. She is not an invalid, and sewing is light work.' She turned to Joanna. 'Take no notice of him, my dear. Men do not understand these things. We will find plenty to keep you occupied, have no fear. There will be no time to brood over the past; we shall keep you very firmly in the present.'

Joanna said, 'You are so kind.'

'Not at all.'

As they eyed each other coldly, Joanna was reminded of two dogs circling before a fight. She heard her uncle draw in his breath as he recognized the first clash of personalities. Leo was also staring from his mother to Joanna with a puzzled frown. Joanna knew that her aunt was waiting for her to back down, but she dared not show any sign of weakness. The unspoken hostility almost crackled in the air between them and she knew with a sinking heart that battle had commenced. It was a relief to them all when Christina put her head round the door to say that refreshments were waiting in the shade on the patio.

*

Later that afternoon Joanna was resting on her bed in the small but attractive guest room which was temporarily hers. Feigning a slight headache, she had come here to escape from her aunt and uncle and collect her thoughts. Her diary lay open on the bedside table, but so far she had written nothing in it. First, she felt, she must find a suitable hiding-place; if she were to continue entrusting her confidences to it, she must be certain that they would not be read by the wrong eyes – by any other eyes, in fact. Leo had departed immediately after the meal on business of his own, although he had offered to show her around. Claiming tiredness after the long journey, she had declined and they had made an arrangement for the following day. Her uncle also had hinted that he would be more than willing to give her a guided tour, but Catherine had reminded him sharply that the mine would not run itself and that she had already taken several messages for him, which awaited him in his study.

From her position on the bed, Joanna surveyed the room in search of a place to hide the diary. Instead of a bed-head there was a large wall tapestry depicting a hunting scene, but she could see no way of affixing a notebook to the back of it. The walls were mainly bare, the wardrobe was built in to the wall. After a quick investigation of the blanket chest she rejected that also, finally deciding to take a calculated risk. She would slide it between two of the books on the small bookshelf which, being in full view, was hopefully the last place where anyone would look. Having settled on a hiding-place, she began to write:

Today I reached San Domingos and met my aunt, who does not want me here and makes no secret of the fact. With her I shall have to be on my guard. On the other hand, Uncle Elliot is almost *too* pleased to see me and watches me most intently. I have met the head servant, who is called Christina and who seems very pleasant. Liliane, the new maid they are training, has not yet appeared. Leo seems to know everyone and everything and fortunately is not going to need my company. The heat is very tiring but I—

Someone knocked on the door and Joanna stuffed the diary under the mattress before calling out a weak, 'Come in!' as she hurled herself into a prone position on the bed.

A large, round English woman looked in. She wore a small white cap, a nurse's apron and sensible shoes. Her podgy face bore an expression of briskness and she oozed competence. This, Joanna guessed, was her grandmother's nurse.

Quickly she sat up, murmuring her excuse about the sick headache, but the nurse paid it no heed.

'I am Nurse Williams,' she announced. 'Your grandmother wants to see you – you'd best come along.'

Before Joanna could refuse she had withdrawn and Joanna was forced to slip on her shoes and follow her. It seemed that Grandmother and her nurse were housed in two rooms which formed part of an annexe built on to the rear of the house, overlooking the large patio where they had enjoyed their refreshments. Once inside the first room Joanna saw an elderly lady sitting stiffly upright in a high-backed chair. In her right hand she held an ebony walking-stick, and both hands fumbled continuously with the carved duck's head which formed its handle. Something in the gaunt face reminded Joanna of Agatha. The old lady was dressed entirely in black, contrasting strongly with her white hair that hung thickly and somewhat incongruously over her shoulders.

Nurse Williams said, 'We wouldn't have our hair done this morning, would we, madam?' She stood beside her patient with her arms folded firmly across her ample chest.

After a moment's hesitation Joanna said, 'I'm pleased to meet you, Grandmother.'

The old lady's skin was remarkably youthful, her nose was thin and a little beaklike, her faded blue eyes narrowed as she scrutinized Joanna. 'Grandmother?' she repeated.

The nurse said, 'Yes, madam. This is your granddaughter, Joanna—'

'Agatha's child?'

Giving Joanna a look which said, 'You see what we have to put up with?' the nurse replied, 'Not Agatha, Maurice. Maurice and Mary. The adopted child – you remember?'

The old lady sighed deeply without answering. Then she

put a clawlike finger beneath Joanna's chin and tilted her head. At the fierce prod of that finger Joanna recoiled instinctively. Her grandmother said, 'Elliot's child! I can see it in her face!'

The nurse tutted irritably. 'Not Elliot, madam. Maurice and Mary. In England. I told you.' To Joanna she said, 'Her memory comes and goes. It's so unpredictable. I do my best, but . . .' She raised plump shoulders despairingly.

The elderly voice quavered now. 'Is Maurice here? I want to see Maurice! Why isn't Maurice here?'

Joanna said, 'My father, Maurice, is in England, Grandmother. I am here for a . . . a holiday. I came over with Leo.'

'Leo?' The old lady brightened. 'Is Leo here?'

'He's in San Domingos, Grandmother, but he's gone off somewhere.'

Nurse Williams said, 'Master Leo has gone riding, madam,' and gave Joanna a wink to show that this was not necessarily true. 'He'll be in to see you later.'

The faded eyes closed tiredly. 'Leo is here?'

'Yes, madam.'

The head drooped momentarily and then snapped up again. Ignoring Joanna, she said, 'Lunch is late today.'

'We've had lunch, madam. You had baked fish, remember?'

'I did?'

'Yes, madam. And a little egg pudding with nutmeg, the way you like it.'

Again the eyes closed as though in sleep, but just as Joanna had decided that this time the old lady *was* asleep, she opened her eyes again and jabbed her sharply with her ebony stick.

'Elliot's child,' she said. 'And don't try to fool me. You've got his voice; I'd recognize it anywhere!'

*

Back in her own room Joanna retrieved her diary and considered what she should write next. After some thought she wrote:

I met my so-called grandmother today. She is quite mad, poor old thing. Her nurse is a bit of an Amazon, so I daresay they are well matched. I begin to wonder how on earth I shall get through each day, and live in hopes that I will receive a letter from Mark, but failing that, I would like Mr Shreiker to be here. At least he is normal, which is more than I can say for the rest of them here . . .

*

Joanna went down to dinner that evening wearing her lightweight blue silk and a brittle smile which hid a mass of anxieties. Someone from the mining company had apparently been invited to join them, but her grandmother would not be present. According to Leo, she rarely dined with the family in the evenings and never when there were guests. He considered this a great pity.

'She sometimes says outrageous things,' he had confided, 'and then Mama and Papa get horribly embarrassed. I don't know why – I think it brightens a dull evening.'

Putting off the evil moment as long as she could, Joanna did not join them for drinks on the patio and was finally forced to hurry into the dining room somewhat ignominiously when the gong sounded. Leo, looking unnaturally tidy, was already hovering near the long table. Her aunt wore a dress of maroon taffeta cut fashionably low which showed to perfection a choker of pearls at her throat. She was talking to a man who Joanna guessed must be in his thirties; Catherine's hand rested lightly on his arm and her eyes were bright. She caught sight of Joanna but glanced away at once so that it was Elliot who came forward and took her hand.

'So there you are, Joanna!' He kissed her hand with mock gallantry. 'You must meet Steven Benbridge, our senior mining engineer. I've been telling him all about you.'

Catherine said, 'You've been *boring* the poor man, my dear!' She laughed lightly and said to Joanna, 'You can't possibly be the paragon Elliot imagines!'

'I'm very pleased to meet you, Miss Grosvenor.' Steven Benbridge's handshake was firm. 'I'm sure your uncle did not exaggerate.' He smiled and his rather plain face lit up. 'Welcome to San Domingos. I'm sure everyone will do their best to make your stay an enjoyable one.'

From the table Leo said, 'Well, she isn't a paragon but she is quite nice – for a girl!'

The laughter this provoked helped Joanna to relax a little, and then it was time for Catherine to seat them. She moved to one end of the table and Elliot went to the other. 'Mr Benbridge, you are here on my right ... opposite Leo ... who is next to Joanna.'

This put Joanna next to Elliot and as far as possible from Steven Benbridge, but she had no strong feelings on the matter. As she sat down Leo was leaning forward earnestly to ask the visitor when he could go down the mine again, and the question was being tactfully fielded. Elliot said, 'Perhaps Joanna would like to see how it's done. You could go down together some time. I'll come with you.'

As Christina came in with the soup Catherine raised her eyebrows in surprise. 'You, Elliot? But your back! You know how much trouble it gives you.' To Steven she said, 'You mustn't encourage my husband, Mr Benbridge. The stooping is so bad for him and he will suffer for it afterwards.'

Elliot flushed slightly. 'What nonsense, Catherine! I have to go down from time to time!'

'Oh, yes, of course, my dear. But why go down when it

is not necessary? It is foolish to ask for trouble. I'm sure Mr Benbridge could take them down and they will be quite safe in his hands. I might even be tempted to go down myself!'

Before Elliot could reply, their attention was momentarily distracted by Leo who began to 'slurp' his soup.

'Leo! Please! What has happened to your manners?' Catherine glared at him. 'I shall write to your matron if you ever make such a horrible noise again!'

Joanna glanced at him, but he returned a look of such innocence that she knew at once he had done it simply to create a diversion and wondered how frequently he felt bound to intervene between his parents. She began to feel rather sorry for him.

Catherine turned to Joanna. 'I hope you won't find it too dull here, Joanna. We do what we can to amuse ourselves, but we are sadly limited. I ride occasionally and paint, of course, but I am kept busy with the various duties which fall to me as your uncle's wife. There are functions to arrange. I visit the sick . . .' She waved a hand vaguely.

Leo said quickly, 'Why haven't you visited Mr Cotton, Mama? He's sick, he's got malaria.'

'I haven't had time, Leo. I have had all the preparations to make for Joanna's arrival. And yours, also. I only have one pair of hands.' To Steven she added, 'I do what I can, but the climate is hard on a woman.'

Elliot nodded and turned to Joanna. 'Your aunt is somewhat frail; prone to sick headaches which can strike at any time.'

'And indigestion,' said Leo.

'Leo! Please!'

He appeared unabashed. 'Is it *cabrita* tonight?' To Joanna he explained, '*Sarapatel*! Remember? The blood! The tripes!'

'Wait and see,' his mother told him. 'I've told you before that it's not polite to enquire about the meal.'

'I bet it *is* kid!'

Christina came in with a large earthenware pot and winked at him.

'It is!' he exclaimed.

Steven smiled at Joanna. 'Don't be deterred; it's an excellent dish. Kid and pork are very popular in Portugal because beef cattle are less plentiful. But you will enjoy it, I assure you. Portuguese cuisine is very tasty and imaginative. The river fish are excellent, too. Lampreys are a local delicacy.'

'Eels to you!' Leo grinned. 'Giant eels! Don't ever swim in the Guardiana, Joanna! But we can fish in the Chanca. If you don't have a rod Papa might lend you his. Would you, Papa? I can show her how to fish.'

'Of course Joanna may borrow it.'

Joanna said, 'I'd like that, Leo.'

Catherine turned suddenly to Steven Benbridge. 'I understand that you are invited to the dinner-party next Saturday at the doctor's house. I shall look forward to seeing you there.'

From the corner of her eye Joanna saw Elliot react to this news with a tightening of his mouth.

Steven said, 'No doubt Miss Grosvenor will also be included.'

Seeing Catherine's expression Joanna said hastily, 'I don't care for parties, as a rule – that is . . . some, not all. I don't expect to be invited to everything.'

Catherine nodded her approval of this sentiment. 'She is still only a girl,' she said.

'She's nearly eighteen!' said Leo. He took a slice of bread and began to mop the gravy from his plate.

'Leo!' Catherine cried. 'You are the most provoking boy I have ever met! Stop embarrassing me, or you will be sent to your room without any dessert!'

'What is the dessert?' he demanded, but now his father remonstrated with him, pointing out that Joanna and Mr Benbridge would not be at all impressed with his manners.

At that moment Christina entered, carrying a tray on which was a dish of fresh fruits and what Joanna took to be an almond cake covered with nuts. After a moment of silent disapproval, Leo declared that he was no longer hungry and asked if he could be excused from the table. Catherine hesitated but Elliot said irritably, 'Yes, and the sooner the better. You are a born fidget, Leo. God knows what you will be like by the time *you* are nearly eighteen!'

'Taller!' said Leo, with a grin, and Joanna wanted to hug him for his impudence. As he slipped from his chair he asked suddenly, 'Are you married, Mr Benbridge?'

Catherine turned her beautiful grey eyes on their visitor as she awaited his reply. It was a question which Joanna had been pondering also, although she tried not to look too interested as he explained that his wife had died some years before.

'She had a weak heart, and when her father died quite unexpectedly the shock was too much for her; she only outlived him by a few days.'

He spoke matter-of-factly and without obvious distress, but Joanna sensed that the memories were still raw and was glad when Leo let the matter drop.

The rest of the meal passed in the same strained atmosphere and Joanna envied her young cousin's escape. She ate an orange as slowly as she could, saying as little as possible for fear of offending either her uncle or aunt. She sensed that Mr Benbridge was also ill-at-ease and felt a sneaking sympathy for him. During the last ten minutes of the meal Catherine established that her husband would be busy all the evening and persuaded Mr Benbridge to ride out with her. When Elliot suggested that Joanna might like to join them, Catherine explained that as yet Joanna had no horse but that she would attend to that tomorrow.

'I'm really too tired to ride,' Joanna told them, hiding her hurt feelings. 'I shall walk in the praca and then rest in my room for a while.'

'Of course,' agreed her uncle. 'You must be very tired after your long journey.'

She made her escape and thankfully went to her room. Closing and locking the door, she leaned back against it. 'Oh, Mark! They don't really want me here,' she whispered, 'and this is all your fault!'

Immediately she felt guilty. This was not entirely Mark's fault; she had been a willing participant, and he was not to blame for the fact that they had been seen together. This exile was the cross she had to bear. His cross was Isobel, and in her present frame of mind she could not resist the hope that it would prove a heavy burden.

Chapter Seven

JOANNA SLEPT LATE the following morning and was finally awakened by loud screams from the direction of the patio. Jumping from the bed and rushing to the window, she was astonished to see Christina struggling with a young Portuguese girl. Her first thought was that perhaps the girl had been found stealing something, but Leo suddenly appeared outside her window to enlighten her. 'Don't worry,' he told her. 'It's not a murder, although you might think so from the din!'

The girl broke free and, seeing that she had an audience, ran towards them shouting, '*Eu detesto-a! Ela é horrivel!*'

Leo translated. 'I hate her! She's horrible!' as Christina, red-faced and furious, ran after the girl. She caught her by the arm, slapped her and marched her inside.

Joanna slipped her arms into her negligée and asked Leo what she had done.

'Nothing. It's what she hasn't done.' He laughed at her confusion. 'That's the new maid. She has to have a bath and she hates it. I expect Christina was the same when she was young. You're going to give her English lessons.'

'Me? Why me?' But she remembered now that teaching the maid English was to be one of the many tasks which her aunt had planned for her.

Leo shrugged. 'Ours is not to reason why. Ours is just

to do or die! Jolly, isn't it!' She looked at him doubtfully. 'They are all quite wild when they first come – almost gypsies. But they soon learn, and Mama gives them shoes and stockings and a nice uniform. Oh, don't look so stuffy, Joanna. Seventeen girls wanted Liliane's job. *Seventeen!* So it's not so bad.' They listened to the sudden silence and Leo said, 'They *have* murdered her, after all!'

'I suppose I've missed breakfast.'

'Ages ago. Do you want me to show you round, or would you rather Mr Benbridge does it? He seemed rather keen, I thought. Oh, Joanna! You're blushing!'

'I'm not! I hardly know the man.'

'I hear you met Grandmother?'

'Yes. She's a bit . . . frightening.'

'It's the nurse who frightens me!' he exclaimed with a shudder. 'But don't be deceived. Grandmother knows more than she tells. Christina thinks she has the gift – you know, seeing into men's hearts and all that stuff. Well, I'm off. I shall be at the stables most of the morning. They're bringing up the underground ponies; they come up for a rest every six months because their coats are green.'

'Green?'

'It's the copper dust in the air; they breathe it in and their hair goes green. It goes brown again eventually and then they go back down.'

Before she could decide whether to believe this snippet of information, Leo had sauntered away, whistling rather unsuccessfully, and Joanna hurried to wash and dress.

Venturing into the large, airy kitchen half an hour later in search of something to eat, she found Christina peeling vegetables while Liliane sat at the table shelling peas.

Christina greeted her cheerfully. 'You don't like eat breakfast?'

'I do, but I overslept.'

'Ah! Then you eat now?' She fetched a pot of butter and a loaf of bread from the pantry and cut a thick slice.

While Joanna ate she watched the new girl cautiously. She seemed to be a few years younger than Joanna, fifteen perhaps. Her face was now scrubbed and gleaming, and her hair was tied back beneath a white cap. She looked quite presentable. Seeing her look, Liliane smiled suddenly and said something in Portuguese to Christina.

'She says you are going to give her lessons in English.'

'Apparently.' Inspiration struck. 'Perhaps she will help me with my Portuguese?'

This was duly passed on and the girl's smile broadened. She pointed at once to the loaf and said, '*Pao!*' To Joanna it sounded very similar to the French *pain*, with a similar nasal sound. She tried to pronounce the word, but her effort sent the girl into peals of laughter.

Christina said, 'She is daughter of one of the miners. Her uncle, he in prison.'

'In prison?'

'*Si.* He is . . .' She searched for the word. 'He is drinking too much. He fights. The other man is in hospital.' She made stabbing motions towards her own chest. Seeing what was being said, Liliane scowled and muttered something under her breath.

'She says they ashamed by him. Always he is drinking.'

'What will happen to him?'

'Senor Grosvenor, he decide. He punish. Maybe he sent to Mertola. Maybe lose his job.'

Seeing how cast down the girl was, Joanna finished her breakfast and suggested that she spend fifteen minutes with Liliane, if she could be spared. Christina agreed, with much finger-wagging in Liliane's direction which Joanna assumed was a warning to behave herself.

For the next quarter of an hour they walked around the patio in the sunshine, telling each other the names of plants and trees. Joanna was rather abashed to discover that the girl was much quicker than she was to pick up the new words. By the time Liliane was called back to her work, however, Joanna had taken a liking to her. She realized to her surprise that the lessons would not prove as boring as she had expected, and found herself looking forward to the time when they could converse properly. Feeling surprisingly cheerful, she went off in search of the stables.

*

A few days later Joanna wrote to Mark.

> My dearest Mark,
> I've been here for nearly a week now and am longing to receive a letter from you. Please, *please* write to me. If you are desperately busy a few lines will do. Just to see an envelope with your handwriting on it would make me happy!
> San Domingos is a strange place, a world within a world. A tiny oasis of civilization surrounded by wild hills and wolves and boar and other unimaginable things ... Inside the stockade (well, it isn't exactly like that!) we even have our own police force.
> One of my tasks is to teach the new maid English, and I have to read to Grandmother most afternoons for half an hour or so. Sometimes she falls asleep in the middle of it and then I just creep away.
> The blacksmith is teaching us (that is me and Leo) to shoot, but I do not think I shall ever want to kill anything. Sometimes we shoot at a row of bottles, and Leo is quite good, but I find the rifle rather heavy and my aim is still a bit erratic.
> Uncle Elliot is very kind (a bit too kind! It is rather embarrassing and does not please Aunt Catherine!).
> Leo is – well, he is just Leo!
> Yesterday we rode in the wagonette to Mertola to meet the new mining engineer, who had come the long way to San Domingos. The poor man was quite exhausted and half jolted to death, and said they had seen

several wolves among the trees but they made no move to attack. He is a charming man and claims to have fallen in love with me.

That ought to give Mark pause for thought, she decided. The mention of a rival should make him reach for his pen.

Mr Benbridge, the senior engineer, came to dinner for the first time since he was promoted and seems very pleasant. Not handsome, but with a kind face. He is a widower, but you need not be jealous for he is much too old for me.

I daresay the wedding arrangements are going ahead. Perhaps *someone* would write and tell me about them. Dorcas promised to write, but a letter from you would be better. Write that you still love me as you did before that day.

Your adoring Joanna

'But do I still love him?' She reconsidered the last line of the letter and thought she had overstated her feelings, but there was no way to remove the words without spoiling the look of the letter. They would have to stand . . . No! On second thoughts she would lightly cross them out so that he would see exactly what she had done . . . No! She would add a P.S.

P.S. Actually I find that I no longer love you except as a brother. Isn't that convenient?

*

Less than a mile away, the new mining engineer was preparing to go underground for the first time in earnest. Not only that, but today he would set his first fuses under the watchful eye of his senior engineer. Having come straight from college in Cornwall, Andrew had only ever blasted rock as an exercise, but today it would be the real thing. Trying not to show just how nervous he was, he followed Mr Benbridge to the mouth of the tunnel which sloped down until it met the main vertical shaft. Alongside the entrance there was a small office built against the rock.

Steven waved a hand towards the interior of the office. 'Everything to do with the underground workings is kept here,' he explained. 'All the paperwork, paraphernalia, lists, maps, rotas, names – everything. Nothing to do with the open-cast mining. OK?'

Andrew nodded. There were a number of boards propped against the window, each one covered with rows of hooks, each marked by a number. From the hooks small metal tokens hung like medals. Seeing his glance Steven said, 'The men's tokens. Each man hands in his token when he goes underground, and collects it again on his return to the surface. At the end of the shift the tokens should all be gone from the board. If one is left on its hook we know there is a man still underground, which means he's in trouble of some kind, and we send down a search party. Luckily that doesn't happen too often. Always check carefully at the end of your shift because you are ultimately responsible for those men.'

'I'll remember.'

'It won't always mean that the man is in danger. It might mean he is up to something; that he's about to cause some trouble. Last year we found a man who had deliberately stayed down so that he could steal some dynamite.'

'Good God!'

'He wasn't planning a revolution, but he wanted the stuff for a friend who wanted to blast some large rocks from his orchard! Or so he said!' He shrugged. 'We shall never know. So be on your guard all the time; they may look innocent but you can't trust them. At least, you can trust most of them, but it's knowing which men you can't trust that poses the problems.'

They signed themselves in and Steven gave Andrew one of the numbered tokens which was hung on the appropriate hook. As he handed him a lamp he smiled at Andrew's expression.

'Did you think we still used candles?'

'I didn't know what to expect.'

'We're very up-to-date in San Domingos and improving all the time. I hear you've brought specifications for new pumps?'

'Several, actually.'

'Good. Mr Grosvenor can have a choice.'

'They're not cheap.'

'Money is no object. Mason and Barry know what they're doing and they don't cut corners. Now here's a map of the workings and we're here ...' He stabbed a finger against the map, which showed a neat arrangement of galleries running at right-angles to the main shaft. From each cross-cut further cross-cuts had been made, so that in effect the ground was honeycombed with workings. Some of them were worked out, however, and were defunct, so the area yielding ore was smaller than it seemed at first glance.

Steven's finger moved. 'We walk along here to the main shaft and climb down. Then it's Shank's pony to the ore face ... here. Oh, yes! Keep well back when we pass the ponies. It's their first day down after being above ground and they're always nervous. They're frisky little blighters at the best of times.'

'So how many levels are there?' Andrew asked.

'Four so far, although we may well go down further if it becomes necessary. So you've never actually *worked* down a mine before?'

'I've been down a coal-mine – for three weeks, to gain experience.'

Benbridge shrugged. 'Coal is a lot less stable than this rock. I've never known a serious rock-fall but, having said that, there's always a first time, I suppose.'

'Let's hope not!'

'There are similarities, however. Temperature, constant water seepage and so on. That will be one of your jobs before too long. Mr Grosvenor wants to improve the pumping system. I understand you've done some work in that field?'

'It was air circulation, actually. Mr Mason thought—'

'Air? Oh, well, you'll have to bluff your way through it. Mr Grosvenor thinks it was drainage! Don't tell him he was wrong; he's the boss and a damned good one.'

Andrew's anxiety must have registered, for the older man added, 'Don't worry. We've got a lot of up-to-date information already. You can get a good idea from that ... Are you ready?'

'When you are.'

'Let's go, then.'

A steep pathway led into the hillside and, as he followed Benbridge, Andrew picked his way carefully over the rails. These he assumed were for the wheels of the trucks which would carry the ore into the daylight, winched up by the winding gear he had already noted. He was relieved to discover that most of what he had been told made sense and he hoped he might aquit himself reasonably well. Normally the men would work in small gangs, and blasting would not be one of Andrew's jobs. However, Benbridge had rightly insisted that he must do the job himself at least once if he was to command the respect of the men under him.

They climbed down the narrow ladder which seemed to go on for ever; the smell of sulphur was strong in the air as they switched to a second ladder. Andrew counted the levels and they finally stopped at the fourth and made their way, half stooping, towards the face of one of the cross-cuts. Here water dripped from the roof, ran down the side and collected in small puddles underfoot. Seepage: the universal problem of underground water which no one had yet managed to solve.

Benbridge said, 'The sulphur is everywhere and costs the company hundreds of pounds. It eats into the men's boots and we have to replace them every six weeks.' He turned a corner, caught his helmet on the roof and swore mildly. Andrew began to think that their trek would never end. Most of the time they could walk upright, but occasionally the ceiling was lower and they had to bend double to get through. Andrew's knees and spine cried out for relief, but he gritted his teeth and said nothing.

They passed various rooms hewn from the rock – a first-aid centre, a store for machinery, a locked door with an exclamation mark painted on it which indicated the presence of explosives. There were even stables cut into the rocks where the ponies were rested and fed. They also passed many men, all engrossed in various aspects of their work: some shovelling the rock into small tubs; others wielding pickaxes; a few leading the small, sturdy pit ponies without which the mine could not function. A few of the men glanced up and one of them, recognizing Benbridge, brought a diagram to him for an opinion. They talked briefly, the man nodded and thanked him. Andrew took the opportunity to crouch down and ease the strain on his back, but almost immediately Steven was moving on and he quickly followed. Somewhere to their left a horn sounded, and immediately the men in the vicinity began to scramble away from the direction of the sound.

'Preparing to blast,' Benbridge explained. 'The horn is the warning to take cover.'

Seconds later the ground beneath their feet trembled, then the blast reached them and dust eddied in the air, hot with the smell of cordite. The older man smiled. 'It's when that doesn't happen that we have to start worrying,' he told Andrew. 'A misfire! Very nasty situation, that. It means some poor sod has to go back and find out what went wrong. It happened once – not here, I'm pleased to say. The chap was experienced enough, but it went up in his face and killed him. You don't forget these stories, and it makes you wary.'

They finally reached the rock face where a drill awaited them, already perched on its spindly metal legs, its hose for the compressed air trailing across the ground. Benbridge stood back as Andrew familiarized himself with the drill, which fortunately was one he recognized. He was told where the charge was to be placed and what weight of rock he was to remove. Then Steven stepped back and left him to his own resources. He aligned the drill and switched it on, and immediately it sprang into life as the bit ate into the rock, boring a neat circular hole into which he would tamp the precise amount of explosive needed. Andrew felt the sweat break out on his skin. The vibration juddered through his arms to his shoulders and thundered in his head.

He was forced to pause. 'How much further?' he asked, controlling his voice with an effort.

'You tell me!'

'Another six inches should do it.'

'I'd say so.'

Gritting his teeth Andrew resumed the drilling, heartily glad that he was not a miner but an engineer. He had done this kind of test back in England, but that was about seven months ago. Under Steven's critical eye, it seemed much harder.

After what seemed an eternity the hole was ready and Andrew prepared the charges with fingers that shook. He was grateful that no comment was made about his obvious nervousness. At last the charge was in place; he attached the fuse, tamped down the hole and reeled the cable backwards, round the corner, to a safe distance. Benbridge sounded a horn to warn that blasting was about to take place, then the fuse was lit. They braced themselves against the rock wall, hands over their ears, and waited. And waited . . . Just as Andrew decided that he had somehow miscalculated the ground trembled, there was a clap of thundrous vibration and then the main blast rocked the air about them, first sucking in the air and then driving it back around them – warmer than before and carrying with it the unmistakable smell of sulphur. Andrew drew a deep breath of relief and raised his head.

Benbridge lowered his hands and grinned. 'Nice work, Shreiker! We'll make an engineer of you yet!'

Smiling with relief, Andrew followed him back to the scene of the explosion. Scattered rock lay in heaps on the ground; soon a gang of miners would be detailed to shovel it into the tubs and the ponies would draw it to the main shaft. From there it would be transferred to the wagons and hauled up and taken to Pomerao by train. Day after day, the work would continue.

As Benbridge led the way back he said, 'Easy to think it will never end, but one day the mine will be exhausted.'

'And then?' Andrew, bent almost double, was finding it difficult to keep up with him.

'And then San Domingos will die! The men will drift away in search of work and their families will follow them.'

'It would be a ghost town!' said Andrew. 'Hard to imagine.'

Benbridge nodded as he stepped out into the light once more and straightened his back. 'It will happen one day,' he said, 'but not just yet. This year's yield is the best ever! The mine is one of the largest and most productive in Europe.' He slapped Andrew on the back cheerfully. 'It will see us out, Shreiker! No fears on that score.'

And Andrew, trying to imagine the thriving mine deserted and abandoned, could only shake his head in disbelief.

*

On Sunday evening, Joanna sat on one of the wrought-iron

seats in the praca and listened to the band which was rehearsing. Catherine had not come down to dinner, claiming one of her headaches, and the meal had been more relaxed without her. Joanna had announced her intention of listening to the band and her uncle had promised to join her later. The band only played on Sundays, so this was the first time she had heard them. They looked very smart in blue uniforms trimmed with yellow and they obviously enjoyed their moment of glory. She could see by their faces that they were proud of their achievements and wondered how much practice had been needed to reach their present level of competence. They ended the piece and she clapped enthusiastically. So far there were very few other people in the praca, but as a rendering of 'The Blue Danube' began Leo slid on to the seat beside her.

'They're going to give a party for you,' he announced, 'and I shall be able to come to the first hour. Mama didn't want me to come at all, but Papa persuaded her.'

Joanna was astonished. 'A party for *me*? But why?'

'I don't know. I heard them talking in Mama's bedroom. She said it would be something for everyone to look forward to. I thought Papa would say "No" because he hates parties, but he said "Yes". I think he's taken a liking to you. Mama said he's always talking about you, and she's getting a little tired of it.'

'Oh, dear!' There seemed nothing else to say.

'They're quite good, aren't they? The band.'

'Yes. Very good. Not much of an audience, though.'

He shrugged. 'People will come out later on. I want to learn the French horn, but Mama makes me learn the piano. Ugh! What use is that? You can't play the piano in a band.' He swung his short legs moodily and Joanna hid a smile.

'Mama is going to invite Mr Benbridge and the doctor and his wife and—'

'Is she inviting Mr Shreiker?' The question slipped out before she could stop it.

'I don't know. He's only a junior engineer but he might be included. Sometimes Father forbids people to come, but I don't know why. Nobody will tell me.'

'What sort of people?'

'Well, there was Mr Sturton who was one of the senior secretaries. He'd been at San Domingos for simply ages. He told me he was one of Mama's closest friends and he was terribly kind to me, too, until Papa found out. Then he didn't come to dinner any more, and he wouldn't even speak to me although it wasn't my fault. Papa said he was a sight too friendly, but *I* didn't think he was. He was sent back to England.' While Joanna was digesting this information he added, 'He gave me a really nice fishing-rod once, but Papa took it away and bought me a better one – so I didn't mind, really, although I could have had two.'

Joanna kept her eyes on the band. 'And who is your Mama's best friend now?'

He frowned thoughtfully. 'I don't know. I think she likes Mr Benbridge now that he's been promoted. She smiles at him a great deal and I think that's a sign, don't you?' He stood up suddenly and went forward to speak to the band's conductor who had just finished 'The Blue Danube' and was mopping his brow with a large, spotless handkerchief. When Leo came back he was smiling. 'They're going to play "Colonel Bogey" for me; it's my favourite. They'll play your favourite tune if you ask them, although if it's new to them they won't play it very well.'

He settled down to enjoy his chosen piece, but before they were half-way through it Steven Benbridge arrived and stood beside them.

'Let me guess who asked for this!' he said and grinned at Leo who promptly stood up and offered his seat, but Steven went on, 'I wondered if Miss Grosvenor would like to come for a stroll?'

As Joanna rose to her feet Leo sat down again and began to conduct what remained of 'Colonel Bogey'.

'He's quite a character,' Steven whispered and Joanna agreed wholeheartedly. As they walked slowly among the trees and shrubs, companionably but not touching, Steven described how the mine and the facilities had grown over the years.

'I saw the trees and shrubs planted,' he told her. 'Carefully chosen for their perfumes.'

'And the bandstand?'

He laughed. 'I'm not *that* old! That was here when I came, although it gets repainted every Spring. I first came the year before my wife died. It was such a tragedy; she had only been here about a year but already loved it. She fell in love with Portugal. She said once that Portugal had "cast its spell" over her! It will, if you give it half a chance.'

She looked at him sharply. 'Meaning what, Mr Benbridge? That I don't?'

'Meaning that you look rather unhappy sometimes and I wonder if you really want to be here.'

She was shocked by his perception and found herself stammering, 'It's not the country, it's . . . Well, it's hard to explain.' Suddenly, however, she was longing to confide in someone. She began, 'There was someone who meant a lot to me – who meant everything. Leaving him . . . losing someone you love to someone else . . .'

To her horror tears pressed urgently against her eyelids and she turned away, her hands over her face, willing back the sobs. She heard him say, 'Miss Grosvenor! I'm so stupid! Please forgive me.'

'No, no! It's nothing. I'm – there's something in my eye.'

'Can I help?'

She thanked heaven for the gathering gloom. 'No, thank you. It's gone now.' With a shaky smile she turned to face him, but was unprepared for the kindly concern on his face.

'Don't!' she cried. 'Don't look at me that way!'

'I'm sorry. I didn't think—'

'Don't be kind to me!' she gasped, and then before she knew what was happening she was sobbing against his shoulder. Before she could speak again he had handed her a handkerchief and his arm was round her. In between sobs she began desperately to try to explain, but quite suddenly a sharp voice cut across her own.

'Well now, what is the matter here? Is that you, Joanna?'

With a gasp Joanna straightened up to find her aunt staring at them with a furious expression on her face.

Steven said quickly, 'I'm afraid I'm to blame, Mrs Grosvenor. I was talking about England and I think your niece is still homesick.'

'I'm sorry,' said Joanna, swallowing hard. She blew her nose and willed her tears to stop. 'It was so foolish of me. Please don't blame yourself, Mr Benbridge.'

Catherine looked from one to the other uncertainly. 'We all feel a little homesick at first,' she conceded. She smiled at Steven. 'We are doing all we can for our poor little exile,' she went on. 'I was just discussing with my husband whether or not we should give a small party for Joanna.'

'A party!' he said. 'That sounds fun, Joanna.'

She took a deep breath. 'It would be very nice.'

Catherine gave a little laugh. 'If you will promise not to cry all over the guests, that is!'

Joanna was silent but Steven said, 'I'm sure she's over the worst of it now. I think tears are a great relief. My wife cried when we left England, but she later grew to love this country and didn't want to go back.'

Catherine said, 'I'll take her in, Mr Benbridge.'

'Oh, there's no need, I assure you,' he protested.

'But there is,' Catherine insisted. 'Joanna is rather highly-strung and apt to dramatize her situation. And you know what they say – sleep is the best cure for melancholy. Thank you for looking after her.'

He asked, 'Is that what you want, Joanna?'

Catherine gave him a sharp look. 'It's not what Joanna wants. It's what I think is best for her, Mr Benbridge. A good night's rest . . .'

She let the sentence die away and Joanna, lacking the strength to oppose her, allowed herself to be led towards the house after a hurried 'Good night'. She glanced back once but saw only Leo who was skulking behind some bushes. Tracking, no doubt! In spite of her misery she could not resist a smile.

'That's better,' said Catherine, seeing her smile. 'You really must make an effort, Joanna. Your behaviour is most unladylike.' She led her into the morning room and brought her a small glass of white port.

'Drink that,' she advised, 'and then go to bed. An early night will do you good, Joanna. We will talk in the morning.'

Joanna's head came up sharply. 'Talk? What about?'

Catherine's smile was enigmatic. 'This and that,' she said. 'I really can't have you bothering the staff. Poor Mr Benbridge—'

'I didn't bother him!' Joanna protested. 'He came up to me and asked me to take a walk with him. That was all.'

'And you began to cry for no reason?'

'He – he told you. I'm rather homesick. I'm sure I'll get over it.'

'I do hope so, Joanna. We can hardly ship you home. Not until after the wedding. Oh, yes!' She saw Joanna's startled expression. 'I've heard all about everything. It seems that you were proving quite an embarrassment to the family. Mark is engaged to a very sweet girl, and you had no right to behave in a way that might have threatened their relationship. Suppose her family had come to hear of it? It could have created quite a scandal. You must see what harm you could have caused.' As Joanna opened her mouth to argue Catherine held up her hand. 'No more, Joanna! I have no wish to hear your excuses. You behaved like a young hoyden and have brought all this trouble upon yourself. Poor Mary was at her wits end with you, and you have been sent to stay with us whether you like it or not. But don't imagine you can ride roughshod over me, because you can't. I am not Mary; I am made of sterner stuff. I shall certainly not allow you to cause trouble here. We are a very small community and everyone must fit in. And don't glare. It is most unbecoming.'

Joanna continued to glare. 'So I have to stay here, is that it? I can't go home even if I want to?'

Catherine hesitated. 'I wouldn't put it quite like that.'

Joanna took several deep breaths in an effort to control her temper. She would not allow this hateful person to goad her into saying something she might regret, but she longed to strike back – to wipe the smile from that perfect face. Before Catherine could dismiss her she jumped to her feet and cried, 'I hate you all! And I loathe Portugal! And don't put yourself to the trouble of organizing a party for my sake because I shan't bother to attend it.' And with one last look at her aunt's astonished face she rushed from the room, slamming the door behind her.

*

Next morning Joanna was up early and, going without breakfast, set out at a quick pace away from the mine in the direction of the hills. She had gone about half a mile when footsteps alerted her to the fact that someone was following, and she suddenly stopped and turned. There was no one to be seen. She walked on, but again the rustle of the grass warned of someone behind her.

'I know it's you, Leo, so you can stop tracking me!'

He slid out from the shelter of a stunted tree and said sheepishly, 'I wasn't really trying. Anyway, where are you going?'

'Nowhere. Anywhere. Away from all of you.' The hurt expression on his young face went straight to her heart so she added, 'It's nothing personal, Leo. I just want to be on my own.'

'But why? What's happened? I heard a most tremendous row going on last night between my mother and father. Mama said you want to cancel the party.'

'Good! I hope she does.'

'Papa said, "Well, cancel it then," and Mama said, "But I've already mentioned it to people and they'll wonder why," and Papa said—'

'Oh, shut up about them, Leo! I don't want to know.'

He scurried along beside her, having difficulty in keeping up with her furious stride. 'But why?' he burst out. 'I thought you liked parties.'

'I'm not in the mood.' She picked up a stone and hurled it into the heather, and at once a large hare broke cover and went loping away. Jolted momentarily out of her ill-humour, Joanna smiled with pleasure.

Leo sighted an imaginary rifle and pulled the trigger. 'Bang! Got it!'

'You missed!'

They both laughed.

He changed the subject. 'Where are you going?'

'I'm leaving home,' she told him airily, not sure in her own mind where she intended to go. 'I shall walk to the edge of the world and then jump off. I shall never be seen again and then I won't be a nuisance to anybody. They'll all be glad to see the back of me.' She turned to Leo. 'They'll say, "Thank goodness she's gone!"'

He blinked earnestly as he considered this. 'No, they won't. They'll send out a search party.'

'They won't find me.'

'Can I come?' He tripped and fell sprawling but Joanna marched on, ignoring his plight. He scrambled to his feet and ran to catch up with her. 'Once I found a wild bees' nest. We could eat the honey. And we could trap hares. I could gather twigs and stuff for a fire.'

The truth was that Joanna was rather pleased with the prospect of some company, even Leo's. She did not really wish to be alone with her resentful thoughts, but had wanted to register a small protest and hoped by her absence to cause the family some anxiety. Possibly Catherine would blame herself for the visitor's disappearance. Maybe her uncle would discover that Catherine had insulted her and would remonstrate on her behalf. After the heated exchange of the previous night she did not want to risk further trouble by continued defiance, but neither did she wish to appear crushed by her aunt's unkind words. The best course seemed to be a total and unexplained withdrawal. Now, however, the sun was shining and her anger was melting away.

She stopped abruptly. 'Where does this lead?' she asked. 'I mean, if we keep on walking where will we end up?'

'Achado do Gamo. It's a tiny hamlet where Liliane's family live. Her mother Maria lives in a tiny house with her old father. I could take you there. I've been there before and they know me.'

She hesitated. 'But how can we talk to them?'

'I know some Portuguese. You don't need words. I'll show you.'

As she still dithered he said slyly, 'I expect she'll give us something to eat. Last time it was a handful of figs she had dried in the sun. Or some *favas* – that's fried beans to you. Do come, Joanna.'

Hunger triumphed over her injured feelings and they went on their way cheerfully. They saw a kestrel hovering above them, and later a stork glided eerily into view. The sense of freedom and the charm of the vast landscape warmed Joanna's heart and she was suddenly reminded of what Steven Benbridge's wife had said – that the country had cast its spell over her.

'Did you ever know Mrs Benbridge?' she asked.

'No, she died when I was very young, but I've seen pictures of her.'

'Was she pretty?'

'I don't know. I don't know why people go on about being pretty. I mean, who cares? It's more important to be fun. I shall marry someone who makes me laugh.'

'You will get married, then?'

'Everybody seems to. Will you?'

'Probably not.'

'If no one else will have you, and you don't mind waiting, I could marry you. You make me laugh quite often, and I'll be taller by then.'

'Oh!' She glanced at his face, but he was obviously in earnest. 'That's very kind of you, Leo, but we're cousins, aren't we?'

He frowned and tutted with annoyance. 'I'd forgotten,' he said, then suddenly pointed excitedly. 'See there! Look, Joanna! Isn't it a wolf?'

Joanna stopped abruptly and followed his pointing finger but saw nothing.

'I'm sure it was!' Frowning, he searched the ground ahead of them. 'A grey shape. I saw it distinctly.' He faced her, his eyes gleaming. 'Once a wolf stole a goat from Liliane's mother. Her uncle went out next day and tracked it down and shot it.' He held out his hands as wide as they would go. 'It was *this* big. They said it was a young male. Its fur was so thick! They sold the head for a lot of money. People like putting heads on the wall – have you noticed?'

Joanna hesitated. 'Do you think we should go on?'

'Oh, yes. If it was going to attack us it would have done so by now.' He clapped his hands several times and let out a great shout. 'That'll frighten it. Come on.'

By the time they reached the cottage where Liliane's mother lived, Joanna had quite forgotten her ill-humour. The furious barking of a mongrel dog on a chain announced their arrival. The house was small and low at one end, rising a little at the other; the rough rock walls supported a worn roof of curved tiles, patched with lichens.

An old man, grizzled and swarthy, was bent over a red-painted chair as his fingers deftly repaired the rush seat. He glanced up briefly at their approach, gave Joanna a sharp look and resumed his work.

Leo whispered, 'Maria's father. He's deaf,' and went forward as Maria herself came out of the house to greet them.

Maria Torres was small and round and looked, Joanna thought, about a hundred years old. She was carrying a pan full of corn which she hurled towards a few chickens who rushed forward in gleeful anticipation. Her face beamed with pleasure when she saw Leo.

Leo introduced Joanna as his cousin – '*Minha prima, Joanna*' – and Maria turned. Then she gave a little cry and dropped the empty pan. Whispering something rapidly in Portuguese, she stared at Joanna almost fearfully. Joanna smiled, but when Maria's expression did not change she glanced at Leo, who was looking equally puzzled. Maria muttered something to Leo and he repeated, '*Minha prima.*'

'What's the matter?' Joanna asked him.

'She asks who you are.'

Suddenly Maria reached out her arm, took one of Joanna's hands in hers and patted it. Then she spoke excitedly to Leo who kept saying, '*Bois.*'

'What is she saying?'

'I don't know, she speaks so quickly. But it doesn't matter. She likes you.'

As though to prove his point Maria smiled broadly and urged them inside, where Joanna looked around her curiously. The house appeared larger than she had expected. Thin wooden beams and a raft of bamboo matting supported the roof tiles, and the walls had been painted white to head height and yellow above. The cupboard, chairs and table were painted red. Pots, pans and a rope of garlic hung from hooks on the walls. At the far end there was a short flight of steps with a hand-rail. Maria talked non-stop and Leo nodded from time to time and said '*Bois!*' at intervals. It sounded like 'Boish' to Joanna's untuned ear. Leo explained, 'They all say "*Bois!*" I don't know what it means, but it seems to do well enough!'

As Leo had predicted they were offered refreshments – a large dish of black olives, some chunks of new bread and goat's cheese and a glass of red wine. 'Her brother made it,' Leo translated, adding in a whisper, 'The one who has been arrested for fighting.'

The early-morning walk had given them an appetite and they both ate hungrily, watched approvingly by Maria. She obviously enquired about Liliane's progress and, to amuse her, Leo mimed a very grand Liliane putting on her new uniform and cap. While they talked a hen wandered in with a brood of yellow chicks around her legs, and Leo and Joanna spent a long time playing with them. A cat with half a tail stalked past disdainfully and sprang on to a basket full of clean washing.

When at last it was time to go, Joanna felt strangely reluctant to leave. Leo was given a small earthenware pot full of olives which Maria was sending as a gift for the ever-patient Christina. As they walked away, Joanna was aware of Maria still waving from the doorway and had to fight down a sudden urge to run back. There was something about the little house and the old woman that caught at her heartstrings.

Leo looked disappointed. 'You're very quiet, Joanna. Didn't you like them?'

'Of course! I liked them tremendously. I'd love to visit them again.'

Her words cheered him. 'We can. Any time you like.'

They walked slowly back towards the mine and much later Joanna saw it spread out in the distance, a tumble of white houses and a red scar that was the mine, tucked between folds in the land.

Leo said, 'It looks so small, doesn't it? I've taken hundreds of photographs of it. I'll show you some time if you like. I'll take one of you.'

She nodded absentmindedly and they trudged on. After a while he said, 'Do let's have a party, Joanna.'

She gave him a friendly push and said, 'We'll see!' They were less than a mile from home when they saw the wolf.

Chapter Eight

JOANNA SAW IT FIRST, out of the corner of her eye: a low grey shape amongst the scrub. As she turned it rose to a standing position and stared at them, unafraid.

'Leo!' she quavered and he followed the direction of her gaze. 'You were right!'

She didn't see the effect it had on him because she dared not take her eyes from the grey shape.

'Is it a wolf?' she asked, hoping against hope.

'Yes!' His voice shook and a frisson of fear ran through her. It was less than twenty yards away and its ears were laid back, close to its head.

For a long moment they both stared at it, mesmerized. The burning question in both of their minds was, was it alone? One wolf was dangerous; more would be disastrous. Slowly she allowed her eyes to wander over the area in the vicinity of the wolf, but saw nothing untoward.

'I think it's alone,' she whispered, still not daring to move. 'What should we do?'

Leo, for once in his life, did not have the answer. He shook his head.

'We could walk slowly backwards,' she suggested. Anything that would take them nearer to the safety of home . . .

'If we wait it might lose interest,' he suggested.

'And it might not!'

The wolf snarled suddenly, lifting its head as it did so, and Leo took an involuntary step closer to Joanna.

'It can smell us,' he announced. 'It's trying to decide what we are. I suppose we're upwind – or is it downwind?'

Joanna looked round desperately, but there was no one in sight except a goatherd in the far distance with his charges. No chance of help there, she decided. By the time their cries for help reached him the wolf would be upon them. Not that he would risk his goats by coming to their aid. Perhaps they should run for it – or would that invite pursuit? Dogs loved to chase people. Would a wolf react in the same way? Or did they only attack when they were in packs? Perhaps this was a pack-leader. If it howled the rest might appear. Her mouth was dry and she could hardly swallow. Her mind seemed to be frozen and she had no idea how long they stood there.

Leo said, 'It might get bored.'

As though understanding his words the wolf lowered its head again and suddenly took a few paces towards them. They clung to each other, terrified by their dilemma.

'Leo, I think we should try to frighten it away,' she whispered. 'Could we throw rocks or something?'

Without moving they scanned the nearby ground, but could see only one small stone the size of an egg.

'I'm not much good at throwing,' she confessed.

'I'll do it.'

Slowly, with infinite care, he handed her the jar of olives and reached for the pebble, but even as his fingers closed over it the wolf took a few more paces forward and snarled again. Joanna bit back a shriek of fear and Leo threw the stone. It flew harmlessly past the animal's head, but gave it cause for alarm and it flattened itself suddenly into the grass.

Joanna put a hand to her heart, which was pounding painfully beneath her ribs.

'You've scared it!' she told Leo shakily. 'Well done!'

'Or maddened it!'

'Don't!'

'It might be a she-wolf.' He glanced at her and his face was white, his eyes large. 'It might have cubs nearby. Maybe she just wants to frighten us away.'

'Then should we run?'

'If it comes after us we won't stand a chance,' he warned. 'I think we should pray.'

'Pray?'

'What else is there? It can't do any harm. We needn't close our eyes. God is supposed to listen to prayers.'

Their eyes met and she nodded.

Briefly Joanna prayed for divine intervention. She apologized for all her wrongdoing and promised to be a better person if He would deliver them safely out of their present danger. As though to mock their efforts the wolf sprang forward suddenly, high in the air, snapping and snarling savagely as it, dropping to the ground and springing up again. It was now less than ten feet away and the sight robbed Joanna of the strength to move. Leo snatched the jar of olives from her, threw them with all his force at the wolf and shouted, 'Run, Joanna! Run!'

Miraculously the jar hit the wolf on the shoulder and the rain of olives and oil that followed seemed to distract it temporarily. Yelping with surprise, it hesitated, and Leo and Joanna fled across the grass without stopping to look back. They ran and stumbled, helping each other, frantic to reach the haven of the village.

'Is it coming after us?' she gasped.

'Don't know! Just keep running!'

There was a painful stitch in her side and her long skirts were hindering her progress. At any moment she expected to feel the snap of the wolf's teeth in the back of her leg. Leo, fleet of foot, could no doubt have run ahead but he kept pace with her, urging her on, until at last the top of the bandstand came in sight and the praca was within reach. Joanna looked up, breathless, weak with relief.

Astonishingly, other people were going about their daily tasks, unaware of the drama. It seemed incredible that while she and Leo had been through such an ordeal life had gone on as usual for everyone else. They staggered to a seat in the praca and collapsed on to it.

'You were wonderful, Leo!' she told him between gulps of air. 'Oh, my side! I've got such a terrible stitch. Oh, God, Leo!'

'Oh, God!' he echoed recklessly.

They looked at each other and began to laugh with relief. Leo took out his handkerchief and wiped his face. 'You were awfully brave, too,' he told her. 'For a girl!'

She began to laugh again and the sound of it pealed across the little park. Still no one paid them the slightest attention. Suddenly Leo leaned forward, a gleam in his eye.

'I think we deserve a restorative,' he told her. 'I know where Papa keeps the port.'

She couldn't resist him, not after all they had been through together. She followed him into the house and through the hall into the dining room. From the sideboard Leo took a decanter and two tall glasses and poured them each a generous measure.

'You'll be drunk!' she warned him.

'So will you!' He raised his glass in a toast. 'Better drunk than dead!' he said.

'I'll drink to that!' she told him and they clinked their glasses and drank deeply. Leo came up spluttering and Joanna coughed herself red in the face. They were still laughing and drinking when Catherine entered the room ten minutes later and stopped in dismay.

'What on earth . . . ?' she began. 'Leo! Catherine! Explain yourselves at once!'

Joanna looked at Leo, who grinned and said, 'It's a long story, Mama . . .'

'Quite long enough!' Joanna added.

And they laughed until the tears ran down their faces.

Catherine glared tight-lipped from one to the other. 'Stop it! Do you hear me!' she cried furiously. She looked at Joanna with barely veiled hostility. 'What do you mean by encouraging my son to drink? You stupid girl! No wonder your poor mother wanted to be rid of you. Stop laughing, Joanna, do you hear me? Stop this nonsense and give me an explanation!'

Finding that these threats merely added to their hysterics, she stepped forward and slapped Joanna's face. If she had expected this to sober up her niece she was sadly mistaken, for after the initial shock Joanna and Leo erupted into giggles and were off once more.

'You will regret this, Joanna!' she cried but, finally admitting defeat, she stormed out of the room. When they had calmed down a little Leo wiped his streaming eyes again and hiccupped loudly. He said, 'Poor Christina! She won't get her olives!'

And because the port was still warm within them and they were so happy to be alive, they found this fact quite hilarious and were still laughing when Elliot arrived to listen to their story.

*

The library was to be found in the Palacio and it was run jointly by Sarah Barratt, the doctor's wife (Monday, Tuesday and Wednesday) and Olwen Jackson (Thursday, Friday and Saturday). It was a large room at the rear of the building and smelt of dried mildew and orange blossom overlaid, when the wind was in a certain direction, with a hint of sulphur. There was a large ceiling fan whirring overhead, a carpet on the floor, chairs, a couple of tables and, today, an arrangement of white daisies which were dying from lack of water. One of the walls was papered in dark red and supported a huge gilt mirror and a few framed hunting scenes; the remaining three were lined with shelves from floor to ceiling.

Many of the books were of general reference and rarely taken from their shelves except by enthusiasts such as Leo, who liked to while away a rainy afternoon with his nose pressed into a book on wild-life or the history of the motor car. Several shelves carried the books specifically connected with mining, and these were used less than Elliot might have hoped. But the fiction section was the most popular with the English; so popular, in fact, that every year the stock had to be carefully examined for signs of wear. Books with frayed pages, torn paper covers or broken spines were withdrawn and new volumes ordered from Foyles in London, to replace them. The system of borrowing was simplicity itself. A book was selected, carried to the desk and noted in the ledger with the name of the borrower alongside it. On its return a line was drawn through the details in red ink. The date was not held to be important; theoretically a subscriber could keep a book for months or years, but they never did. There was great rivalry to see who could read the latest books first, because the merits of each new novel could then be described over the dinner table.

On the day following the wolf episode Catherine, the only person present apart from the librarian, stood in front of the far wall and ran her fingers thoughtfully along the books. She was still smarting from the events of the previous day and her husband's foolish acceptance of Joanna's unlikely story. Oh, Leo had backed her up, but those two were getting too close and no good would come of it. Elliot had laughed at the escapade. Laughed! After all she had said to him beforehand. The man was a fool – but then she had known that for years.

She jumped as Sarah Barratt appeared at her elbow. Sarah was a nonentity in Catherine's opinion. Her manner was nervous to the point of shyness; her clothes were uninspired and her fine hair resisted all attempts to shape it into a style that was recognizable as such. She wore it in a wispy bun and Catherine frequently referred to her in private as 'the frightened rabbit'.

'Can I help you, dear?' she asked, her voice tentative. 'There's the new Ethel M. Dell, if you're interested. Unpacked only this morning. It's under my desk.'

Catherine gave her a brittle smile. 'Under your desk! Whatever is a new book doing under your desk, Sarah?'

Sarah flushed. 'Oh ... I ... I was just going to put it out when I caught sight of you and ...' She trailed into silence.

Catherine said, 'I'm not usually impressed by first novels. Do they think she is any good?'

'Good? Oh, yes! The reviews were most promising. A new star in the firmament – I think that's how one of them put it.'

'My father used to say, "Never trust a critic!" but I'll give her the benefit of the doubt. I'll take it and let you know what I think of her.'

Sarah nodded, placed the book on the table and carefully wrote the date and Catherine's name in her ledger. Then she smiled and Catherine guessed she was hoping for an invitation to Joanna's party, which everyone was talking about. Let her wait, she thought impatiently.

'Don't let me keep you from your work,' she said, and moved on to the next wall, apparently engrossed in her search once more. It was tiresome having to invite people like Sarah, but the English-speaking community was so small that there was very little choice. Everyone visited everyone. It would be pleasant if one of the steamships put in at Pomerao because then she could invite the English captain. And Steven Benbridge, of course. Her pulse quickened, for she was actually loitering in the library in the hope of seeing him. Christina, who knew everything that went on in the English compound, had said he was a keen reader. Catherine took out a volume at random – Gene Porter's *Freckles*. She had read it. A second random selection produced a book by Mary Rinehart. Catherine flicked through it and with feigned interest asked Sarah's opinion. Before the older woman could answer, however, the library door creaked open. Arranging her face into a sweet expression Catherine glanced round, only to be disappointed for it was Joanna.

Sarah was across the room in a flash, her hands outstretched in welcome. 'How nice that you've come to find us at last, dear!' she said. 'I knew you were here, naturally. Well, my husband would have to know for his records, you see; he's our doctor. So you're Joanna. How lovely to see a new face! I can see the family likeness; you are obviously a Grosvenor. And I hear your aunt and uncle are giving a party for you.'

Joanna said, 'Yes. I'm looking forward to it.'

'And I heard all about your fight with the wolves! My husband heard about it from—'

Catherine said sharply, 'It was hardly a fight, Sarah. Young people exaggerate, you know. A rather silly incident, actually.'

Sarah looked at her in confusion. 'Oh, but I heard that it chased them! That it was going to attack!'

Joanna said, 'I'll tell you all about it some time, Mrs Barratt.'

'Oh, do, dear! Do! I'll be thrilled! And have you met Mr Benbridge? I said to John only yesterday that it's such a shame about that man – still unmarried after all these years. And we're all couples, you see, and it's awkward for him to fit in. John thought you would be just the person to cheer him up.'

'He's very pleasant. We have met.'

From the corner of her eye Catherine saw that Sarah's thin shoulders were hunched with excitement.

'Oh, you have met! Well, you do your best, Joanna, to

bring the poor man out of his shell. John thinks he's what they call a "loner" but I'm not at all sure. I think he needs a wife, Joanna! He might talk to you. You see—'

Catherine interrupted her. 'If Steven Benbridge needs anybody, Sarah, which I doubt, he will find someone without our help. Please don't put any more ideas into Joanna's head. She has enough of her own already.'

Joanna turned, a bright flush in her cheeks. 'How on earth can you say that? Do you know me that well already, Aunt Catherine? I have only been here a little over a week.'

There was a hush in the room. Sarah, her hands clasped nervously in front of her, was obviously trying hard to hide her pleasure at Joanna's cutting reply. Catherine gritted her teeth and swallowed a spiteful comment. She must not allow the girl to draw her. It would never do to brawl in the library of all places and if she lost her temper, Sarah would have the details all round the compound before nightfall.

Without another word she snatched a book at random from the nearest shelf and walked with it to the desk. She banged it down with unnecessary force and watched, simmering, while Sarah glanced at the title.

'Are you sure this is the book you want?' she asked.

'Of course I'm sure!'

Sarah wrote carefully in the ledger while tears of vexation pricked at Catherine's eyelids. Damn them both! Why did people go out of their way to aggravate her? Joanna and that pathetic Sarah – she longed to bang their heads together. There was no point in waiting now for Steven Benbridge to show up; she would get no chance to speak with him with Sarah and Joanna watching like hawks!

When the librarian handed her the book Catherine thought she saw a glimmer of malice in the older woman's eyes. She was smiling like a Cheshire cat.

'*An Introduction to Russian Literature in the Seventeenth Century!*' Sarah said loudly. 'That sounds fascinating, my dear.

You'll have to tell us all about it when you next dine with us.'

*

Promptly at 2.30 p.m. Joanna knocked on her grand-mother's door and was answered by Nurse Williams with a brisk, 'Come in!' She entered, the books under her arm, and hesitated. Her grandmother still sat at the small table on which her meals were served. A large napkin was tucked under her chin and several stains revealed that some of the food had not found its way into her mouth. The nurse, who sat beside her, laid down the spoon with an expression of relief and said, 'There! I told you there would be a visitor if you ate all your rice.' She reached for the napkin and wiped the old lady's chin.

Joanna said, 'I brought your books, Grandmother. The ones you asked me for.'

'Books!' snapped the old lady. 'Books? What's this about books?' She glared at Joanna who had started to cross the room but now stopped again, uncertain.

The nurse shook her head and sighed. 'We're not having a very good day, I'm afraid. We're a mite tetchy – and very trying!'

'Perhaps I should just leave the books?' Joanna hoped she could put them down and go, but the nurse would not hear of it.

'No, no! You stay!' she told her. 'A visitor might be just what the doctor ordered. Something to take her mind from her grievances. Or should I say *imagined* grievances!'

She attempted to wipe the old lady's chin again, but the napkin was snatched from her hand and thrown to the floor.

'Don't fidget with me! I've told you before!'

Her grandmother beckoned imperiously to Joanna. 'Give me the books, girl. Hurry up!' Joanna hurried forward and handed them over, but before she could withdraw a bony hand clutched at her wrist. 'Who are you, eh? What's your name? Speak up, girl!'

As the nurse gathered the dish and spoon on to a tray she said soothingly, 'Now, I've told you before. This is your grand-daughter from England. This is Joanna.'

'What? Joanna?'

Joanna smiled. 'Yes. I'm Joanna from England. I'm having a . . . holiday here.'

'Here?'

'Yes, Grandmother. In Portugal. In San Domingos.'

'Hmm!'

For a moment she regarded Joanna suspiciously. The nurse whipped off the white tablecloth and replaced it with a small pot of violets. Before either of them could stop her, the old lady had sent them flying with a deliberate sweep of her hand. The pot rolled across the carpet, the earth scattered and the small blooms were crushed and broken.

'Now that was naughty!' To Joanna's surprise Nurse Williams slapped the withered hand. 'Very naughty! We don't behave like that here.' To Joanna she said, 'Some days we are so childish.'

Joanna knelt to pick up the fallen flowers and the nurse recovered the pot and swept the earth into a small dustpan.

Grandmother said, 'Where's your brother, eh? Why isn't he here?'

'I don't have a brother here, Grandmother.'

'Of course you do! Where is he. Young whatsisname!'

'Leo is my cousin.'

'Don't talk back to me, child! I know who Leo is.'

'He's gone fishing, Grandmother, with the doctor. They've gone to the Chanca River to fish for eels.'

The old lady suddenly lost interest in her grandson and took up the books Joanna had brought. 'I didn't ask for this!'

'Yes, you did,' said Joanna. 'They are the two books you—'

'I don't want them! Take them away at once!'

She thrust them towards Joanna, who took them patiently. Was this what old age was about, she thought unhappily. A second childhood? She hoped not. Her own childhood had been traumatic and she would not relish reliving it.

'Shall I read to you?' she suggested.

'Certainly not! If I wanted you to read I would say so.'

The nurse said, 'Now then! That's not very nice, is it? We mustn't forget our manners, must we?'

'Talk to me, Joanna,' demanded her grandmother. 'Tell me about England.'

Eagerly the nurse provided Joanna with a chair and retired to the small ante-room which served as a kitchen.

Joanna could hear her washing up. She wondered where to begin. 'Well, England is ... er ... It's summer ... Everyone sends their best regards, Grandmother. Dorcas, Suzanne ... Mark ...'

'Mark?'

From the kitchen the nurse prompted, 'Tell her about the wedding preparations. She'll like that.'

Joanna took a deep breath and launched into details of the coming wedding.

'And Juanita?' the old lady asked suddenly. 'Will Juanita be there? At the wedding?'

'Juanita?'

The nurse reappeared, with a flannel and towel in her hands. She sidled behind Joanna's grandmother and suddenly pounced, washing her chin and drying it before the old lady could fight her off.

'There now! We're nice and clean!' she murmured soothingly with a wink at Joanna.

Joanna asked her, 'Who's Juanita?'

The nurse shook her head. 'I don't know. She often speaks of Juanita, but nobody knows anything about her. A figment of her imagination, perhaps.'

'Juanita!' the old lady insisted. 'She went to England and never came back. Very dark, Juanita.'

Joanna said, 'I'm sorry, Grandmother. I don't know her.'

'Will she be at the wedding?'

'I – I don't think so.'

'Poor Juanita!'

Joanna became aware suddenly that there were tears in her grandmother's eyes.

'That poor girl! It was very sad.'

'What happened, Grandmother?'

The nurse said, 'You may well ask. I've asked her time and again but she won't tell. Or else she doesn't know. Or nothing happened. Who can tell with a mind like that?'

The old lady's lips trembled and two tears ran down her face. 'I blame myself,' she whispered. 'She was so young. So afraid . . .'

She began to cry in earnest and Joanna at once regretted her questions. 'I'm so sorry,' she said. 'I shouldn't have asked. Now I've upset her.'

The nurse was fetching a large white handkerchief from a pile on the windowsill. 'It doesn't hurt her to shed a few tears,' she told Joanna. 'It won't be the first time she's cried for this Juanita person. Nor the last. You pop along now; you've been very kind. Sometimes she's better than others. This is a bad day, that's all.' And she hurried Joanna from the room.

Joanna stood outside the door, feeling not relief but a kind of dissatisfaction. For a moment she wondered what was troubling her. Was it the reminder about Mark's wedding? Or thoughts of England? Slowly she walked through the house and out into the garden.

Christina called to her. 'Letter for you, Miss Grosvenor. You like letter from home!'

Joanna was opening the letter when it dawned on her. She wanted to understand her grandmother's tears for Juanita.

She read the letter, which was from Dorcas. Enclosed was a picture which Suzanne had drawn for her; a picture surrounded by kisses which made Joanna smile. She slipped it into her pocket and went through to the kitchen where Christina was rolling out pastry. Liliane was watching, a scowl of concentration on her face. They both looked up as Joanna entered and smiled a welcome.

'Good letter?' asked Christina. 'You happy now you get letter?'

'It was the wrong letter, but it doesn't matter. Christina, did you ever know anybody called Juanita?'

To her surprise Christina's smile vanished, she stopped abruptly in mid-roll – and then spoke sharply in Portuguese to Liliane, who replied shrilly in the same language and was then pushed roughly towards the door, presumably for her impertinence. She went sulkily, banging the door behind her.

To Joanna, Christina said, 'No. I not know Juanita. Never.'

'But why are you cross? What have I said?'

'I not cross. Liliane is lazy girl. She must work.'

She would not meet Joanna's gaze and Joanna could see that the normally cheerful woman was upset. Reluctantly she persisted with her questions.

'Grandmother spoke of Juanita. She cried, Christina.'

The maid glanced up, shocked, then returned to her pastry.

'Grandmother said Juanita was so young and so afraid. What did she mean?'

'She mean nothing. She is old woman. She imagines – here!' She pointed to her own head. 'Miss Grosvenor, you must forget what she says. Juanita never here. Is not good talk about Juanita in this house.'

Joanna fixed her with a look. 'Grandmother said that it was very sad and she blames herself. What did she mean, Christina? I think you *do* know!'

Slowly Christina put down the rolling-pin and sat down heavily on a nearby stool. Her face was inscrutable as she regarded Joanna. 'Please!' she said. 'You must not ask. Is all forgotten and Juanita . . .' She bit her lip. 'You should forget the tears. Forget everything you hear. Everything.' She was twisting her hands in her lap and her expression was less guarded. Joanna thought she saw anguish in the dark eyes. 'Is long time ago, Miss Grosvenor. Long, long time.'

'What is?' cried Joanna, leaning forward. 'What is a long time ago? Juanita? Was she a long time ago? Is that what you mean? That whatever it was happened a long time ago. Someone must know. Perhaps I should ask my uncle.'

'No! He will tell you nothing.'

Joanna stared at her triumphantly. 'He will tell me nothing. So he *knows* something!'

'He knows nothing.'

'Aunt Catherine, then?'

This suggestion did not provoke the same resistance, but Christina was shaking her head.

'You don't think I should ask anyone, then?'

The woman looked at her helplessly. 'Is best.'

Joanna stood up, realizing she would get nothing else from Christina. Either she did not know any more or, for some reason, dared not tell. Her mind raced. Who else had been here a long time? Who else could she ask? Leo was too young. Andrew was too new to the mine. What about the doctor? The Barratts might know. She would go back to the library and ask Sarah Barratt.

*

Joanna found the older woman standing on a low set of steps dusting the shelves. There was nobody else in the library and she went straight to the point.

'Mrs Barratt, I'm trying to find out about someone called Juanita.'

'Oh, my dear!' cried Sarah. She came quickly down the ladder. 'I really don't think . . .' She looked flustered – almost guilty, Joanna thought curiously. 'Whatever makes you ask such a question, my dear? You really shouldn't . . .'

'My grandmother keeps talking about her,' said Joanna, choosing her words carefully. She would not lie, but she would make it sound as though the old lady had spoken at length. 'She was so upset when she told me.'

Sarah's mouth fell open with shock. 'She *told* you?'

'She tried to. You know how confused she becomes. She blames herself, you know – for what happened.'

'Well,' said Sarah self-righteously, 'so she should! At least—' She broke off, alarmed by what she had said; aware that perhaps she had given away too much. 'What exactly did she tell you about her?'

'About Juanita? Oh, a rather garbled tale. The nurse says that she often rambles about the past and is always talking about Juanita. I thought perhaps you or your husband might recall such a person.'

Joanna waited, fascinated by Sarah's obvious discomfiture. Was the luckless Juanita a skeleton in everybody's cupboard?

Suddenly Sarah took her by the arm and led her to a table where they could both sit.

'My dear, I think you should try to forget all about this – this person,' she advised. 'There is nothing to be gained by digging into the past. You know what they say – let sleeping dogs lie! It really would be best to ignore the old lady's ramblings. John says she is hardly ever lucid these days.'

Joanna frowned. 'How long has she been like this? Do you know?'

'How long? Oh dear! Let me think . . . About three years or maybe four. Something like that. It is very sad. Your grandmother was a very fine person before . . . well, let's just say that we all had the greatest respect for her.

She knew what was right and she wasn't afraid to—' She broke off in some agitation and Joanna felt a sneaking compassion for her as she stumbled on. 'I'm sure – that is, we all believe her intention was honourable—' She looked at Joanna, her expression wretched. 'It is always easy with hindsight!' She turned away, her hands tightly clasped in front of her chest, but after a moment she collected herself, faced Joanna once more and said firmly, 'Well, that's enough about that.'

Joanna ignored this broad hint. 'The nurse believes that Juanita is a figment of my grandmother's imagination,' she persisted.

Sarah's eyes widened gratefully. 'Why, there you are then, my dear! That answers your question, doesn't it?' Relieved, she patted Joanna's hand. 'Don't give it another thought. Forget all about it and enjoy yourself. Mr Benbridge came in earlier, just after you had left. I was talking to him about you. He seemed . . .' She smiled archly. 'He seemed rather *taken* with you, if you'll pardon the expression. John does so hate me to use slang, but I rather like some of it.' She regarded Joanna wistfully. 'Language should grow, shouldn't it?'

'I suppose so.'

'I believe you've made a conquest there, Miss Grosvenor, and in spite of what your aunt said, I think a new wife would be good for him. Men get so set in their ways, don't you agree?'

'I've never thought about it.' Joanna stood up suddenly and smiled. 'I think I must go now. I thought I'd walk out and meet Leo and your husband. I wonder if they've caught anything. Oh, and thank you for being so frank with me, Mrs Barratt. I appreciate it.'

'Frank? Oh, but – Miss Grosvenor, I don't think . . . that is, I hope I haven't been *frank* . . .'

As the librarian's voice faltered Joanna closed the library door behind her and leaned against it thoughtfully. There seemed to be a conspiracy of silence on the subject of Juanita. Something had happened at San Domingos; something everyone hoped had been long forgotten.

'A mystery!' she whispered and her eyes gleamed as she made her way along the corridor and down the stairs. Here was something with which to while away the long hours of her exile. She would unravel the mystery of Juanita!

Chapter Nine

WHEN ELLIOT AWOKE the following Saturday he found his wife already seated at the dressing-table, brushing her hair with long, even strokes. Her eyes were closed and he was able to watch her for a moment, unobserved. He thought with regret that once he had brushed her hair for her, in the far-off days of their early marriage. She had liked him near her and he had imagined, in his innocence, that she loved him. Only gradually did she allow her true feelings to emerge and then he knew that it was his position in the company which had attracted her; that Mason and Barry had great faith in him and would eventually entrust the day-to-day running of their enterprise to him. His mother had insisted that he should wed and had been taken in by Catherine's apparently sweet and dutiful nature. Only later did they realize how strong-willed she was — when she insisted on entertaining to a lavish degree and finding the most expensive dress-maker for her clothes; when she refused point-blank to have a second child; when, much later, she insisted that Elliot's ailing mother be confined to separate accommodation. Too late then, he thought, and wondered if his mother had ever regretted the choice she had made for him.

She caught his eye in the mirror suddenly and swung round. 'You're spying on me, Elliot! Stop it!'

'Surely a man can look at his own wife!' He sat up, propping himself on one elbow. 'You don't object to other men looking at you.'

'What does that mean, I wonder?' She laid down the brush and began to coil her hair. 'You are quite ridiculously possessive, Elliot. You are so quick to remove any possible rivals, I wonder there is anyone left in San Domingos about whom you can feel jealous! If you had your way, you would soon find yourself without any staff at all!' She laughed. 'First it was Captain Marryat; you forbade him the house.'

'With good cause, Catherine!' He groaned inwardly: another exchange of insults. But Catherine appeared to thrive on them and her face in the mirror wore the familiar, challenging look which he had learned to dread.

'Then Senor Borella was out of favour. Next it was David Sturton—'

'You can't pretend that *that* was an innocent friendship!' He threw back the bedclothes.

'We were very good friends, nothing more. He told you that over and over again, but you wouldn't believe him! I swore to you that there was nothing between us but you called me a liar! Oh, yes, my dear. A liar! And then you had him sent back to England to satisfy your precious vanity.'

'I sent him away to protect our marriage and your reputation, Catherine. Everyone was talking about you; laughing behind your back, but you could not – or would not – see it!' He stared at her reflection. 'Yes, I called you a liar and it was the truth.'

'How can you say that?' She swung round to face him, two bright spots of colour burning in her cheeks. 'You don't love me, and you cannot bear it if anyone else does! You are a small-minded tyrant, Elliot, and I wish I had never married you!'

A silence followed her outburst as Elliot wondered whether to confront her with the letter.

She cried, 'And don't think I haven't seen you with Joanna! Your own brother's child! Leering at her and touching her hair – you can't keep your hands off her, can you? God knows what she thinks of you – a nasty, lascivious old man, probably. Oh yes, I've seen you flirting with her, and I'm disgusted. It's *you* they'll be gossiping about next, Elliot. You and that chit of a girl!'

He drew a deep breath as he made up his mind: he would do it. His heart was heavy as he moved to the chest and from the top drawer he withdrew the letter and held it up so that the handwriting was visible to her. He saw the sudden fear in her eyes.

'You recognize the writing, no doubt, Catherine?'

'David Sturton has written to *you*!' she whispered. Her anger had been replaced by apprehension. 'He wrote to you after he—'

'Yes, Catherine. He wrote to me after he reached England and he—'

She darted to her feet, but he moved quickly to hold the letter out of her reach.

'He wrote to me to tell me the truth, Catherine! To *apologize*! You wouldn't understand his motive, would you? Oh no, he wasn't trying to cause trouble – merely to satisfy his conscience and to ask my forgiveness. That must have taken a lot of courage, Catherine. I finally began to feel some respect for the fellow.'

Her face had a pinched look that he rarely saw and he felt a moment's pity for her.

'I don't believe it!' she whispered.

Elliot handed her the letter and watched her face as she read it. Three closely-written pages of contrition. He knew it by heart, and it still had the power to hurt him. Yet now his moment of triumph had a hollow ring to it. His own conscience was not clear and never would be, but since his marriage he had been faithful to his wife – lonely but faithful. He had never looked at another woman.

Catherine gave a little cry that was part anger and part pain and tore the offending pages in half. She tore them again and again and threw the pieces into his face.

'So he told you! Why should I care? What difference does it make now, Elliot?'

He pulled his dressing-gown round him and tied the cord. 'None at all, I daresay. No doubt it will be someone else before long. Benbridge, perhaps, or the new chap. Shreiker's a bit young for you, but you're not choosy, my dear, are you?'

She ran towards him, flailing her arms, wanting to hurt him, but he caught her wrists and held them tightly. As they struggled his thoughts were sombre. Had they really sunk so low that his wife wanted to scratch his eyes out? Was this all he had to look forward to for the rest of his life? Was this, perhaps, his punishment for his treatment of Juanita? If so, then maybe he deserved it. Perhaps the ghosts of the past demanded retribution. He would suffer without complaint.

'Let me go!'

Warily he released her and she made a great show of massaging her reddened wrists. He turned away and went into the bathroom and as he closed the door something smashed against it and Catherine began to cry.

*

He felt too ill to eat any breakfast and went early to the Palacio and tried to immerse himself in work. But his thoughts returned constantly to the quarrel he had had with his wife. He could not concentrate and Catherine's remark about Joanna worried him. She had accused him of flirting, and only he knew how far that was from the truth. But how did it look to Joanna herself? Surely she did not see him as a rather lascivious old man! Old? Yes, he must be old in her eyes, but lascivious? Surely not? He could not bear the thought of her disapproval; she was the one person in the world who still might learn to love him.

He reached for a sheet of paper and dipped his pen in to the brass inkwell Leo had given him the previous Christmas. He smiled as always at the thought of his beloved son, but then his smile faded. What did Leo think of his father's treatment of his cousin? Did he, too, believe there was something odd about the relationship? He felt cold at the mere idea. Leo loved and respected him and he must do nothing to jeopardize that; he dare not lose the boy's affection.

He wrote the date and 'Dear Senor da Silva', and a few sentences about the eucalyptus saplings he had provided. The tall, fast-growing trees were used for fuel and needed to be replanted regularly, but da Silva's contract would soon be up for renewal and now was the time to complain about the quality of the last plantation. He would demand another twenty saplings to compensate for the weedy specimens he had noticed on his latest tour of inspection. He wrote rapidly for half a page and then threw down the pen. Damn Catherine! He would not be easy in his mind until he had spoken to Joanna. He blotted the unfinished letter and reached for his jacket, deciding that he would go and find her now. There must be no risk, now or in the future, that Catherine could turn the girl against him. Somehow he must convince her that his affection was normal and in no way suspect. He hoped the right words would come.

He found her sitting in the praca with an easel set up in front of her. A palette and tubes of colour were set neatly beside her and she had made a reasonable attempt in charcoal of the lines of the bandstand. Seeing him, she turned and smiled and he was relieved to see nothing in the smile to disturb him.

'May I watch?' he asked.

'Certainly, but it will be a slow business.' She considered the sketch with her head on one side. 'Have I got the proportions correct, I wonder? I think it is a fraction too low – or is that my imagination?'

158

'It looks about right to me.'

'Well, maybe.' She made a few adjustments to it and sighed. 'What are you doing here, Uncle Elliot? I thought you would be in your office. I thought you were *always* in your office!' She laughed to show that the remark was kindly meant.

'I wanted to speak to you.' He hesitated and she glanced up quickly into his face. She laid the charcoal on the ledge of the easel and stood up. The smile had gone. 'Is this going to be a reprimand?' she asked, and he was aware of her anxiety.

'No, no! My dear girl! Nothing of the kind.' He looked at her in surprise. 'Why do you ask such a question?'

'I thought perhaps . . . oh, never mind.'

'I feel I'm neglecting you, Joanna. I had such good intentions, but the mine takes up so much of my energies and time. I thought perhaps we might walk a little. But I'm disturbing your painting.'

'The bandstand is still going to be there when we get back!'

'Of course.' As she fell in beside him he resisted the urge to tuck her hand into the crook of his arm. Would she misunderstand? Would it hint at a lascivious nature? Oh, damn Catherine to hell!

They walked away from the bandstand and for a while neither spoke. Then they both spoke together and laughed awkwardly.

'Do go on,' he said.

'I was just going to ask how the new man was getting on – Mr Shreiker.'

'Well enough, I daresay. I've heard no adverse reports from Benbridge. No news is good news in this business.'

'And what were *you* going to say?' she prompted.

He took a deep breath. 'I just wanted to reassure myself that you are settling in here. That no one is . . . treating you unkindly. I want you to be happy here; I had rather hoped that you might stay with us a long time. As long as you wish, that is. What I mean is, you don't have to look upon San Domingos as simply a holiday. It could be your home. I mean,' he amended hastily, 'your second home.'

After a rather long pause she asked, 'Has Mama suggested that I don't return home? Is that it?' Her voice trembled. 'If she has, I would rather know.' She would not meet his eyes.

Appalled, he said, 'But of course not! It is entirely my own idea. Not that I want to coax you away from your family but – but we are also your family. Do you see, Joanna? This could equally be your home. I just want you to know how much I care about your happiness. How happy I am that you are here with us. With Leo. Everything . . .' He was aware that he was not making very much sense, but it was harder than he had expected. 'You are happy here, aren't you?'

She nodded slowly, then raised her head and he was surprised to note her anguished expression. 'Has Aunt Catherine said anything? Is that why you're asking?'

'She – she does want you to be happy.' It sounded horribly false. 'Your aunt has a rather quick temper. If she says anything to upset you, try to ignore it. I mean, don't brood on it. Ten minutes later she has probably forgotten all about it. She is not a very happy person, I'm afraid. She doesn't mean to be unkind.'

The excuses sounded so lame that he felt ashamed.

Joanna stopped abruptly and faced him. 'Uncle Elliot, I know she dislikes me but I'm not sure why. I don't mean to cause trouble but I wonder what she might say about me. To you. If she said anything bad about me, would you come and ask for my version? Would you give me the benefit of the doubt?'

She looked so terribly vulnerable; so young and defenceless. He felt a terrible longing to take her in his arms and hold her close. That his own daughter should have to ask such a thing! It was terrible . . . humiliating.

Weakly he said, 'Of course. But she does not speak ill of you.'

Joanna gave him a look which told him that she knew better, but she said nothing. Was she wiser than he was, he wondered. Were these things better left unsaid? Bringing them out into the open might prove a dreadful mistake, yet he had to convince her that his own intentions were entirely honourable. There was always the risk that Catherine would poison her against him.

'I think very highly of you, Joanna!' he stammered. 'I would never do anything to offend or displease you. You are family. My brother's daughter. Any affection I show you is that of an uncle; nothing more. I don't want you to misunderstand ... If anyone ever infers anything else you must ignore it.' He swallowed hard, cursing himself for his blunt words. He really was very bad at this sort of thing. Expressing himself on an emotional level had always been a problem to him. Perhaps he should have stayed in his office, out of harm's way, he thought wearily.

Joanna took his hands in hers and her look was very direct. 'I know you are fond of me. That perhaps you love me.'

'My dear, I do!' he cried.

'And I'm grateful.'

Grateful? Grateful for what? His love? His hospitality? His frankness?

'And I think one day I shall love you in return.'

'Joanna! My dearest girl!' His fears were abruptly swept away by her words. 'I shall wait for that day! You make me so happy!' He was smiling and his heart raced with delight. The girl would love him!

'I'll try hard not to antagonize Aunt Catherine,' she said earnestly.

He nodded eagerly. 'She did so want a daughter,' he confided, 'and after Leo she didn't— Well, the doctor thought ... These things happen, you know how it is.'

She nodded and he rushed on. 'I think she is a little jealous – just between you and me. It's a difficult thing for a beautiful woman to grow older, Joanna. A younger woman is a possible threat. She makes comparisons. Do you know what I mean?' She was nodding her head, her dark eyes on his face. Those dark, dark eyes. The little heart-shaped face. So dear. So very familiar. It was as though time stood still and he was a young man again . . .

'Please don't worry about me, Uncle Elliot.' She stepped forward and kissed him gently on the side of his face. Before he knew what he was doing he had taken her into his arms and kissed her in return.

'Your mother—' he cried hoarsely. 'Oh, Joanna! If your mother could—'

He became aware that she was struggling in his arms and guiltily he released her. 'My *mother*?' she whispered.

Oh, God! She was so quick, so bright. He must think quickly. He had been a fool; he had alerted her, frightened her, even. He must be calm and choose his words carefully.

'I meant that . . .' Think, Elliot! Think! he told himself. 'That if your real mother . . . whoever she is . . . or was . . . could see you as a young woman, she would be so very proud.' His smile was uneven, he knew, and she would notice that too. 'That is all I meant, Joanna. She would want to hug you as I did; that's all.'

There was a long silence. Her face was flushed and her expression guarded. He wanted to weep with frustration. He had undone all the good! She had offered one chaste kiss and he had overwhelmed her with his own passion. But at that moment she had looked so like her mother. Heart-wrenchingly so! The tragedy was that she must never be allowed to understand the depths of his feelings for her.

Miserably he said, 'You will remember what I said earlier? And what you said?'

'Certainly I will.'

She looked around as though for rescue from an

awkward situation, but they had the praca to themselves. Tentatively she said, 'Perhaps I should get back to the bandstand; to my painting.'

'Yes, you must.' He forced a smile. 'I've detained you long enough. Perhaps you will show me the finished painting when it is done?' And without waiting for her answer he stumbled away. Back to the office. Back to the letter that awaited completion. Letters, papers, documents. Yes, those he could manage. Matters of business were his forte, he told himself bitterly. In matters of the heart he was out of his depth.

*

10th July, 1912. Today I painted a picture of the bandstand in the praca with a mimosa tree in the background. I cheated a little, but the result is rather good. I surprised myself. Maybe too much green, but the sunlight striking through the leaves was difficult so I left it out. Apparently Mr Benbridge is a good artist, or so Leo assures me, but I would not ask him for help. After the way that dreadful Sarah woman has been pushing me down the poor man's throat, I can hardly bear to face him and have deliberately kept out of his way.

Uncle Elliot came out to talk to me and was in a very strange mood. I think he is sorry for the way Aunt C. treats me and is trying to be extra nice. He tried to make excuses for her, but he is a rather intense person and I have to be careful what I say to him. At one point he hugged me so tightly that I could hardly breathe, but he said my mother would be proud of me. My real mother. That was nice of him. He said he would like this to be a second home. I didn't have the heart to tell him that I am counting the days until I can go back to England.

Still no letter from Mark. Surely he has not forgotten me already! Please God let it rain on their wedding day!

Andrew Shreiker sent me a little note this morning

asking me to go riding with him for an hour or so this evening, before dinner. I shall not mention it to Aunt C. in case she tries to spoil things. It's a shame she is so unpleasant. She is definitely the fly in the ointment here . . .

She glanced up as Leo appeared in the doorway. 'You never knock!' she grumbled half-heartedly.

Unabashed, he sat himself on the end of the bed and said, 'The jungle drums tell me you want to see me. So here I am.'

'Do I?'

'Christina said you were looking for me.'

'Oh, that! Well, I wanted to ask you something. What do you know about Juanita, Leo?'

'Nothing,' he said promptly. 'Nobody would say, and Papa gave me a bit of a talking-to. He says Grandmother has imagined it all, and it's very bad form to ask about it.'

'Bad form?'

'You know – not the done thing, and stuff like that. He said it upsets people and I'm not ever to mention her to Mama, so I don't. And you'd better not, either.' He shrugged. 'Actually I'd already asked Mama, but she didn't know what I was talking about.'

'Christina got rather upset when I mentioned it.'

'I asked Christina, and there are going to be little fishy things on sticks and chicken vol-au-vents and smoked salmon sandwiches sent out from Harrods – the salmon, not the sandwiches – and—'

'Leo! I don't know what you're talking about – and take your feet off the bedspread, please! I shall get the blame if you make it dirty.'

He swung his legs down as slowly as he dared. 'The party, of course. Your party. And petit-fours and champagne to drink. I've never had champagne.'

She grinned. 'You've had port, though!'

'Coming out of my ears!' he agreed.

They looked at each other like two conspirators.

Joanna said, 'Thank goodness your father believed us.'

Leo looked serious. 'The doctor says that my father is a very decent sort of cove. I hope I shall grow up like him.'

'I'm sure you will.'

'They're going to borrow some records from Mr Jackson at the lab. Dance records!'

'Good heavens!'

'Do you dance, Joanna?'

'Of course.'

He regarded her earnestly. 'I wondered if you'd teach me a few steps. I shall feel rather left out of things if I can't dance. We do have a few records, but nothing like the ones Mr Jackson is lending us. His were brought out earlier this year when his brother came for a visit.' He slipped purposefully to the floor and stared at his feet. 'I know a bit of the "Gay Gordons". I know it's three steps forward and three steps back.' He hummed under his breath and began to dance.

'Leo, I have to get ready,' she told him. 'I'll show you some steps another day. I promise.'

'Get ready? Where are you going?'

'Riding with Mr Shreiker, if you must know. So please scoot, Leo.'

He thrust out his chin. 'And if I don't scoot?'

'I won't teach you to dance!'

With a grin he leaped towards the door and was gone.

*

They rode towards Mertola because Andrew had not properly appreciated the landscape on his previous trip. He confessed, shamefaced, that the long ride on the back of the mule had so exhausted him that even when he was comfortably seated in the wagonette he had been unable to enjoy the scenery. Joanna, resplendent in her new riding-habit, rode a dark bay mare by the name of Tabor — one of two horses kept for the use of visitors. Andrew rode Blue Boy, Steven Benbridge's grey gelding which stood at seventeen hands and almost dwarfed Joanna's mount. Andrew had told her that as soon as he could find a suitable horse, he would buy it.

For the first ten minutes they admired the vastness of the land over which they rode; commented on the birds which neither could name and the hares which occasionally bolted across their path. There were few flowers remaining and the short, rough grass, scorched by the sun, had withered and turned brown. Joanna recounted her adventure with the wolf and Andrew promised that no harm would befall her under his protection. They talked quite generally about the mine and their first impressions of the small world which Mason and Barry had created in the vastness of Portugal. Joanna found Andrew very pleasant company, but was surprised to learn that for him the mine was simply a jumping-off point for Australia. His mother's brother, who was childless, had promised a well-paid job in his mine when Andrew had had three years' mining experience. San Domingos had a good reputation and Andrew had decided to start there.

'Have you ever thought about Australia, Miss Grosvenor?' he asked. 'It's a wonderful country. The land of opportunity, that's what they call it. You don't need to have been to the right schools or come from the right family. Out there you can make your own way and people respect you for what you do, not who you are. My uncle was nobody when he went there. Now he owns a small mine. Owns it, Miss Grosvenor! No offence intended towards your uncle, but there's a world of difference between administering and owning.'

'I just want to go home,' she told him simply. 'I've never thought of Australia or anywhere else for that matter. I suppose I thought I'd get married and live in England.'

He turned shining eyes upon her. 'Wouldn't you like to get up in the morning, step out on to the veranda and see for miles and miles and say, "That's all my land!"?'

She smiled. 'I can see *you* would like it!'

'Land is so cheap, you see. The country is so vast. It's so new, Miss Grosvenor. That's what makes it exciting! A man who's prepared to work can save up and buy his own "spread". A man who will work can become rich. I'm a hard worker, Miss Grosvenor.'

'I'm sure Australia will welcome you with open arms, Mr Shreiker,' she said. 'I'll settle for England.'

He was looking at her thoughtfully. 'Don't you like Portugal?'

'Sometimes. At other times I hate it.'

'Aren't you happy, Miss Grosvenor?'

She recognized the compassion in his voice and at once said firmly, 'Of course I am. What makes you ask such a thing?' When he made no reply she added, 'At least I'm not unhappy. Not all the time. It's just that ...' She shrugged. 'My aunt doesn't like me very much and—'

'Doesn't like you? Oh, but that's impossible!' His indignation was so genuine that Joanna had to laugh.

'She doesn't!' she insisted.

'But how could she not like you? How could anybody not think you the finest—' He stopped, embarrassed, and looked at her anxiously. 'What I mean is, Miss Grosvenor, that you are one of the finest people I have ever met! There, now! I've said it and I meant to be so circumspect. I shouldn't have spoken. My heart rules my head.'

Taken by surprise but deeply flattered, Joanna said, 'You're very kind, Mr Shreiker, but you don't really know me very well. I am not the paragon you think I am – far from it.'

He was shaking his head vehemently. 'No! I won't listen to a word against you – not even from you!' He laughed. 'I mean what I say, Miss Grosvenor, even if I haven't chosen the right time. To me you are the most dear and precious girl—'

With a shock of dismay she realized exactly what he was trying to say. 'Oh, no, Mr Shreiker! Please don't!'

But he had reined in his horse and was leaning forward. As he caught hold of her bridle, his expression was one of deep sincerity and Joanna's heart sank.

'Ever since we first met on the *Lanfranc*,' he said, 'I've thought of no one else. I was bowled over – yes, that's the truth, Miss Grosvenor. I was bowled over by you, and I still am and I always will be. It's like a bolt from the blue, to be quite honest with you, as I had made up my mind to think of nothing and no one but making my way in the mining profession. I planned to go to Australia and look there for a wife.'

'Mr Shreiker, I have to tell you—' she began, but he rushed on, the words tumbling over each other.

'Please! Hear me out, I beg you. I must say it. I must tell you how I feel, although I know it is too early and I am probably making a fool of myself, but—'

'Not a fool, Mr Shreiker. No, of course not, but—'

'I love you, Miss Grosvenor! I love you. That's the long and short of it, and you must love me in return. Oh, not just yet. I realize I must give you time, but I cannot let you go because I know we are right for each other. I know it in my heart!'

He stopped, out of breath, and Joanna experienced a wave of pity for him. She could not love him, but she must say something kind.

'I do like you, Mr Shreiker,' she said cautiously, 'but at the moment I—'

'You *do* like me? Oh, you dear girl!' His face glowed with hope.

'*Like*, Mr Shreiker,' she insisted hastily. 'I only said "like". We hardly know each other and you really shouldn't commit yourself to loving me.'

'But I *do*, Miss Grosvenor. I adore you!'

At this moment, perhaps fortuitously, the two horses – their heads held uncomfortably close together – became restive. Andrew's horse backed away, prancing irritably and shaking his head. Joanna took advantage of the brief respite to compose a short speech.

'Mr Shreiker . . .' she began when at last he had quieted his mount. 'I am very honoured that you—'

'May I not call you Miss Joanna?' His look was pleading. 'Miss Grosvenor sounds so very formal.'

'Oh! Very well, then. But, Mr Shreiker, honoured though I am . . .'

'Miss Joanna, I am not asking for an answer – not now. I wouldn't be so foolish. You need time, I can see that, and I will give you time.'

Inspiration struck her. 'I am not yet eighteen, Mr Shreiker. My uncle would disapprove, I'm sure, if he knew of your declaration.'

She looked at him hopefully. Surely her uncle's disapproval would count for something?

His face crumpled. 'Not yet eighteen? No, of course! I remember now. You told me on the ship coming out here. All the more reason why I should give you time – and I will, Miss Joanna, and I beg you not to mention this to your uncle. Not yet. Not until you can tell him that you return my love.'

To gain time Joanna leaned forward and stroked the neck of her horse. What could she say? How to reject him without wounding him? He was such a nice man and he was paying her a great compliment. Suppose she said 'Yes'! Just suppose she took a chance and threw in her lot with this stranger! For a moment she wondered how Mark would feel if he suddenly heard that she was engaged to be married – and to a man who was preparing to carry her off to Australia. One who intended to be rich and own hundreds of acres of land. Would Mark care? Would he regret his wasted chances? She wanted to think so, but there was a niggling doubt at the back of her mind.

She straightened up. He was looking at her with such devotion that for a moment she was almost afraid. She had the power to bring him happiness or grief, but the responsibility weighed heavily upon her. She wished desperately that he had kept his feelings a secret from her.

'Please, Mr Shreiker—'

'Won't you call me Andrew?'

'Oh, no!' she protested.

'Not all the time, just when we are alone. Please!'

'Oh dear! Maybe. Oh, very well then, Mr ... I mean Andrew.' His smile was radiant. 'But will you please give me time?'

'All the time you need.'

'And if I have to say "No" ...'

He beamed at her. 'Oh, but you won't! I promise you. You will love me, Miss Joanna, and you will make me the happiest man alive!'

'But in the meantime we will not speak of it?'

He looked a little crestfallen but finally nodded. 'If that is your wish.'

'It is!' she said firmly.

He reached across to take hold of her free hand and tried to kiss it, but Blue Boy had other ideas and neatly side-stepped so that Joanna and Andrew were drawn apart. An omen, thought Joanna, as they rode on, but the seed had been sown. Although she chattered cheerfully throughout the ride her mind was busy. She could not help wondering how it would be if she *did* fall in love with Andrew Shreiker.

Chapter Ten

JOANNA WOKE UP the following morning with one startling thought in her head. Juanita was Aunt Agatha's daughter! She had had an illegitimate child while she was in Portugal and somehow the child had conveniently disappeared. The more she considered her theory, the more likely it appeared. If the widowed Agatha had been forced to part with her child, it might explain why she was so kind towards Joanna. Agatha was giving her the affection she would have given to her own child. So that was why her aunt took such an interest in her! She lay in bed, staring at the ceiling, examining the possibilities, trying to fit together the pieces of the jigsaw. Firstly, Juanita was not to be mentioned. Talk of her had been frowned upon, if not actually forbidden. So where was she? When exactly was she born? Was she born secretly and then handed over to a Portuguese family? To allow Agatha to keep the child would have created a scandal, so did Grandmother insist that she should be adopted? Maybe Aunt Agatha wanted to keep the child and the family persuaded her to give it up – and it had broken Agatha's heart, and that was why Grandmother had a guilty conscience. Perhaps that was why Agatha went back to England ... Did she still keep in touch with the child? Perhaps she sent money for her upkeep.

Secondly, who was the child's father? With a name like Juanita, presumably he was Portuguese. Maybe he was already married. Perhaps it was the same as in Italy, where a woman's brothers would retaliate if her honour was tarnished. An unfaithful husband might expect violent retribution . . . It was all quite fascinating.

As she rose and washed, her mind continued to wrestle with the problem. Why did everybody get so *sad* when Juanita was mentioned? Had she died, perhaps? Yes, that was it! She had died and that was why Aunt Agatha had not been back to San Domingos for eleven years. There was nothing to draw her back. Her child was dead . . .

She began to pull on her clothes, paying them scant attention as she frowned in concentration. There was something wrong with her theory, for Grandmother had said that Juanita went to England and didn't come back. So either she was still in England, or she had died there and that's why they were all sorry and didn't want to be reminded of her tragic life . . . Grandmother had said that, 'It was all very sad!' So that must be it. She was dead – and that was why Agatha took such an interest in her, Joanna. Because Joanna had also been abandoned by her parents. That is why Agatha favoured her, giving her the writing desk and the silver-backed dressing-table set. In Agatha's mind Joanna was taking the place of Juanita!

She had just begun to smile with delight at her own cleverness when a fresh thought struck her. Grandmother had said, 'She was so young. So afraid.' Afraid of what? So young for what?

'Juanita!' she exclaimed. 'What happened to you? Where are you?'

The more it eluded her, the more determined Joanna became to discover the truth. If Juanita had gone back to England and died there, then why perpetuate the mystery? It hardly mattered now, surely . . . Dare she write to Aunt Agatha and ask for the truth or would that be cruel? She had no wish to stir up unhappy memories, but if it was all in the past the pain would surely have faded by now?

Impatient to try out her theory on her cousin, she went down to breakfast and found the room empty. Christina told her that Leo had eaten already and was working in his room.

'Working? At what?' Joanna wondered aloud.

'He must do his lessons.' Christina wagged a finger. 'He no do any lessons and his Mama she say, you do lessons, Leo.'

'What sort of lessons?' She helped herself to scrambled eggs and toast and Christina poured a cup of tea for her.

'His teachers in England, they give him lessons to do while he in Portugal. Master Leo, he not do them yet. Not do any!'

'Oh, I see.' She smiled. So, Leo had been given homework but had instead been skipping off on his own adventures and his mother had found out. Poor Leo. 'And Aunt Catherine?' she asked.

'She has cold. She have breakfast in bed.'

Joanna deliberated silently. Her uncle would almost certainly be at his desk in the Palacio.

'Were there any letters for me?' she asked hopefully.

'He not here yet. He very late.'

When she had gone Joanna returned to her problem. Christina had said that Uncle Elliot would tell her nothing, so obviously there was something to tell. Suppose she asked *him* . . . But Christina had been really shocked at the idea. Sarah Barratt had hinted that the old lady should blame herself for whatever had happened to Juanita . . . Could she have fallen overboard on the way back to England? No. Rather unlikely . . . And Grandmother's intentions had been honourable, except that with hindsight they were not so honourable. She sighed. The most likely explanation was that Agatha's illegitimate child had been shipped to England and had somehow died. The end of the story and a great relief to some people, thought Joanna resentfully. Very convenient for them all to have no one to reproach them for whatever it was they had done . . .

She was still brooding somewhat moodily upon this thought when Liliane bounced into the room waving a letter.

'Lettah!' she pronounced carefully. 'You – lettah!'

'A – letter – for – me. Thank – you, Liliane!' Joanna glanced at the handwriting and saw that it was from her mother. To Liliane she said, 'Letter. In Portuguese?' She waved the letter.

'Ah!' Liliane beamed. '*Letra ou carta.*'

'*Letra* or *carta*? Thank you, Liliane.'

The girl pointed accusingly. '*Nao!* "Sank you" eez Engleesh! You spik Portuguese! You spik "*Obrigada*"!' she cried.

'Oh, yes! Sorry, Liliane. *Obrigada!*'

She waved the girl away, but Liliane was enjoying herself and wanted to prolong the lesson. She darted to the table and snatched up a fork. '*Garfo!*'

'*Garfo, si.* English – fork.'

'Fork?'

'Yes. *Si.*' Joanna was opening the letter. Wasn't Mark ever going to write to her?

Liliane now waved a spoon aloft. '*Colher!*'

'*Colher* . . . Now I have to read this letter, so go away, please, Liliane.'

Liliane was hurt. 'Go? Me go way?'

'Yes, ple— I mean *se faz favor.*'

The door eventually closed behind the maid and Joanna began to read with a sense of growing alarm.

Dear Joanna,
This letter is very painful to write, but I must put pen to paper. Your father and I agree that you must know that I read your letter to Mark. I opened it in error and was

shocked and hurt by what I discovered there. That it was you and Mark! It is almost unbelievable. My first instinct was to think you had invented it all for some perverse reason of your own, but Maurice insisted we must speak to Mark. He tried hard to protect you but it is painfully clear to us that you must have encouraged him. He obviously accepted some of the blame, but Mark is our son and we know him so well. Whatever the circumstances and your feelings towards each other all *you* had to say was, 'No'. I still find it hard to believe that you lived with us all these years and have repaid us so unkindly. We loved you, Joanna. We thought you returned our affection and yet all the time you were trying to seduce Mark who has been like a brother to you. Legally *is* your brother! It is so sordid. Mark tried to be generous towards you and suggests that you acted from a misguided jealousy of Isobel. Even if that is so, it does not exonerate you in any way from blame.

Poor Mark is quite distraught. No wonder he told me that you had been seen with someone in the wood. It was the only way he could think of to get you out of our house before you caused more problems. Fortunately Isobel knows nothing of all this. It would break her heart. The wedding will go ahead in spite of your efforts to stop it.

After long discussions with your father we have reluctantly decided that we do not want you to return to us. By now you may have discovered that you are with child. If such a thing should occur I suggest you throw yourself on the mercy of your aunt and uncle. Tell them everything and ask for their help. You will get none from us.

I hope this is the last time I shall ever have to write to you. You have broken our hearts with your ingratitude.

Mama

For a long moment Joanna sat stunned by what she had read; shattered by the extent of the disaster. 'Oh, Mark!' she whispered. 'What have you done to me?'

'But why, Mark? Why?' It was incredible. She realized that her hands were shaking and she crumpled the letter fiercely in her hands. What could she do? Nobody would believe her version of what had happened.

'Oh, my *God*!' Too late, though, to pray. Too late even to hope. She had no home now except San Domingos but if her uncle and aunt ever heard what had happened they, too, presumably, would turn her out. Panic seized her, there was a terrifying blackness before her eyes and she felt desperately alone. Was there no one she could turn to for help? She cast around in her mind and suddenly thought of Andrew Shreiker's offer to take her to Australia. For a wild moment it seemed to offer a way out – maybe the only way out – of her predicament. Then she shook her head regretfully. That was out of the question. She could never make use of Andrew Shreiker to escape from her own mistakes. He was an honourable man and did not deserve such callous treatment.

On legs that would hardly support her she pushed back her chair and stumbled out of the dining room, thankful that she met no one. The few yards to her room felt like a mile. She felt ill and weak and her whole body now shook and she was icy cold. Her one thought was to lie down before she fell down, but first she must destroy the letter. Clumsily she tore it into shreds and dropped it into her waste-paper basket, then fell on to the bed and drew the bedspread around her. Gradually the irony dawned on her. Here she had been teasing out well-kept secrets of a long-dead scandal, and all the time her own disaster was looming. Presumably this would be the shameful secret about which *she* would ramble in her old age. She cringed at the thought. Years from now people would pretend it had never happened, would disown Joanna, would discourage outsiders from ferreting about for the ugly truths. Perhaps this was her punishment for her own investigation. There was a pressure behind her eyes and she longed to cry, but perversely the tears would not come. She lay dry-eyed and alone and desperately frightened. Her mother's remark about being with child worried her. Mark had said he would see to it that nothing happened to her, but now she wondered if that had been a lie. How would she know if she was with child? She felt the same and thought she looked the same. Were there signs? The awfulness of the situation appalled her and the unfairness of it choked her.

And Mark had done this to her!

'I hate you, Mark!' she whispered, though still it did not quite ring true. But she would practise hating him. It would take a little time but she would learn to hate him. Hate was easier to deal with than fear, she told herself. She would learn to hate him and then she would punish him. Somehow. Some day!

She was feeling no better when, some time later, Leo put his head round the door.

'Joanna! What's the matter?' he asked in surprise. 'Are you ill?' She did not answer, pretending to be asleep, but he ventured further into the room, eased back the bed-spread and peered into her face.

'Go away, Leo!' she muttered. 'Just go away!' She saw kindly concern in his large grey eyes and suddenly the tears flowed. There was no way she could hold them back and after the first few moments she no longer attempted the impossible. Regardless of Leo's presence she sobbed without restraint, helplessly, wordlessly, for a long time until it seemed she could have no more tears left to shed. And to her surprise Leo did not go away but hovered nearby, watching her anxiously. He said nothing, but when she occasionally glanced at him she saw that his eyes were troubled and from time to time he leaned forward a little self-consciously to pat her shoulder. He was still with her when, with no tears left to shed, she finally fell into an exhausted sleep.

*

When Steven Benbridge came out of the Palacio at 5 o'clock Leo, shrouded in gloom, was waiting for him.

'Hullo, young sprout!'

This greeting usually earned a smile, but Leo's face remained grim.

'What's the matter?' Steven asked, as the boy fell into step beside him.

'She can't come,' Leo told him. 'She's indisposed.'

'She's what?' He hid his amusement.

'She can't come, but she says to say "Thank you" for the invitation. So I suppose I can't come either.'

Steven hesitated. 'Of course you can come,' he said, hiding his disappointment. 'But what is the matter with your cousin?'

To his surprise Leo appeared to find this rather difficult to answer. He pursed his lips, shook his head and sighed heavily.

'She's not ill, is she?' Steven asked.

'I don't think so, Mr Benbridge. I think it's an affair of the heart.'

'Good heavens!' He glanced down at the boy's face. 'What makes you think that?'

'I'm not supposed to tell you. I mustn't tell anyone.'

'Not even me?'

Leo kicked a pebble and watched it dispassionately. 'Well, just you, maybe. She was crying. She went on and on. The paper-basket was full of bits of paper and Christina says she had a letter from England.'

'Ah!'

Leo looked up at him. 'I think it's called crossed in love.'

'Oh, dear. Poor Miss Grosvenor.' It was not his business, he told himself. Better not to ask.

But Leo was suffering under the burden of knowledge which he was eager to share. 'She had an unhappy love affair; that's all I know. I did warn her about love and all that stuff. I suppose she's pining. She looks pretty awful and her eyes are all swollen and she didn't have any lunch. Do you know anything about love affairs, Mr Benbridge?'

'No. Not really.' He had invited them both to supper this evening. The prospect of supper alone with Leo was not exactly inspiring but he did not want to disappoint the boy.

'Suppose I give you a little note for your cousin,' he said. 'Maybe I could change her mind. What are red eyes between friends? Maybe we could somehow cheer her up. We might play a few records?'

Leo's face brightened. 'I didn't know you had a gramophone, Mr Benbridge. You don't have any dance records, do you? Joanna is going to teach me to dance before the party. We could practise at your house!'

Steven imagined that his own face brightened at the possibility.

'You're brilliant, young man!' he told him. 'I think she might fall for that. Come back to the house while I write the note, then you can run all the way there and back.'

He wrote:

Dear Miss Grosvenor,
I have always been very partial to red eyes. Do please come to supper. We can teach Leo to dance.

Steven

*

That evening, as he waited for his guests to arrive, Steven sipped his drink and thought about Joanna and wished he could help in some way. His own wife, Sue, had been so vulnerable at seventeen, hovering between child and woman. Joanna, too, had that defensive air which brought

179

out all his protective instincts. He picked up the photograph of his wife and stared at the small, elfin face with its mop of bright curls. They had been childhood sweethearts and had never doubted that they would one day marry. When Steven went away to college in Camborne she had waited for him. When he arrived home with his engineering degree, she had been on the station platform to meet him and he had proposed for the second time. She had accepted, threatening him with a large family of boys.

'Poor little Sue,' he whispered, turning the photograph frame so that it caught what remained of the light. Sue looked shy but happy, her hair blowing in the breeze as she smiled up into his face. If only she had left him with a child, he thought, with the familiar stab of loss. That way something of their life together would have remained but she had never had the family she craved. The plan had been to start their family after they took up the posting to San Domingos. They had been married just over a year and had returned to England on holiday when her father, whom she adored, collapsed with a heart attack. Steven had had to break the news to Sue, and she appeared to take it very bravely at the time. The funeral had been a sad affair conducted in heavy rain. That night Sue had cried herself to sleep in Steven's arms and he found her dead beside him when he woke the next morning. The post mortem had revealed a weakness in her heart that no one had ever suspected.

After the shock and grief had taken its toll, Steven had somehow carried on, resigning himself to a lonely life, unable to imagine how any other woman could ever take Sue's place in his heart.

'Oh, Joanna!' he said softly and wondered what had happened to cause her such heartache. Seventeen! The world could be so hard at that age. He wished Sue was with him, because she would have found the right words to comfort the girl. A man was at such a disadvantage when the problem was a broken heart. Sighing, he swirled his drink until the ice chinked cheerfully and wondered if his note would do the trick. If she came he would cheer her up, would make her forget her troubles, if only for a few hours. He took out his watch and decided it was time to light the barbecue. As he busied himself with the matches he found himself humming. He was looking forward to the evening more than he would admit.

'You must come, Joanna!' he whispered. 'You must come!'

*

The meal, eaten in the garden, was a simple affair – chicken cooked on the barbecue, a tomato and onion salad and a bottle of the local red wine.

'Ah! Vinho tinto!' Joanna said casually.

Leo said, 'You cheated! You looked at the label!'

'I did *not*! I'm learning Portuguese, but it's a slow process. I have a sneaking feeling that Liliane is learning English faster than I am learning Portuguese!' She was making a big effort to be sociable, to shut out the horror of that letter and its significance. Her eyes were still puffed and her cheeks were blotched, but Leo and Steven treated her as though nothing untoward had happened and she felt as though she was waking from a nightmare. Her mother's words crept repeatedly into her mind, however, and her anger simmered somewhere below the surface.

For dessert they had a fruit compote and then coffee. By the time they had finished she was feeling a little more human and when Steven produced a small stack of records, a little of Leo's enthusiasm touched her. In no time at all she and Steven were demonstrating the 'Gay Gordons' and then it was time for Leo to dance with her.

His expression was earnest, his body taut with the effort of concentration. Steven wound up the gramophone and set the needle carefully into its groove.

'Bow!' Joanna reminded him as the first chord sounded. She took his hands and held them aloft. 'Now forward, two and three, and turn and go backwards! ... And three and turn again ... and back and stop ...'

She was aware of Steven's eyes on her, but by this time the wine had lightened her mood and she no longer cared what he thought about her. 'I am very partial to red eyes,' he had said. Well, they didn't come any redder than hers! If he could bear it, so could she. As a gesture of defiance she had not changed into another dress, nor had she done her hair. She had marched across the praca looking thoroughly dishevelled and miserable, daring anyone to cheer her up. Fortunately she had passed no one.

'How kind of you to come,' Steven had said by way of greeting. 'I hope you like your chicken spicy.'

He had led her at once to the barbecue area at the rear of the house. There, portions of chicken were already sizzling above the charcoal and he had explained about the ground pepper known as piri-piri. He had poured her a glass of wine and had not once referred to her awful appearance. He had even ignored her initial attempts to remain morose and awkward. In the face of so much goodwill she had found herself surrendering and now, much to her surprise, she was actually beginning to enjoy herself.

'... And waltz – one, two, three, no, no! Clockwise! one, two three, that's it! You've got it, Leo!' They collapsed, breathless and laughing on the garden seat, and Leo appealed eagerly for an opinion.

'What do you think, Mr Benbridge? How did I get on?'

'First class, young sprout! You'll be the star of the evening!'

'I think I made a couple of mistakes,' he confessed modestly.

Joanna said, 'But it's early days, you see. We'll practise again and—'

Leo turned hopefully to Steven. 'I suppose it's a bit

of a cheek to ask if we could borrow your records for tomorrow?'

Steven smiled. 'Borrow my garden *and* my records,' he offered. 'I'm a bit rusty myself and I could do with some more practice.'

'I think you're very good for your age,' Leo told him ingenuously, and Joanna said, 'Leo! How could you be so tactless!'

Steven laughed. 'That put me in my place!' he said. 'Perhaps I should order my Bath-chair!'

Leo was full of contrition. 'Oh, Mr Benbridge! I didn't mean that you were old, just that . . . well, I just meant—'

Steven slapped him cheerfully on the shoulder and said 'I'm not offended, Leo. I may sob into my pillow tonight but – oh! Sorry, Joanna.'

Leo said, 'Now who's being tactless?'

'I'm sorry, Joanna. I didn't mean . . . do forgive me.'

They both looked at her anxiously.

Dramatically she pressed a hand to her heart. 'I'm terribly offended and hurt. I shall probably throw myself into . . . a puddle!'

Leo's laughter pealed out, relieved. 'I told you you were funny, Joanna!'

Steven said, 'Don't expect me to go in after you! I can't swim!'

Joanna laughed, and as she did was aware once again that Steven was watching her. He had nice eyes, she thought suddenly, and she liked his mouth and the sound of his voice. He was kind, and being in his company was – was what, exactly? Reassuring, perhaps? Relaxing? Probably because he was so much older than she was. He was fatherly, somehow. Comforting, even. She tried to imagine him as a father with several children; she would envy them his love. And how sad that now he would never have any children. He must be lonely without his wife, yet he hadn't married again. Perhaps he preferred being solitary – or could never love anyone else. She recalled Sarah Barratt's hints about a wife and found herself wishing that she were older.

Leo said, 'Joanna!' He snapped his fingers. 'You're miles away!'

She caught Steven's eye and said, 'Sorry! I was. Where were we? Oh, yes! Well, now that we've all finished being tactless, what about the "Valeta", Leo? Are you still game?'

'Rather!' He rushed to find a suitable record.

Steven said, 'And this time Leo can wind up the gramophone. We elderly wallahs just don't have the stamina!'

As Leo bent to his task Joanna said quietly, 'You're not at all elderly, Mr Benbridge. At least, I don't think of you that way.'

'You're most kind, Miss Grosvenor.'

'Won't you please call me Joanna.'

'Do you think I should?'

'Mr Shreiker does.'

As soon as she had said it she regretted the careless words, but he did not react in any way to the news that his junior engineer was already on more intimate terms with her than he was.

'Thank you, Miss Joanna.' The light was fading fast and she could not see his expression, but there was something in his voice she did not recognize. Was he mocking her? No, he was not that kind of person.

She said, 'I'm very glad I came tonight. It was so kind of you to bother with me. I know I'm a nuisance at times.'

'A nuisance? Never! In fact, it was very selfish of me to insist, but I had been looking forward to your company.' He leaned forward suddenly. 'Being older means that I have more experience of the world and its woes, Miss Joanna. I doubt if you could shock me. If you ever need someone to confide in, you could always try me. I'm a very good listener and most discreet.'

'Are you?' She wasn't really doubting the validity of his claims, but testing her own reaction to his words; wondering if she would ever dare accept his offer. 'Thank you,' she said uncertainly. 'I hope I never have to burden anyone with my problems, but if I do I'll remember your offer.'

'We all have problems. Sometimes they get out of proportion and then a new viewpoint . . .'

At these kind words Joanna felt a sudden and overwhelming urge to confide in him, but a sense of shame held her back. With an attempt at lightness she said, 'If I ever do have a terrible secret . . .' and then she fell silent. Her throat felt tight at the thought of losing his good opinion of her.

'There is always another pebble on the beach,' he said. 'A cliché, perhaps, but true.'

She said sharply, 'Leo has been telling tales!'

He shook his head. 'No. It was just a guess,' he said.

Leo shouted, 'Right! We're ready! Come on, you two. The "Valeta"! Before it gets too dark.'

Joanna jumped quickly to her feet, glad of the interruption. She had been too tempted by the offer of a confession. Abruptly she said, 'I daren't tell anyone, Mr Benbridge, but if I could, it would be you.' And as the music started she turned and seized Leo's hand and led him back on the lawn to continue the lesson.

*

The following morning Catherine was still at breakfast when Joanna entered the room. Leo passed her on the way out.

'Good morning, Aunt Catherine,' Joanna sat down at the table. 'I hope you are feeling better today.'

'Well enough, thank you.' Her aunt's tone was somewhat frosty.

Joanna prayed that Catherine had not received a letter from her mother about Mark's disclosures. She had convinced herself that it would not be in Mama's interest to write since she would not want Joanna forcibly returned to Folkestone like an unwanted parcel.

Catherine said, 'Nurse Williams is unwell today. I have told her that you will spend the morning with your grandmother so that she may go back to bed for a few hours. It is a bilious attack, and she has been up and down all night.' She pursed her lips. 'This is not the first time; I had no idea her health was so uncertain, or I would have thought twice about employing her. The doctor will call during the morning and give her something suitable.'

'I'll do my best.' Her heart sank at the prospect. She abandoned the idea of egg and bacon for a slice of toast, which would be quicker.

'I would sit with her myself,' Catherine told her, 'except that I have the dressmaker coming. I'm sure you will manage perfectly. Nurse has a weekly menu and the food is in the larder. She has already given your grandmother her wash.'

She dabbed at her mouth with her napkin and looked at Joanna sharply. 'I understand that you and Leo spent some time with Mr Benbridge last evening. Wasn't that rather inconsiderate of you?'

Joanna forced herself to look at her aunt. 'Was it? In what way?'

'In what way? Why, because Christina had expected all of us to dine. Food was wasted, Joanna.'

'But Leo told Christina in plenty of time.'

Catherine hesitated and Joanna guessed that she had not checked first to find out.

'It is not up to Christina to decide what you should be allowed to do! If you had asked me, as you should have done, I would have said "No".'

'Why is that, Aunt Catherine?' Joanna tried to keep her voice level. She knew it would not be sensible to antagonize her further. On the other hand, she did not want her aunt to treat her like a child when she was nearly eighteen.

'Because I don't want you and Leo bothering the staff. I have spoken of this before.'

'But it was Mr Benbridge's idea. He invited us and I think it would have been churlish to refuse. And we were not distracting him from his work, because his day's work was over.'

Seeing the angry colour in her aunt's face, she made a great show of spreading marmalade on her toast and waited for her to reply.

After a moment her aunt threw down the napkin and said, 'You are a very stubborn girl, Joanna. And not very intelligent. If you want to stay on in San Domingos, you really should try to fit in. You seem determined to cause trouble. I shall speak to my husband about you.'

Joanna stared hard at her plate as Catherine stood up. Christina came in and Catherine said, 'You can clear the table now. We've finished.'

This was patently untrue, since Joanna still held toast in her hand, and Christina hesitated. Catherine stared at Joanna, willing her to comply, but Joanna said deliberately, 'Give me five more minutes, please, Christina. I think I shall have a second cup of tea.'

With a look at her mistress's furious face, the maid went out and Catherine drew in her breath.

'I don't want you or Leo to visit Mr Benbridge's house again. Do you hear me, Joanna? It is most unsuitable and I will not have it. I shall speak to him and I shall speak to my husband.'

Joanna experienced a moment's panic. Was this part of a deliberate plan to isolate her from all those who befriended her? Steadying her voice with an effort she said, 'I think I am old enough to decide such matters for myself, Aunt Catherine.'

'You are a mere child!'

'I am nearly eighteen.' To hide her nervousness Joanna began to pour herself another cup of tea but suddenly, with an exclamation of anger, Catherine leaned forward and tried to wrench the teapot from her. The lid flew off and hot tea splashed out on to Joanna's hand. In spite of herself she could not hold back a cry of pain and for a moment Catherine was unable to hide her satisfaction. She watched silently as Joanna wrapped her napkin around her hand and did not utter one word of apology. In that moment, Joanna's dislike of her aunt became loathing.

She said, 'Don't worry about my hand, Aunt. I'm sure you didn't intend to scald me, and I doubt if it's too serious. I'll ask Doctor Barratt to take a look at it when he calls to see the nurse.' And she pushed back her chair and stood up. As she left the room, she was uncomfortably aware that Catherine was now her enemy.

*

Joanna found her grandmother in a cheerful frame of mind and surprisingly lucid. The old lady asked how she was settling in and ate her breakfast without too much trouble. She talked to Joanna about the coming party and insisted on showing her a large photograph album.

'My husband was a very keen photographer,' she explained. 'From the moment it first became possible for the ordinary man to take photographs, your grandfather was obsessed by it. He spent hours under that black cloth! I used to tease him about it. Look, here are the boys, Maurice and Elliot, taken at their school at the end of the summer term.

'They were very close. Always have been . . . And that's me, taken on my birthday with all the children around. Agatha was such a pretty child. So sad about her husband. Poor man. They would have been happy together, I believe. Marriage is such a lottery, isn't it?'

There was a knock at the door and Leo came in with the doctor. He greeted his grandmother and then said to Joanna, 'Mama says you spilt hot tea on your hand. Is it painful?'

'It smarts a little; nothing much.' She held out her hand for the doctor's examination and was reassured that it was not serious. He promised to send up a soothing cream for it. There would be no need, he said, for a bandage, but if it became at all inflamed she should see him again. He then went through to the nurse's bedroom.

'We're looking at old photographs, Leo,' Joanna told him. 'I expect you've seen most of them before.'

He agreed eagerly and turned the pages. 'Here I am as a baby.' The youthful Leo stared up, podgy and beaming, from a rug on the lawn.

Joanna smiled. Even at that age the likeness was there.

'And here I am on my first pony! I can still remember him. His name was Griffin and he was a lazy little devil. Five miles an hour was his usual speed!' He laughed and turned the page.

Grandmother said, 'And this is one of me with the staff in their new uniforms ... I had had them sent out from England, and they were so proud of them. Lace straps on the aprons ... Now which was which, I wonder?' She peered more closely at the three members of staff and Joanna saw a woman who was obviously a much thinner Christina.

Leo said, 'Look at Christina! She's not so fat!'

Grandmother said, 'Leo! Please! That's not very gallant! But yes, that's Christina. She was much younger then. And we had a cook. That's the cook. You won't remember her, Leo – a good cook, but so bad-tempered. A difficult woman. Funny, I can't recall her name. She left suddenly when her mother became ill ...'

Leo pointed to the third person – a young woman, obviously Portuguese, with a small elfin face, high cheek-bones and small, dark eyes. She was holding out the straps of her apron as though to emphasize the fact that they were lace.

'Who's that?' he asked.

189

Grandmother stared at the photograph. She put a hand to her mouth and her lips moved soundlessly. Joanna, watching her closely, saw a shadow pass across her face.

'That's Juanita,' she whispered. 'Poor girl! Oh dear!'

Leo and Joanna exchanged glances and Leo prompted, 'What happened to her, Grandmother? What happened to Juanita?'

The old lady stared up at him and her mouth trembled. 'She . . .' She turned to Joanna. 'She—'

They both waited breathlessly, but suddenly Grandmother shut the album with such force that dust flew from it. She held the book close to her chest, hugging it as though it were a child, rocking it to and fro, her face frozen.

Before anyone could speak again the doctor came back into the room. 'Nothing to worry about!' he told them. 'Nurse will be as right as rain shortly. The worst is over. Plenty of liquids.' He looked at the old lady and noted the change in her. 'Aha?' he said and smiled at her. 'Mrs Grosvenor! It's me, Doctor Barratt. How are you today?'

She seemed unaware of his presence. Joanna said, 'She was just showing us a photograph of Juanita. Then she seemed to close in on herself.'

'Juanita!' He avoided her eyes. 'You mustn't mind her. It's very sad, this complaint. So unreliable, these sudden recollections – these *fantasies*.'

'You mean it wasn't Juanita?'

After a deep sigh he looked at her. 'Miss Grosvenor, the past is best left alone. I know you're curious; my wife told me you were asking questions. There was a tragedy, and many of us now regret it. But with all the goodwill in the world, we cannot undo past mistakes; they simply live on in our memories to reproach us. It should not be your concern, my dear, so let me just make this one appeal to you. Don't try to resurrect the past. It can do no good.' He took out his watch and made a pretence of consulting it. 'Is that the time? I must be on my way.'

He gave them each a quick nod and was out of the room before Joanna could think of a way to detain him. She looked at Grandmother – who now rocked to and fro with the album clutched to her chest – and then at Leo.

'So that's that!' she said. 'We're warned off!'

He stared at her. 'But that *was* Juanita! Grandmother said it was!'

'So are we any nearer the truth?'

He gave her a mysterious look. 'We may be,' he told her in sepulchral tones.

'Leo! What on earth do you mean?'

He lowered his voice. 'I went out early this morning. To the *cemetery*. The English one, not the Portuguese one. I found something there that you might like to see!'

She gasped. 'What was it? Tell me, you awful boy!'

He shook his head. 'When you can leave Grandmother, come and find me and I'll show you. I'll be in my room doing my beastly lessons.'

*

It was nearly two hours later before Joanna was free, and then she and Leo made their way to the small, stark cemetery built on high ground beyond the miners' houses. Its plain high walls were painted white, but the gateway was framed in a blue design and a wrought-iron cross surmounted the arch. In a dark corner, almost hidden beneath a tangle of weeds, there was a small wooden cross. It stood about eighteen inches high and there was no inscription . . .

Except the letter 'J'.

Chapter Eleven

THE INSIGNIFICANT GRAVE, narrow but turfed, was tucked away in one corner and the letter 'J' told them nothing. There was little else to be gleaned in the way of information. They looked at it for a moment or two and then turned to examine the other grave. It was that of Agatha's husband, and with some difficulty they deciphered the inscription which was already becoming weathered.

Leo read aloud: 'Sacred to the memory of Charles Warren ... Requiescat in Pace ... A bit of Latin,' he told Joanna airily. 'It means—'

'Rest In Peace.'

'How did you know that?' He looked at her indignantly. 'Girls don't know Latin.'

'An enlightened guess!'

He snorted irritably but let it pass.

Joanna said slowly, 'One grave is marble and obviously quite expensive, while the other is cheap and made of wood.'

'And only two graves so far,' Leo observed.

'So San Domingos must be a healthy place to live!'

'Of course it is.'

'If Aunt Agatha's husband had lived longer, we might have had some more cousins.'

'I don't want any more,' Leo told her. 'I've got you and Dorky and Suzanne and Mark. That's enough.'

She looked at him. 'Do you wish you were going to Mark's wedding?'

'Not really. I'm not interested in weddings and stuff, but do you wish you were going?'

Joanna hesitated. 'Not any more,' she said, surprised. 'I thought I did, but it all seems such a long way away now.'

'So what do you think about the "J" grave? Do you think it's hers?'

'Hard to say.' They turned to look at it once more, and Joanna noticed the remains of dead flowers. 'Someone still puts flowers on it,' she said, puzzled. She glanced around her, strangely oppressed by the lack of space and the high walls. Claustrophobic, she thought – yet if you were dead it wouldn't matter.

They left the cemetery and walked thoughtfully back down the slope towards the miners' cottages, none the wiser about Juanita.

In the village all was peaceful. Many of the miners were sleeping after their shift and the wives moved quietly about their work – small, solid women and slim girls with swarthy skins and eyes like currants. When they met they talked in shrill, excited tones. They smiled readily but shyly when they saw Leo and Joanna.

'Papa says that they are totally trustworthy,' Leo informed her. 'He says they are generous to a fault and would share their last slice of bread with a stranger.'

Joanna nodded. Presumably this was the time the women liked best . . . their time. The time to shop and wash and mend; the time to sit outside their doors and slide the beans from the pods or scrape the small white turnips. The scraps would go to feed the goat or the hens, or maybe a pig shared by several families. A time to think back on their carefree youth and ponder the years to come. A time to gossip among themselves, to grumble at the hours the men worked and to commiserate with those who fell sick; to lament the dying. Joanna was dimly aware that knowing almost no Portuguese set her apart from these friendly people. She felt a great longing to talk with them and be accepted by them, and made up her mind to work harder at her lessons with Liliane. Perhaps there was a Portuguese phrase-book in the library at the Palacio. Once she could speak the language more competently, she would go back to visit Maria.

'The children are at school,' said Leo. 'The school my father had built for them, although the company paid for it. Papa says they should think themselves lucky to get such an education.' He looked at Joanna, eager that she should appreciate his father's good qualities.

She smiled and imagined how the children would scamper home, laughing and jostling, their feet bare, their clothes makeshift, making their way along the terraced, whitewashed houses built low with tiny windows to keep out the sun. She found herself envying them their simple lifestyle and sighed deeply. They might be poor, but they did know exactly who they were.

Leo, chattering non-stop, led Joanna through the streets, proudly pointing out geraniums in pots and basking cats as though his father was personally responsible for those also. As they picked their way carefully along the narrow, cobbled streets, they occasionally passed a bread oven from which round flat loaves were being withdrawn on long-handled shovels. Each time they stopped to sniff appreciatively at the warm, yeasty smell. They also paused and dutifully patted a variety of rangy mongrel dogs with lop-sided ears, whose owners obviously adored them.

'*Boa tarde, senora!*' Leo cried again and again, bidding them 'Good afternoon'. He enquired after their health – '*Como esta?*' – and said how good it was that they were well. '*Ah, bem!*'

Before long Joanna had learned these phrases from him and began to venture a few words herself.

One elderly woman brought a very young child to the door to be admired; the first grandchild, Leo explained. It was the smallest baby Joanna had ever seen, with a wonderfully peaceful expression and a mass of straight dark hair.

'*Vera!*' said the old woman.

'*A nome bonito!*' Leo grinned at Joanna. 'A pretty name. Vera.'

'Oh, I see.' She repeated it and the old woman nodded happily and withdrew into the dim interior of the house.

There was a savoury smell of spices from dozens of stews which simmered in unseen cooking pots; woodsmoke also lingered in the air. The hot sun, trapped within the narrow streets, warmed the houses, and the whitewashed walls added their own distinctive scent to the air. Joanna wanted to absorb it all; longed to stand still with her eyes shut and allow it to seep into her soul. There was an air of such simplicity and contentment that her own life seemed fraught and extravagant by comparison, and suddenly she felt ashamed of her spiteful thoughts towards Mark and the anger towards her aunt. She imagined that if she could creep into the gloom of one of the tiny houses, close the door and be entirely alone, she might somehow come to terms with her life. Might even become reconciled to her tempestuous existence or, better still, make some order from the chaos.

'Joanna!' Leo was regarding her with exasperation. 'You're not listening. I said, do you know what I think?'

'Sorry, Leo. What do you think?'

He narrowed his eyes and pursed his lips thoughtfully. 'I think Juanita was murdered! I think they killed her!' His eyes gleamed. 'She did something they didn't like – or she discovered a terrible secret – and they killed her!'

She stared at him. '*Killed* her? You're mad, Leo! Of course they didn't kill her. They wouldn't dare!'

His face fell. 'Why not? Murders happen all the time!'

'You really think someone in your own family could commit a murder?'

'Why not?'

'Because they're just ordinary people, that's why. Ordinary, law-abiding people and – and they wouldn't dare.'

'But you do think that was her grave, don't you?'

'It might be. It might not. There could be lots of people whose names start with "J" – and it could have been a man. It might stand for Juan; it might even be the grave of someone's pet.'

Leo was not listening. He had stopped to stroke a mangy-looking cat. 'I wonder if it's meowing in Portuguese,' he said. 'And if I meow back in English it won't know what I'm saying. Or cat language might be universal. They'd be awfully lucky if it was; they'd be able to go anywhere in the world and talk to the other cats. Then they'd be one up on us!'

Joanna was not listening. 'It wasn't a small grave, Leo,' she pointed out. 'So she couldn't have died when she was very young. Maybe she grew up somewhere secretly and then killed herself – or died of cholera or something.'

'You *do* think it's a her!'

'Yes, I think so – but why don't they put a proper headstone with an inscription? "Rest In Peace" or something like that.' She frowned. 'Unless it's because they don't want anyone to know who it is. Is it a sin to kill yourself, I wonder? I suppose it is.'

They walked in silence for a few moments, leaving the village behind, then Joanna said, 'I'm not supposed to go to Mr Benbridge's again. Your mother's forbidden it. What about you?'

He looked stricken. 'Nor me. Sometimes I hate Mama! How does she expect me to learn to dance?' He kicked irritably at a small stone. 'You mustn't blame me for my parents, Joanna. People don't choose their parents, you see. It's a bit of a gamble, isn't it?'

'Parents can't choose their children either. They have to make the best of what they get.' She smiled at him. 'They might be hoping for a sweet, demure little girl but get a noisy, bouncing boy!'

He grinned. 'I might ask Papa if we could go to Mr Benbridge's. He'd probably say "Yes", but then Mama might find out and be angry with him. I don't like it when they quarrel.' He glanced up at her. 'Do you hate my mother, Joanna?'

She bit back her first reply. 'Not exactly, but I do get very angry with her. But I also get angry with other people at home in England.'

'Which people? Your parents?' He thrust his hands into his pockets with a quick glance at Joanna, but she did not comment on this flagrant breaking of the rules so he left them there and went on, 'Parents can be a great worry. My mother came to my school at the end of term once. She was wearing a new jacket with a fox tail round the collar. Trimming, you know? I suppose she thought it was smart, but all the boys laughed at her and called her Foxy. Then they teased me when she'd gone home. I know she didn't mean it, but it was awfully embarrassing.'

'Poor Leo!'

He shook his head wearily and then, with his characteristic abrupt change of direction, said, 'Pity you're no good at Latin. I've got this boring homework to do – I thought we could do half each.'

'Isn't that cheating?'

'Only if you're found out! At least, that's what the boys say at school, but since you don't know any Latin it's no good anyway.'

They came in sight of the English compound and suddenly he snatched his hands out of his pockets, cried, 'I'll race you to the Palacio!' and went bounding off, whooping and hollering for her to try and catch him. Joanna continued on her sedate way, a slight smile on her face. When he finally turned to look for her, she would be nowhere in sight.

*

Below the ground the miners' work continued. Shifts worked around the clock, blasting the rock free and shovelling it into the tubs. It was soulless labour, with little variation – a daily grind that had to be borne for the money at the end of each week. The men sang sometimes, but talk was difficult because of the continuous noise of scraping shovels and the clatter of falling rock, interspersed with the thump of the explosions and the roar of the hot, dust-laden wind. They breathed in sulphur and they walked in sulphur, and the sour smell clung to their clothes and hair. The presence of the ponies made matters worse, for they dropped dung and fouled the air with their breath. Their plaintive braying and the shouts of the men leading them all added to the general confusion of sounds and smells which the miners scarcely noticed, so accustomed were they to their environment. Their sole intention was to get through their allotted number of hours without calling down the wrath of their superiors for a misdemeanour which might mean a fine. That, in turn, meant a scolding from the wife and less to spend in the market.

The miners themselves were a mixed group, mostly Portuguese, but other nationalities were represented. A few Englishmen, many of them from Cornwall; some German and some Dutch. All tough, wiry men, proud of their skills and their strength, united by their shared experience and knowledge.

Steven knew some of them by name, most by sight. He had worked alongside them for many years and earned their grudging respect. He was considered hard but fair when he dealt with the men. The mine's safety record was good and that was due to his insistence on the rules. Output had risen steadily until this year, when it looked as though the production would top that of any previous year. The vein had proved immensely rich, and Mason and Barry had seen to it that the shareholders benefited.

Share prices soared and investors grew wealthy on the proceeds.

On this particular day one of the men had come in search of Steven to report on a new area of 'hot ground'. This had been uncovered by the morning's blasting. It was the result of long-dead volcanic activity in the area which had once heated the strata.

'Damn!' Steven straightened his back as far as the height of the tunnel would allow and asked in Portuguese, 'A large area?'

The man shrugged. It could be.

'Have you moved back?'

Yes, they had gone deeper and had found the heat increasing rather than decreasing. The hot rock was difficult to work and less stable. The usual solution was to seal off the area and abandon the cut. But first he would send for Shreiker – it would be useful experience for him. He spoke to a man who hurried away. Left to his own devices, Steven made his way towards the hot ground where he would meet his junior engineer. He thought of Joanna and wondered when he could arrange another dancing lesson for Leo. He would dearly love to know what had caused the girl so much unhappiness; Leo had mentioned an unhappy love affair, which was possible. Or he might be able to take them on a picnic. He liked the young lad, but most of all he wanted to see Joanna laugh. There was a tenseness about her which concerned him. She was young and she deserved to be happy. A picnic should be possible . . .

Andrew Shreiker arrived about five minutes later. At least he was willing to learn, thought Steven; a bit wet behind the ears, but keen. He seemed to be a very cheerful chap, always whistling or smiling. Suddenly Steven remembered that this young man was on first-name terms with Joanna, and felt a twinge of jealousy which he quickly suppressed. They were not too far apart in age and a friendship would be perfectly natural, he told himself, and was annoyed that a small uneasiness lingered. He began quickly to explain the situation and the younger man listened intently.

Then he asked, 'Is it something to do with the hot springs? Like the thermal springs they have in New Zealand?'

'The same.' He explained the technical reasons for abandoning the cut. 'We'll simply wall it in and forget it.'

'Shame, really,' said Shreiker. 'I mean, all that natural heat being wasted. Pity we can't heat water with it or something.'

Steven did not bother to answer. To him, the hot ground was simply a nuisance to be dealt with. He explained how the wall should be built, then Shreiker said, 'Will you be around?'

'Doubtful. Why?'

Shreiker looked sheepish. 'Nothing, really. It's just that I've had a bit of trouble with one of the men. Had to reprimand him for turning up late, then he starting slacking. Deliberately. I had to report him and he was fined.'

'You did the right thing. What's the problem?'

'I've seen him — well, I think he's plotting something with one of his chums. I can sense it.' He looked anxiously at Steven.

'Mmm! Keep an eye on them. Any more trouble and I'll have a word with them. Better, though, if you deal with that sort of thing yourself.'

'Yes, I see that. I just wondered how to — that is — what to—'

Steven shook his head. 'There's no set way to deal with them. You have to play it by ear. My feeling is that if you have to be firm, make sure you're being fair. They can accept that. It's injustice they hate; they jib at it, and it seems to smoulder on. Just keep your eyes open. Be on your guard.'

He sent Shreiker off to organize a small team of men. A

glance at his watch told Steven that it was time to go off duty, and he put the problems of work behind him and began to think again about Joanna.

He was half-way back to his house a little later when he saw Catherine Grosvenor waiting for him. He groaned inwardly but arranged his features into a smile; the woman made him nervous.

'Good morning, Mrs Grosvenor! How are you?'

'Very well, thank you, Mr Benbridge.'

She smiled and he thought how attractive she looked. The pink dress suited her and her parasol cast a soft light over her face.

As she fell into step beside him she said, 'I was hoping to catch you, Mr Benbridge. I wanted to apologize for the young people; they do tend to monopolize one, if allowed. You were kind enough to entertain them the night before last, but I have told them they must not take advantage of your hospitality. I don't think you will be troubled by them again.'

'Oh, but I wasn't in the least troubled by them, Mrs Grosvenor. I enjoyed their company. Young people are so – so buoyant, so invigorating. We enjoyed ourselves tremendously. Your son wants to dazzle you at the party with his newly-acquired dancing skills. He's a nice boy; I'm sure you and your husband are very proud of him.'

'Well, we are naturally very proud, but Leo is a rather effervescent boy, I will admit. There are times when I find him quite exhausting!' She laughed. 'And young Joanna is not an easy girl to be with. She may have been on her best behaviour with you, but with family she can be—' She shrugged. 'What can I say without sounding unkind? At her age I was much more controlled, Mr Benbridge. I put her lack of finesse down to her lack of breeding. A foundling is at a great disadvantage, don't you think? One has no idea who the parents are, and they could be anyone! Her mother was obviously no better than she should be, and presumably some brute of a man took advantage of her.' She shuddered. 'Animals! That's all one can say.'

He dared not meet her eyes in case his anger was too apparent. 'But the girl cannot be blamed for her parents' behaviour,' he protested. 'And it might not have been as sordid as you fear. It might have been a love-match.'

Catherine's laugh rang out. 'A love-match, Mr Benbridge? Oh, now we are moving into the realms of romantic fiction.' She laid her hand on his arm. 'Believe me, I pity the girl and we do what we can for her. At present her adoptive parents are in need of a rest, and we are looking after her – but hopefully, not for too long! My patience is wearing thin; I have tried to like her, but she resists all my friendly overtures and seems determined to aggravate and upset me. I don't want her to fall into those ways with you, Mr Benbridge, and I have warned her to stay away from you.'

Disappointment surged through him at these last words and he strove to demonstrate his loyalty. 'I find her a most charming girl, Mrs Grosvenor. Your husband's brother and his wife have brought her up well. She is a credit to them.' He sensed that she did not want to hear this and her next words confirmed his impression.

'I am so pleased to hear you say that, Mr Benbridge. I only wish I could say that I, too, find her charming, but as I have told you, she has taken against me for some reason and I cannot get close to her. Still, I am so pleased she has found someone to admire her.' She laughed lightly. 'Oh, I don't mean you. No, no. Young Mr Shreiker is quite enamoured of the girl; he told me in confidence that he hopes to win her hand. Can you imagine that? He hardly knows her – although of course they travelled from England together on the same ship.'

He was aware that she was watching him intently, and hoped that his dismay was not too obvious. Young Shreiker? Good Lord! The youngster was barely out of school! How could he be thinking of marriage?

'Not that she is ready for marriage yet,' Catherine continued. 'She is much too immature. I don't blame my brother and sister-in-law for packing her off to foreign parts. They have done their best for her but — and I hate to say this — she is most unappreciative of all they have done for her. If Mr Shreiker feels he can help her to grow up, then good luck to him, say I!'

He searched for something to say. 'He *is* rather young,' was all he could manage.

'But nice enough, I think. The trouble is, she is receiving rather too much attention here at San Domingos. My husband dotes on the girl . . .'

He saw her eyes narrow.

'Is there any chance,' he asked, 'that her real parents might be discovered? Was any attempt made to trace them when she was found?'

'I imagine so. But obviously without success. My own view is that we are probably better off not knowing. Lord knows what problems we might create or what skeletons we might uncover!'

He was aware that her hand still rested on his sleeve, but he could see no polite way to remove it.

She went on, 'But enough about our little Miss Nobody! I came to ask you to join us for dinner this evening. We need one more to make up a four for bridge. Sarah Barratt is coming but—'

'I'm sorry,' he said, 'but I have rather a lot of work to catch up with. We struck hot ground again today, and will possibly have to abandon the cut. I want to be ready to start again tomorrow morning.' He tried to speak lightly but inwardly he was seething. The woman was trying so hard to discredit Joanna and was making no secret of her dislike. His refusal to accept Catherine's verdict on the girl was obviously annoying her. He did not underestimate her power but could not commit himself to an evening in her company.

She removed her hand abruptly and her lips tightened. 'As you wish. I'm sorry you put work before pleasure, Mr Benbridge. That is not a recipe for a happy life.' She smiled thinly but her eyes were cold. 'Never mind. Perhaps Mr Shreiker will join us instead,' she said. 'I suspect he will jump at the chance to be near his beloved Joanna! Another time, perhaps.'

He watched her go, longing to wipe the smile from that lovely face. He was old enough and wise enough to recognize that she was trying to gain his interest. He had known about her affair with Sturton and had wondered in which new direction she would cast her net. She would find him an impossible fish to land! Steven knew her better than she could ever imagine; he knew that she was vain, unprincipled and potentially dangerous. He thought Elliot Grosvenor deserved better.

*

Joanna wrote '*3rd August*' and then sighed deeply. She stared around the room and saw the watercolour of the bandstand displayed on the easel. It wasn't too bad. She wrote:

> My painting of the bandstand has finally turned out rather well. Perhaps the bandstand is a little too low, but it is still recognizably *our* bandstand. I would like to ask Mr Benbridge's opinion, but daren't. Aunt will be furious if I make contact with him again. I thought he might have invited us to dance at his house again, but maybe she has frightened him off . . .

Several weeks had passed since the arrival of her mother's letter, and still it appeared that no letter had been sent to Joanna's aunt and uncle. Perhaps God had heard her prayers.

I have been in Portugal for a month now, and I suppose I am beginning to feel at home. At least I feel a little less frightened, and my Portuguese is improving under Liliane's tuition. Today it is 'Pargo' day (the market) and Leo and I are off shortly to see what we can buy. I missed the last one because I had a sick headache. I might find a small gift for Dorcas – *if* Mama will let her keep it. Perhaps she will think it contaminated and throw it away. I can try, anyway.

Still no letter from Mark, and now I think there never will be. How I wish I could undo that terrible day. Looking back, it seems that my whole life turned sour that afternoon – and all for nothing because he doesn't love me, and now I think I no longer love him.

Because of Mark I can feel sorry for poor Mr Shreiker. I know what agony it is to love someone who does not love you in return. Yesterday he brought me a small posy of flowers, but I can hardly bear to look at them. Catherine keeps reminding me how fortunate I am to be courted by such a fine young man, meaning that he is too good for me. I am sure she does it to upset me because she knows how unromantic I feel towards him. Uncle Elliot also referred to him, but he said I must not rush into anything. I feel I am being sucked down into a bog. The more people who know, the harder it will be to say 'No' to him. Perhaps I should say it now, and save the poor man a lot of heartache. If only Mark had disillusioned me years ago, I should not be in all this trouble today . . .

There was a knock at the door and Leo came in; a Leo whose hair had been reduced to a severe shortness.

He said, 'Amo, amas, amat—'

'Stop trying to impress me,' she told him. 'You know I don't know any Latin. And you look awful! Like a shorn sheep.'

'The barber came,' he said unnecessarily. 'Papa looks terrible, too; we all do. What are you writing? Another love letter?'

'My diary!' she closed it pointedly. 'Are we ready now, then? Is it Pargo time?'

'It is.'

She waited for him to leave the room and when he remained she said, 'Go on, Leo! You know I have to hide my diary.'

She shut the door firmly behind him and put the diary away. When she re-opened the door Leo was rubbing his right eye.

'Such a draught through that keyhole!' he said.

Laughing, she aimed a fist in his direction and he ducked, grinning.

'There's a key in the keyhole!' she told him. She collected her parasol from the wardrobe and said, 'Lead on, Macduff!'

On Pargo day, which was a monthly event, the neighbouring traders brought their wares to the market-place in San Domingos. On this day the normally sober area was full of noise and bustle and music. It had expanded to five times its normal size and was crowded with people. All the goods had been laid out on the ground beneath huge, colourful umbrellas which cast a welcome shade. Although it was not yet 11 o'clock, the sun was very hot and Joanna was grateful for her parasol. Leo wore his boater at a jaunty angle, but otherwise appeared quite unaffected by the temperature. Everywhere they looked there were tethered donkeys and the carts that had brought people into the village.

'They come from miles away,' Leo informed her. 'Look at those chickens.'

He pointed to five large brown hens, each with a string around one leg tethering it to the wheel of a low cart. A woman stood beside the cart, guarding a straw 'nest' in which a few dozen eggs nestled.

Joanna said, 'But if she sells the hens as well, she won't have any more eggs.'

'They've probably finished laying. They're for the pot!'

She looked at him with mock exasperation. 'Do you have to know everything about *everything*?' she asked, but he was now bending down to peer into a cage full of live rabbits. To one side of her, Joanna saw a man examining the ears of a young kid which bleated shrilly. Beside the old woman a child of maybe ten or eleven shelled peas into a bucket. There were wicker cages full of bright finches who fluttered ceaselessly from branch to branch. A large white gander rested royally in a shallow basket. Something in a large sack moved restlessly, but without any sound.

Leo said, 'You could give your sister a piece of pottery – except that it might get broken in the post.'

'There's Suzanne, too.'

It was noticeable that most of the shoppers were women, although there was a sprinkling of elderly men. All the rest were underground, she supposed. Many of the traders were men, however; they all wore large-brimmed hats, and many had divided leather aprons tied round their legs. Some of the women wore brighter clothes, shawls and headscarves, even straw hats which Joanna would have called panamas. The older women were all in black and Joanna assumed that these were either married or widowed; however, determined not to allow Leo to show off his knowledge again, she did not ask.

Beyond the flowers, fruit and livestock they came upon the handicrafts. Brightly painted plates and mugs, earthenware pots in an amazing array of shapes and sizes. There were dozens of handwoven rugs in blues and pinks and multicoloured stripes; there were tables full of lace and hand-embroidered shawls. Amongst so much colour and excitement Joanna felt her mood lighten and she found herself humming to the music supplied by five guitar players.

Leo sidled up to her and whispered, 'I spy the doctor's wife on the port beam!'

But Sarah Barratt was engrossed in her shopping and did not see them.

'What are the young trees people are carrying, Leo?' Joanna asked.

'Orange and lemon trees. You haven't bought anything yet.'

'I think I'll buy them each some lace. Then Mama can make it up into new collars.'

She was paying for the lace when a voice behind her said, 'Miss Joanna! Oh, what luck!' and she turned to find Andrew Shreiker, his face wreathed in smiles. A little way behind him, Leo grimaced in despair and she struggled to keep her face straight as she greeted him.

'Mr – I mean Andrew. What brings you here? I thought you were all at work.'

'I've got the morning off; I put in some extra hours when we walled off the hot ground. You really must try to get permission to go underground. I'll ask your uncle, if you like.'

'That's very kind, but Mr Benbridge has made some kind of arrangement already.' This was not quite true. She held up the lace. 'For my sisters at home,' she told him. Leo, she noticed, had slipped away into the crowd. She was at the mercy of her admirer, she thought wryly.

'I'm looking forward to the party,' he told her. 'I hope you will save me a great many dances. I shall be first in line with my programme.'

'I'm sure we will dance together, Mr . . . Andrew.'

He gazed at her earnestly. 'Would you allow me to hold your arm, Miss Joanna? The crowd is rather boisterous, I think.' Without waiting for an answer he tucked her left arm through his and, with a proprietorial air, patted her hand. Leaning closer, he whispered, 'You have made me the happiest man in San Domingos!'

She came to an abrupt halt. 'I have?'

'But of course! Knowing that some day you and I will be—'

She pulled her arm free and stared at him in growing agitation. 'Mr Shreiker! You should not take anything for granted. I have only said that I would consider the matter, I have never said anything definite. It is most unfair of you to . . . to assume . . . oh, no, Mr Shreiker. You must not assume . . .' Her voice trailed away and she regarded him helplessly.

He looked stricken. 'But, Miss Joanna! Your aunt led me to believe . . . Oh, do please forgive me if I have been presumptuous.'

'What has my aunt said?' she demanded. 'Please tell me. Andrew, I think I have a right to know what has been said about me since I have said very little to my aunt on the subject.'

His expression was abject. 'It is a little difficult,' he began. 'That is, I'm sure she meant it kindly—'

'I doubt that very much!'

'She suggested that she would use her influence to persuade you – that for your sake it would be best. She hinted that – well, I already knew there had been an unhappy . . . affair of the heart and she rather— Oh dear.' Oblivious of the crowd around them, he took hold of her free hand. Her other hand fidgeted with the handle of her parasol. 'No, please don't draw away from me, Miss Joanna. If you only knew how much I care for you! If you knew that I would never willingly make you unhappy . . .'

Joanna withdrew her hand and clasped them both round the handle of the parasol. She took a deep breath. 'Mr Shreiker –'

He mouthed the word 'Andrew' but she ignored him.

'I have not committed myself to you *ever*, and until I do I beg you not to take anything for granted. I may discover that I love you and that will be—'

'That will *be wonderful*, Miss Joanna!'

'Wonderful, as you say.' She swallowed. 'But I may not discover anything of the kind. In the meantime, I beg you not to put your trust in my aunt. She does not like me, Mr – Andrew. Oh, yes! I can see exactly how it was. My aunt suggested that I was lucky to find such an upstanding young man who would be prepared to take on such a difficult young woman. Isn't that about it?'

He looked embarrassed. 'Not exactly but – I said I adored you and I wanted to marry you in spite of any . . . any problems. I told her that your father might be a dustman for all I cared! You see, I do really love you.'

'I wish you didn't!' she cried. 'Suppose he was a common thief? What then?'

'It would make no difference at all!'

She had started to walk on and he hurried to keep alongside, elbowing a way through the crowd. She thought suddenly of the grave in the English cemetery and said, 'He might be a murderer!'

'I don't *care!*' he cried. 'He could be Attila the Hun! I would still want to marry you! Please don't turn me down, Miss Joanna. Won't you wait and see? A few months . . . a few years . . . I'll wait for you.'

Suddenly she realized there were tears in her eyes and she rubbed them away impatiently. 'You're a good, kind man, Andrew,' she said, 'and I won't turn you down just yet if you don't want me to, but I'm not saying "Yes" either. Please don't rush me. I need time – a lot of time.'

Now she saw the relief in his nice brown eyes and fleetingly wondered yet again if she could ever return his love. It would solve so many problems.

He said, 'And you will save me plenty of dances?'

'Of course I will.' She looked round and saw Leo hovering hopefully nearby. 'Oh, there's my cousin!' she said quickly. 'Let's join him, shall we?'

And, taking hold of Andrew's hand, she hurried towards Leo, telling herself in no uncertain words that she had had enough romance for one day.

Chapter Twelve

THE NEXT DAY the carriage was being connected up to the train to collect the captain of the *Roda*, one of the steamships which had docked the previous day at Vila Real. Hugh Simpkins had been invited to dinner with the Grosvenors and Elliot decided to take the morning off and go down to Pomerao to meet him. It was really an excuse to spend time with Joanna, who willingly accepted the invitation to accompany him. Leo pleaded to be allowed to join them but his father refused; he had missed too many study hours, Elliot insisted, and was sadly behind with his homework. He reminded Leo that the long periods he spent in Portugal were only to be justified if he accomplished plenty of work so that he was not at a disadvantage when he returned to his school. Normally he was prepared to spend a couple of hours working most mornings, but Joanna's presence was proving a great distraction.

'You've been idling, young man!' Elliot told him sternly. 'And now you must catch up. An hour's Latin and an hour's arithmetic. Tomorrow I shall ask Joanna to give you some mental arithmetic.' Leo groaned. 'You *need* it, Leo. Everyone needs to be able to add up without the help of pencil and paper!'

'But I'm good at it already. I got good marks at the end of last term.'

'Did you? What are eight nines?'

'Um. . .' Leo looked appealingly at Joanna who mouthed the answer, but too late.

'Eleven elevens?' Elliot demanded. 'Seven twelves? Nine —'

'It's not fair! You're going too fast, Papa!' His round face was flushed with indignation and the humiliation of being found wanting in front of Joanna.

Elliot pointed to the door. 'Go to your room and work, young man! And no slacking! I shall want to see how much you have done when we get back.'

Leo went out looking very disgruntled and, leaving him to his solitary labours, Joanna followed her uncle down to the yard where the carriage was being coupled on to the back of the line of wagons. The rear of the train was still in the loading shed, part of a vast structure with a high ridged roof which deafeningly reflected the sound of metals on metal. The front of the train projected outside and consisted of three small engines each with a tall smokestack, harnessed one behind the other. There were perhaps a dozen wagons in the line and each of them groaned under a full weight of ore. To Joanna's inexperienced eye it seemed that the engines would never be able to cope with their heavy load, although she remembered from the day of her arrival that this could not be the case. She found the bustling railway yard noisy, dusty and utterly bewildering, but presumed that to the initiated there was order to be found amidst the chaos.

Elliot held Joanna's hand tucked into his arm, as though he was proud of her and wanted everyone to know that he was her uncle. If her conscience had been clear she would have found this quite touching, but in the circumstances she felt a fraud. She was thankful when, after much shunting and shouting, the train was declared ready and they could climb inside the empty carriage, away from the curious eyes of the men.

They settled themselves comfortably, and she was pleased to see that her uncle, sitting opposite her, appeared to be in a very happy frame of mind. She waited for the inevitable question.

'So how are you enjoying my little kingdom?' he asked.

'It's quite fascinating,' she replied. That, at least, was true.

'You think you're going to like it here, then? You may want to stay – is that it?'

He looked so eager to hear her say 'Yes' that she said it, stifling the doubts that surged into her mind. She might not want to stay, but now it seemed she had no alternative.

'And my mother, poor soul – she is not proving too tiring for you? Catherine was sure you would be a comfort to her. She is difficult at times, but then at others she can be almost her old self. Old age is never easy – so I'm told!' he added hastily.

'I think she likes me.'

'I'm sure she does, my dear. Who could *not* like you? I'm quite delighted that you've joined us. We all are – especially young Leo. It is company for him. He manages well enough alone – he's very independent – but it's always more fun to have a companion.' He leaned forward. 'Not that you must let him monopolize your time, Joanna. Be firm with him if you must. He can take it, he's a most resilient child.'

'We get along splendidly,' she assured him.

From outside there was a flurry of shouts and the train shuddered. It gave a jolt and then another, and then with a loud whistle was finally in motion, grinding its way along the track. Faces flashed past the window, then the train was out of the yard and gathering a little speed.

Elliot smiled. 'Not the fastest form of transport, but pretty reliable. Can't recall when we had the last breakdown – can't afford them. Time's money, and the ships at Pomerao are waiting on us. Ships at Vila Real are waiting on *them* – that's how it goes.' He settled back with a satisfied smile, and Joanna thought that if it were not for his dreadful wife he would probably be a happy man. Maybe he managed to be happy in spite of her . . .

He leaned forward and patted her knee. 'I want you to be happy here, my dear. If anything troubles you, come and tell me and I'll soon put it right. Can't have you being unhappy.'

She wondered uneasily if he had heard about her distress after the arrival of the letter from her mother. Leo would have said nothing. Catherine did not know. Steven Benbridge certainly would not have mentioned it.

'I'm not unhappy, Uncle Elliot,' she said, and smiled to reassure him.

'You enjoyed the Pargo, I hear? Quite a gathering, isn't it? Quite a sight. Leo says you bought some lace.'

'Yes. And a painted plate for my bedroom.'

'Splendid! That's what I like to hear. We may be in the back of beyond, but we do find plenty to do. We amuse ourselves here. Have you had a game of tennis yet? You must have noticed the court near the Palacio. Not the best in the world – it needs some attention. I could give you a game one day, if you like – when it gets slightly cooler. Too hot at present until late evening, and then of course you can't see the damned ball!' He laughed aloud and slapped his knee. 'You do play, I suppose?'

'A little.'

'We might make up a foursome: you, me, Leo and – Mr Shreiker?' He laughed again.

'Oh.' She groaned inwardly. 'You've heard about that.'

'A little bird told me. And why shouldn't he fall for you, eh? A pretty girl like you! I'm surprised they haven't all declared themselves head over heels!' He beamed proudly at her.

Quickly she said, 'I haven't encouraged him. I told him I'm not yet eighteen.'

'But you soon will be, my dear. Your birthday is this

month! I'm wondering what you would like for your eighteenth birthday? A rather special day!'

'Oh, please! I really don't expect anyone to make a fuss.' She was puzzled. How on earth did he know her birthday? He had never remembered it while she was in England.

The train had now settled into a steady if somewhat erratic pace, juddering and swaying along the narrow track. Wisps of smoke from the engines occasionally floated past the carriage window. Joanna sat quietly for a while watching the softly rounded countryside, soothed by the emptiness of both land and sky. Then, hardly knowing why, she asked, 'What happened to Juanita, Uncle Elliot?'

The effect on him was sudden and in some way unnerving. He sat bolt upright and stared at her, all the good humour gone from his face. At once she regretted her question, but it was out and she could only curse her stupidity.

It was a whisper: 'Juanita!' He shook his head and added, 'Oh, my dear girl!'

'I'm sorry . . .' she began, but there was no way she could undo the mischief. He had paled and his right hand was a tight fist balled against his chest as he turned away from her and stared fixedly out of the window. Miserably she waited, silently, appalled at her mistake. When at last he turned back to her he asked, 'Who told you about her?'

'Grandmother. She showed us a photograph of the three maids in their new uniforms . . .'

'Oh, yes!' For a moment a smile touched the corners of his mouth, then it was gone. 'The new uniforms! I had forgotten.' He drew a deep breath and looked straight into Joanna's face. 'I won't hide the truth,' he said. 'At least, I'll tell you what I can . . .'

He looked so sad that Joanna could hardly bear it. Leaning forward, she told him urgently, 'It doesn't matter, Uncle Elliot! Don't tell me. Why should you? I've no right to ask. Please forgive me.' She had taken his left hand in hers, and now he brought down the right to cover it.

But he went on as though she had not spoken. 'Juanita was one of our maids. A very sweet girl. Clever. Quick to learn. She – she ...' He closed his eyes as though in anguish and Joanna found herself squeezing his hands. 'We discovered – that is, my mother discovered that Juanita was with child. Five months pregnant, in fact. She had been so frightened that she had told no one. Poor Juanita!' He opened his eyes and they were dark with grief.

'Wouldn't the child's father marry her?'

He said slowly, 'It wasn't that simple. The father was ... one of us.'

Joanna stared at him. 'You mean English?'

'Yes. He wanted to marry her, but my mother was against it. She was a very strong woman – morally I mean. She was against the marriage; said it could never work. In those days it wasn't done to intermarry – still isn't, of course – and she feared the scandal.' He released her hands suddenly and leaned back in the seat as though the telling of it exhausted him. 'She sacked the girl. She was quite ruthless towards her ... showed her no pity. My sister Agatha was here at the time and she argued Juanita's case quite passionately. She also thought the marriage should go ahead and there was a terrible quarrel.' He shook his head at the memory. 'A most dreadful scene. She and my mother were well matched! The weeks drifted by and rumours started, the way they do; it even seemed we might have trouble at the mine because of it. Time passed and nothing was decided, then suddenly Juanita went into an early labour. No one was prepared for it. We were playing bridge, and they came for the doctor. My mother insisted it must be a false alarm and she and Agatha argued. The doctor wanted to go to his patient, but my mother insisted we should finish the rubber! Told them to fetch the midwife instead.' He shook his head. 'I can still hardly believe how badly we all behaved that night ... it was quite shameful. I don't excuse myself; I should have insisted that Barratt went to her. I have never forgiven myself – or my mother!'

Softly Joanna asked, 'Did she die? Juanita?'

He nodded. 'By the time the doctor arrived she was beyond help, though he did what he could.'

Joanna felt a shiver run through her as she imagined the scene all those years ago. 'And that cross in the English cemetery. Is that her grave?'

'Yes and no. She was buried in the Portuguese cemetery, but – somebody put up that cross in the English cemetery. A reminder, lest we forget.' He put both hands over his face.

'And the child? Did the child live?'

Slowly he lowered his hands, but did not look at her. 'They said not,' he muttered. 'They said it had died, but that was a lie. It was adopted secretly. Agatha arranged it all without my mother's knowledge ... My mother has never mentioned the tragedy from that day to this; not one word of regret. A very hard woman ... until now, that is. Now that her mind is confused, she doesn't know what she says. Obviously it comes back to her and preys on her mind.'

'How terribly sad.' The words sounded so inadequate.

He swallowed hard and Joanna longed to take him in her arms and comfort him.

'We all have to live with that, Joanna,' he told her. 'It's not easy. Remorse is such a burden. You know you cannot undo the wrong, so you are never going to be free of the guilt. A young woman lost her life and we are to blame – as guilty as if we had taken a gun and shot her. I remember Juanita every day of my life, do you know that? It's the first thing I think of when I wake in the morning, and it's with me when I fall asleep ... How different it all could have been! How much happier. I was such a coward. I should have stood up to my mother; supported Agatha. Instead I said nothing.'

'But it wasn't up to you,' said Joanna. 'It was up to the child's father, surely?'

He looked confused, then said quickly, 'I mean that I

should have supported him against my mother.' He drew a long shuddering breath and stared out of the window.

The train veered unsteadily round a curve in the track and then they were upright again. Joanna searched for something to say that might ease her uncle's sorrow, but words eluded her. Then suddenly he frowned and faced her once more. 'Joanna, I must ask you never to let your aunt know of this. It all happened before we were married, and there seemed no point in telling her – no reason to burden her with such awful knowledge. Do you understand, my dear? I felt I could trust you. That you were entitled to know – since you asked. But not Catherine; she would never understand. In her eyes it would blacken the family name, and I think it would destroy her.'

'I won't tell her; I promise.'

'Nor Leo.'

'Of course not.' She thought quickly; she would have to pretend to lose interest in the mystery.

He smiled shakily at her and, without quite knowing why, she moved to sit next to him. He put an arm around her shoulders and drew her close.

'Our secret then, Joanna,' he whispered.

'Our secret,' she agreed.

And they sat together for the last ten minutes of the ride and Joanna, drawn to him by his grief, hoped that she was of some comfort to him.

*

When the train stopped they climbed down and returned the greetings of Senor Louro.

To Joanna he said in English, 'And how you like San Domingos? How you like Portugal? Is good country, no?'

Leo had taught her to say 'Very good' and she thought she might venture a short phrase. '*San Domingos muito bem!*' she replied, and was rewarded with a bellow of laughter for her atrocious accent.

'She loves Portugal,' said Elliot. 'Adores it!' He winked at her, but she could see that he was still shaken by their recent conversation. 'We'll walk out to the end of the jetty, Senor, and see if we can spot any fish. Oh, don't worry. I won't let her fall in!' To Joanna he whispered, 'He's a bit of an old woman on the quiet! Fusses a lot, but he's sound enough; takes it all very seriously. A good man for the job. I'll be hard put to find a successor when he gives up.'

They walked to the end of the jetty, where the first engine now stood silent but steaming. The driver had dismounted and was wiping his hands with a rag. He nodded to them both but said nothing.

'Not a word of English!' said Elliot. 'After all these years. Very shy with us, but he's a damned good driver.' He peered down over the end of the curving jetty and Joanna, beside him, felt rather insecure. She was not particularly good with heights and the drop from the jetty to the surface of the water was at least thirty feet.

'You can sometimes spot a lamprey or two from up here,' he told her. 'Big beggars, like large eels. Quite a delicacy.' He shouted something in Portuguese to a woman who watched from the roadside, but she shook her head. 'I was asking if anyone had caught one recently. Sometimes they are happy to sell one, and Christina prepares it in the traditional way. Delicious! But no luck today.' Together they stared down into the dark, quickly-flowing river. 'Flounders, too, but less common. And something called "saboga". Don't know that fellow.'

At last, to Joanna's relief, they made their way back along the jetty to the road, and from there down the steps to the little landing-stage where the ship would tie up. They stood in the shade of the jetty and chatted to Senor Louro, who had joined them. It seemed an eternity since Joanna had arrived at this same landing-stage, tired and apprehensive after her long journey from England. Then she had been determined to hate everything and everybody but so much had happened in the past few weeks. Was she the same person, she wondered? She had had almost no time to consider the implications of her uncle's confidences, but she did know that she felt closer to him because of them. The glimpse into his heart had moved her, and the anguish he expressed over his mistake found an echo in her own heart. It was possible, then, to live with the shadow of regret and to make something of what remained. If that were so, then might she not have a chance to salvage what was left of her own life? Her uncle's revelations had saddened her, but they had also given her hope and she no longer felt isolated by the 'crime' she had committed. Her uncle, too, had sinned – and so had Grandmother and the doctor. No wonder they wished to forget! No wonder that they resented her questions. Such a past was best forgotten. Perhaps, in some distant future, her own particular skeleton would be relegated to the cupboard . . . And just when she thought she had lived it down, a pert young nobody like herself would spring up and rattle the cupboard door, demanding the key! How she would hate her prodding and prying . . .

'Here she comes!'

A shout from her uncle broke into her uneasy thoughts, and she relinquished them gratefully as the neat little steamship nosed her way round the bend and puffed towards them. Five minutes later the ropes were made fast and the *Roda* was secure. Their visitor had arrived.

*

Dinner that evening was a comparatively grand affair and Catherine, at one end of the table, took pleasure in the elegant scene as she sipped her wine. There were nine at table: the family (excluding her mother-in-law), the doctor and his wife, Steven Benbridge (seated on her right), Andrew Shreiker (opposite Joanna) and Hugh Simpkins. The Italian crystal sparkled the length of the table and the finest bone china dinner service, a family heirloom, was in use. Catherine felt that she was shown to best advantage on these occasions – a beautiful woman of wealth and breeding playing host to a group of people who could surely recognize her qualities. She could have wished for a more prestigious group of visitors, but San Domingos lacked society as such and she must satisfy herself with her husband's staff.

She had married slightly beneath her, nobody could deny that, but she had been eager to escape from an ailing mother and Elliot's posting to Portugal offered exactly that. Elliot had been astonished when she accepted him, but they had been brought together rather hurriedly by his mother, an old friend of the family, who had been determined to see him settled – and 'out of mischief' as she had laughingly put it! They had now been married for many years, but Catherine had enjoyed only one of them. The first year had been exciting – meeting new people, making a new life, refurbishing the house at San Domingos. Friends had come out from England to see her in her new role as wife to the General Administrator of San Domingos but, sadly, few of them came more than once. Elliot was inclined to be moody, and she quickly discovered that his mother was a power to be reckoned with. Two women sharing the reins was disastrous and there were quarrels. Elliot, torn between his mother and his wife, withdrew from the fray and immersed himself in his work. At that time the English compound had been a dull place and in desperation Catherine had initiated a round of dinner-parties with bridge, picnics and outings. With some justification, she felt she could claim the credit for whatever social life existed.

Now with a quick tilt of her head she emptied her glass and, catching Leo's eye, put a warning finger to her lips. He was talking too much as usual, and poor Sarah was having to listen. No doubt she was longing to talk to the captain, who sat opposite her and was telling rather outrageous stories about life at sea. Dear Leo! He had arrived late in their marriage, but was none the less welcome. For a long period after their wedding Catherine did not conceive; when at last she did, she had lost two girls in succession, both stillborn. Leo's arrival had been greeted with huge delight and, with the doctor's approval, Catherine had then felt able to declare the prospect of further childbearing dangerous. Elliot, happy with his son and heir, had promptly agreed that to risk Catherine's health was out of the question. So now she had a child, a husband and plenty of money – an enviable lifestyle, in fact – but she was not happy. Deep down she doubted that she ever would be, for her husband could not, or *would* not, give her what she longed for, which was worship.

Catherine's mother had been set upon a pedestal by the man she married, and had enjoyed his passionate devotion until the day he died. As a child Catherine also had basked in her father's adoration, and had tried to be all that he wanted. Pretty in ribbons and flounces, a doll-like child whom her father could show off to his friends, she had endured nightly discomfort with her hair in curling-rags so that during the day she could toss the little ringlets which Papa found so charming. She had sat on his knee and recited her nursery rhymes and he had been enchanted. Always enchanted. He had called her 'the little princess', and she had felt safe and loved and aware of her true worth.

Catherine expected nothing less from Elliot. She craved the continued appreciation which she felt was due to her as a beautiful adult; she was still the same person, still the princess. However, Elliot had never adored her. He had said flattering things to her, and had bought her lavish gifts, but something was subtly lacking in his attitude towards her. He did not appear to consider himself the fortunate man Catherine imagined him to be. He could be moody and quiet at times, and sometimes she believed that he invented work so that he could escape from her to the Palacio. She had waited in vain for him to show her the blind devotion she felt to be her due. In time she began to think he took her for granted.

She glanced now along the table to where he sat, immaculate in his evening-dress suit and black bow-tie. Handsome, perhaps, but there was no way she thought resentfully that he could take her father's place in her heart. Catherine saw in other men's eyes what she wanted to see in his – admiration and passionate desire – and she encouraged them to express these feelings in the hope that Elliot's eyes would be opened to her finer qualities. She had been physically unfaithful only once, and Sturton had been stupid enough to confess! What fools men were! But she did flirt unashamedly. However, far from becoming more appreciative of his lovely wife, Elliot had simply become jealous and then disenchanted. Now he paid her so little attention that she was forced to rely totally on other men for it.

Catherine knew that she had lost her youthful bloom. Her complexion was still good, but there were shadows under her eyes. The Portuguese climate had not helped, and without the many creams she used her skin would have been dry and lifeless by now. Soon she would not be a 'pretty doll', and she dreaded the eventual approach of old age with something akin to panic.

But tonight, with the help of the wine, she was keeping those dark thoughts at bay. She inclined her head gracefully towards Steven Benbridge and smiled brilliantly at his humorous remark, imagining herself as he would see her – soft mouth curving, even white teeth, bright eyes, shining hair. So far Steven had not fallen under her spell, but she was determined that he should. Sturton's summary departure had hurt her more than she would ever admit, and his letter to Elliot had left her lonely and afraid. But if Elliot thought that he was safe, he had made a big mistake. Soon Steven Benbridge would be putty in her hands. He would desire her as fiercely as Sturton had done; would cherish her as she deserved. Catherine lifted her wine-glass and drank deeply, then signalled to Christina to refill her own and any other empty glasses. Probably she was drinking too much, she thought vaguely, but she no longer cared. She wanted to be rid of her inhibitions and a few drinks would help her to take a few risks.

'The captain is captivating the ladies!' Steven remarked with a smile. 'I always think seafaring men have an advantage over the landlubbers – theirs is a tough but glamorous existence.'

She leaned a little closer and murmured, 'He doesn't attract *me*, Mr Benbridge. Don't most sailors have a wife in every port? That doesn't impress me. I fly my kite a little closer to home.'

A quick glance at his face showed her that either he missed the significance of this remark or chose to ignore it.

He said, 'Your husband is a very fortunate man, Mrs Grosvenor. We are all envious.'

Charmingly said but rather general, she thought impatiently. Why didn't he make the first overture? It shouldn't be left to the woman.

'I sometimes feel a little neglected, Mr Benbridge,' she told him with a small pout. Her eyes felt heavy and for a moment she closed them and pressed her fingers against the lids. Too much red wine; she should have stayed with the white. 'My husband's first love is the mine. San Domingos has stolen his heart!' she said carefully. 'You might call it an obsession.'

'Or a passion.'

She shook her head a little too sharply and felt dizzy. 'Oh dear!'

'Is anything wrong?' he asked kindly.

'No. Nothing . . .' She tried to remember what they had been talking about. 'Oh, yes! My husband's passion for the mine. San Domingos is the other woman in my life!' She laughed and it sounded a little tipsy. 'San Domingos!' she repeated. 'Oh, Lord! A mistress would be so much easier to fight!'

As she laughed she saw his gaze stray towards Joanna and her impatience grew. The girl was no beauty. Not yet. Later she might well be, but her face and form were still too gauche. 'I almost envy that child,' she said. 'You see how Mr Shreiker looks at her? He adores her. No doubt if he were a poet he would write verses to her! I daresay he dreams about her and whispers her name in his sleep.' The smile she attempted was a long time coming and felt a little lopsided.

'Do you think so?'

She fancied his tone was a little colder. 'That's why I envy her.' Was her voice a little slurred? Did it sound soft and alluring or merely foolish? If only she knew ... She went on regardless, 'My husband has never worshipped me, Mr Benbridge. Can you believe that? He is not that kind of man, you see. My father was; he was a perfect gentleman and they are rare. An endangered species like the dodo. They will soon be extinct!' She wanted to put her hand over his, but for that she was still a little too sober. If only he would put *his* hand over hers!

'Are you that kind of man, Mr Benbridge?' she asked. 'Are you the worshipping kind – Steven?' There! She had gone as far as she dared and the rest was up to him. If he could not see an opportunity when it bit him on the leg, then damn him!

He said coolly, 'I don't think so,' and went on, 'Andrew Shreiker is a very promising engineer. He should do well here – and then apparently he wants to move on to Australia. Quite an adventurous young man.'

It was almost a slap in the face! It was most certainly a snub, she thought hazily. He had chosen to ignore her use of his Christian name. What was the matter with him? Had he meant to insult her? Was that it? Was she being insulted

at her own table by one of her own guests? If she was . . .
For a moment she thought she swayed and gripped the
table edge tightly for support. Breathe deeply, that was it.
Breathe deeply . . .

'Please, ma'am, shall we clear the main course now?'

She realized with a start that Christina had come into the
room with Liliane. Well, let them clear away. She nodded,
one hand to her head which was beginning to ache. She
had drunk too much and only knew for sure when it was
too late. Looking vaguely around the table at her guests,
she saw that they all seemed to be enjoying themselves
heartily. Everyone except her. The boar had been excellent,
cooked to perfection. The dessert was a delicious trifle, and
there were cheeses and fruit to round off the meal. Catherine leaned back in her chair, trying to concentrate but
finding it difficult. They were all having a wonderful time,
but she was being snubbed at her own table. For one
dreadful moment she thought she was going to cry but
she held her napkin up to her lips and willed back the
tears. She heard Steven Benbridge ask, 'Are you unwell,
Mrs Grosvenor?'

What a hypocrite! Oh, how she hated the man! He insulted her and then pretended to care . . .

As though from a great distance, she heard her own
voice say, 'Elliot, I think I —'

And Steven Benbridge said, 'Excuse me, doctor, but I
think Mrs Grosvenor is a little faint. The heat, perhaps.'

Then the old fool of a doctor was fussing round, and
that little madam Joanna was helping her to her feet, and
they were taking her out of the dining room and up the
stairs to her room . . . Well, let them. What did she care?
They would never miss her. Elliot would hardly notice her
absence. Damn Elliot! Damn them all . . .

Five minutes later she was tucked up in bed and fast
asleep. It would have been the final blow to her pride to
know that she snored.

Chapter Thirteen

THE FOLLOWING DAY Joanna had just come down to breakfast when Liliane arrived with a note for her from Nurse Williams, which said, 'We are having some trouble with our bath. Can you help? Wear an apron!'

Joanna smiled, swallowed a few mouthfuls of stewed figs and then abandoned the idea of having any more.

'Serves you right,' she told herself cheerfully, 'for being so late up.'

She made her way into the kitchen and was greeted by Christina and Liliane. Her request for an apron was quickly met; Christina hurried to the linen cupboard and returned with a large, highly starched pinafore with frilly straps which she slipped over Joanna's head, while Liliane giggled delightedly. Joanna tied the straps behind her back and found that the apron covered most of her blue dress. In fact, the maids' dresses were almost the same colour and Liliane was quick to point out the similarity.

'You maid!' she told Joanna. 'You *criada*!'

'*Criada?* Is that what I am?'

Liliane pointed to herself, to Christina and then to Joanna. '*Tres criadas!*'

Smiling, Joanna twirled round to give them both a better view. Excitedly Liliane held up a hand to delay Joanna's departure; she rushed out of the room and quickly returned with a starched cap with trailing white ribbons. Laughing, Joanna bent her head and the girl fastened it on for her.

'Is that better?' Joanna asked.

Liliane clapped her hands with delight, but Joanna caught a strange expression on Christina's face – confusion, shock, perhaps, and not a little doubt. But as soon as their eyes met Christina glanced away and when Joanna looked up again she was smiling.

'You go quickly!' she told Joanna. 'Nurse wait for you.'

Joanna needed no second bidding and hurried along the passage to the rear of the house. She knocked on the door of her grandmother's room and entered. The hip-bath was standing in the middle of the room half-full of water, and three jugs containing more water stood ready beside it. Two large, fluffy towels waited on a chair beside the bath, and a bath-mat was in place. A tall three-sided screen blocked the view from the window, and clean clothes had been hung over the wooden clothes-horse at the end of the bed.

Nurse Williams, looking flustered and cross, said, 'Oh there you are!' to let Joanna know that she was later than expected. With a toss of her head she indicated her patient who was sitting up in bed in a blue silk bedjacket, with her crossed arms held close around her chest. The photograph album was open on the coverlet in front of her.

'We don't want our bath!' Nurse explained. 'We don't even want to get out of bed, do we?' This last question was addressed to the old lady, who glared in reply.

'It's too cold!' she said in a peevish voice. 'Too cold!' She looked down at the album and said, 'It's gone, Nurse. I tell you it's gone!'

The nurse tutted impatiently. 'It's fallen out, that's all. I've told you already. We'll soon find it.' Her voice changed slightly. 'After we've had our bath, I'll find it. How would that be, eh? First the bath, then the photograph.'

The nurse looked at Joanna to make sure she understood just what a problem her grandmother could be. In a low voice she said, 'Last night she slept with that wretched album under her pillow. She's suddenly refusing to be parted from it, like a child with a teddy bear!'

'What does she mean about the photograph?'

'Oh, a big fuss about nothing! One of the photographs is missing. She knows every page like the back of her hand, so I suppose it's fallen out, but it can't be far away.'

Joanna nodded.

'It's gone!' the old lady repeated. She gave Joanna a sharp look and asked, 'What are you doing here? You shouldn't be here.'

Joanna said cheerfully, 'I've come to help you with your bath, Grandmother.'

'Grandmother?' She stared at Joanna. 'Don't call me Grandmother!'

'But she is your grand-daughter, Mrs Grosvenor,' said the nurse. 'Joanna from England. You've seen her before – she comes to read to you.' She shook her head and sighed. 'The sad thing is she can only get worse,' she murmured. And in a hearty voice she tried again: 'Time for our bath! The water's all ready for you. Joanna and I—'

'It's too cold, I tell you! I want to stay in bed!'

'Of course it's not cold!' the nurse told her. 'It's August in Portugal and the temperature's way up high!' To Joanna she said, 'Sometimes she is like this. She gets it into her head that the weather is either too hot or too cold, and nothing I can say will persuade her otherwise. Wants to wear all the wrong clothes. It's very vexing! It makes such a late start to the day.'

'I suppose she can't help it,' Joanna ventured, but re-alized immediately that she had said the wrong thing.

The nurse stiffened. 'Of *course* she can't help it. I know that. You know it. We *all* know it. But the fact that she can't help it doesn't make it any easier to deal with!'

She glared at Joanna, who said quickly, 'I'm sorry. I know you're doing your best.'

'Young Mrs Grosvenor gives her a shaking sometimes, and that does the trick, but I'm not family and I don't think it's my place to shake her.'

She looked expectantly at Joanna who, seeing the direction of her thoughts, said hastily, 'I don't think I should shake her, either.'

They both looked at the old lady, who was staring at Joanna. Suddenly she pointed a quivering finger and said, 'What are you doing here? You shouldn't be here. I've told you I don't want to see you again.'

Nurse bridled. 'Now that's very naughty! Very unkind when Joanna has come to help us.' To Joanna she whispered, 'We'll try to take her by surprise, if you see what I mean. You pull away the bedclothes and I'll try to swing her legs round so that she's sitting with them over the side. Then before she knows what's happened she'll be half-way there.' Seeing Joanna's doubtful look she added, 'We have to be cruel to be kind, my dear! She can't stay here all day! Once we allowed her to get her own way, she'd never get up. Then she'd be bedridden in no time. At least she can still take a few steps, even if it's only into a chair on the patio. That helps the circulation and keeps the leg muscles flexible. It also varies her day, and the doctor says that's very important.'

The old lady pointed again at Joanna. She looked agitated. 'She shouldn't be here. She's dead!'

The nurse was shocked. 'Dead? Why, that's a wicked thing to say! I'm so sorry,' she said to Joanna. 'Take no notice of her. Dead, indeed! Whatever will she think of next?'

But Joanna's thoughts were slowly crystallizing. She had suddenly realized that her grandmother was confusing her with someone else. Now, too, she understood the expression she had seen on Christina's face. With her dark hair and eyes, and wearing the frilly apron and cap, she obviously reminded them of the young maid long since dead.

'Don't scold her, Nurse,' she said. 'It doesn't matter.' She could hardly explain to Nurse Williams what her uncle had confided to her about Juanita.

Looking thoughtfully at her grandmother, she said carefully, 'When you've had your bath I'll go away, Mrs Grosvenor. Not before. Do you understand me?' Ignoring the nurse's puzzled expression she went on, 'You don't want me here, do you?'

'No!' It was barely a whisper.

'I'll go when you've had your bath.'

The old lady hesitated, glancing from Joanna to the nurse and back again. 'You'll go? You promise?'

'I promise.'

Grandmother sighed deeply. Then she laid down the album and clumsily pushed back the bedclothes.

'Well I'm blessed!' exclaimed the nurse, looking at Joanna in astonishment. 'You certainly do have a way with you and no mistake.'

Together they helped the old lady from her bed, removed her clothes and held her steady while she stepped into the bath. Docile as a kitten, she allowed herself to be soaped and rinsed. She said nothing throughout the proceedings, but her eyes never left Joanna's face. At the appropriate time she dutifully stepped out again and Joanna and the nurse employed the fluffy towels to good effect. After dressing her, they guided her few faltering steps outside. There they sat her in a chair on the patio in the shade of a large palm tree from where she could watch Juan-Carlos. He was watering the plants which spilled from various earthenware pots on to the rough paving-stones, and gave them all a shy smile and said, *Bem dia, senoras.*

The tedious job of emptying the bath now began, and Joanna helped scoop out bucket after bucket of soapy water, which was emptied on to the soil around the trees and shrubs. Since fresh water was brought to San Domingos each day by mule, and water was a precious commodity, it was never wasted. When the bath had been emptied, wiped out and stowed away in the small kitchen, the damp towels were taken off to be washed. The soap was returned to its china holder, and the flannel was wrung out and laid across the window-sill to dry in the sun. Nightdress and bedjacket were shaken, folded neatly and stowed away in the appropriate cupboard. When at last the room had been restored to normal, Joanna went out alone on to the patio.

'I'm going now, Grandmother. Goodbye.'

The old lady stared at her for a long time without answering, then she reached out a trembling hand to touch her. Her expression was anguished. 'I'm so very sorry!' she said.

The words, hardly audible, were spoken with such genuine regret that Joanna's heart was touched. She knew exactly why her grandmother was apologizing; she too had made a mistake which could never be put right; for which she could never be forgiven. Joanna wondered if the burden of the guilty secret had been responsible for at least some of her grandmother's present condition. She wondered too if Juanita would have wished this frightful punishment upon her one-time enemy. How would she react if she were alive today and could see the old lady, broken both in mind and spirit? It seemed to Joanna that even Juanita would be moved to compassion if she could see her distress. And hadn't Jesus preached about the forgiveness of sins?

She leaned forward and said softly, 'Forget the past. Do you hear me? Let it go now,' and dropped a light kiss on her grandmother's cheek.

*

Leo stared rebelliously at the page of tables in front of him. Where on earth was Joanna? She had said she would be in after breakfast; she must be eating enough to feed an army! He lay face down on his bed, propped up on his elbows. He wanted her to come to put an end to this misery, but when she did there would be the further misery of mental arithmetic. He was quite pleased to have her around and she wasn't too bad . . . for a girl. She had been jolly brave over the wolf; most girls would have cried or fainted or sprained an ankle. But there were snags to her presence in San Domingos and mental arithmetic was one of them. Andrew Shreiker was another. On the ship coming out he had promised to teach Leo some card tricks, but instead he spent his time mooning about over Joanna. One or two polite reminders about the card tricks had fallen on stony ground, which was a pity.

'Five sevens are thirty-five, six sevens are thirty — No, forty . . . Six sevens are forty something – forty-two! Yes! Six sevens are forty-two, seven sevens are forty-nine, eight sevens are . . .' It was a funny thing, but figures always tripped him up. He was 'consistently sound' at Latin, and he wrote jolly good essays, and his Geography teacher said he had 'a good visual memory'. His piano tutor said he was 'very promising', although he hated practising. He could whack a cricket ball to the boundary on a good day with the wind in the right direction. (He had never actually done this, but he knew in his heart that it was only a matter of time.) And he could remember dates: 1066, the battle of Hastings! So why was he such a rabbit when it came to mental arithmetic?

'One nine is nine, two nines are —'

There was a knock on the door and he called out eagerly, 'Come in, whoever you are!'

'It's me.' Joanna came in, smiling. She was dressed like one of the maids. 'Who were you expecting?'

'I thought you might be Beelzebub,' he told her, 'come to offer me success in mental arithmetic in return for my soul. Beelzebub is the King of Darkness who —'

'I know who he is, thank you, Leo!' She sat down

without being asked. 'Sorry I'm so late, but I was summoned to help bath Grandmother.' She held out the apron as proof. 'I had a distress signal from Nurse Williams.'

He grinned. 'Didn't we want our bath this morning?' he mimicked.

'No, we didn't! Well, are you ready for the test? What do you want first?'

He pursed his lips and considered his options gloomily. 'Addition,' he said at last.

'Ten and ten and ten.'

'Thirty!' At least she was starting with something easy, he thought.

'Right.' She grinned. 'Subtraction?'

'Is that all?' He could hardly believe his luck. 'Is that all the addition?'

'That's all. Subtraction. Ten minus ten.'

A wide smile spread over his face. 'Nought! Division?'

'Fifty divided by ten.'

'Five!'

'Multiplication. Ten times ten.'

Gleefully he hurled himself off the bed. 'One hundred!'

'You're obviously a mathematical genius!' she told him.

'Will you tell Papa that?'

'I might. What's it worth?'

He closed the book with a bang and pushed it into the drawer of his desk. 'I could give you an interesting piece of information,' he told her.

She waited, eyebrows raised.

'Liliane's Uncle Jose is in the kitchen – at least, he was. The one who—' He mimed someone drinking deeply. 'They are trying to get rid of him before Mama finds out that he's here. He's been forbidden to come here on pain of sudden death, but they can't keep him out! Mama's gone to the library.' He suddenly assumed an air of tremendous innocence and said, 'I'm feeling rather thirsty, Joanna. Shall we go to the kitchen for a glass of lemonade?'

'What a good idea!'

They made their way along to the kitchen and, as Leo had promised, found Jose sprawled on the chair beside the stove. His head rested on the wall behind him and his eyes were closed. He breathed deeply as though asleep, but Leo knew better.

'He's drunk!' he whispered to Joanna. 'They're both a little scared of him.'

A subdued Christina, mixing a cake in a large white bowl, watched their unwanted visitor warily. She threw in some chopped almonds and cast an anxious look at the kitchen clock. Leo folded his arms firmly and studied the man, trying to see him through Joanna's eyes. He was overweight and his swarthy face was set in sullen lines; he reeked of alcohol and his clothes were stained.

Liliane glowered at her uncle from the direction of the sink, where she was up to her elbows in soapsuds and crockery.

Leo said loudly, 'Mama will be back soon from the Palacio.'

The sleeping man snored on.

Liliane hissed something in Portuguese and Leo said, 'She says he's a bad man; she doesn't like her uncle.'

Joanna said, 'It's not your fault, Liliane.'

Christina translated this, then to Joanna she said, 'We try send him away but he not go. He fall asleep.' She lifted her shoulders in a gesture of helplessness.

At that moment they heard the front door open and Leo recognized his mother's footsteps in the hall.

'It's Mama!' he cried and his words galvanized Liliane to further efforts. Darting forward, she caught at her uncle's sleeve and shook his arm until he woke, grumbling and belching. She began a torrent of Portuguese, obviously designed to urge him on his way, but he regarded her stupidly and shook himself free of her hand.

Christina stepped forward and also spoke sternly to him.

Leo could see that she was very nervous, and it suddenly seemed to him that as the only male present and as his father's representative, he ought to take command. He stepped forward and said loudly in English, 'It's time for you to go now, senor.' Pointing to the door so that there should be no misunderstanding, he repeated, 'Go, senor! *Compreendo?* You – go!' He hoped that Joanna was suitably impressed.

A positive flood of Portuguese greeted his efforts and the bleary eyes were turned menacingly in his direction. The heavy brows contracted into a frown, but somehow Leo stood his ground. He could not back down in front of the women. He stepped closer to Jose. 'You must go, senor!' he repeated, hoping no one would notice that his voice shook.

'Eh?!' A large hand shot out suddenly and grabbed him by the arm. More Portuguese – which Leo was glad he did not understand. He was beginning to think that coming into the kitchen had not been such a good idea after all. He wriggled to free his arm, but the man's fingers dug deeper and painfully into his flesh. Suddenly they heard Catherine's voice from the hall: 'Christina! Come here, please!'

Christina appeared paralysed with indecision, unwilling to leave them but reluctant to disobey her mistress's call.

Leo summoned all his courage and said sternly, 'Let go of my arm, you brute!' His voice, when it came out, was a little shrill, but he thought his words had an authoritative ring to them of which he was rather proud. However, the man seemed unimpressed and continued to mutter under his breath.

Liliane darted to the back door and flung it open, then indicated to her uncle in no uncertain manner that he should take himself through it. Her face was white and pinched and Leo knew what shame she must be feeling. Suddenly Christina rushed forward and took hold of Jose's arm, but he threw her off so roughly that she fell back against the dresser with a sharp cry of pain. Liliane screamed at her uncle as Joanna hurried to Christina and helped her to her feet.

To show his contempt for them all, Jose released Leo's arm and took a small knife from his belt. As he began to clean his fingernails, Leo hesitated. He was longing to step back out of reach of the man's hands, but that would look suspiciously like a retreat. Instead he said, 'Jose!' and pointed once more towards the back door. The whole incident was taking on nightmare qualities, and Leo was definitely regretting his suggestion that they visit the kitchen. He was also aware that he had brought Joanna into what was proving to be a dangerous situation. Joanna had helped Christina to a chair, but there was a small gash on the side of the maid's head from which blood trickled. Leo was beginning to wonder how it would all end. Perhaps it would be a good thing if his mother *did* come into the kitchen and discover Jose.

Joanna said, 'Leo! What can I do to help? Should I fetch Juan-Carlos?' She was obviously frightened and again he felt the weight of responsibility of his position. Rashly he grabbed hold of Jose's shoulder and tried to prise him forcibly from the chair. To his horror, the man put a brawny arm round him, pinioning him against his chest so tightly that he could hardly breathe.

Then he held the knife against Leo's throat.

For a moment there was a horrified silence, and then everything seemed to happen at once. While Leo gasped for breath, Christina gave a little moan and began to mutter something which he guessed was a prayer. Joanna rushed forward and began to tug at the arm which held the knife. Jose started to curse and mutter in Portuguese and, incongruously, Catherine's voice again called from the hall for Christina.

Liliane, at first frozen into inactivity, suddenly came to life and took matters into her own hands. Snatching a heavy saucepan from the sink, she swung it upwards and brought it down heavily upon her uncle's head. There was a horrible thud, then Leo felt the pressure on his chest relax as the arm fell away. Seizing his opportunity, Leo slipped to the floor and then scrambled away to the comparative safety of the far wall. They all watched, shocked and silent, as Jose stood up with a roar of anger, both hands to his head. No one spoke as he stumbled forward, his mouth open in dismay. He tottered, groaned, then fell slowly to his knees. Still no one moved. Leo's heart thudded within his chest as the big man closed his eyes, slowly lost his balance, crashed to the kitchen floor and lay still.

They all exchanged looks in which relief mingled with fear.

Leo was the first to recover, muttering, 'Serves him right!' but Liliane gave a little scream and dropped the saucepan with a clang. At a loss now, Leo looked hopefully at Joanna. Again Catherine's voice came, this time tinged with anger: 'Christina! Do you hear me?'

Ignoring her aunt, Joanna said, 'We must get him outside, quickly!'

Leo said, 'Yes. Let's drag him out!'

And without further consultation Joanna and Christina each took hold of one of Jose's arms while Leo and Liliane reached for his feet. Somehow they dragged the unconscious man out of the door and on to the patio.

'Well done!' said Leo as they rushed back into the kitchen and closed the door. He gave Liliane a pat on the back, and wished he had been the one to fell the wretch.

He looked up as his mother appeared from the hall and said, 'Christina! Are you deaf? I've been calling you for ages. I need —' She broke off abruptly. 'What's the matter with your face? It's bleeding.'

'My face? Oh —'

Leo said quickly, 'She bumped into the cupboard door.'

'How careless of you!' his mother replied. 'Well, ask Nurse to cover it for you and then come along to the morning-room.'

As Christina left the kitchen his mother's eye fell on Leo. 'What are you doing here?' she demanded.

'Er – I was – I came in for a glass of lemonade, Mama.'

Catherine turned her icy gaze on Joanna. 'And you, Joanna?'

'I came in to return the cap and apron. I've been helping to bath Mrs Grosvenor.'

Leo wondered if he dared nudge the saucepan further under the table, but already his mother's eyes had spotted it. 'What is that doing on the floor, may I ask? One of my best saucepans!'

Liliane, now thoroughly unnerved by events, burst into loud tears and Joanna murmured something about her not feeling too well. Catherine rolled her eyes expressively and said, 'Well, pick it up, Liliane, and stop this foolishness!' She turned on her heel and swept out of the kitchen.

As soon as she was out of earshot they all made a rush for the back door, where Liliane's uncle lay exactly as they had left him.

'*Esta morto!*' whispered Liliane, and crossed herself fearfully. Leo's heart skipped a beat; events were rapidly getting out of hand once more. He stared down at the still figure. Prone, Jose looked pathetic, but Leo was taking no chances and kept a respectful distance between them. *Was* he dead? Had Liliane saved his life by murdering her own uncle? Already he could see the headlines in all the newspapers:

Well-known local man battered to death in English compound in San Domingos! The murder weapon has been identified, and a young kitchen-maid is helping the police with their enquiries . . .

He wished that it had been Liliane whose life was threatened and he, Leo, who had wielded the saucepan. That way, he would have been the hero of the articles instead of the victim. Still, victim was better than mere onlooker. Joanna and Christina had not contributed very much to the drama. Probably he and Joanna would be called as witnesses, and they might even get their photographs in the paper. Papa would be furious because it would all reflect badly on the mine. But it would be a whole lot worse if Jose should die. Leo wondered how thick his skull was, and tried briefly to imagine how the saucepan would have felt on his own head. It was all wonderfully exciting, but on reflection he was glad that it *was* Liliane who had wielded the saucepan. He wondered if he and Joanna would save Liliane from the gallows by explaining that it was self-defence. She might not hang, but she would almost certainly go to prison. Leo imagined himself returning to his schoolmates, who would all be agog at the news of his adventure . . .

As one, they regarded Jose's prostrate form.

Leo asked, 'Is he dead, Joanna?'

'He's still breathing! See his chest move?' They watched it rise and fall.

'Oh, good!' said Leo, trying to hide his disappointment. 'What shall we do with him? We can't just leave him here. Or can we?'

Just then the big man opened his eyes and stared round at the three faces above him. He groaned and sat up, one hand to the back of his head, then said something explosive which made Liliane shiver.

Joanna asked, 'Are you all right now, senor? You fainted.' She winked at Leo. 'We carried you out here for some air.'

Quickly Liliane translated and her uncle nodded slowly. His earlier aggression appeared to have vanished – knocked out of him, Leo thought smugly. Jose shook his head in a bemused fashion as though he could not remember what had happened. Then he caught sight of Joanna in her white apron and cap and, as his jaw dropped, a look of horror came into his eyes. He struggled to his feet and began to back away.

'Juanita!' he whispered. 'Juanita!' His eyes rolled and he staggered a little but clutched at the nearest tree for support before continuing to back away down the path. Suddenly, with a muttered oath he turned and ran, stumbling wildly and almost missing the gate in his eagerness to be gone.

They watched him go with relief.

'So he's not dead, Liliane,' Leo told the maid.

She looked at him, still worried by what had happened.

'You saved my life,' he said, but she did not understand and he could not find the necessary Portuguese. He turned instead to Joanna. 'He thought you were Juanita! I wonder why.'

To his immense surprise she merely shrugged.

'He *did*, Joanna,' he insisted. 'He thought you were a ghost! He was scared to death!'

Strangely, she still showed very little interest and he followed her back into the kitchen feeling rather deflated. Probably still suffering from shock, he consoled himself. Liliane, sniffing loudly, went back to her washing-up, and Joanna took off the cap and apron. She appeared rather distracted and he began to feel a little sorry for her. Perhaps being mistaken for a dead person had unnerved her.

'It's not an omen or anything,' he assured her. 'You mustn't let it worry you.' When she still didn't answer, he said, 'Do you fancy a game of tennis? We've just got time before lunch. You can borrow my racquet and I'll use Papa's; he doesn't mind.'

For a moment he thought she was going to refuse, but then she nodded. She asked him if he felt all right after his ordeal and seemed really pleased when he said 'Yes'. Recalling the mental arithmetic test, he remembered how much he liked her and grinned as he hurried away to collect the racquets.

*

In the cool of the evening Joanna watered the plants in the garden at the front of the house. The small area of grass was shrivelled and brown from the intense heat, in spite of their best efforts to keep it green. The geraniums thrived somehow and the cacti were in their element — tall and grey and spiky. She had volunteered for the job because she knew Leo was unlikely to want to help her, and she particularly wished to be alone. Weeding was anathema to Leo, as he had explained on one occasion, proud of the word 'anathema'. A small yellow butterfly fluttered into her line of vision and she watched it briefly, telling herself that she really ought to make an effort to learn about the flora and fauna. Her increasing grasp of the language pleased her tremendously; she would branch out into botany and surprise Leo. Tomorrow she would go to the Palacio and look for a suitable book in the library.

After refilling the watering-can at the well, she continued with her task, but her mind was not on it; she was thinking about the morning's encounters with her grandmother and Jose. Both of them had mistaken her for the long-dead Juanita, and it could not only be because of the uniform. Liliane wore the same uniform and yet, so far as Joanna knew, she had never aroused the same misunderstanding. True, her uncle was hardly likely to confuse his own niece with anyone else, but Grandmother had done so. Grandmother had thought she was Juanita's ghost and, rather unkindly, Joanna had taken advantage of the fact. A startling suspicion was taking root in her mind. During the afternoon she had gone back into the old lady's room while she was taking her afternoon nap, and had asked to borrow the photograph album. As she suspected, the missing photograph which had so disturbed her grandmother was the one of the three maids in their new uniforms. Joanna believed that her uncle had taken it.

But why?

Why should her uncle want a photograph of a maid-servant who had died in childbirth many years ago? The obvious answer was that he feared it would distress his mother to see a constant reminder of an unhappy episode in her past. That was perfectly logical – so why did doubts crowd her mind? Because there was an alternative explanation that was almost too bizarre for her consideration. Forcing the suspicion to the back of her mind, she concentrated on what she knew. She looked like Juanita; Jose, too, had been confused by the likeness, and even Christina had given her a strange look when she had first dressed in the apron and cap.

She took a deep breath and felt a shudder run through her – not of fear but of anticipation. Joanna looked like Juanita, who had been in love with an Englishman by whom she had had a child. Her uncle had not said whether it was a girl or a boy, but Agatha had arranged for the child's adoption. The question was, was that in England or in Portugal? Her uncle had not specified. It might have been a boy and it might have grown up in Portugal. But suppose, just *suppose*, that the child had been a girl and that Aunt Agatha had taken it back to England with her and . . . Joanna took another deep breath . . . had taken it back to England and persuaded her own brother to adopt the girl!

She clasped her hands tightly together and closed her eyes. Suppose that had happened . . . then she, Joanna, was Juanita's illegitimate daughter and one of the men on the English compound was her father!

'Oh, God!' she whispered fearfully.

What had her uncle said? That the doctor wanted to go to her (meaning Juanita), but his mother (meaning Grand-mother) had insisted that he finish the rubber of bridge. So was the doctor the father of Juanita's child? Was he *her* father? Had her uncle said the man was married? It was all possible. And impossible! She was a foundling. Mark had told her all those years ago, and her parents had agreed. But that could have been a convenient lie. Presumably the doctor dare not tell his wife about the affair, so he agreed to the adoption. And Juanita had died. How convenient for all of them!

'Oh, my God!' she whispered. Did she want to know the truth? If the doctor was her father. . .

She pulled herself together. It could have been any of them. It could have been Oliver Jackson in the Assaying Department; or the Sturton who was banished for his relationship with Catherine . . . but that was not very likely. More likely that the man concerned had long since been dismissed, or had moved on where his crime was not known. If it was a crime. She thought about it; it was not a crime to love someone, but maybe it was a crime to let that person die and then to abandon the child . . .

With a flash of inspiration Joanna knew the way to settle the problem. She would go the church where Juanita was buried and ask to see the church records. The date of death might be recorded. The *date* of the burial would most certainly be recorded, and that would be close enough. Suddenly it was imperative that she knew. Was she really Juanita's daughter and, if so, who was her father? She sat abruptly on the damp grass and put her hands over her face. The suddenness of events had overwhelmed her. The certainty was growing in her that she had stumbled on the truth and she was not a foundling at all. Today she would find out the name of her mother; it was a step in the right direction. If the church records proved her theory, then she would go straight to her uncle and demand to know the name of her father.

Abandoning the watering-can, she jumped to her feet. Steven Benbridge would be home by now; she would ask him to go with her to the church and translate for her. She need not explain the details to him; he would have to trust her. She ran across the praca, past the bandstand to his house and pushed open the gate. Now that she was so near to the truth every second was an agony. She rang the bell and banged on the knocker, and when he opened the door she cried, 'Please come with me. I have to go to the church and I need you. I can't explain but – I mean, I don't speak Portuguese and — Oh, please, *please* do come right away!'

She took his hand and began to tug him out of the doorway, desperate to be on the way. To her relief he asked no questions but said simply, 'Let me fetch my keys.'

Having done so, he closed the door behind him and accompanied her to the gate.

'Don't ask me to explain,' she begged. 'I can't, because I've promised someone – and I may be wrong, but I don't think so. I hope I'm not.'

He looked at her with concern. 'Something's terribly wrong,' he said. 'You're as pale as death! You can trust me, Joanna. I've told you that already.'

'I can't tell anybody – but I must know!'

She knew she was not making much sense, but in her present state it did not matter. He must remain in ignorance. They half ran to the church and had just reached the gate when Leo appeared from nowhere.

'What's happening?' he asked, obviously startled.

Joanna wanted to weep with frustration. More delay. 'Go away, Leo!' she cried urgently. 'I'm sorry, but you can't come with me. I daren't let you – look, *please*, Leo. Don't follow us inside.'

His face was pink with the hurt of rejection. 'Why can't I?' he demanded. 'What's happening?' A new expression crossed his face. 'You're not getting *married*, are you?'

Even Joanna laughed. 'We are *not* getting married!' she assured him. 'But I can't tell you, I can't explain. It's so —' She swallowed hard. 'It might be something rather terrible – no, not terrible but – oh, Leo. I can't explain.'

Leo looked at Steven. 'Can you?' he asked.

'I'm really sorry, Leo, but even *I* don't know what this is all about. I'm just being dragged along here. Joanna won't say.'

'Please go away, Leo!' she begged, in an agony of impatience.

'Well!' he said huffily. 'If I'm not wanted!'

Seeing his hurt expression, Joanna said, 'It's not that, Leo. Of course you're wanted but . . . look, if what I think is true – and if I'm allowed to tell you – I will.'

'Cross your heart?'

'Cross my heart. Please, Leo. Trust me!'

Leaving him thoroughly confused, she ran into the church with Steven close behind her. Fortunately for Joanna's peace of mind, when their eyes became accustomed to the gloom they found the priest at prayer, kneeling before the altar. After a few moments he stood up and turned towards them.

Joanna looked at Steven. 'Ask him if he keeps a record of burials as far back as – about eighteen years.'

He gave her a strange look but repeated the question in Portuguese.

'He does,' Steven told her.

'Ask him if we may look at it. Tell him it's *very* important!' Her heart was thudding with a mixture of hope and dread.

The priest nodded and beckoned them to follow him into a small room. From a cupboard he took a large ledger, placed it on a table, and with a wave of his hand indicated that they could examine it. For a few seconds Joanna could not move; then tentatively she stretched out her hand and with trembling fingers began to turn back the pages. She was aware of Steven and the priest, puzzled, beside her.

1896, 1895, 1894 – she closed her eyes and prayed: 'Please God, don't let it be Sturton!' She stared at the page, but her eyes refused to focus.

Steven asked, 'Have you found what you were looking for?'

The priest said something that she didn't understand. She ran a finger down the page of spidery writing.

May ... June ... August ... She turned the page. And suddenly there it was, staring back from the brittle page in faded brown letters.

9.1.1894

Of course. They put the month first in some countries. The first of September and she, Joanna, had been born on the twenty-ninth of August! Two days. And there, incredibly, was the name –

'Juanita Torres!'

And another name! She drew in her breath sharply as she read it with total disbelief.

'Elliot J. Grosvenor. Pai.'

But of course! Her uncle had probably had to register the death because she had been a servant. But where was the father's name? She turned to Steven and said shakily, 'What does "*Pai*" mean?'

'It means "father".'

She stared at him and for a moment the walls of the tiny room seemed to press in against them. She felt stifled.

'Father?' Her voice sounded very faint and seemed to come from a great way off. '*Father?* Are you sure?'

He nodded. 'Quite sure. Joanna, what is it?' He took a step nearer and glanced down at the page, and she should have closed the ledger but was not fast enough. Suddenly his eyes widened and she knew that he had seen and read the entry. But her own name was not mentioned, and he surely could not understand the full significance of those other names. They looked at each other as she struggled to remain calm. The priest was gazing at her suspiciously; he said something and Steven asked her if she had finished with the ledger. Had she seen what she wanted to see?

Robbed of speech by the shock of her discovery, she

could only nod her head. There was a whirl of emotions within her that threatened to take her breath away.

As the priest closed the book Joanna shook her head, as though dazed. Steven took some money from his wallet and pressed it into the priest's hand.

'Uncle Elliot?' she murmured to herself. She was mesmerized by the unexpected nature of the revelation, almost afraid to trust her own eyes. Dimly she was aware that Steven's arm was around her.

'Oh, Steven!' she whispered.

He was looking at her with concern. 'Good news?'

'Yes. At least, I think so.'

'You look as though you need some air,' he told her gently. Without a word she allowed herself to be propelled gently back towards the church door. Once outside she was quite unable to contain her growing excitement, and turned towards him with shining eyes. Oblivious to the presence of Leo lurking nearby, and dizzy with excitement, she succumbed to a moment of pure recklessness.

'No wonder he loves me!' she cried. 'He's my *father*!' And, unable to contain her excitement, she threw her arms round Steven's neck and kissed him.

Chapter Fourteen

THEY STEPPED OUT into the sunlight to find Leo still loitering, a hurt expression on his face. As soon as he saw them he said, 'Don't bother to tell me anything. I don't care. I don't want to know, anyway.'

Joanna looked at him and a huge smile lit up her face. This was her brother – or rather a half-brother. Or step-brother? She was not sure.

'What's so funny?' he demanded.

'Nothing,' she told him. 'I'm just happy, that's all. And Leo, I'll tell you when I can. I promise.'

'Huh!' He managed to put a wealth of meaning into the exclamation but he looked at Joanna with surprise. Five minutes earlier she had been tense and nervous, snapping his head off. Now she looked radiant.

'I swear on the grave of Julius Tobin!' she told him with a smile. 'You wouldn't know him. He was a housemaster at your prep school when Mark was there.'

'But you can't swear on his grave,' Leo protested. 'He's still alive! Worse luck.'

'Still alive?' Her eyes narrowed. 'He can't be still alive. He died in an accident; he fell from a train in the Austrian Alps. Mark said —'

'He's still alive, I tell you!' Leo glared. 'I ought to

know. He teaches us history, and it's so boring. We call him Caesar because his name's Julius.'

But Mark had sworn on Tobin's grave! It took Joanna a few seconds to understand his treachery. No wonder he had felt free to tell his parents everything – his vow had never meant anything at all. He had tricked her! She stood stock-still, shaking her head at his duplicity, then suddenly she began to laugh. In the initial glow of her new-found happiness, she found she did not really care. Over the past weeks she had gradually revised her opinion of Mark and this new revelation merely served to confirm it. Charming, maybe, but certainly devious, Mark was not the paragon she had once thought him and she had had a narrow escape. She would put it down to experience. She could still love him as a brother, but as a husband – Isobel was welcome to him!

Steven said in a low voice, 'So what now? What will you do?'

'I don't know,' she said. But deep inside her she *did* know. She must go to her father, tell him of her discoveries and hear the truth from his own lips. Only then would she be satisfied. Abruptly she came to a decision: she would seek him out after dinner that very evening.

The hours passed so slowly that by evening Joanna was in a state of feverish excitement and the meal was an agony. It seemed that everyone ate so slowly – she wanted to shovel the food into their mouths and shout, 'Swallow it, damn you!' Christina appeared so fastidious as she served the dessert; each time she spilled the tiniest speck of cream on the rim of a plate she wiped it clean with a cloth. Who cared about a few drips of cream? Eyeing Catherine surreptitiously, she thought of the world-shattering news that, if revealed, would wipe the supercilious smile from her aunt's face. She stole a few glances at her 'uncle' and wanted to hug him.

It was a quarter to ten before he finished his glass of

port and made his way upstairs to his study. A few moments later Joanna made her own excuses and followed him. In answer to his 'Come in' she opened the door, closed it behind her and crossed the room to stand directly in front of him.

Without preamble she said, 'I went to the church today and saw the date of Juanita's burial. It was two days after my birth.'

He stared at her speechlessly and she went on, 'I also saw the name of the child's father; it was yours.'

For what seemed an eternity he gazed up at her. Then he said, 'Oh, Joanna! My dear girl!'

They stared at each other wordlessly.

'Am I your daughter?'

He was so slow to answer that for a moment Joanna thought he was going to deny it, but at last he stood up and said, 'Yes, you are!'

Yes, you are ... Yes, you are ... The words seemed to echo in her brain. Three wonderful words – but what could she say in reply that would not sound trite? She continued to stare at him until he suddenly held out his arms and she stepped forward and felt them enclose her. Then she was crying and he was kissing her.

'I'm glad you know,' he murmured. 'I'm so very, very glad. I've wanted you to know; I've wanted to own you all these years. You must believe me, my dearest girl. Do say you do.'

'I believe you —' She wanted to say 'Papa', but the word wouldn't come. After all these years she had found her real father and the word stuck in her throat! More tears sprang to her eyes but she willed them back.

He led her to the little sofa and they sat together with his arm around her and her head against his chest. She could hear his heartbeat and thought she had never heard anything so beautiful. Slowly the rest of the story came out and painfully the remaining pieces of the jigsaw were dropped into place.

'My mother was furious when she knew about Juanita,'
he told her. 'I wanted to marry her, which would have
been unthinkable in those days – still would, I suppose. Of
course, Juanita's family were shocked too. Maria Torres
was a widow but one of her brothers, Jose Torres, was
very angry that his niece was disgraced. He is a bit of a
bully and —'

'I've met him!' she laughed.

'He tried to find out the name of the father and said he
was going to kill him. Juanita wouldn't tell, and I daren't.
Not just because he carried a rifle, but because even if he
hadn't shot me it would have been all over the mine. I was
prepared to admit the paternity if I could have married her
but my mother was adamant. Maria didn't want the marriage, either; she wanted Juanita to marry a young Portuguese man who was very much in love with her. It had
been "understood" in the vague way things happen here.'
He shrugged. 'That poor little grave!' he said softly. 'Because we were not married she couldn't be buried —'

'My mother,' she corrected him gently.

His arm tightened across her shoulder. 'Your mother
couldn't be buried —'

'I just wanted to hear you say it!' she explained. 'My
mother! My father!'

'I know, my dear. I understand. You don't have to
justify yourself to me. Not ever.'

She nodded.

'Your mother is buried in the Portuguese cemetery; I'll
take you there tomorrow. But because I couldn't visit the
grave, I had a cross put up in the English cemetery. I used
to put flowers there when I could, but it was difficult
because no one outside the family – and the Barratts of
course – was to know the truth.' He sighed. 'I should have
insisted on a marriage. I should have given up my job here
and taken Juanita and you to Australia. Or South Africa.
Anywhere! We should have made a fresh start but – I was

weak. I have to accept the blame.' He looked down at her. 'I robbed you of your mother. Will you ever forgive me?'

'Of course I will.' She squeezed his hand. 'Your mother is also to blame. You wanted to do what was right.'

'Agatha insisted on taking you back to England and Maria finally agreed. She would have brought you up, but she was very poor and Agatha finally persuaded her that you would have a better life in England. Since my second name is John, Agatha decided that you should be Juana. Juan is Portuguese for John, you see.'

'So who changed it to Joanna? My parents?'

He nodded. 'Agatha wanted to keep you in the family. She was determined that you wouldn't be brought up by strangers; she said you were a Grosvenor, and she was right. So she persuaded Maurice, and he finally talked Mary into it. At first my mother protested strongly, but Agatha fought her. At last Mother agreed as long as you were never told the truth, so it was decided to pretend that you had been abandoned. And that's how it happened. Maurice thought Juana sounded too foreign, and I think they were probably right. You blended in better as Joanna.'

'They've been very good to me,' she said soberly, thinking how badly she had rewarded their generosity. 'Were they ever going to tell me the truth?'

'Probably not, because of the trouble it would cause to whoever I eventually married. You would have been perfectly happy believing that Maurice and Mary were your parents. But of course young Mark had to blurt it out. I never did know how he found out.' He frowned. 'He must have snooped around – probably read something very private. I could never take to him somehow. Was it very terrible for you? Finding out like that?'

'I was dreadfully upset,' she admitted. 'I remember I couldn't stop screaming and they had to call the doctor. Mama – I mean . . . well, Mary – she thought I was going to have a fit. But I don't blame you!' she added hastily. 'Really I don't.'

He was silent for a long time and then said, 'I shall tell Catherine.'

'Oh, no! Uncle—' She sighed. 'Will I ever be able to call you Papa?'

'Yes. And soon. I shall tell Catherine. Whatever happens she should know; it will be a shock, but truth must out. I want everyone to know, you see.' He blinked rapidly and brushed a hand across his eyes. 'You must think me an old fool, but I want everyone to know that Juanita and I had a daughter. I don't care what they say, I can't have you skulking about on the fringe of my life any longer.' His voice cracked and Joanna realized that he was dangerously close to breaking down. That would never do. Catherine would want to know what was wrong, and he was not yet ready to tell her.

'I'll go now,' she said quickly, standing up. 'You must have time to think it out. It's been a shock to both of us.' She reached up to kiss him. 'I love you,' she said. 'Whatever you decide to do, I love you.'

'I love you, too, my dear.' As she turned to go, he cried, 'Wait!' He called her back and kissed her again. 'That was from your mother!' he whispered and she ran from the room before the tears began.

*

In the gloom of the third level, Andrew Shreiker wiped the sweat from his face and blinked his tired eyes. He was queuing to reach the ladder, crammed against the rock wall by the throng of weary, dust-caked men who, like him, were going off duty at the end of the shift. The rock pressed into his shoulders and an occasional drip of water from above him splashed on to his helmet. In the light of the men's lamps faces appeared darker and eyes whiter, so that everyone seemed to be staring fearfully like tormented souls in hell. The air was unpleasantly thick – a rich mix of sour breath spiced with sweat, the exhaust fumes of the countless carbide flames and the ever-present sulphur. The voices around him were sometimes harsh, sometimes an exhausted whisper, a background of mutterings in a variety of languages which to Andrew were mostly meaningless. He was slowly becoming used to being underground and no longer thought of himself as being entombed in the rock. Having mastered his earlier fears – the fears he had not dared to share – he had come to terms with the crudeness of their unnatural existence and had taught himself to ignore the plight of the ponies who spent six months at a time away from the light of day.

Close by, two men jostled each other irritably, their patience exhausted, their tempers fraying. Their actions sent another man cannoning into Andrew, and he responded angrily which provoked a ripple of resentment. But he understood. The last minutes below ground were tense with longing to be above ground, where they would find the sunshine and clean air that was fit to breathe. As they stepped off the ladder they would shed all memories of their incarceration and their other life would begin. They would hand in lanterns and tokens, shout a cheerful '*Adeos!*' to their workmates and make their way home to their families. For the luckier ones a welcoming kiss and a bath, for most a wash-down, for all a welcome meal.

Andrew waited impatiently, and wondered suddenly what his mother would think if she could see her son. Like the rest of the miners he wore a scarf tied round his forehead to stop the sweat from running into his eyes. Like them, his feet were encased in the special boots provided by the company. Like theirs, his clothes clung damply to his body, uncomfortably gritty against his skin. His ears still rang with the sound of metal on rock. She would be appalled, he thought with a brief smile; she spoke of him as an engineer and thought him a cut above the rest.

Joanna, too, would be astonished by the Andrew she had never seen. He began to think about her. One day, he would not be going home to lonely bachelor quarters but would also have a home and children waiting to greet him. That knowledge would buoy him up through the long dark hours. Joanna! Her very name was enough to cheer him, and he acknowledged his good fortune. But then, he thought happily, he was the obvious choice for a girl like Joanna. The rivals for her interest were in another class altogether. Paul Jackson, the son of the Senior Assayer, was young but not exactly attractive with that long nose and weak chin. A nice enough chap, but hardly a rival for Joanna's hand. Benbridge was a decent, steady sort but much too old. Masters, the secretary, already had a wife although she had gone back to visit her mother two years ago and hadn't yet returned. The doctor was spoken for; the wages clerk was a total idiot and that left Leo!

The queue of men shuffled forward and Andrew moved with them. He was glad that it was a ladder that awaited him and not a cage. His experience in the coal-mine had made him wary of the clanking iron 'box' into which the miners were packed. At least here his safety was in his own hands. He could keep the necessary distance from the man above, and the strength of his own legs and arms would carry him to the top. Inside the cage he had felt like a trapped animal.

When his turn came he grasped the first metal rung which was cold and slippery. As he climbed, the muscles in his legs protested and his shoulders ached, but all his thoughts were of Joanna and he was still thinking of her when he reached the top and stepped thankfully on to firm ground. There he drew in a deep breath of clean air and joined the miners in their rush up the slope towards the welcome daylight at the mouth of the tunnel.

Tonight he had determined to write to his parents and tell them about Joanna. No doubt they would be delighted;

they had never really taken to his first love – Veronica, from the solicitors' office – nor to Louise who had replaced her in his affections. And he had never taken to podgy Olwen, the daughter of his mother's best friend. In fact, he thought regretfully, his parents refused to take any of his women seriously. His mother always insisted that he was far too young to know his own mind, and his father considered it unwise to marry before he was financially secure. They had met and married in their late thirties and were fond of saying that 'later is better than sooner'. The fact that Joanna was a foundling was also going to be something of a problem, but Andrew thought he need not tell his parents about that until much later. They would have to know sometime, but after they had met Joanna those details would be irrelevant. They were planning to spend a few weeks in Mertola over Christmas and would meet her then.

He went to the head of the queue where Benbridge was checking the men out.

'Any chance of having Friday off?' Andrew asked him.

Benbridge frowned. He could be a bit surly sometimes, thought Andrew, but he was basically a sound chap.

'Must it be Friday?' Benbridge asked. 'I was planning to sort out that special detail to start the new cut on D7. I thought you could supervise it. What about Monday?'

Andrew shrugged. 'I was going to take Miss Joanna shopping in Mertola,' he told him, unable to keep the pride out of his voice.

Benbridge appeared unimpressed. 'The shops will still be there on Monday,' he said.

'They might be closed on Mondays,' Andrew began. 'I know they're open on —'

'Look, Shreiker, you can't have Friday off just to go gallivanting with Miss Grosvenor! We've a mine to run, in case you had forgotten. Make it some other time. Be here half an hour early on Friday and we'll check it all through.'

Mortified, Andrew found himself pushed aside by the next man who was eager to get off home. 'Arrogant sod!' he muttered, but not loudly enough for Benbridge to hear. 'Who the hell does he think he's talking to?'

He brooded on Benbridge's high-handed behaviour all the way back to his house, feeling mortified and resentful. By the time he had had his bath, however, he had realized that the wretch was obviously jealous of the special relationship which he, Andrew, had with the boss's niece. That Andrew could forgive. On reflection, he was surprised that the jealousy had not shown itself before now. It would be more than a little awkward for the fellow when he and Joanna were man and wife and he, Andrew, was in Mr Grosvenor's confidence.

He dressed in cool cotton slacks and a cream shirt and then sat down to write to his parents. He had written once to assure them he had arrived safely; this would be the second letter. When it was finished, he would prepare a salad and sit out on the terrace to eat it. Then he would stroll in the praca and would almost certainly meet Joanna or Leo. Preferably the former, naturally, but the lad could be trusted to take a message to Joanna.

He found paper, pen and ink and without preamble began to write:

> Dear Mother and Father,
>   I hope you are both well. I am fine. San Domingos is as good as can be expected for foreign climes, but work goes well. Some of the men try to take advantage of my inexperience but I can handle it. My boss tells me they always 'sound out' the new men and I just have to stand firm . . .

He was not the world's best letter writer – in fact he normally hated the job – but today was different. Today he had something important to say and he plunged right in.

You will remember that I mentioned Joanna Grosvenor when I last wrote. You will love her, I know, as much as I do.

Not quite as much, perhaps. That was expecting too much, but they surely could not resist her sweet face and innocent ways.

She is not yet eighteen, but I can wait a few years. Did I tell you that she is the niece of the General Administrator – but that is simply a coincidence.

A very opportune coincidence, however, he thought happily, and one that would certainly impress his father. It was the icing on the cake!

I think I told you that we met on the SS *Lanfranc*. It was love at first sight for me, but I did not know how Joanna felt about me. Now I think, in fact I'm sure, she returns my affections, although she cannot bring herself to say 'Yes' on such a short acquaintance.

Carried away with enthusiasm, he continued to sing Joanna's praises for another three pages and by the time the letter was signed and sealed it was dark outside. If he wanted to see Joanna, he would have to miss his supper, but he smiled cheerfully at the prospect as he let himself out of the house. It was a small price to pay for happiness.

*

About 9 o'clock that same night, Steven was sitting in an easy chair, looking out of the French windows towards the miners' houses, strung out in the darkness like glow-worms. He had tried many times to picture San Domingos from the air, a bird's-eye view of Mason and Barry's tiny world. An eagle soaring high above the plain would see hundreds of white houses clustered together, and the huge lake formed by the dam. It would note the scarred hillside of the open-cast workings where the surface miners blasted their way into the rock. The bird would see the little church and the school and, further over, the praca and the bandstand, surrounded by more white houses. No doubt the beady eye would catch the glint of steel where the railway lines sped out towards Pomerao, and would ponder the white steam puffing from the train's engines. It would have no conception of the much vaster world below ground. And on all sides it would see the heathers and ferns and wild thyme. From the air San Domingos would appear exactly what it was – a tiny oasis of civilization in a vast desert of arid plain.

He closed his eyes, letting the stillness wash over him. The daylight had gone and he had not bothered to light the lamp, preferring to sit in the gathering dusk alone with his thoughts. On this occasion he was troubled by the knowledge of Joanna's discovery. Her joy was undimmed, although she was not a fool and could no doubt see the difficulties ahead. He had not seen her since she had visited the church and did not know whether she had spoken to Elliot Grosvenor. Catherine was going to be a serious problem and, knowing her nature, Steven suspected that she would react against the news by rejecting Joanna. Even if she did not throw the poor girl out she could – and probably would – make her life a misery, and there was little her husband could do about it. Knowing that Elliot had been in love with another woman would be hard enough to take, but discovering that the illegitimate daughter of that union was living under the same roof would be intolerable – for many women, he reflected fairly, not only for Catherine. It would not be so bad if the two had ever liked each other, but they did not.

Steven shook his head. He would not like to be in Elliot Grosvenor's shoes when he broke the news to his wife!

Sparks would fly and the marriage, already rather fragile, would receive a shattering blow from which it might not recover. He smiled suddenly. Probably the only one who would be pleased was the young 'sprout'. It was strange how well he and Joanna got on; they might already be brother and sister. His line of thought switched abruptly to Andrew Shreiker and his request for a day off. With hindsight, Steven thought he had been a bit hard on the man. Friday was not possible, but he might have been less churlish in turning him down. Apart from his youth, Steven could not fault his new junior, although he did sometimes remind him of a puppy, too willing to please and too eager to be loved. Such an innocent, he thought, and so vulnerable. And did Joanna really intend to marry him? Somehow he could not imagine it succeeding – she was so young and vulnerable herself.

'But what's wrong with that?' he asked aloud. Who was he to scorn young lovers? He sighed heavily. It was ironic, he thought, that for years he had never looked at another woman and now that he had, she was still a girl at heart and in a few years he would be forty.

*

The day before the party Clementine Grosvenor awoke from a bad dream and lay awake, staring at the ceiling, while her heartbeat slowed. There was a faint perspiration on her face and she felt hot and restless. Turning her head, she saw that it was just after six o'clock. She knew it was Friday; she knew who she was; she knew that she was often confused, but that this was going to be one of her good days.

'I am Clementine Alice Grosvenor,' she whispered. 'I am seventy-nine years old, and my nurse is a martinet called Williams.' A smile softened her face momentarily, then was gone as she frowned in concentration. 'My son is Elliot John, and his wife is a spiteful creature called Catherine.'

She sighed, closed her eyes, then snapped them open again. If she went back to sleep now, she might wake confused, so she would cling on to this delightful clarity of mind. Her bad days were a nightmare of doubts, unwarranted fears and minor irritations, mostly the fault of the nurse who seemed to take a perverse pleasure in thwarting her every whim. She straightened herself in the bed. At least she still had the use of her limbs, if only for a limited period each day. The doctor was such a fool, but he was all they had. Still, he had been right about Juanita and she had been wrong, but she had finally admitted that to him. Not that the wretched girl deserved to die, but the death had been almost convenient. If only she would stay dead! But she seemed determined to haunt the house; Clementine had seen her several times. Unless she was confusing her with the niece, Joanna, who did look remarkably like her. The trouble was, she thought wearily, that even on the good days the confused episodes of the bad days were still hazy to her.

She heard the nurse splashing water in the little bathroom and thought disparagingly how dreadful it must be to be plain, podgy and totally lacking in charm. No wonder she had never married! The poor soul had been invited to Joanna's party and was in a fine fever of excitement about it, though who she expected to meet there was a mystery. They would be all the same old faces. Elliot had suggested that she, Clementine, might join them for a short while, but she had refused. Garden parties were such clumsy affairs. Satin shoes were ruined by the grass stains, and the mosquitoes were a constant hazard. What little energy she had could be put to better use, she had told him. That had wiped the smile from his face. Poor boy! He had been such a fool, had ruined his life. Now all he had was a discontented wife whom he had married on the rebound. He had taken Catherine when she was suggested to him, but had blamed his mother for introducing them. If he hadn't wanted her, he should have said so; he had only himself to blame. Catherine? Huh! Kate, more likely! A shrew if ever there was one!

'Where did I go wrong with that boy?' she wondered. Elliot had been a sickly child – and was now a sickly man. No spirit, that was his trouble – no gumption! She sighed. All her children had been a disappointment to her. Agatha was so quarrelsome and had a very sharp tongue. Maurice was too docile – would always take the easy way out. Agatha should have been the boy; she had enough courage for all of them.

At that moment Nurse Williams bustled in, adjusting her cap, wearing the usual simper on her face.

'Good morning. And how are we this morning?' she asked briskly.

This was a question that did not require an answer and Clementine ignored it. The nurse came to the bedside, said, 'Awake, are we?' and smiled to show the one gold filling of which she was so proud. She peered into Clementine's face and Clementine knew why: she wanted to gauge how lucid her patient was.

'Brighter this morning, are we?' she chirruped, hauling her into a sitting position and plumping the pillows with a few deft blows.

'Don't bother me,' said Clementine. 'I'm thinking.'

Nurse looked pleased as she reached for the thermometer. 'Thinking, are we? That's good.'

Clementine started to say that it might *not* be good but was silenced by the thermometer. She spat it out immediately and said, 'Just ask me how I am and I'll tell you I'm very well. Now please hurry up with my washing water.'

Her tone was slightly hectoring, but the nurse simply smiled, retrieved the thermometer and held it out. 'The washing water comes *after* the thermometer,' she said in a steely voice. 'We don't know how well we are unless we know our temperature.' She folded her arms across her chest and stared challengingly at her patient, her expression clearly indicating that she had time on her side.

She reminded Clementine of the various nannies who had cared for her as a child; it had always been a battle of wills between them and their determined young charge. Her father had been an army man who spent most of his service life in India. His wife accompanied him and Clementine, the only child, had stayed with her maternal grandmother and the inevitable succession of nurses, nannies and governesses. Her parents had been rare beings who intruded occasionally into her life. She hardly knew them, yet she loved them passionately and clung to the idea that they adored her in return. Now here she was, old and alone, and still having to battle it out with a nurse. She sighed; it was all so foolish. She stared at the woman, who stared back.

Nurse Williams glanced at the bedside clock and said, 'My! We *will* be late for our breakfast, won't we?' Her expression was triumphant. So, thought Clementine, you think you will win? We'll see about that.

'I'm not hungry.' She sat a little straighter. 'I don't want a wash. I may go back to sleep.'

The nurse's face sagged slightly. 'Go back to sleep? What a thing to say! What about our routine?'

Clementine bit back a sharp rejoinder and began instead to slide down a little into the bedclothes. She closed her eyes and pretended to doze. After what she imagined to be about a minute she heard the rustle of the nurse's apron as she leaned over to replace the thermometer in its holder. Hidden by the sheets, Clementine smiled. She might be in her dotage, but she was not entirely helpless after all.

'I've put the thermometer away,' the nurse conceded, in a tone which suggested that it had been her own idea. 'Shall we have our wash now, in case young Leo calls in to see us? We don't want him to see us looking frowsty, do we?'

Clementine, having made her point, surrendered gracefully and allowed herself to be washed and dressed and helped out to her chair on the patio. Nurse Williams had chosen the shadiest place where any slight breeze might reach her. The temperature was climbing, and it was going to be another very hot day.

'I'll fetch your ivory fan,' Nurse told her. 'The one your father sent you from India.'

'I don't want that one.' There was no point in making her life too easy! 'I want the Spanish fan with the lace edge and the picture of the bullfighter.'

Nurse made a tutting noise. 'And where is that one, may I ask?'

'In one of the drawers – I think, Nurse.' Let her go and look for it, she thought cheerfully.

Five minutes later Clementine sat fanning herself and turned her thoughts away from the past to her grandchildren – those beings for whom she was partly responsible; for whom she had had such high hopes. Leo of course was a bright young spark, much brighter than either of her own sons. He would go far. Dorcas? Well, she rarely saw Maurice's children, but they had sent her a photograph which did not inspire much hope. Poor Dorcas was plain as a pikestaff, and Suzanne looked too pretty for her own good; she would be hopelessly spoiled. A great pity ... Mark? Ah! There was a sly child who would probably grow into a sly adult. He had visited once many years ago, and she had been unimpressed. Handsome in a pretty way which did not appeal to her. No. At Leo's age, Mark had 'played to the gallery' as the saying goes. He could twist Mary round his little finger even then. He lacked Leo's directness ... And then there was Joanna. A strange, fiery child – but what else could one expect from such a mother? Still, she was bright enough and perhaps, after all, Agatha had been right to keep her in the family ... She sighed. Perhaps Agatha had been right about a lot of things, with hindsight, but a marriage between Elliot and Juanita would have forced them to leave San Domingos. It would also have meant that she, Clementine, would have had to surrender her position in Elliot's home to a servant girl — and that would have been quite impossible. On reflection it had probably all worked out for the best, with the exception of Catherine. Unfortunately that marriage *had* proved a mistake, but that was a cross her son must bear. Why, oh why was life so difficult, she asked herself petulantly, when it could all be so much nicer? There were times when she seriously wondered why she had wanted a family. Children were such a worry . . .

Juan-Carlos drifted into view, armed with a small gardening tool with which to dig out the weeds. He gave her a shy smile and bent dutifully to his task. When he dropped the weeds on to the flagstones she tutted irritably.

'You need a basket,' she told him. 'A *basket*! To put the weeds in.' She raised her voice imperiously and repeated loudly, 'A basket to put the weeds in!' She had always refused to speak a word of Portuguese and now Juan-Carlos was regarding her nervously, not understanding a word she had said. It really was too exasperating.

'Oh, get on with it!' she told him with a dismissive wave of her hand, and he understood that and bent once more to his work. She closed her eyes . . .

And then it happened.

Just for a moment she was conscious of a sudden break with reality, as though all her senses had been switched off for a second or two. She felt as though she was existing in a vacuum. Thoroughly alarmed, she opened her eyes and was relieved to find that they still focused. Had she imagined that small but frightening lapse? Her heart thudded with fear. What had happened? Was it a warning? A forerunner of something else? She waited, reluctant to call the nurse; unwilling to declare her dependence after her recent victory. Time passed and she watched Juan-Carlos, willing herself back to normality. 'Please, God, don't let it happen again,' she pleaded silently. For a few moments she was reassured and then, without warning, she felt a wave of dizziness and tried to cry out. Too late. The Spanish fan fell from her hand. There was a roaring in her ears and she sank into unconsciousness. Without uttering a sound, she swayed forward in the chair and fell heavily on to the ground.

Chapter Fifteen

12th August

Grandmother is very ill. They have taken her to the small hospital in San Domingos where Doctor Barratt is looking after her, although he says he can do very little. Just 'monitor her progress' and pray! She was found yesterday, lying on the ground unconscious, and has still not regained consciousness. Juan-Carlos was there when it happened and thought she was dead. Poor man, it gave him a terrible shock. The doctor is not very hopeful because of her age and because she struck her head when she fell. Nurse Williams is in a terrible state and blames herself, although she could not watch Grandmother every minute of the day. When I went in to speak to her she was clutching a lace-edged fan which Grandmother had been holding before she collapsed. She was crying and muttering and almost hysterical, and the doctor had to give her a sedative to calm her down. He thinks Grandmother had a brainstorm or a seizure of some kind, and has warned Papa that if she does regain consciousness her sight or speech might be impaired. Poor soul, it would be so terrible.

Naturally, the party has been cancelled. Aunt Catherine was not very pleased. The food had been ordered and some of it had been prepared in advance; twelve coloured lanterns had been bought and the wine had been delivered. She said she thought that probably Grandmother would like the party to go ahead, but my father (I can call him that in here!) insisted that it be postponed. He is very distressed and I tried to comfort him by saying that G. had had a good, long life. Christina and Liliane are looking very gloomy and sighing a lot, and even Leo is cast down. It is a very sad day for everyone.

I have come to a decision about Andrew Shreiker: I shall tell him that the answer is definitely 'No', and hope he takes it well. I don't want to hurt him, but I cannot let him hope any longer. I think he is too young for me.

Sarah Barratt is working herself into a fever because she has visitors coming to stay for five weeks, and they should arrive tomorrow if the ship docks on time in Lisbon – her sister, Harriet, and a grand-daughter, Lucy, who is twenty. They have been once before. I hope Lucy is not as dull as her aunt Sarah! I asked Leo, but he wasn't here when they last came to San Domingos so for once doesn't know.

The heat is still rising. Yesterday it was over ninety at midday. Today it is already ninety-four, and it is only 11 a.m. Christina can't keep the butter solid, and my bedside candle is melting and leaning to one side. It looks very odd! The level in the lake has fallen quite noticeably. No one is venturing far except Leo, who has gone off with Juan-Carlos's brother to watch him swim the horses in the lake to cool them down. And no doubt to take a photograph or two. I would have liked to see it myself but cannot face the heat.

This evening the family (and any English who want to join us) are going to the church for a special service to pray for Grandmother. I don't know whether to pray that she lives or dies . . .

*

The little church at San Domingos stood on a slight rise of the ground and was surrounded by a small area of grass which looked somewhat sparse and brown in the late summer heat. A low white wall formed the boundary. The walls of the church itself were limewashed under a red-tiled roof, and the two massive doors were of solid wood. There were no gravestones amongst the grass, for Mason and Barry had built a Portuguese cemetery on the outskirts of the village, as custom decreed. Inside the building the walls were also white, and there were rows of wooden pews with a central aisle. The altar itself was a simple affair resembling a tiered table covered with several white cloths, each tier bearing two lighted candles. The Virgin Mary and several appropriate saints were represented by small statues set into recesses in the white walls. To the left a flight of wooden steps led up to a small pulpit. The windows were circular, with plain glass. It was relatively cool inside the church, as one by one the family and friends arrived to take part in the ceremony. The English community were not sufficient in number to fill more than the first four rows, but the priest appeared unperturbed by his small congregation and began the service promptly at 7 o'clock. It was in Latin and Joanna, understanding none of it, had plenty of opportunity to gaze around her. Andrew Shreiker had managed to find a seat almost immediately behind her, and had leaned forward before the service started to squeeze her shoulder. She had smiled at him rather guiltily, aware of the bad news which awaited him. To her right, across the aisle, she saw Steven Benbridge and was comforted by his presence. The doctor's wife sat to her left two rows back, but the doctor himself was absent for obvious reasons. In the third row to her right Nurse Williams knelt with head bent. She had arrived at the church in tears and Joanna felt sorry for her; she reminded her of a dog who has lost its master. The rest of the English were dotted around. Juan-Carlos, Christina and Liliane were also there, but further back. After the first ten minutes Elliot himself took over the service, and they prayed in English and listened to a short address by him in which he asked for God's mercy and a total recovery for his mother. There was no singing, and after a blessing by the Portuguese priest they all filed out into the heat of the evening.

They were met by the curious stares of the Portuguese who, enjoying the evening, were surprised by the unexpected service. Christina answered the first hesitant question, and news of the old lady's condition quickly spread by word of mouth. Soon most of the villagers had crossed themselves and murmured words of sympathy, adding appeals to the Virgin Mary to be merciful.

Joanna felt her arm grasped by someone and turned to see Andrew, his face creased with concern.

'I was so sorry,' he told her. 'What a terrible shock for you. I had to be with you, Joanna, at such a sad time.'

'That's very kind, Andrew.'

'It's the least I could do,' he protested. 'If there is any way I can help – at times like these, family must rally round.'

Family? She registered the word with a lurch of the heart. Did he already consider himself *family*? The sooner she disillusioned him the better. Steeling herself she said, 'Andrew, we must talk. I have something to say to you—'

'Talk?' His face lit up. 'But of course we must. Oh, Joanna! I must tell you this. I've written to my parents about you! I felt they should be the first to know.' He took her hand in his and lifted it to his lips.

'Your parents?' Her voice was full of dismay. 'Oh, you shouldn't have done that!' She caught sight of Steven Benbridge watching them and her heart sank as she realized how it must look to him. 'Where can we talk?' she asked desperately. 'Somewhere private.'

He hesitated. 'I would suggest my house, but that would be rather unconventional and likely to be misconstrued. The library, perhaps?'

'But it's closed.'

'The praca?'

It was Joanna's turn to hesitate. The praca was certainly not a private place, but on the other hand she did not want to be somewhere *too* private.

Triumphantly he held up a finger. 'The English cemetery!' he suggested.

She agreed reluctantly. 'After dinner? At nine-thirty?' He nodded, kissed her fingers again and hurried away.

Elliot came up to her just then and said, 'Shall we walk back together?'

Joanna glanced round for Steven; she saw that he was deep in conversation with Catherine and was immediately aware of a distinct pang of jealousy. No doubt she was telling him how hard she had tried to go ahead with the party. No doubt she had hoped to flirt with him on that occasion. Certainly she had spent a lot of money on a new dress, Joanna thought crossly. She wanted to have a few words with Steven herself, but now her father was slipping his arm through hers.

Nurse Williams hovered nearby, casting pathetic glances in their direction. She had wanted to accompany her patient to the hospital but had been refused; there was a trained nursing sister there, and another pair of hands was really not necessary. Elliot, understanding the woman's loneliness, said, 'Won't you walk with us, Nurse Williams?' She joined them gratefully, and together they walked back to the house.

*

In the late evening light the English cemetery had an eerie atmosphere and Joanna, arriving just before nine, shivered a little and hoped that Andrew would not be late. Scolding herself for her timidity, she pushed open the gates and went inside. In the gloom the marble gravestone gleamed dully and she fancied it reproached her for her frivolous errand. The wooden cross in the corner was almost invisible.

'Hurry up, Andrew!' she whispered, deciding that if he were even a minute late she would be on her way home. She began to wonder what she would say to him; all through dinner she had tried to put together a few kindly sentences, but had been unable to concentrate on the problem. Perhaps she should come right out with it: 'I can't marry you, Andrew. I'm sorry.' It was blunt, but was it too unkind? Should she lead up to it gradually? 'I've done a lot of thinking, Andrew, and I can't marry you.' Was that better? Sighing deeply, she leaned back against the wall which was warm to her back. She could be more subtle: 'I don't want to hurt you, Andrew, but I've something rather painful to say to you . . .' But she didn't want to prolong his agony. Nor did she wish to sound too reluctant in case he thought she was merely wavering – or too young to commit herself – or afraid of marriage. The reason for her rejection of him was that she did not love him and was sure she never would, but how could she convince him that time would make no difference to her feelings?

'Joanna!'

He had arrived.

'I'm in here,' she called, relieved, and saw him come through the gates.

He hurried towards her with hands outstretched and, before she could stop him, he took her in his arms and kissed her.

'Do you realize, Joanna, that this is the first time we have ever been truly alone?'

She could hear the excitement in his voice. 'Andrew,' she began, 'I've something to—'

'Truly alone!' he repeated. 'Oh, my sweet girl! My dear, *dear* Joanna!' He kissed her again and she tried to free herself.

'Andrew, I must tell you!' she cried. 'I've been thinking a great deal and—'

'I told you I'd written to my parents, didn't I? They'll be so thrilled. I can just see them, especially my mother! She'll adore you, Joanna! As I do.'

She pulled herself away and said quickly, 'Andrew, you must believe me that I don't want to hurt you but—'

'Hurt me? My dearest girl, you could never do anything to hurt me. When two people love each other as we do . . .'

She put her hands over her face. He was making it impossible for her to tell him gently, the way she had planned, and she felt like an ogre. Taking a deep breath, she said loudly, 'I don't want to marry you, Andrew. I've made up my mind! I'm terribly sorry.'

To her dismay he put an arm round her shoulders and gave her a comforting squeeze. 'I know,' he said.

'You *know*?'

'I mean I guessed this might happen. Don't worry, we'll survive a few nerves. It's my fault, I rushed you into it. I shouldn't have told you about the letter to my parents. You've panicked, that's all.'

Unbelievably he was smiling, still cheerful.

'No, Andrew, it's not all. I mean it. I truly *am* very sorry, and you are such a nice man, but not the man for me – that is, I'm sure you'll meet someone else and realize that . . .' She stared at him. '*Andrew!* I'm serious. Please don't take it this way. There is truly no point in hoping. Do you understand me? Please believe me. I am not going to marry you.'

He was silent for a moment and when he spoke again a little of the excitement had faded from his voice. 'You can't possibly know that, Joanna. You hardly know me. That's my point. You need time.'

'Andrew! Please *listen* to me.' She felt a sense of desperation. 'If I were to know you for another month or another year, you would still not be the right man for me. Oh, Andrew, I did beg you not to set your heart on this match, but you wouldn't listen!' Now he was staring at her. 'I told you that I wasn't sure, but you were convinced it would work out and I rather hoped it would. Now I see that—'

'But that's what I'm saying, Joanna. I'm saying it's too early for you to make up your mind like this.' He tried to take hold of her hands, but she clasped them to her chest and shook her head.

'Can't we just be friends, Andrew? Good friends?'

'I don't want friendship! I want *love*!' he cried. She saw that he was beginning to realize that she was in earnest, and the ache in his voice told her how deeply he was suffering. 'I don't think you understand, Joanna. You are the only girl in the world for me. The *only* girl! If I can't have you, I'll be alone for the rest of my life. Is that what you want? Could you really be that cruel?'

'It would be much more cruel to let you go on hoping,' she said wretchedly. 'Buying the ring and telling everyone, and then I turn you down at the church! That would be cruel, too, wouldn't it?'

'You wouldn't do that, Joanna, because by the time we were due to marry you'd know that I'm the right person for you.'

She was silent, unable to meet his eyes, wishing she could somehow end this terrible meeting. She could not imagine how they would ever walk away from the cemetery. Together in an awful silence? One walking ahead? She seemed to have created a problem that couldn't be resolved; they were locked in an impossible situation.

'I'm sorry,' she repeated inadequately.

He turned away and stared out through the gates. Then

suddenly he said harshly, 'I could take you here and now and *make* you mine! No one would hear you if you cried out. I could! Do you know what I'm talking about? I don't suppose you do.'

He turned back to face her and Joanna thought of Mark. Yes, she knew what he meant.

'You're not that kind of man,' she said.

'But I could do it!'

His grief was giving way to anger and she hoped he could bear that more easily.

In a low voice she said, 'I would never be able to make you as happy as you deserve.'

'That's for me to decide.'

'I'm sorry. I don't know what else to say.'

'I was a fool to trust you, then.'

'If that's how you see it.'

'Oh, God, Joanna! You've broken my heart!'

He turned and began to pace round the little cemetery and she was miserably aware of his agitation. A new and frightening possibility entered her head. He would never take his own life? No, surely not. She could never mean that much to him.

'You'll find someone else, Andrew. I'm not the only girl—'

Abruptly he stopped and turned to stare at her. 'There's someone else, isn't there?' he cried. 'Don't deny it, Joanna. There's another man! Why didn't I see it before?'

'Another man?' she echoed. 'You can't mean that, Andrew. You know there's no one else at San Domingos. Believe me, there's no one else, that's not the reason.'

But he was unconvinced. He came close to her and caught hold of her hand. 'Who is it, Joanna? I just want to know. I think I have the right to know. You were promised to me and now—'

'I was never *promised*! Not to you, not to—'

She stopped. No, she was never promised even to Mark.

She had loved Mark too well, but there had never been a promise. How could there be?

'Not to whom?' he challenged. 'There *is* someone else!'

'No, Andrew. Only the man I told you about on the boat. I loved him, but he didn't return my love and I have never been promised to any man. Not even you.'

There was a long silence and suddenly his anger seemed to evaporate. He stared at the ground and said, 'Forgive me. I've behaved very boorishly. I'm ashamed.'

'There is no need, Andrew. I'm so sorry it had to end like this, but I shall always hold you in the highest regard. I hope we'll always be friends.' He drew in his breath and let it out slowly without replying. She guessed he was wondering how to tell other people that his dream had been shattered. She said, 'I think it best to say simply that we are giving ourselves more time. Then people will forget.'

'*I* shall never forget.'

Wanting to comfort him, she took a step towards him, but he said hoarsely, 'Don't come near me! I couldn't bear it.'

She stood there miserably, knowing exactly how he felt – just as she had felt when Mark had betrayed her. It was the saddest pain in the world! Time would heal it, but she dare not tell him that. In his present state he would never believe it.

'I'll go now,' he said. 'Will you walk back with me? I don't like to leave you here. It's nearly dark.'

Together they left the cemetery and began the short walk back to the compound. Joanna's heart was heavy and she longed to console him, but there were simply no words which could undo such a hurt. She knew from bitter experience that no one could help at such a time. As they walked she went over their conversation in her mind, wishing she had handled things differently; wondering if her own clumsiness had been to blame for his short-lived anger. They parted at her gate with polite 'Good nights' that were really 'Goodbyes'. As he walked away, downcast, she said softly, 'I'll pray for you, Andrew,' and knew she could do no more.

*

A week passed and there was no change in Clementine's condition, a situation which cast a gloom over the entire household. Catherine, disappointed by the cancellation of the garden party, grew tetchy and impatient as the days went by. It seemed to her that her husband was making too much of his mother's illness. Obviously it was very sad, but there was little anyone could do about it. Either the old lady would survive, which Catherine believed she would do, or she would die. Why, therefore, should Elliot feel it necessary to go about with a hangdog look on his face? He was upsetting the servants. Liliane mooched about the house talking in whispers and Christina snapped at her. Nurse Williams was positively wallowing in self-pity; she seemed to *enjoy* her guilty feelings and, whenever anyone would listen to her, blamed herself for the old lady's collapse. It was too ridiculous and Catherine was finding the whole situation tiresome. If Clementine died she would be one of the first to shed tears; crocodile tears, perhaps, for there was no love lost between the old lady and herself, but she would express her grief in a suitable manner. *If* she died. If she recovered, all this gloom would have been in vain.

Finally, Catherine decided to make her husband aware of her feelings and the first opportunity occurred at the end of breakfast on the Saturday. Leo and Joanna had gone off to fish in the Chanca, taking a picnic, so they were safely out of the way. Catherine waited until Christina had cleared away the crockery and then smiled at Elliot briskly.

'Elliot, I think we have suffered this doom-laden

atmosphere long enough. Don't you think you should pull yourself together?'

He looked at her in astonishment. 'Pull myself together? My mother is *dying*!' he said.

'We don't know that. She may well recover.'

'Barratt is not at all hopeful, Catherine.'

'Barratt is an old fool, Elliot. You have said so yourself many times.'

'In this instance I think he may be right.'

'You have no medical knowledge, Elliot. How could you possibly know?'

He passed a hand over his eyes. 'I have this awful premonition. Last night I dreamed that Mother was—'

'Dreams! Premonitions! For heaven's sake! You should be setting an example. You should at least make an effort instead of moping around with a long face and sighing all the time. I'm getting very tired of it all.'

He stood up. 'You always were callous, my dear. I shouldn't expect you to understand. You have never loved anyone in your life except yourself!'

She stared at him incredulously. 'Elliot! How dare you!' She too rose to her feet as the angry colour rushed into her face. 'That was an abominable thing to say and you will apologize immediately!'

'I won't, because it's true!' He was white-faced and there was something in his expression that made her nervous. 'You are a cold-hearted bitch, Catherine, and it's time you knew it!'

She was lost for words. Whatever had come over him? Whatever he had thought in the past, he had never spoken so cruelly. 'That's despicable!' she said at last. 'No gentleman would ever speak to a lady like that!'

He did not deny this statement and after a moment he said, 'I'm sorry.' But he did not *look* at all sorry. For a minute neither spoke and she regarded him curiously. She sensed a desperation within him and wondered whether something disastrous had happened at the mine. His next words confirmed this fear.

He said, 'I have something to tell you and I don't think it will wait. I should have picked a better time but – I must tell you now. Please sit down.' He himself sat down, his elbows amongst the crumbs, and put his head in his hands.

Catherine felt a wave of panic. It was not his words that alarmed her, but the manner in which he uttered them. She *knew* she did not want to hear whatever he had to say. 'I prefer to remain standing,' was all she could manage, but her throat was dry with apprehension. Perhaps he was ill ... Dying perhaps ... Or there *was* something wrong at the mine ... Or they had lost all their money! Were there financial problems? Oh, God! Not that! They were ruined ...

'Tell me!' she demanded.

'I think you should sit down, my dear.'

'My dear'? Now she was really worried. One moment he was calling her a bitch, the next it was 'My dear'!

'Elliot! Tell me!' She felt her fingernails dig into her palms as she curled her hands into two tight fists.

'Very well.' Very slowly he looked up at her and she was shocked to see compassion in his eyes. *Compassion!*

She sat down at once, trembling. 'What is it?' she whispered.

'It's Joanna, Catherine. She—'

'Joanna?' A wave of relief broke over her. 'What has she done?'

'She has done nothing.' His lips moved soundlessly as though he could not utter the words. After an agonized silence he said, 'She is my daughter.'

She heard the words but they meant nothing. How could they? Joanna his *daughter*. It was quite ridiculous.

He went on, speaking carefully, watching her face. 'Joanna is my daughter and I love her, and from now on this is to be her home. I have written to Maurice and Mary and—'

'Your *daughter*? But how ...' she stammered. 'I mean – I—'

'She is my illegitimate daughter, born before I met you. Her mother ...' He swallowed. 'Her mother was a young Portuguese woman.'

Catherine could hardly believe what she was hearing and yet her husband's expression told her that he meant every terrible word. Joanna his ... A Portuguese woman? It was impossible! 'I don't believe a word of it!' she said shakily. 'Not a word.' She tried to stand up, but her legs buckled under her. She wanted to call for Christina to fetch the sal volatile, but she dared not let the servant see her in this state. Breathless and trembling with shock, she sat down heavily.

Now he was fiddling with his table napkin and she snatched it away. 'Tell me it's not true!' she demanded, her voice shrill.

'It is true, Catherine, and I am sorry I lacked the courage to tell you years ago ... before we were married. I should have done.'

'I would never have married you!' She was almost screaming and fought to hold down her rising panic.

'I'm sorry,' he said. 'This must be dreadful for you.'

'Dreadful? It's more than dreadful! It's – it's disgusting! Abominable!' Her mind began to run round in frightening circles until she felt dizzy with fear. Did he know what he had done to her? Did he have any idea what this would mean? She would be a laughing-stock. They would all gloat over her downfall. This was worse than losing their money; worse than Elliot being ill. This was humiliating and – oh, God! She wanted to kill him! She wanted to reach out with her two hands and strangle him. He had ruined her utterly!

A fresh thought struck her. 'Does she know? Does Joanna know?'

'Yes.'

'And anyone else?'

'The family knows. They've always known.'

'The family? You mean your mother, Mary, Maurice — they all *know*? Oh, my God!' More thoughts crowded her feverish mind. 'And the mother? Joanna's mother? Where is she? Not Christina? Oh!' She felt faint. 'It's Christina, isn't it?'

'Not Christina, no. Joanna's mother is dead.'

'Dead? I don't believe you. I can always tell when you're lying, Elliot. It *is* Christina! Well, she can go too. They can both get out of my house!'

'It was *not* Christina!' he insisted. 'If you assume that, you will make a fool of yourself.'

Anger gave her a moment's strength and she cried furiously, '*You* have already done that. You've already made a fool out of me!' Her mouth worked feverishly; she could hardly get the words out fast enough. 'Oh, Elliot! How you must hate me to do such a terrible thing to me!'

'I don't hate you,' he said. 'All this happened before I even *met* you, remember. Do please try to calm yourself a little. You will make yourself ill if you go on like this.'

She tossed her head. 'Oh, yes! That would suit you very well, wouldn't it? You'd like me out of the way, wouldn't you, so that you and that bastard daughter of yours can live here.'

He shook his head. 'That's not true. I would like the two of you to be friends. Is that so impossible, Catherine? Can't we make a fresh start?'

'Friends?' She stared at him wide-eyed. '*Friends?* Are you out of your mind? The girl already hates me . . . is rude to me. Defiant little bitch! How can you—'

He reached out suddenly across the table and slapped her face and she fell back. 'Elliot!' She put a hand to her cheek, which stung with the force of the blow.

'Don't ever call Joanna a bitch again. Never! Do you hear me?'

She could only stare at him, shocked and trembling. He had never struck her before. This was the end of their marriage, the very end. She would leave him. Somehow she would free herself from a man who dared raise his hand to her. Somehow she would revenge herself for that blow. Tears of rage trembled on her eyelids, but she would not shed them. He would be glad to see her cry, glad to see her brought low.

When she had regained a little of her self-control she asked, 'Then if it wasn't Christina, who was it?'

'One of the servants.'

'A servant? Good God, Elliot!' Her mocking laughter was slightly hysterical. 'The master of the house and a slut of a servant! It's pathetic, Elliot.' She regretted the words as soon as they were out because his face was suddenly contorted with rage. He sprang up from his chair, which fell backwards, and as he came round the table towards her she thought for a terrible moment that he meant to kill her and felt the rush of adrenalin. His hands were outstretched, but instead of closing round her throat they seized her shoulders and she felt herself dragged up from the chair. She wanted to cry out, but her throat was constricted with fright and no sound came. He shook her savagely, then pushed her violently back on to the chair. She could see that he was horribly shaken by what he had done.

He said hoarsely, 'Don't ever speak of Juanita in that way again. I have tried to be a good husband to you, Catherine, but I *loved* her.'

His chest was heaving and suddenly she wanted him to die. She wanted his heart to give out under the strain. Let him collapse and die like his mother! She would be glad to see the back of both of them. Damn them! Damn the Grosvenors! She hated all of them . . .

So her name was Juanita!

He stalked to the window and stood staring out, trying to regain control of himself. She knew how much he despised violence. At least she had pushed him to the edge; at least he now knew that he was no better than any other brute of a man. She clutched at this small crumb of comfort, deciding that she would say nothing more to him. She would listen, and then she would walk out of the room. He would never know until it was too late that she intended to leave him. Then *he* would be the one to face humiliation. He would be the butt of everyone's jokes.

For a moment or two the room was silent. Catherine, one hand to her heart, waited for her own fear to subside. He began to speak again and now his voice was quieter.

'When Joanna was born, Agatha took the child back to England. She wanted to keep her, but then she thought it unfair to deprive her of a normal family life. So Maurice and Mary—'

'They've all known, all these years. My God! A conspiracy!' She tried to breathe normally, but there was a tightness in her chest. 'And your mother never said a word! How she must have laughed at me – the poor innocent dragged into the family to save your reputation. To satisfy your needs before you took another servant! You can't think how that cheapens me, Elliot. You will never understand how—'

'They called the child—'

'I don't want to know!' Unable to prevent it, she heard her voice rise shrilly. 'You stupid wretch! Do you think I care twopence for the whys and wherefores?' She took a deep breath. She *would* tell him. 'I shall leave you, Elliot!'

He said nothing; made no effort to dissuade her, and she suddenly wondered if he *wanted* her to go. Perhaps this was a trap to get rid of her. Perhaps she had fallen straight into it. She said hastily, 'At least I shall take legal advice. You won't get away with this, Elliot. I warn you.' But her mind was filled with dread and she knew that her threats lacked credibility. The law was on the side of the men and he knew that. There was probably nothing that she could do legally, and she was consumed with a passionate rage at her own helplessness.

'She's got to go!' she declared suddenly. This was the best way to punish him; possibly the only real weapon she had. 'Joanna must pack her things tonight, and you can arrange a crossing for her. I won't allow her to stay in this house, Elliot. I won't live under the same roof as your bastard child! One of us has to go!'

'Then you must go, Catherine, for I will not turn her out.' He spoke so calmly; he was turning her out of her own home, yet he spoke as though he were commenting on the weather. 'Joanna is not to blame, and there is no reason to punish her for what happened years ago. I did not even know you then; it was all over before we met. There was really no need for you ever to know.'

'So why tell me now?' She wanted desperately to know.

'Because Joanna has discovered the truth. She thought she was a foundling and now, suddenly, she knows the truth. I couldn't lie to her. She is a lovely girl—'

'I hate her! And I hate you! Oh, God, how I loathe you, Elliot. You think you can treat me like this and get away with it? Well, you will learn that you are wrong! Nobody is going to trample on me, Elliot! Oh, no!'

He stood up wearily. 'Joanna has gone fishing with Leo, but when they return I shall tell her that you know. I shall tell her that if you try to make her life miserable she is to come to me. If you try to persecute her in any way, I shall stop you, Catherine – no matter what it takes. Joanna, my daughter, is staying here! When I feel the time is right, I shall tell Leo too.'

He walked heavily from the room and Catherine watched him through the tears that blurred her eyes.

Crossing her arms on the table with a cry of anguish, she began to cry wild, passionate tears, and when Christina came in twenty minutes later she was still there and still crying.

Chapter Sixteen

L EO WAS VERY DISAPPOINTED in the Barratts' niece,
Lucy. She was only two years older than Joanna but,
in his opinion, she behaved like a prim old maid. He
had confided his thoughts on the matter to Joanna, who
had cautiously agreed with him. However, Lucy was very
pretty, he would not deny that. She was sweetly plump,
with rather bulbous blue eyes and bright golden hair which
she wore in dozens of tantalizing ringlets. Her laugh was
high and trilling, and she was obviously proud of it because
she was always laughing. In Leo's opinion, she laughed at
the silliest things. She did not want to go fishing or rowing
on the lake; she did not want to watch the horses being
shod, and she did not want to explore the countryside
around San Domingos. What she did want to do, it seemed,
was sit with her mother and aunt, talking interminably
about the Barratt family. She also liked to sew and crochet
and work on her tapestry. Fashion interested her too, and
something called 'the London season', which she had just
enjoyed, was another favourite topic. Best of all, she liked
to discuss marriage and children. Apparently men also interested her very much, and she had asked Leo several searching questions about Andrew Shreiker. All in all, he thought
her a bit of a failure and quickly stopped offering to show
her what he had rather grandly termed 'the sights'.

However, the fishing trip to the Chanca river with Joanna had been fun. As usual they had caught absolutely nothing, and Leo was certain that this was a fault of the bait they were using. Alternatively, it might have been the rod itself but, since it was a gift from his father, this seemed a rather ungrateful opinion which he kept to himself. However, the picnic had been very satisfying and they had seen a wild cat, and as he and Joanna made their way back into the compound he was feeling very pleased with life.

They went straight to the kitchen for a glass of Christina's freshly squeezed orange juice and immediately discovered that something was wrong. To Leo's surprise Christina murmured something in Joanna's ear and Joanna looked startled and sat down suddenly.

'She knows!' she whispered.

Leo asked, 'Who knows what? It's rude to have secrets.' He glared at them both and then glanced towards Liliane to see if she was more forthcoming. She hunched her shoulders and rolled her eyes dramatically, then clapped a hand over her mouth.

Christina said to him, 'Your mother, she not well. She in bed.' She put a hand to her head, miming a headache.

'Oh, is that all!' said Leo. He looked at Joanna and his eyes narrowed. 'It's not all, though, is it?'

'No, Leo.'

He stared from Joanna to Christina and then to Liliane. 'Why should you all know and not me? It's my family; I've a right to know what Christina said.' He felt hot and nervous without knowing why. There was something in the air which troubled him and made him uneasy. They had had such fun at the river and now it was all spoilt.

Joanna looked very upset. She beckoned Christina to her and whispered something else, and Christina nodded.

'Joanna! Don't do that!' he cried. 'Tell me! It's not fair!' He heard the break in his voice and Joanna stood up.

'Come to my room, Leo,' she said quietly. He thought she looked rather sad and even a little frightened, which made his heart lurch uncomfortably.

Leaving the orange juice on the table, they went slowly along the passage to Joanna's room. As they went in Joanna gave a small exclamation of alarm. On the pillow there was a sealed letter in an envelope, and Leo recognized the handwriting. It was his mother's! Why on earth should she write Joanna a letter, he wondered anxiously. It didn't make any sense.

Joanna sat down on the bed and picked up the letter while he sat on the bedside chair, swinging his legs to suggest that he was not in any way intimidated by whatever it was that was happening. He watched Joanna draw out the folded paper and read it. Her face paled and her lips trembled, but with an effort she steadied herself.

'A letter from Mama,' he said unnecessarily.

She looked at him and nodded. Then she said something very odd. She asked, 'Would you mind, Leo, if we were brother and sister instead of cousins?'

It was such a funny question that it took Leo some time to understand it. Brother and sister? But how could that be? She was a foundling and he wasn't. Did she mean that he, too, was a foundling? Were Mama and Papa not his real parents? He felt a shiver of apprehension and couldn't think of anything to say.

Joanna was looking as though she might start to cry. He hated women crying, so quickly he said, 'I don't know. Would you?' It seemed a silly thing to have said, but it was too late now.

'You see, Leo ...' Joanna was looking at him very kindly and he felt a lump in his throat. 'A long time ago, before your father met your mother ...' She put a hand over her eyes for a moment and Leo wondered if someone had died. Had Grandmother died? Was that it? He waited, hearing his heart bumping around inside his chest.

She looked at him and went on, 'Your Papa was in love with another lady, but they didn't actually get married — but they had a baby. A girl.'

So Grandmother wasn't dead. Nobody was dead. But his father had once been in love with ... he stared at Joanna. 'Do you mean ... a girl?'

She nodded, watching his face intently. Her gaze disconcerted him and he said, 'It's rude to stare!'

'I'm sorry.' She immediately looked down at her hands and he tried to think. Papa had been in love with another lady, and they had had a baby. But that was ...! He daren't even think the word, but he knew it was the wrong thing to do. His father had done something very wrong. Had he been found out? Was he now in terrible trouble? Is that why they were all so frightened? His own fear increased and he heard himself ask, 'Will he go to prison, is that it?' He tried to imagine his father in a small, dark cell with leg-irons and it seemed quite impossible. Poor Papa!

'No!' she cried, so vehemently that he believed her and was instantly reassured. 'Nothing bad will happen to your father, Leo. It's just that — you see, for a long time it was a secret, and your mother has only just found out about it and she's very upset.'

'You mean Mama is very angry?'

'Yes — but that's understandable, I think.'

So that was why Mama was in bed with a headache. Perhaps a few pills would put her right; they usually did. So that was what all the whispering was about. It didn't seem quite so terrible. He thought about the baby girl, and something else that Joanna had said came back into his mind. Was it possible? Was that what she had meant? He felt a rush of excitement that dispelled the last of his fear.

'Was it *you*, Joanna?'

After a pause she said, 'Yes, it was me, Leo. Do you mind terribly?'

Joanna was ... No, his father was ... Joanna and his

father ... He made two fists with his hands and pressed them together. When he found his voice he asked rather squeakily, 'So are we – I mean, is Papa your Papa as well?'

'Yes, Leo.'

She was looking terribly worried and he felt sorry for her. 'Does it matter?' he asked. 'Do *you* mind? Is it a rather dreadful thing to have happened?'

Now her mouth was going all wobbly and his heart sank; she *was* going to cry!

'No. Our Papa is happy about it but your Mama . . .'

Ah! Now he could see it all. His Mama was not Joanna's Mama and that made all the difference.

Rather doubtfully he said, 'I see. Yes.'

She said, 'Your Mama and your Papa both still love you a tremendous amount, Leo. It's only me.'

He frowned. 'You mean that Mama is finding it difficult to – to love you.'

'Yes.' She waved the letter. 'She wants me to go away and I may have to, Leo. I'm not sure. But I do want to know that you and I are still good friends.'

'What does it say? The letter.'

She hesitated. 'It's rather private, Leo.'

To his horror two large tears rolled down her cheeks and he stood up, embarrassed, and walked past her to stare out of the window. He had always wanted a sister or a brother, and now he had Joanna and Mama wanted to send her away. It was all jolly difficult. No wonder Mama was in bed with a headache. These little problems always affected her. He listened to Joanna and noticed that she was crying harder than ever. Now there were tears in his own eyes!

He suddenly heard himself cry out, 'Don't go away, Joanna!' And then he turned and flung himself into her arms and they were both bawling, and having a girl's arms around him was not as bad as he'd expected.

When it was over and they had blown their noses and

laughed a bit, she said, 'I'm going to talk to Mr Benbridge, Leo. He might be able to help me. I don't really know what to do.'

'Can I come with you?'

'I think it will be a bit embarrassing,' she told him. 'I think I might feel better if I went alone.'

He nodded reluctantly. 'But you won't go away, will you? You won't just disappear?'

'I promise I won't. If I have to go anywhere, I'll tell you first.'

Leo was rather reluctant to let his new sister out of his sight. 'I'd like that,' he said.

*

Steven read the letter which Catherine had sent to Joanna. It was short and to the point:

> Joanna,
>   My husband has told me about his affair with his servant. You will understand, I'm sure, if I tell you I no longer want you under my roof. I feel that you have trespassed on my hospitality under false pretences. Now that I know exactly who and what you are, I would like you to leave San Domingos before seven o'clock today. I don't think we have anything to say to each other.
>   Catherine

He was aware that Joanna watched him nervously. 'I'll have to go,' she said.

Steven folded the letter slowly. 'What about your father? Won't he have something to say about this? Have you seen him since he told Catherine?'

'No. Leo and I were at the Chanca all day, fishing. I suppose Papa is at the Palacio or the mine. I wanted to talk to you first.' She looked at him anxiously. 'You said that I could come to you.'

'I'm glad you did.'

She waited, then she said, 'We didn't catch anything; we never do.'

'Maybe there are no fish!'

'Maybe.'

They were sitting on his veranda, watching the sun go down.

'I shall have to go back to England, I suppose,' she suggested, without much enthusiasm.

'Is that a possibility?'

For a moment or two she rocked slowly and then said, 'Not really. At least it would be very difficult, actually. You see, I left under a kind of a cloud.' She sighed. 'I seem to cause trouble everywhere I go, although I never mean to; it just happens.'

'What has happened here is not your fault. How could it be? You weren't even born.'

'No, but – it's because of me, isn't it? In France it was partly my fault. I can't blame it all on Mark.' She looked the picture of dejection and he was full of compassion for her plight. She seemed very young for her age and hardly able to cope with life's hard knocks. He wondered what had happened in France but, hearing Mark's name, almost wished he had not.

'Oh, dear!' He smiled at her. 'Do you want to tell me about France? It's not compulsory.'

'You won't think much of me if I do tell you,' she said in a strangled voice. 'But I would like to tell someone.'

'Try me!' he told her.

There was another long silence. In the soft twilight she looked very beautiful, with her dark eyes and sharp little cheekbones. Very Portuguese, he thought. She also had some of the Portuguese characteristics: she was at once trusting yet reserved; she had a sense of humour but also the capacity to feel deeply. He wondered how different her life would have been if she had been brought up by Portuguese grandparents. Presumably that had been an option at the time. Obviously she took after her mother, but there was something in her voice that reminded him of Elliot Grosvenor. What characteristics had she inherited from him, he wondered? There was no trace of the family arrogance, but perhaps a hint of their resilience.

She had begun haltingly, but her voice grew stronger as she went along. He made no attempt to interrupt her.

'My adopted brother Mark is ... was—' she corrected herself, 'a most charming person. I have loved him – *had* loved him for years. He was the sun and moon to me. It was Mark who told me I was a foundling, and I trusted him because he had told me the truth. I was shocked and bewildered, but I trusted him. It seemed that the others – my mother and father – had lied to me. Of course, I realize now that they might have told me eventually, but I didn't see it that way then. I thought I could be in love with Mark because he was no relation. Not really, only by adoption.'

She looked at him anxiously, but he simply nodded.

'When he met Isobel and became betrothed to her I was devastated. I had always believed that he loved only me. Childish, I suppose ...' She sighed. 'One day he said that I could prove my love for him by allowing him to ...' A hand crept up to hide her mouth as though she dared not permit the words utterance. 'To do something ... as though we were man and wife ...'

Nodding, he stifled an exclamation of anger and hoped that his expression gave nothing away.

'I wasn't sure. It seemed a very final thing to do and I didn't know – I wasn't happy about it but ...' She lowered her voice so that he could hardly hear her. 'I didn't know how people had children.' She looked at him and swallowed hard.

She is probably still ignorant of such matters, he reflected. His own wife had known nothing on their wedding night; he had been very gentle, very reassuring, but still she had been shocked. Trying to imagine Joanna with a young man, he was appalled to feel a strong surge of jealousy. He still said nothing. Talking about such a delicate subject would be very hard for her.

She went on, 'But Mark said he knew all about it because he had already done it, and nothing would happen. I had to trust him. There was no one in whom I could confide about such a thing. It was to prove my love for him ... I think I believed that if I – if he was *pleased* with me – he would give up Isobel. I thought that if we were not really brother and sister, we could marry. I suppose you think me very stupid.' She looked at him with a flash of defiance, daring him to agree.

'No,' he told her, his heart aching. 'Not at all. Any woman would have thought the same in the circumstances.'

Her face brightened immediately. 'Oh, Steven! Do you think so? I mean, honestly?'

'Honestly!'

'Oh!' She appeared quite overcome by this judgement, and he began to understand how deeply she had been burdened by her guilt.

She continued, haltingly. 'I – that is we – did what Mark wanted.' She waited for an exclamation of disapproval but Steven managed to remain impassive and she took a deep breath. 'It was all a terrible disappointment,' she told him.

He hid a smile.

'He was very pleased, but I thought it was – well, not at all romantic. Anyway, it didn't make any difference to their betrothal.'

A sudden thought shocked him into an involuntary exclamation. Had she had a child by this wretched man? Was that the disaster for which she had been banished to Portugal? If so, then Fate had come full circle. He stared at her.

'What is it?' She was anxious. 'What have I said?'

'It's nothing. Truly!' The thought of Joanna with another man's child was not as unbearable as he had expected. Children were children, and all needed love and attention; he could accept a child. But the more he explored the idea, the more unlikely it appeared. He could not imagine Joanna giving up her child. Or had it died? He fought down his impatience, knowing he must wait for her to tell it in her own time.

'Go on,' he encouraged. 'I'm listening.'

'I thought it was all over, but then somebody told Mama that we had been together in the wood . . . and they were very disappointed in me. They thought I was ungrateful, which I was. They thought I should come here for a few months.' She swallowed hard. 'I daresay they wanted to be rid of me! I came here, and then—' Her lips trembled. 'Then they read a letter which I had sent to Mark and they blamed me for what had happened and . . . they said they don't want me home. Not ever.'

Steven thought he had never heard such a sad story and he said, 'Poor Joanna. The world can be a cruel place.' He wanted to say a lot more; he longed to take her in his arms and promise that he would never let anything hurt her again. But he dare not. Instead he asked, 'So you feel you cannot return to England?'

'How can I?' She sighed again, a deep sigh from the depths of her soul which tore at his heartstrings. 'They don't want me at home and Catherine doesn't want me here.'

'But your father? He will want you to stay.'

'But she will make it impossible. I can't stay if she hates me so much! It would be intolerable.' She glanced at him miserably. 'One way or another, I seem to have ruined my life before it's even started! You must despise me! You must think me a dreadful fool.'

'No. I think you've been treated very badly by young Mark. You made an error of judgement by trusting him, but can't you see that you have been the victim of circumstance? I don't see how you are in any way to blame.'

So Joanna was not a virgin. She had been persuaded into a seduction by her unscrupulous 'brother', who was in fact her cousin. That was bad enough, but at least she had not been as unlucky as Juanita. She appeared to have escaped conception. A young and vulnerable girl had been exploited by a young man old enough to know better. It was scandalous, but Joanna was not to blame.

Joanna stood up suddenly. 'Well, now that you know it all I expect you would rather I went. It's not a very nice story, and I'm not proud of myself.'

Abruptly he said, 'Does young Shreiker know all this?'

She shook her head and he felt a glow of pleasure that she had confided only in him.

'If you went back to England, where would you go?'

'Aunt Agatha might put me up for a few weeks, until I find somewhere else. I wouldn't go the wedding; I'd be a terrible embarrassment to them all. I could find work of some kind. I could be a companion, maybe? Or a children's governess. I've been well educated.'

He hated the idea that she might go away. 'What about the Barratts? Would they offer you a bed, temporarily?'

'They have no room. Harriet and Lucy are staying with them.'

'Of course! I'd forgotten.' He hesitated. 'You could stay here. There's only one bed; I could make do on the sofa, but I suppose that would do your reputation no good. It would probably make things worse.' Reluctantly he asked, 'What about young Shreiker? Will you tell him?'

'Oh!' She glanced away. 'That's all over. I told him last night. Suddenly I feel so old!' she said. 'I suppose it's all this anxiety ... I daresay I could go to Maria Torres. She is my other grandmother — although she doesn't know who I am. If she did, she might give me a bed, but I can't speak enough Portuguese and anyway I would be a terrible shock to her and that might cause more trouble. I don't quite see what I can do.'

'You could marry me,' he said, and was astonished to hear the words spoken aloud. 'I mean, Joanna, that—'

'Oh, please don't!' she cried, springing to her feet in alarm. 'You don't have to feel sorry for me! I just need to get away from here. I don't care what happens to me! I don't care what people think! I can go away and I'll survive somehow! I don't want your pity, Steven!'

'I'm not offering pity, you idiot!' he shouted. 'I'm offering *love*!'

She looked at him wildly. 'I don't want anyone's love. I want respect! Oh, God! I don't want to stay here! I knew I'd hate Portugal and I do. Damn San Domingos! Damn you all with your stupid secrets and — Coming to Portugal has just made everything so much worse!'

He regretted his rash words, but it was too late to unsay them and now he felt a wave of panic. She was going to disappear from his life, and his own stupidity had precipitated the event. 'I'm sorry,' he said. 'Please forget that I said what I did. I was just afraid that you would leave San Domingos. Surely you can't leave your father? You'll break his heart. He has risked so much for you by telling Catherine. Go to him, Joanna, and show him the letter. Ask his advice. Give him a chance to help you.'

He saw that she hesitated, saw the glint of tears and cursed himself. She had wanted calm reassurance and he had simply added to her confusion by declaring a love he had hardly known existed.

'Maybe,' she said wearily. 'I must go, but thank you for your time.'

His *time*! Damnation! He would have given his life to help her and instead he had added to her worries.

In another moment she was gone. He watched her speechlessly until her slim form blended with the dark night.

'Steven Benbridge!' he murmured. 'You are a damned fool!'

*

The room in which Clementine lay was small, with a high ceiling and shutters which kept it dark and cool. Nurse Williams sat beside the bed, writing notes on her patient's condition. She wore her uniform and hoped that she was using her time in a way that Elliot Grosvenor would approve. She had begged Sister Sammon to be allowed to spend time with her patient and at last she had relented. Since Mrs Grosvenor's collapse there was little to do at home, and the fear loomed large in Nurse Williams' heart that her services might prove dispensable. Certainly, if the old lady died there would be no reason for her to remain in San Domingos, and she would almost certainly be paid off and despatched back to England. That would mean a return to her sister's mean little house in Edmonton while she searched the columns of the *Nursing Gazette* and applied for another post. She would be very reluctant to return to England. San Domingos and the old lady suited her very well.

Every day when she turned up at the hospital she read the night nurse's report and spoke to Doctor Barratt. Then she wrote all this information in a small notebook which she showed to either her mistress or master at some time of the day. She also relieved the hospital nurse of some of her duties – changing the bed-linen, washing the patient and so on. In this way she felt she was making herself useful, and each day brought hope that old Mrs Grosvenor might make a sudden recovery. Nurse Williams prayed hard, too, for this to happen.

'Temperature normal at 98.4°,' she wrote. 'Pulse fluctuating slightly but not significantly so . . .'

'What else?' she thought desperately.

'Skin colour a shade warmer . . .'

Maybe it was not a little warmer, but it was a small lie which no one would bother to dispute.

'Bladder and bowel condition unchanged . . .'

'Eyes still closed. Breathing light but stertorous . . .'

She liked that word. 'Stertorous'. She had read it in the *Gazette* and thought it had a nice medical ring to it.

The so-called sister put her head round the door and said, 'Cup of tea, dear?'

'Please!' She glanced up from her writing and forced a smile. She hated being addressed as 'Dear'; it sounded so unprofessional, but she did not want to antagonize the hospital staff. Mildred Sammon was probably about thirty, thin, ginger-haired and covered with freckles. A mess, poor woman. True, she was pleasant enough but hardly out of the top drawer. There were very occasional hints of London's East End in her speech. Nurse Williams prided herself on her ability to spot these small details.

She stared round with a sigh. To one side of her was an empty bed, high, with a metal frame which had been painted white. There were two small lockers and two small chairs. Two small *uncomfortable* chairs, as Nurse Williams had discovered for herself. It was possible to pull a blue curtain between the two beds, but since the other was unoccupied this was not necessary. There was also a small table holding various bottles; three white enamel bowls of different sizes; a syringe; two glasses. On the wall was a small cupboard which contained bandages, lint etc. The window looked out across rooftops to the plain that surrounded San Domingos. All very correct and clean and clinical.

It was fine for the hospital staff, she thought. They rarely had more than one bed in use at a time. Last month there had been the man with malaria; before that a miner with a gash on his shoulder from a falling rock. Whatever did the staff do with their time, she asked herself with a disparaging sniff. How did they justify their wages?

Normally, Nurse Williams had a patient who required attention twenty-four hours a day, day in, day out. Not that she was complaining, but there it was. *Had* had a patient, she reminded herself nervously.

'Here you are, dear!' The sister smiled her thin, professional smile as she laid a small tray on the table. 'Milk and sugar.'

'Thank you very much.' Nurse Williams indicated the notebook in which she had been writing. 'Just bringing the records up to date,' she said, 'for my employers. They expect to be kept fully informed of my patient's condition.' She laid the faintest emphasis upon the word 'my'.

'That shouldn't be difficult!' The sister laughed. 'Just write "No change!"'

Typical of the woman! Nurse Williams stuck out her tongue at Mildred Sammon's retreating back. No change, indeed! That just showed the level of her imagination — and her attitude to her work! No change! The easy way out. How very typical of today's nurses. They seemed to recruit just *anybody* these days, and modern training left a lot to be desired.

She heaved herself off the chair, poured out a cup of tea and stirred in three spoonfuls of sugar. Glancing at the old lady, she saw that beneath the closed eyelids the eyes seemed to flicker convulsively. They had done that several times during the last two days. Carefully, Nurse Williams put down the cup and saucer and picked up her notebook.

'Eyelids fluttering from time to time. Might be a hopeful sign.'

'And might not,' she muttered as she went back to her tea, sipping it carefully, relishing its sweetness. She smiled faintly. Old Mr Lubbard used to say she shouldn't take sugar, that she was sweet enough. Dear old boy, she had missed him when he went. Eighty-one years old, and he had been bedridden for twelve of them with never a word of complaint. She let her mind dwell on some of her patients, the good and the bad. Miss Jules, with that terrible wasting disease — and so virulent that after Nurse Williams arrived the poor soul had only seven months left to live. And Mr Harris. *Hubert* Harris. Nurse Williams' chest heaved with a huge sigh. She had been ready to marry Hubert Harris, and he would have married her if those daughters of his had not interfered. Oh, well! It was all water under the bridge now, but she often wondered how things might have been. She had nursed him too well! He had recovered from his broken hip, and the daughters had been quick to dispense with her services, for which they were paying. Dear Hubert . . .

Suddenly her patient groaned! She actually groaned! Nurse Williams was so startled that her hand shook and she spilt tea down the front of her uniform. Carefully she put down the cup. She had not imagined it, she *had* heard a groan — but what kind of groan was it? Was this the end? Was the groan a precursor of death or a sign that all might once again be well? Would Nurse Williams' life in San Domingos resume, or was her employment about to be terminated?

She leaned over the bed and whispered fiercely, 'Mrs Grosvenor! We mustn't give in! We can fight this! I know we can!'

She was rewarded by another sound, almost a groan yet more deliberate. A grunt, perhaps, as though the old lady was trying to speak. The eyelids remained closed but suddenly the grey lips twitched uncontrollably. Nurse Williams' heart leaped. Her patient was coming round! Excitedly she caught hold of the nearest frail hand and patted and rubbed it vigorously. 'Come on! Come on!' she cried, as though urging on a racehorse to the winning- post. Her training told her that she should summon the doctor, but she wanted to make the most of this unexpected development; she needed to savour the sweet fruits of success. Already she could imagine how the story would be told.

Nurse Williams was *there* when the breakthrough finally came! The devotion of Mrs Grosvenor's *personal* nurse had surely been the crucial factor in her recovery! The family would be eternally grateful to her. She stared at the pale face, willing another sound from the bloodless lips. When it came it was not a groan, nor was it a murmur. It was a distinct word – faint and quavering, but recognizable as a word. Clearly the old lady said, 'Elliot!'

She had *spoken*! At last Nurse Williams allowed herself to accept the fact that her prayers had been answered. She relinquished the withered hand and rushed joyfully out of the room in search of the doctor.

Doctor Barratt was in the reception area talking to a young Portuguese man, but he immediately abandoned him and followed Nurse Williams along the corridor, his white coat flapping. As they passed the dispensary he called to Sister Sammon, and she too hurried along.

Nurse Williams told her, 'She's rallying!' and added triumphantly, 'I thought she would. I never gave up hope.'

The three of them stood round the old lady's bed and were astonished to see that the patient's eyes were now open.

'Elliot! I want to see Elliot!'

The doctor said, 'You will, Mrs Grosvenor! We'll fetch him at once.' To Nurse Williams he said, 'This is wonderful and, to be honest, most unexpected.' He lifted the patient's eyelids and peered into her eyes. 'Splendid! Splendid!' he muttered.

Nurse Williams beamed, happy beyond belief. She turned towards the sister and saw that she, too, was impressed by events.

'Splendid indeed!' said Nurse Williams and then, to be sure she would be first with the good news, she said, 'I'll fetch Mr Grosvenor myself,' and was off on winged feet in the direction of the Palacio.

Chapter Seventeen

ELLIOT WAS DELIGHTED with his mother's unexpected recovery, although the doctor warned him that they were 'not out of the wood yet'. His joy was tempered, however, by a second, equally pressing problem. As soon as he left his mother's bedside he went in search of Joanna and learned from Leo that she was with Steven Benbridge. He thanked him and was about to hurry away when Leo stopped him in his tracks.

'I know, Papa!' he said. 'I know all about Joanna. Does she have to go away?'

Taken by surprise, Elliot stared down into the large grey eyes of his son. 'Go away? Joanna? Of course not.'

He was going to ask Leo *how* he knew, but the boy said quickly, 'Mama has sent Joanna a letter. She says she has to go away.'

Elliot hesitated. Anxious though he was to find Joanna, he must not neglect his son at such a traumatic time. He laid a hand on his shoulder and said gently, 'I'm glad you know. I was going to tell you myself, Leo. You do believe that, don't you?' The boy nodded. 'Was it Mama who told you?' He hoped not; he could imagine what a garbled account Leo would have received from Catherine.

'It was Joanna.'

'And how do you feel about — about everything, Leo? Do you think we can all still be happy? And friends?'

'Yes, Papa. I wish Joanna wasn't going away.'

'I'll see that she doesn't, Leo.' He patted his arm reassuringly. 'I'll go and talk to her now. Don't worry, I won't let her go. We both want her to stay, and maybe Mama will change her mind.' He did not think this at all likely, but he hoped that it would satisfy Leo for the present.

Leo asked, 'May I come with you?'

'I think not, Leo.'

'Nobody ever lets me go anywhere!' he grumbled, and ducked pointedly as Elliot reached out to ruffle his hair.

'Some things need to be said privately, Leo. You are wise enough to appreciate that, aren't you?'

His son nodded reluctantly and Elliot left him to his thoughts and went in search of his daughter. As he approached Benbridge's house he saw Joanna leave; she was almost running down the path, and he wondered what prompted her haste.

'Joanna! Wait!' he called, and she slowed her pace at once and turned to smile a welcome; a smile that was so genuine that at once he knew how worthwhile all this present disruption was. Catherine would come round eventually, he told himself. She *must*, and then his family would be complete. He had to expect difficulties at this stage, but matters would resolve themselves with a little patience.

'Joanna, I know about the letter. Leo told me.' He thought she looked very agitated, but it was hardly surprising. 'You must ignore it; I'm sure it was written in the heat of the moment. I shall speak to the doctor. It may be that Catherine needs a strong sedative. She's at breaking point, I'm afraid . . .' When she merely nodded he asked, 'You were not going to leave, were you? Leo says you think—'

'I decided I should go away for a few days at least,' she told him. 'I thought about Maria Torres; she is my grandmother, after all, but I don't know how to tell her. And is it fair to her? I wish I knew.'

He slipped an arm through hers and led her across the praca to one of the seats. 'Maria will have to be told,' he agreed, 'but why don't you go to see her when all this is straightened out? There is plenty of time. As to whether or not it's fair to her, I imagine she will be delighted.' He took hold of her hand. 'As for Catherine's letter, I suggest we go back to the house and you go to bed as usual and I – I sit out the storm!' He laughed wryly at his choice of phrase. 'Catherine is very highly strung. She always over-reacts, and now she has a genuine excuse for a little melodrama. Not that I'm underestimating the shock to her pride, nor her sense of betrayal. In her place I should feel very upset, but in time she will adjust.'

'Mr Benbridge says that I am not to blame myself.'

'He's very wise!' He raised a hand in greeting to Oliver Jackson as he passed the bandstand. One by one the members of the band were assembling to practise their music; each one nodded to Elliot and he acknowledged them politely.

To Joanna he said curiously, 'What else did Benbridge say?'

She hesitated. 'He said that he loves me,' she replied, rather crossly. 'He offered to marry me. It was very kind of him but—'

In spite of his worries, Elliot grinned. 'Not another one! It seems my daughter is quite a heart-breaker!'

To his surprise she did not laugh but said, 'I like older men, Papa.'

'Do you now?'

'Especially Mr Benbridge. Because he's not romantic like some men – at least, not usually. He's quite sensible.'

'Oh!' Elliot was silenced by this comment. 'Did you know he had once been married? His wife died soon afterwards.'

She nodded. 'Leo told me.' She smiled suddenly. 'Leo is a mine of information!'

They became aware of Leo hurrying towards them over the grass, as though summoned by the use of his name. One of the bandsmen called out to him, but he paid the man no heed.

'Papa!' he called breathlessly, and Elliot sensed with a lurch of the heart that this was more bad news. His first thought was that Clementine had had a relapse. The incredible improvement in her health had seemed too good to be true.

'Is it Grandmother?' he asked, bracing himself for the worst.

Leo shook his head. 'It's Mama! I've just been talking to Juan-Carlos and he's been talking to the groom. He says that Mama's gone riding; she took Star and rode off towards Mertola.'

'Gone riding?' Elliot exclaimed, while beside him Joanna gave a cry of alarm. 'But I thought she was resting. The doctor said she needed to rest.'

'Perhaps she has gone riding to clear her head,' Joanna suggested.

'At this hour? And in her condition?'

Leo said, 'Juan-Carlos says she's gone away. She said "*Adeos*" to the groom and thanked him for everything. She's never said that to Senor Jorge before.'

'Oh, Leo!' For a moment Elliot was stunned by this new calamity and could not think rationally. He felt dazed and disorientated.

Leo stared at his father. 'Papa! *Papa!* You must bring her back!' He was near to tears. 'You must go after her!'

With an effort Elliot forced himself to face the problem. 'Yes, of course.' For his son's sake he tried to appear calm. 'Go and find Juan-Carlos, Leo. Tell him to saddle up my horse and one for himself. I'll find Mama and bring her home, don't you fret.'

As the boy raced away he turned to Joanna. 'Catherine cannot be in a fit state to ride after all the sedation she's had.'

'What can I do, Papa?'

Papa! His daughter had called him 'Papa'! It sounded so right. Even in the midst of a worsening crisis, Elliot felt his spirits lift a little, but this was no time to rejoice.

'Find the doctor, Joanna, will you? Tell him what has happened, but don't broadcast it.' He put a hand to his eyes and tried to clear his thoughts. 'I expect Christina knows; Juan-Carlos will have told her. I'll have to go now.'

'I'm so sorry!' she said.

He took hold of her hands and looked at her earnestly. 'And please don't blame yourself, Joanna! I take full responsibility for Catherine's actions — d'you understand? You cannot possibly be held responsible for all the world's woes.' He attempted an encouraging smile. 'Don't worry, I'll find her. She won't have gone far; she's very angry and probably wants to frighten me. I know her better than you do.'

Joanna nodded.

'And take care of Leo for me. He's so bright we sometimes forget he's only a child.'

He watched her go and hoped he had reassured her, although in reality he felt far from confident and hurried towards the stables with a sense of impending disaster which he could not shake off.

*

Somehow Catherine clung to the reins with a determination fuelled by anger. The tears in her eyes blurred her vision, and her legs were so weak she could scarcely keep her foot in the stirrup. She rode side-saddle as usual, but she had not changed into her riding-habit and her full skirts bunched round her legs disconcertingly. Her head ached from the brandy she had drunk, and the alcohol mixed with the doctor's sedative was playing havoc with her mind. All she knew was that she must get away, and that she would never go back. The letter to Joanna had been her last chance, but the deadline had arrived and Joanna's clothes were still in her room. So she had not left for England as instructed. The little bitch thought she had called Catherine's bluff, but she would soon know better! When Elliot was faced with his wife's disappearance he would blame Joanna! That would not only cast a blight on their relationship, it would also cause him maximum embarrassment — the kind of embarrassment he would have inflicted on her!

As she rode she fought to stay awake, to remain alert, but found herself swaying erratically in the saddle. Star was usually very reliable, but she was dimly aware that she was alarming him by her constantly changing position and conflicting signals. More than once she almost fell, when the horse stumbled or swerved, but miraculously she remained in the saddle and her anger was mixed with a kind of elation that she could undertake this desperate escape and succeed. 'You'll be sorry you crossed me, Elliot Grosvenor!' she muttered. 'And I'll see you rot in hell, Joanna!'

Illogically, most of her anger was directed towards Joanna, the cuckoo in her nest. That cheap little slut! That sly little bitch! Worming her way into Elliot's affection and turning him against her!

She had wanted to kill them both, had seriously considered how it might be done without incriminating herself, but finally acknowledged that it was impossible. So she was leaving; she would disappear from their lives, and they would never know what had become of her. The mystery of her disappearance would haunt her husband until the day he died, and the burden of guilt would finally crush him.

'Oh, Elliot! Just you wait!'

Her smile was crooked and for a moment her grip on the reins slackened, but with an enormous effort of will she sat up straight and urged the horse to greater efforts. Her lungs were straining and her back ached from the jolting as Star pounded across the uneven ground at a pace that, in her right mind, she would never have attempted. With her crop she whipped the horse on, faster and faster, regardless of her safety, concerned only with the urge to put a hundred miles between herself, her husband and Joanna.

After a while she reined in, breathing hard, and tried hazily to take stock of her position. She had started out towards Mertola with the vague idea that from there she would find some form of transport to Vila Real, and from there a ship back to Lisbon. After riding for nearly thirty frantic minutes, however, she was not at all sure where she was. Her confused signals had changed her mount's direction so many times that she might have been anywhere. And now it was getting dark. A curse rose in her throat as the first hint of fear touched her. If she was not going towards Mertola, then where was she? There were wolves around San Domingos, but surely she was safe enough while she had the horse? Overhead a large bird swooped low with a mournful cry and, startled, Star reared up. Catherine grabbed his mane, hung on grimly and somehow kept her seat. She stared around as her anxiety grew. Suddenly her anger was replaced by fear.

'Where am I, for God's sake!'

The land lay about her, grey and unfamiliar. There was no landmark that she recognized. Feeling the beginnings of panic, she spoke sternly to herself: 'Just ride on. You must be near Mertola.'

More circumspect now, she allowed her horse to move at a trot, but a few minutes later a hare sprang out of the grass ahead of them and, with a shrill whinny of fear, Star dug in his front hooves, lowered his head and pulled to an abrupt halt. Unable to stop herself, Catherine slipped forward and over the horse's head and fell heavily to the ground. She screamed with pain and fright, and the unexpected sound finally unsettled the horse and sent him racing away into the gloom, the thunder of his hooves diminishing until she was left alone with the silence.

Catherine lay where she had fallen and wept tears of frustration and rage. Damn the animal! It felt as though every bone in her body had been broken in the fall. Her head ached and her thoughts swirled helplessly as the brandy and the medication continued to affect her bloodstream. She wanted to lie there and sleep, but her strong sense of survival would not allow it. Cautiously she sat up, amazed and relieved to discover that although she ached all over there were no bones broken. Was it possible that she could still walk? She scrambled unsteadily to her feet and stood swaying, arms outstretched to balance herself. Her legs shook with fatigue and weakness, but she remained upright, staring round her into the gathering gloom. Clutching her skirts she stumbled forward a few paces, then stopped and tried to clear her eyes which were again filling with tears. A wave of dizziness swept over her and, searching for the worst word she had ever heard, she whispered, 'Bloody Joanna!' She stumbled and fell to her knees and for a long moment she remained there, sobbing, but then her instinct for self-preservation rose once more.

'Get up!' she told herself furiously. 'Get up, you fool!'

On her feet again, she moved forward once more but now her wits, addled by abuse and weariness, deserted her. Her footsteps wandered crazily, so she made very little progress. All about her the sounds of the night echoed disconcertingly: the screech of a bat, the rustle of a snake in the grass, the dart of a racoon across the hillocky ground in front of her. Her resolve, once so strong, began to falter and for the first time she wondered if Elliot would come in search of her . . . If not, the wolves would get her. Later they would find what remained of her body and Elliot would not shed a tear. He hated her . . .

She wandered for more than an hour until the moonlight shone eerily on the landscape and her fears intensified. The cool night air did nothing to clear her head and, dazed with exhaustion, she was on the point of giving up when she tripped and fell. She had stumbled over the railway line!

'The railway! Oh, thank God!'

At least she knew vaguely where she was now and she tried to concentrate her mind. She was somewhere between San Domingos and Pomerao. She stared along the track in both directions. One way led to home and comfort – but also to Elliot and Joanna. The other way led to the little town of Pomerao, where she would have to explain who she was and what she was doing – wandering on foot, dishevelled and half-crazed in the moonlight. Catherine shook her head helplessly.

'I can't!' she admitted.

With a gasp of relief she surrendered and chose home. The problem was, which way *was* home? The railway extended for twelve kilometres, and she might be only a few kilometres from either end. She shrugged wearily and stared up at the cloudless sky, but the position of the stars meant nothing to her. North or south? Or should it be east or west? The moon could not help her, either. It was in the lap of the gods! She told herself that she was past caring and began to walk.

*

The two men had been riding for less than twenty minutes when they spotted Catherine's riderless horse. Star was cantering sedately back towards San Domingos, and when Elliot whistled he came obediently and allowed him to take hold of the reins.

'So where in hell is your mistress, eh?' Elliot demanded.

Star shook his head and stood patiently beside him while Elliot tried to decide what to do. Juan-Carlos shrugged and spread his hands, palms upturned, to show that he was at a loss also.

'I'll keep Star with me and ride straight on,' Elliot told him, in Portuguese. 'You weave across my track, first to the right, then to the left. If either one of us finds her we whistle, so don't go too far in either direction. If she's been hurt in the fall, don't try to move her. Wait for me, do you understand?'

Juan-Carlos nodded, his eyes large with importance. Elliot had a vision of his wife lying dead somewhere. He would never forgive himself for not realizing the extent of her distress. He should never have gone to the Palacio, leaving her to the mercy of the doctor. It was not Barratt's fault; he could never have appreciated the depths of Catherine's hatred or the lengths to which she would go. The shock might well have unhinged her mind and he, Elliot, should have foreseen the possibility.

He rode carefully, skimming the path on either side as far as the eye could see in the twilight. If injured, she would be easy prey for wolves. If uninjured but undiscovered, she could die of exposure in her present condition. She was heavily sedated, and there was always a likelihood that she might have drunk brandy. She had turned to the bottle once or twice before, in times of trouble, a fact which he had successfully hidden from everyone else.

'Catherine! Catherine!' he shouted. 'It's me. Elliot!' His voice carried in the stillness, but there was no answer. He wondered how far she had gone towards Mertola before she had been thrown, or had fallen. He did not want to blame the horse since he could not rule out the possibility that, under the influence of a lethal cocktail, his wife had simply fallen asleep and slipped from the horse's back.

'Catherine! Catherine!' he shouted, again and again, but still there was no answering shout. From time to time, in the distance, he could hear Juan-Carlos's voice calling her. She seemed to have vanished into thin air.

He knew now that, without the horse, there was no way that Catherine could have reached Mertola; but he pressed on nevertheless until he gained the outskirts of the town, where he met Juan-Carlos who had also drawn a blank. Elliot alerted the Chief of Police and informed him simply that his wife had been thrown while out riding. The official shook his head emphatically; they had heard of no such incident, they had found no such woman. He could do nothing in the dark. Did Senor Grosvenor want a search party organized as soon as it was light?

'Most certainly.' Elliot gave a description of Catherine, her height, colouring and so on, but did not know exactly what she had been wearing. 'A creamy-coloured dress, I think you'd call it. Or maybe pale yellow.' He watched as the Chief of Police wrote down the details while Juan-Carlos, holding the three mounts, watched gloomily.

Elliot remounted and took the reins of Catherine's horse. They would ride back to San Domingos, he announced, and they would vary their route so that even in the dark there was a chance they might find her. The long ride home seemed to take an eternity, but they arrived back at the mine in the early hours of the morning. As soon as it was dawn, the anxious household awoke to the grave news that Catherine had apparently vanished.

*

In fact, Catherine had only been five kilometres from Pomerao and seven from San Domingos, when she found the track; but, not knowing this, she had made the wrong choice and walked towards Pomerao. Her confusion was giving way to a kind of delirium in which the past mingled unhappily with the present, and there were moments when she wondered where she was and what she was doing, alone and in the darkness. The one fact that she clung to was the double thread of silver which stretched interminably ahead, as the moonlight was reflected from the railway track. With every step she reminded herself that she would soon be home. By the time she eventually staggered into Pomerao's main street it was deserted. To the left, the rows of houses rose up the steep sides of the valley, and here and there a few lights gleamed. To the right there was only an inky blackness, a puzzling void.

Convinced that she had reached the mine, Catherine stared round her, trying to pick out the Palacio or the bandstand. Suddenly, while she was still trying to get her bearings, her failing strength deserted her, her legs buckled treacherously and she pitched forward on to the road. Bruised and badly shaken by yet another fall, she lay there for a long time, too weary and dispirited to rise to her feet. Her anger, grief and fear had left her; she was aware only of an overwhelming desire to sleep. She had come home. Now it was up to Elliot to find her. Tomorrow seemed a long way off, and she would worry about that when it came.

It was a cold nose that finally roused her. She felt it pressed enquiringly against the back of her neck and gave a small scream. The dog barked, sprang away, sprang back and thrust its nose against her face. Excited, it growled and barked again, to be answered by another dog and then a third. By the time Catherine opened her eyes the three long-legged creatures were regarding her curiously, and she shuddered. From her position on the ground they seemed larger than was natural, apparently towering over her threateningly. The hounds of hell!

'Get away, you brutes!' she cried weakly, but the sound of her voice merely served to increase their interest. One of them darted forward and worried at her shoe. When she tried to kick it away it nipped her ankle, and she shrieked in distaste and lunged towards it. The dog snatched lightly at her outstretched hand, enjoying the game, and a fourth shape materialized from the surrounding gloom. In the darkness the animals appeared menacing, and a sudden suspicion entered Catherine's tortured mind. *Hounds* did not attack defenceless people.

'Oh, my God!' she whispered. They were not hounds but wolves – a threatening pack of wolves! It was the realization of her worst nightmare, and with a scream she struggled to her feet and tried to kick the nearest one. The effort unbalanced her and she fell back, crashing heavily to the ground again, where one of them pounced on her and she could feel two paws scrabble at her shoulders.

'Help me!' she screamed. She struck out with her fist and managed to hit one of them in the face so that it leaped back, howling with fright. She managed to stand again and began to back away, but her foot caught on the railway line where it curved towards the river and she almost fell – but somehow regained her balance. The air seemed full of snapping and snarling and she was surrounded by writhing, threatening bodies. From somewhere among the houses she heard a door open and voices. Foreign voices. Where was Elliot?

'Elliot!' she screamed. 'Help me!'

Another door opened, but all the voices were Portuguese. The 'wolves' crept after her, snapping and snarling, as she backed away; then suddenly two of them lunged towards her. One had leaped high and she thought it was going for her throat. With all her remaining strength she turned and ran. At first her footsteps rang out on the wooden decking but then, abruptly, they were stilled as she reached the end of the railway track and plunged into the darkness beneath. Catherine fell thirty feet into the swiftly-flowing river and her thin screams went unheard. She couldn't swim but she thrashed about wildly, sobered by the sudden immersion.

'Elliot! Ellio-o-t!'

Astonished by her sudden disappearance the dogs rushed

to the end of the jetty and peered down at her, barking hysterically, leaping perilously close to the edge and threatening to fall down after her. Catherine heard them dimly but the sound receded rapidly. She went under but struggled to the surface again, coughing and spluttering, unable to scream. As the current carried her swiftly round the bend of the river, the sodden layers of her clothing dragged her down deeper and deeper until her lungs were full of the dark water and she felt strands of river weed clinging briefly around her legs. Panic-stricken, she knew that she was going to die and her last anguished thought was of Leo. The moon shone on her clutching hand as it rose desperately from the river for the last time, and the droplets of water that fell from it were darkly silvered.

As she died two women arrived at the curve in the track and made their way carefully to the edge of the jetty, where the dogs still stared intently downward. An elderly man with a rifle over his shoulder joined them and, puzzled, they all stared into the river while the dogs, robbed of their sport, began to whine and whimper. One of the women shouted at the dogs to stop their noise; she shook her fist at them and went back to her sleeping children. The second woman grabbed her own dog by the scruff of the neck and dragged it away. The man, unconvinced, remained alone, frowning into the darkness that was the river. He held his rifle at the ready, for the dogs' barking told him that something or someone was around. He waited, straining his ears to catch the slightest sound, but there was only silence. Eventually he too shrugged dismissively, shouldered his gun and went home.

*

As soon as it was light a search party was organized at San Domingos to parallel that in Mertola. The Chief of Police in San Domingos rode through the miners' quarters with a megaphone, explaining the problem of Catherine's disap-

318

pearance and asking for volunteers. There were plenty of these, and before long they were grouped in the praça around the bandstand, mingling with half a dozen policemen who would supervise the search. A map of the surrounding area had been pinned to a large makeshift easel set up on the bandstand where Elliot, Doctor Barratt and the Chief of Police waited impatiently. The Police Chief addressed the assembled men just before 6.30 a.m. when the sky was lightening.

Joanna and Leo stood on the fringe of the crowd, listening intently to the instructions for the search, which Leo translated to her.

In Portuguese, the Police Chief explained simply that Mrs Grosvenor had gone riding the previous day and had not returned. Her riderless horse had been found, but she was still missing. The news was greeted with a rumble of concern.

'She is known to have been riding towards Mertola, but that area was searched last night with no result. We must therefore assume that the horse bolted for some reason before throwing Mrs Grosvenor. We shall therefore spread the search to these areas.' He tapped the map and all heads craned eagerly forward. 'Some of you will comb the southern area around Sapos and Achado do Gamo; others will concentrate here, around Serralhas, Corvos and Quinta, on the north side of the track. Remember that she may be wandering, dazed by her fall, or she may be on the ground, unconscious.'

There was another murmur of dismay and Leo glanced up at Joanna who said, 'They'll soon find her, Leo. There must be a hundred men here.'

'Call her name repeatedly as you go. Don't stop calling for her. As soon as you find her, send a runner back to alert Mr Grosvenor and we'll take over from there.'

It was now the doctor's turn and he came forward somewhat self-consciously and cleared his throat. His Portuguese was quite adequate for what he had to tell them.

'If Mrs Grosvenor is unconscious, don't try to move her,' he warned. 'She might be suffering broken limbs or ribs, and you could unintentionally make the injuries worse. If she's conscious, of course, you can ask her about her injuries. You might be able to carry her, or she might need to wait for a stretcher to arrive. I'm sending a few bandages with one or two of you, but that's about the extent of the first aid. I'll have morphine, splints and so on with me, and I'll arrive with the stretcher. I think that's all.'

Elliot stepped forward. 'I just want to thank you for giving up your time. I and my family appreciate it more than I can say. God speed and good luck!'

The men were divided into groups and given last-minute instructions by the policemen, and ten minutes later they had all moved out. Joanna and Leo walked slowly up to the bandstand where Elliot was still talking to the Chief of Police. The doctor had already left to make a few early calls on his patients so that he would be free to go to Catherine as soon as she was found.

Leo said, 'I saw Mr Shreiker amongst the crowd. He wants to find Mama.'

'They all want to find her, Leo.'

'They *will* find her, won't they?'

'Of course they will. I promise!'

He returned her smile dubiously. 'I wish we could have gone with them.'

'Well, we did offer, but Papa thought we would slow them down and I expect he's right.'

'That's not the real reason,' he told her. 'He's afraid that they'll find her and she'll be dead.' His tone was as matter-of-fact as he could make it.

Joanna hesitated, then said, 'That may be so, Leo, but we mustn't give up hope. Do you want to go to the church and pray? We prayed for Grandmother and God has made her better.'

His face brightened. 'Yes, he has! Let's go there, then.'

Having prayed for Catherine's safe return, they went to watch the horses being shod and then in desperation they went to the library. Still there was no word from the searchers that Catherine Grosvenor had been found. After lunch they went to visit Grandmother in the hospital and talked to Nurse Williams about a cat she had once owned which was missing for three days and then turned up alive. Then they went to Leo's room and did some mental arithmetic. By 5.30 there was still no news, and everyone was getting very anxious and a little irritable from the strain of waiting and trying not to admit that hope was fading.

At a quarter to six Steven found Joanna and Leo sitting on the edge of the bandstand, staring towards Mertola.

'You should be searching for Mama!' cried Leo indignantly.

Steven smiled. 'I volunteered, Leo, but your father insisted that I stay underground for another shift. That released Mr Shreiker, who really isn't sufficiently experienced to take charge. I've been down there for sixteen hours, and I'm beginning to sympathize with the ponies!'

'Oh!' said Leo, immediately ashamed of his outburst. 'I'm sorry.'

'That's OK, young sprout!' He sat down beside Leo and said, 'Well, no news is good news.'

Joanna met his eyes over the boy's head. 'Leo doesn't think so,' she said warningly. 'He was just telling me he had a bad dream, and he's got a cold feeling in his stomach.'

'Not cold,' Leo corrected her. 'Icy. An *icy* feeling — here!' He demonstrated it to Steven and said, 'I wonder if it's a bad omen?'

'People always get bad dreams when they're worried, Leo.'

'But this was about Mama. She was flying in the air and she went higher and higher until I couldn't see her any more.' He swallowed quickly and stared at his shoes.

'Flying? That sounds quite pleasant, doesn't it?'

'She was waving to me. I tried to call out "Goodbye" but no words came out.'

Steven put an arm round his shoulders. 'You'll forget all about bad dreams when she's home again, you'll see. In a day or two we shall all have forgotten what a fright your Mama's given us.'

He spoke reassuringly, and for a moment or two Leo felt comforted.

'Have you two eaten?' Steven asked.

'I'm not hungry,' said Leo, 'and neither is Joanna.'

Steven stood up. 'Then if I can't tempt you to share my supper, I'd better get back to my work. I've got enough paperwork to keep me busy for hours! Let me know as soon as your Mama is found and we'll celebrate—' He put his mouth close to Leo's ear and added, 'Maybe a small glass of my best sherry!'

Leo smiled half-heartedly. Time passed and they were still sitting there an hour later when one of the train drivers who lived in Pomerao was telling the station-master at San Domingos about the strange behaviour of the dogs on the railway jetty the previous night. The station-master promptly hauled him along to the Palacio to repeat his story to Elliot Grosvenor. Elliot tried hard not to connect the event with Catherine's disappearance, but dared not dismiss the possibility. He accompanied the train driver to the police station to repeat the story and by nightfall, when the unsuccessful search had been abandoned, word was sent to the authorities in Vila Real. The Spanish authorities were alerted, a watch was kept on both river-banks and the agony of waiting continued.

Chapter Eighteen

IT WAS DAWN, two days later. Pedro Picarra made his way slowly along the river-bank, his eyes still heavy with sleep, his mouth dry, his legs leaden. He walked with a heavy stick, but this was not to lean upon; it was to protect his charges from wolves, snakes or other predators. The stick was rarely needed and today he did not expect to use it. The sky above was a pale, clear blue-green and it would be hot again, even under the trees where he would rest to eat his breakfast – a chunk of bread and an onion. Ahead of him thirty-two goats of assorted colours and sizes moved slowly over the ground, their heads down, their eyes searching for the lichens and mosses which, at this time of year, replaced the lush grass of spring. Small leaves, dried stalks, a very few flower-heads – all disappeared as the goats passed over them. The goatherd knew them all. The oldest nanny, half blind, brown dappled with white, who would soon die but who had given him seven kids; the youngest kid, a billy, only three months old and black as soot but already as independent as his brothers. He would end up in the pot before the year was out and would make succulent eating; the white nanny, larger-boned and with long legs, who gave the sweetest milk . . .

Occasionally they glanced back and always he urged them on with a soft whooping sound which they knew. He glanced around him, on the alert for trouble if it should seek him out. The herd was valuable and he understood his responsibility towards it. He was fond of telling his old woman that he would lay down his life for them, though she always laughed at this. But then she didn't understand. How could she? She was a woman. He had tried to explain it to her, but without success. What could she ever know of responsibility? For as long as he could remember, and for as long as he could foresee, there would be him and the goats ... He thought of his wife now with a hint of a smile. She was small and round, and she talked too much and knew very little, but she had given him six children. Three had died in infancy, but that was the Lord's affair. Neither the goatherd nor his wife could be blamed. It happened ...

Overhead an eagle hovered and swooped, watching them. If a newborn kid was left unattended, he would snatch it in his great claws and carry it off. Beautiful birds — but Pedro hated them; they were his enemies. He glanced to his left where the sides of the valley sloped steeply, brown and dry from the heat. To his right the Guardiana flowed still and deep towards the sea. He had no idea what lay beyond his own territory, for he had never ventured further than a few miles from his home. In one direction he went as far as the look-out post which watched the river and the Spaniards on the other side of it. Pedro Picarra had no truck with them, keeping his eyes well down so that he would not meet the sharp eye of officialdom. They were knowledgeable men with long spy-glasses, and they watched for smugglers.

Across the river! Now that was another place of which he was very wary. Portugal and Spain had always been enemies; he knew from his father and grandfather before him that the Spaniards of old had been bloodthirsty pirates, and he was glad he was separated from such people by the width of the river!

To the north of his territory he often spotted the squat shape of a windmill, its painted sails whirling in the wind. When he and his goats moved westward they went as far as the dirt road, and once he had seen an enormous wagon loaded with tree-trunks and drawn by six horses, and the driver had waved his hand to him.

A small movement in the rushes at the water's edge caught and held his eye. Frowning, he stared at the glimpse of yellow. Not flowers. Not an animal. Too large for a yellow bird. Something washed down by the river, perhaps? He hesitated, calling his herd to wait. They stopped, bleating their resentment, for the juiciest food always grew right ahead, just a few steps further. They waited, milling unhappily, eager to be off. The goatherd climbed down towards the water; as he did so he realized that what he had seen was yellow clothing, and a cold certainty came upon him that he would not like what he found. Yellow clothing did not fall into rivers unless there was somebody wearing it. He stared fearfully at the yellow bundle which rocked very slightly with the water. There was hair; long, floating hair! There was a slim, yellow-clad arm floating limply among the tall rushes! A hot bile surged in his throat as he looked at it. He wanted to look away but his gaze was fixed. There was a dead woman in the water! He, Pedro Picarra, had found a drowned woman! It was a long time before he could believe it. He stepped into the shallow water and pushed at the body with his stick. It rolled over with a gurgling sound, and he saw a grey, bloated face which made him want to vomit. He coughed and spat into the reeds, wiping the back of his hand across his face. Then he stepped hurriedly back on to dry land. Behind him the goats bleated restlessly and he shouted to them angrily to stop fussing and let him think.

He sat down, his two hands clasping the heavy stick which prevented them from trembling too badly. A woman in a yellow dress! He was tempted to walk on without a backward glance. What was a dead woman to him? She would interrupt his day's work, and all to no purpose. He could leave her where she was until someone came looking for her. Or he could push her out into midstream and let her float away for other eyes to find. These alternatives held a great appeal. He could pretend to know nothing about her; if someone mentioned it, he would be surprised. His life would continue and, after a while, he would forget her. He shook his head and sighed and called again to calm the goats. The trouble with casting the dead woman adrift again was that he wanted to tell his wife about the adventure, and he could imagine her scorn and the scolding he would get. He could almost hear her voice, shrill and accusing.

'What?' she would cry. 'You did nothing? You found a poor dead woman and you told no one? Pedro! So much for responsibility!'

She would never let him forget what he had done – or rather, what he had not done! The sharp, reproachful tongue of a woman could be a terrible scourge! He sighed again. He would have to tell someone. He would have to tell the men in the look-out post; they would know what to do. His heart began to thump, uncomfortably loud. He would have to approach the look-out post and call up to them; he would tell them where the body lay, and then he would tell them that he must go about his work. His goats needed their food; they must graze. He wondered if they would ask him to put his cross on a piece of official paper – and if he must, then he would. But he would not like it. The idea appalled him. But there was this dead woman and there was his wife – and there was responsibility. He stood up and at once the goats bleated excitedly.

'I'm coming!' he told them, but his heart was heavy with dread and his very soul shrivelled at the prospect of the encounter ahead of him.

*

Catherine's funeral service was held in the little church in San Domingos. Leo stood in the front pew between Joanna and his father, his back straight as a ramrod. He was wearing his best suit with the Norfolk jacket, and he was terribly hot, but he stared straight ahead of him and tried not to think about the contents of the smooth, shiny coffin. His father had explained that because his mother had been in the water she had looked very pale and ill, so nobody had been invited to view the body. He knew he would never see her again, but he did not want to accept that she was inside the coffin and would shortly be buried in the English cemetery near to the wooden cross marked with a 'J'. He felt very confused. If Joanna had never come to San Domingos, his mother would still be alive. Yet it was not Joanna's fault. And Papa loved Joanna. It was Mama who had wanted Joanna to go away, and Joanna had said she would. Not that he, Leo, had wanted her to go, but she had been willing. So why had Mama ridden away and got herself drowned? It all seemed very unnecessary.

His father leaned down with an English hymn-book opened at the correct page, but Leo discovered that his eyes were strangely blurred and the writing in the book was unreadable. He opened and shut his mouth and hoped that no one would notice. There were lots of flowers on the coffin and Mama liked flowers. Or rather, she *had* liked them when she was alive. Now she could never see flowers or smell them or arrange them in vases – or stuff like that. In a secret kind of way he felt that it was Grandmother who should have died, because she was old and her memory had gone and she was about the right age to die. But she was back home again and Nurse Williams was looking after her, just as though nothing had happened – as though she had never fallen out of her chair – and everyone said how marvellous it was. It was so unfair.

The hymn ended and they all knelt to say the Lord's

Prayer. Leo whispered it, and listened to his father's strong voice beside him. He did hope his father wasn't going to die. Maybe a rock would fall on his head while he was underground; it did happen from time to time. Or he might have a seizure, or die of malaria. Then he, Leo, would be alone, except for Joanna. He glanced sideways at his father and saw with relief that he looked well enough. A trifle sad, perhaps, but they were all sad. Leo did so wish he had not said that dreadful thing about Mama; it was on his conscience. He had told Joanna that sometimes he hated his mother, and he had told her about the time the boys at school had called her 'Foxy'. He wished very much that he hadn't told her that. He wondered if, now that she was dead, his mother knew all these things. If so, could she ever forgive him? He thought he might ask Mr Benbridge, who seemed a very sensible man.

They stood up again for a little more Latin and Leo was mortified to discover that, despite his flair for Latin and a 'B' in the end-of-term test, he couldn't understand any of it. Suddenly Joanna was squeezing his hand, and he looked up and she was smiling at him. He smiled back dutifully. Joanna had said that it was quite all right to feel horribly sad and to cry when someone died. It was natural. She had cried, too, even though Mama had tried to send her away. She had said that no one is a hundred per cent good and kind; not even mothers and fathers. Everybody did good things and bad things, but if you loved the person you forgave them the bad things and went on loving them. She had said that his mother was a very good, very kind person who now and then did bad things, but she should be forgiven. Joanna had forgiven her for the letter she wrote, which was jolly good of her.

Now the men were carrying Mama's coffin outside – Mr Benbridge, Mr Jackson, Papa's secretary, Mr Shreiker, Senor Louro and even the doctor. Everyone in the church had to follow it for 'the interment' – which meant lowering it into the deep hole that someone had dug. He was glad he was so young, because it was going to be a long time before they had to lower him into anywhere. Mr Shreiker had said that drowning was very quick; Leo didn't exactly believe him, although he wanted to. Papa had said that now Mama was at peace with God and the angels, and that was rather nice. Perhaps she was looking down on them from somewhere above the church, and would watch them all as they made their way up towards the cemetery. Nurse Williams had said that, whenever he wanted to, Leo would be able to bring flowers and put them on Mama's grave. The doctor's wife had said that only his mother's body would be in the ground; her soul and her spirit would be in Heaven. He glanced across at the doctor's wife, and thought that her tiny black hat with the bits of black gauzy stuff was terribly silly. It looked as though a large black gnat had settled on top of her head.

Joanna had taken hold of his hand again and he didn't really mind. He supposed that because it was a funeral it didn't matter. He'd noticed before that women liked to hold people's hands; Grandmother was always holding his hands, if he got near enough to her. They hadn't told her about Mama being drowned in case she had a relapse; later, the doctor had said, when she was stronger. Now they went in through the gates of the little cemetery and there was hardly room for some of the people to get in. One or two, he noticed, were standing on the other graves, but presumably dead people would understand and make allowances. The mourners crowded round the coffin and the men began to lower it into the ground while the priest muttered away. It was horribly hot inside the cemetery and the Barratts' niece, Lucy, was fanning herself. She was very red in the face and he wondered hopefully if she was going to faint. He watched her surreptitiously in case she did, so that he wouldn't miss it, but she caught his eye and smiled and he quickly looked away.

Then his father stepped forward and said something about his beloved wife, and going to a better place and remembering her always with esteem and affection. The doctor's wife started to cry and Christina blew her nose rather loudly, and Liliane rolled her eyes humorously at him over the rim of her hand and he had to try hard not to giggle. Which was awful at such a time, but he blamed Liliane entirely and he would tell her so later.

When the earth started to fall on the coffin he felt a bit strange, but his father put a hand on his shoulder and Joanna was still holding his hand. When it was all over they walked away in silence and headed back to the house where the food was waiting. Christina had cut up a large ham, and the doctor's wife had made a large tart of sliced peaches with cherries round the edge. He remembered then that Mama loved cherries and tears came into his eyes, but he blinked them back and wondered if the worst was over.

*

29th August, 1912
Today I am eighteen. Not a great age, although I feel ten years older than when I first came to Portugal. So much has happened that it is hard to believe I am the same person. Papa gave me a wonderful present – the photograph of my mother and the other two maids. It is in a beautiful silver frame which is engraved with flowers and leaves. It is on the table by my bed, so that I see her as soon as I open my eyes. I cannot think of a better present, and I shall treasure it until I die.

He also gave me £100, which almost frightened me. I have never had any money of my own and I feel like a millionaire. The first thing I did was to buy a lace tablecloth and matching place mats in a shop in Mertola, and send it to Isobel as my wedding gift to her and Mark. I sent a card wishing them happiness, and I think I meant it.

We also went to the cemetery on my birthday, and put a small posy of flowers in a little earthenware pot by the wooden cross. It must have been a strange sensation for Papa, to be laying flowers for Juanita so close to Catherine's grave. Her flowers are just about dead now, but nobody has had the heart to take them away. There were tears in Papa's eyes when we stood by the cross, and I cried, but he said that my mother would be so happy if she could see us there together, and I am to remember that when I feel particularly sad.

Good news. Aunt Agatha is coming out to San Domingos to keep house for us. Papa did not need to ask her; she simply wrote when she heard about Catherine's death and said she was coming and would brook no argument. Papa was so pleased. He said she has always longed to come back, but felt there was no place for her here. Now she will feel loved and useful and we shall all be together.

I wrote a long letter to the family at home yesterday. I hope it will help to mend the rift. I am so happy now that I want everybody else to be happy.

We also went to see Maria, my grandmother, and she was so excited to know who I am. She said she had never expected to see me again. I can visit her any time I wish. She said very little to Papa, but I can see that she might never be able to forgive him for what happened. Papa said that he did not expect forgiveness, and did not blame her, which made me feel better about it.

I have this strange feeling that I have truly come home, and I think myself so very fortunate. Leo and I played tennis this evening for more than an hour; he's not very good at it, so I won. He doesn't like losing, but when he played with Andrew he grumbled that Andrew *let* him win. He says that cricket is really his game and he's a 'pretty good all-rounder'. He seems to be

331

recovering from the shock of Catherine's death; Papa says he is very resilient. I do hope so.

No more for now.

*

The following day Leo went fishing with Juan-Carlos, and Joanna strolled over to the Palacio to change her library book and then spent an hour with Grandmother. Then, when she could think of no further errands which might delay her, she walked over to see Steven Benbridge. She knocked at the door and, receiving no answer, made her way round to the rear of the bungalow where she found him sitting on the grass in the shade of a carob tree, an empty glass beside him. He was reading, but he jumped to his feet when she appeared.

Smiling, he waved the book and said, 'I'm a Sherlock Holmes addict! Would you like a deck-chair?'

'No. The grass is fine.' As she sat down beside him he regarded her with his head on one side. 'Do I detect a hint of bad news?' he asked. 'You're looking very solemn.'

Joanna cursed her lack of guile, for she had wanted to approach this matter circumspectly. She shook her head. 'Not bad, exactly,' she told him. 'At least, I'm not sure.'

He put a leather marker into the book and laid it on the grass beside him.

'Where's young Leo today?' he asked.

'Fishing with Juan-Carlos. Papa wants us to keep him busy so he doesn't have too much time to think.'

Steven nodded. 'The nights will be plenty long enough for that,' he agreed. 'May I offer you some lemonade? Or something stronger?'

'No, thank you.' She shook her head nervously.

'Is something wrong?' he asked gently.

'Yes, it is.' Joanna saw that she was twisting her hands in her lap, and folded them quickly. She knew he was trying to help her, but wished he would just sit quietly until she was ready to deliver her prepared 'speech'.

Suddenly, without intending it, she said, 'I saw you playing tennis yesterday – with Lucy Barratt!'

'Poor Lucy! She's a bit of a rabbit, but she tries for every ball – I'll grant her that.'

Joanna sensed rather than saw that he glanced at her, but she continued to stare straight ahead. 'Leo said she was only interested in sewing and crochet.'

'I think that's true, but her aunt thought she should have some exercise. They needed someone to make a four.'

'So they asked you!' It came out like an accusation and Joanna bit her lip, annoyed with herself.

'No, they asked Shreiker, but he was just going back on duty so had to refuse. I was second best, but I'm not proud!' His tone was humorous; he was willing her to be amused, but she could not manage it.

'She's rather pretty,' she suggested.

'Not my style but yes, she's pretty enough. The ringlets are her trump card!' He laughed. 'Even Leo is bewitched by the ringlets.'

'But you're not?'

'No. I'm not a ringlets man!' He laughed softly.

Desperately she asked, 'What sort of woman would you marry – if you were ever to marry again?'

She thought that if he treated this question humorously she would tip him out of the deck-chair, but he appeared to be thinking seriously about it.

'A woman with integrity,' he said at last. 'A woman with a mind of her own. Not necessarily beautiful but with something about her – nice eyes, glossy hair, perhaps ... a trim figure. I don't have a vision of "the perfect woman", if that's what you mean.' He looked at her. 'How am I doing?' he asked.

Joanna ignored the remark. 'What sort of age?' she asked.

'Anything from sixteen to sixty!'

'Steven!' She glared at him.

'I'm sorry, Joanna. I just don't understand the need for all these questions.'

'Well—' She took a deep breath. 'The reason is that I think you should get married again, and I need to know if there are any things about a woman – I mean that you may feel—' She closed her eyes so that she need not see his face. 'The most important thing is if the woman would have to be a . . .' He was waiting, but she could not bring herself to utter the word and she swallowed. 'Would it matter if she were not a – a . . .' She wanted to weep with frustration; this was an unaskable question.

'A virgin?' he prompted. She dared not look at him, but his voice was surprisingly matter-of-fact.

'Yes!' It was a whisper. 'You see, I know it is terribly important but—'

'Not to me,' he said. 'The other things I have mentioned matter much more.'

'They do? You mean that?'

'Most certainly.' He swatted at a mosquito as though the topic of conversation was not of particular interest.

Her relief was overwhelming. 'Oh!' After a long silence she said, 'Would you consider someone who has been rather foolish – no, very foolish?'

He looked thoughtful. 'I think I would prefer someone who was less than perfect. Perfection is surely difficult to live up to – wouldn't you think so?'

'Oh, I would, yes, but . . . Well, some people wouldn't agree.'

'Whoever it was would have to put up with my vices,' he said. 'I hate getting up in the morning; I am not averse to the occasional white lie; I don't like cats; I—'

'Then would you consider me?' she asked.

'I've been considering you for a long time.'

His tone was so calm that Joanna was not sure she had understood him correctly. He wasn't even looking at her, but bending down to retie the laces of his right shoe.

'Steven? Do you mean that? You have been thinking about me?'

He turned towards her. 'I've been waiting for you to let Mark go,' he said. 'Hoping that then I might have a chance.'

She stared into the grey eyes. 'A chance with me? Oh, Steven! Do you love me then?'

'Apparently!' he laughed.

'Because I've just realized that I love *you*, but I wasn't sure ... Well, I wished I hadn't confided in you about Mark. I thought perhaps I'd made a terrible mistake.'

'I don't think so. Now there are no secrets.'

'No.'

She watched a small yellow bird in the branches above them. 'So will you?' she asked. 'Will you marry me?'

'It would give me great pleasure to accept your proposal!' A huge smile lit up his face as she checked to see that he meant it. She thought how wonderfully handsome he was, and wondered why she had never seen it before.

Still she hung back. 'In a few years,' she said, 'when I'm older.'

'When you're twenty?'

'Yes.'

'That will give you two years to be with your father.'

'How did you know?' she asked, astonished.

'When you love someone, you just know these things.' He took hold of her hand.

Joanna looked at her hand and his. 'Do you think our hands look right together?' she asked.

'I think so.'

She found herself grinning ridiculously. 'So this is what it's like to be ... Are we betrothed, do you think?'

'As you wish. If you want to keep it a secret for a while, that's fine with me.'

She thought about it. 'I want everyone to know, yet it seems too soon after Catherine's death to be so happy when everybody else is miserable . . .' Her voice trailed off.

'I agree. Let's wait a month or so.'

She nodded. 'Should we kiss, do you think?'

'Why not!'

He put a hand under her chin and tilted her face towards his. The kiss was not as exciting as she had expected, but she imagined Steven was a little out of practice.

'That was nice!' she said breathlessly.

'It wasn't one of my best,' he laughed. 'You have rather taken me by surprise.'

'I think I can do better,' she told him. 'We can practise together! Steven, do you think your first wife would be happy that you have found someone else?'

'Most certainly. She wouldn't want me to be a lonely old man. And she would approve of you.'

'Really? Why do you say that?'

'Your heart is in the right place.'

'Oh, Steven—'

Recognizing the tone of her voice, he rolled his eyes. 'Now what's coming?' he said, with mock alarm.

'It's just that, when I was with Mark – on that day – I thought it was all rather . . .' She swallowed. 'Rather disappointing. Did your wife – I mean, would it matter if I found it disappointing? We may have got it wrong; I don't know.'

His laugh was so genuine that she was immediately reassured.

'These things take time,' he explained gently. 'How shall I explain it? Sue and I were both very happy with the way things were and I'm sure you will be, too. It's nothing to worry about.'

'I'm glad about that.'

She squeezed his hand and then shook her head in amazement. 'I've just realized that I have Mark to thank for all this. If it hadn't been for him, I would never have been sent here and I would never have met you! Isn't Fate strange?' She leaned towards him and he put an arm around her. 'Is it legal to be so happy?' she whispered.

She felt his quiet laughter. 'It's legal!' he said, and she felt his kiss, light as air, as his lips touched her hair.

*

Five weeks passed before Agatha was able to travel to San Domingos. She had sold the house, leaving the details to be finalized by her solicitor, and had found a dealer who gave her a good price for her antique furniture; she was so impatient to be gone from England that she could not be bothered with goods and chattels. After all, she would live with Elliot and he had goods and chattels enough for two. In some ways she would be sorry to be leaving England, for she had made a few good friends, but San Domingos called her with the soft, insistent voice of a lover and she longed to be there. The sea journey was mercifully good, and she was not seasick; she suffered the long train journey with growing impatience. She was longing to see Joanna, whose letter had given her so much pleasure. The girl loved San Domingos as Agatha had known she would. And with Catherine gone, there was no reason why Joanna should not be happy there. It was her birthplace, Portugal was her real home . . . And she had announced herself to Maria! Agatha had brought Maria a small mirror with painted flowers and gilding around the edge. Even an old woman had vanities! It seemed incredible that the wrongs of so many years ago had somehow been righted.

If only Elliot had had the courage to marry Juanita, he would never have married Catherine. Their mother had a lot to answer for! A strong woman, but terribly misguided. But now even Clementine had been brought low, her power and her memory both gone. Still, presumably she would have forgotten all the quarrels they had had in the past, so it was an ill wind . . .! But then if Elliot had not married

337

Catherine, he would never have had Leo. A delightful boy; she had brought him an eyeglass as a present – a good one. He would appreciate that. Leo was a credit to his parents. God works in a mysterious way, she told herself as she climbed thankfully from the train at Vila Real and was greeted by Senor Pavao, who would escort her to the steamboat. He smiled broadly, pumped her hand enthusiastically, and told her how good it was that she had come back to Portugal.

She settled herself in the little steamship and prepared herself for the next part of the journey. She had always loved the river trip from Vila Real to Pomerao. It gave her time to absorb the sights and sounds of the country and to cast off the trappings of civilization – to forget the outside world with its harsh veneer of sophistication, and prepare herself for the gentler pleasures of life at San Domingos.

As the little ship chugged its way through the dark waters, Agatha thought of her long-dead husband. Now he shared the little cemetery with Catherine, and they would make strange bedfellows! They had never met, but he would have disliked her on sight. Charles had had no time for artifice; he had been a most un-pompous man, kindly and ordinary. Nothing spectacular about Charles. She had once called him 'a thoroughly good egg', and he had taken it as a great compliment. She smiled and, leaving her seat, crossed to stand in the bow of the ship, watching the cool green water part for it. The smile faded as she thought that this same water had closed over Catherine's head and forced its way into her lungs, driving out the last gasp of air and ending her life. She had a momentary vision of Catherine falling from the jetty and shuddered. But that was all in the past, and it was the future that held Agatha's interest. Staring intently ahead, she mentally urged the ship's engine to greater efforts . . .

*

Leo and Joanna stood together on the narrow wooden trolley, shaded by the small, striped awning. The little shunting engine pulled the trolley along the track as the land beneath them rose imperceptibly. Leo's hand was on the brake, but that was for Joanna's benefit. The brake would not be needed until they entered the last stage of the run, downhill into Pomerao; then it would be very necessary to prevent the little platform from gathering speed and bouncing off the track. This could, and did, sometimes happen when a young engineer with an adventurous spirit allowed it to get out of control. Elliot was not amused by these little accidents, but fortunately they were few and far between. Leo knew better than to risk his father's wrath, and Joanna felt sure she was in safe hands.

'Are you quite sure Aunt Agatha wants to travel this way?' she asked him for the third time, as they rattled and lurched along. 'If I were her, I'd want to sit down in the special carriage in comfort.'

He grinned. 'But you're not her,' he pointed out. 'Aunt Agatha loves the trolley; she rode on it several times with her husband. Last time I visited her in England I talked about the trolley, and she said she remembered it. It makes her laugh just to think about it. She said it's the only way to travel from Pomerao to the mine! She *did*!'

'Well, I hope you're right. There won't be much room for three of us if she's brought a lot of luggage.'

'She won't. People never do. It all comes the other way by mule.'

They reached the changeover point and now the shunting engine was uncoupled; the driver waved and reversed the engine. Joanna looked round. 'What happens now?' she asked, disconcerted.

'The engine goes back to San Domingos and we coast down to Pomerao. It's quite safe, Joanna. I can handle it. When we collect Agatha, another little engine tows us back to this point—'

339

'And we "coast" back to San Domingos, which presumably is all downhill from here! Very ingenious.'

'Now,' said Leo, grinning wolfishly, 'you are in my power! Hold on to your hat!' He released the handbrake and the trolley began to move slowly. 'There's nothing to it!' he told her. 'When we come to the tunnels you duck your head. That's all.'

She looked around them nervously, feeling remarkably vulnerable without the company of the shunting engine and its driver. For a while she was conscious of Leo watching her, and she tried to look relaxed and carefree.

'What do you think of it?' he asked as the trolley rounded a bend and swayed alarmingly. 'Do you think Aunt Agatha was right?'

'Yes, she was!' cried Joanna, albeit a little breathlessly. 'It's certainly not boring!'

'Boring?' cried Leo. 'I should think not . . . First tunnel up ahead!'

Joanna, who was looking the wrong way, ducked instinctively and he roared with laughter. 'Not *yet*!' he told her. '. . . *Now*!'

They both lowered their heads as the trolley ran through a short tunnel and out again into the sunshine. 'Lucky old Agatha!' thought Joanna, but she was beginning to enjoy herself.

Leo grinned. 'You can have a turn, if you like,' he offered. 'A short one, that is.'

For a few kilometres the trolley bounced and jolted on its way with Joanna's hand on the brake; it was certainly exhilarating. She handed the controls back to Leo and watched the countryside pass.

'How fast are we going?' she asked.

'A hundred miles an hour!' he laughed. 'No, more like five, but it seems faster because we're not closed in.'

Joanna thought how good it was to see him looking happy again after so many wretched weeks of adjustment.

He really was making a tremendous effort to come to terms with the loss of his mother, but Joanna had sat with him through some tearful nights and knew exactly how he had grieved.

Through another tunnel, around another bend. Was it her imagination, or were they going faster?

She said, 'Leo!'

But the wind was ruffling his hair, his lips were parted and his eyes shone with excitement. Faster still . . .

'*Leo!*'

Just as she was about to make a grab for the brake, the trolley rounded a last bend, then they were on the flat and she could see Pomerao and they were slowing down.

He laughed. 'Had you scared there for a minute!'

'Just for a minute!' she admitted.

And then they were jumping off and the other shunting engine was being coupled to pull them back to the change-over spot. The little steamer was already tying up and Aunt Agatha was waving to them from the bow of the ship – and suddenly Joanna's heart was full. These were *her* people. This was *her* country. And back at San Domingos her future husband waited for her. She blinked back tears of happiness as she followed Leo down the steps to welcome Aunt Agatha with a bearlike hug. For it was Agatha, all those years ago, who had made it all possible.

TURN OF THE TIDE

Pamela Oldfield

1911 marks the turning point in Grace Martin's life.

During that year she takes up the job of nursery maid to George and Victoria at Berwick House – and falls in love with their father, Alexander Latimer.

Grace quickly learns that beneath the calm surface there are dangerous undercurrents at Berwick House. Alexander's wife has succumbed to the sophisticated charms of a rich American visitor, and the children's Nanny Webster is a tyrant whose evil influence spreads far beyond the nursery.

But nothing has prepared Grace for the cruel twist of fate that will tear her from the man she secretly adores, as with her two young charges she sets sail for New York on the *Titanic*'s maiden voyage . . .

FICTION
0 7515 0868 **3**

THE STATIONMASTER'S DAUGHTER

Pamela Oldfield

Tom Turner could have hoped for a better position than
stationmaster of Gazedown, a small village in the heart of
Kent. But a long-buried scandal had blighted his career –
and dashed the hopes of his only daughter Amy. Instead
of going to London to become a teacher, she has to look
after the three menfolk in her family.

But previously unknown emotions erupt with the arrival
of a fascinating stranger, the writer Ralph Allen – though
there are rival contenders for his attention.

And Ralph provides the mysterious lure that sparks off
events leading to final tragedy . . .

FICTION
0 7515 0132 8

☐	Green Harvest	Pamela Oldfield	£3.99
☐	Summer Song	Pamela Oldfield	£3.99
☐	Golden Tally	Pamela Oldfield	£3.50
☐	The Gooding Girl	Pamela Oldfield	£5.99
☐	The Stationmaster's Daughter	Pamela Oldfield	£5.99
☐	Lily Golightly	Pamela Oldfield	£5.99
☐	Turn of the Tide	Pamela Oldfield	£5.99
☐	A Dutiful Wife	Pamela Oldfield	£3.99
☐	Sweet Sally Lunn	Pamela Oldfield	£4.99
☐	The Halliday Girls	Pamela Oldfield	£4.99
☐	Long Dark Summer	Pamela Oldfield	£4.99

Warner Books now offers an exciting range of quality titles by both established and new authors. All of the books in this series are available from:

Little, Brown and Company (UK) Limited,
P.O. Box 11,
Falmouth,
Cornwall TR10 9EN.

Alternatively you may fax your order to the above address. Fax No. 0326 376423.

Payments can be made as follows: cheque, postal order (payable to Little, Brown and Company) or by credit cards, Visa/Access. Do not send cash or currency. UK customers and B.F.P.O. please allow £1.00 for postage and packing for the first book, plus 50p for the second book, plus 30p for each additional book up to a maximum charge of £3.00 (7 books plus).

Overseas customers including Ireland, please allow £2.00 for the first book plus £1.00 for the second book, plus 50p for each additional book.

NAME (Block Letters) ....

....

ADDRESS ....

....

....

☐ I enclose my remittance for _____

☐ I wish to pay by Access/Visa Card

Number ☐☐☐☐☐☐☐☐☐☐☐☐☐☐☐☐

Card Expiry Date ☐☐☐☐